THE SEVEN THUNDERS

AN ALTERNATE HISTORY
ADVENTURE

Book One from the *Annals* of
Zebulon

WILLIAM WHITTENBURY

ZENNA
BOOKS

ZENNA BOOKS

The Seven Thunders: An Alternate History
Adventure

Paperback Edition ISBN: 978-1-7349976-0-6
Library of Congress Control Number: 2020907988

Published by Zenna Books
WilliamWhittenburyAuthor.com

This book is dedicated to Beth Whittenbury, my best friend and constant source of inspiration; to Auntie Doll, who always supported my dreams; and to all who fight the good fight.

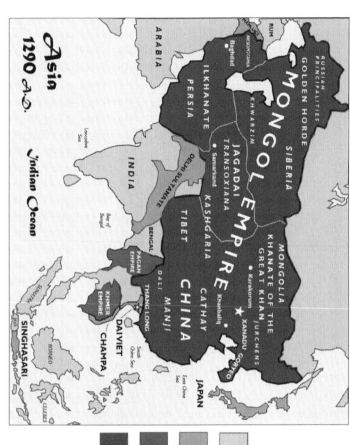

Asia
1290 A.D.

Indian Ocean

RUSSIAN PRINCIPALITIES

RUM

ARABIA

MESOPOTAMIA
• Baghdad

GOLDEN HORDE

MONGOL EMPIRE

ILKHANATE
PERSIA

KHWARIZM

SIBERIA

JAGADAI
TRANSOXIANA
• Samarkand

Laccadive
Sea

INDIA

DELHI SULTANATE

KASHGARIA

TIBET

MONGOLIA
KHANATE OF THE
GREAT KHAN
• Karakorum
JURCHENS
★ XANADU
Khanbalik •
CORYO

Bay of
Bengal

BENGAL

PAGAN
EMPIRE

DALI

THANG LONG

MANJI

CATHAY

CHINA

KHMER
EMPIRE

CHAMPA

DAIVIET

South
China Sea

East China
Sea

JAPAN

SUMATRA

BORNEO

CELEBES

SINGHASARI

Mongol
Empire

Mongol
tributaries

Nations resisting
the Mongols

Non-aligned
nations

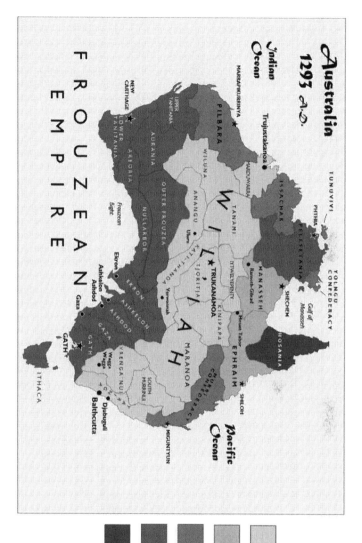

Australia
1293 A.D.

Indian
Ocean

Pacific
Ocean

FROUZEAN EMPIRE

Hosania
Frouzean Empire
Wil'iahn allies
Ephraim-Manasseh
Wil'iah

AUTHOR'S NOTE

Wil'iah is not a real country. Nobody really knows what happened to the Tribe of Zebulon and the other lost tribes of Israel. There are many theories, but none of them posit that they fled to Australia. Thus, this is a work of pure imagination and does not pretend to endorse any actual anthropological or historical theory. However, many plot points in this book are grounded in real historical events, and this book is faithful to the historical timeline regarding these occasions. Kublai Khan really did conquer China and go to war with the Southeast Asian kingdoms of Dai Viet and Champa, and he really did try to invade the Javanese kingdom of Singhasari. Many of the characters in this book are real historical figures, and though the author has taken some artistic license regarding their response to the fictional events of this story, he has tried to ground their characters in reality. A full list of characters and a pronunciation guide can be found at the back of this volume, including information on which ones are real historical figures and which are entirely fictional..

PROLOGUE

The Pearl River Delta, southern China, 1279 AD

A line of a thousand Chinese ships formed a grim chain across the brackish mouth of the Pearl River, the last desperate strength of the Southern Song Dynasty of China. Zhang Shijie, Grand General of what was left of the Song Army, nervously paced the deck, eyeing the fifty Mongol warships that drifted just out of range, festive music emanating from their decks. The blockade that had severely weakened his forces and forced them to start drinking seawater continued. Zhang winced as he heard a man vomit over the side of the ship.

He nervously cast a glance toward the large junk at the center of the Song formation, the ship that contained the last hope for a free China- seven-year-old Emperor Zhao Bing.

Zhang looked back over at the merriment on the Mongol ships, suspicion filling his eyes. He could have sworn that the enemy ships were getting closer.

They definitely were.

Still, the festive tunes wafted over the water.

Suddenly, the air was pierced with the screech of a horn, and great tarpaulins were flung back from the decks of the Mongol ships, revealing hundreds of soldiers, armed to the teeth. Zhang's head whirled around in panic as similar formations of Mongol ships appeared on all sides of the chain of Song vessels. Forty-four years of valiant resistance against the Mongol hordes had led to this moment -- China's last stand had begun.

Zhang sounded the alarm, and his weakened soldiers, emaciated and exhausted, staggered into their positions. Wave after wave of deadly arrows arced through the angry sky and rained down on the Chinese fleet, met with thousands of anguished cries as Zhang's men were cut down in droves. Dread rising in his chest, Zhang helplessly watched as seven of his ships sank beneath the waves. Chained together, the Chinese ships were unable to maneuver, and the battle soon degenerated into a chaotic melee. Zhang's heart leapt into his mouth as he realized the main group of Mongol warships was headed directly for the emperor.

"Cut us loose!" he yelled frantically at the sailors on his ship.

"I thought the chain was to keep any ships from deserting!" yelled back the ships' commander.

"It's far too late for that!" Zhang bellowed.

With painful sluggishness, the twelve ships around him freed themselves from the chain and began to inch their way toward the emperor, fighting their way through formations of Mongol junks.

They were too late.

Aboard the Imperial flagship, Zhao Bing cowered in wide-eyed terror as bellowing Mongols hacked their way through hundreds of Chinese soldiers and courtiers on the deck of the ship, heading directly for him. The boy emperor's slight frame trembled as he was dwarfed by the titanic struggle that roared around him. The timbers of the ship groaned ominously beneath his diminutive feet as a gurgle of water announced that it was beginning to sink. The young boy squeezed the arm of Prime Minister Lu Xiufu, who watched in helpless horror as annihilation bore down on them. Lu winced as he realized what he had to do. A horrible fate awaited the terrified boy if the Mongols captured him.

"We have no choice, Your Majesty," he said, his voice cracking with tears. He turned from the ravening hordes that cut their way like a cyclone across the deck of the ship next to him and led the boy by the hand to the starboard railing near the ship' stern. The angry, churning water awaited them below.

Lu took a deep breath and looked at the boy.

"It's been a privilege serving you. None of this is your fault. You have comported yourself with honor. Your courage will not soon be forgotten."

With that, he prepared to climb to the top of the railing, trailing the boy behind him.

Suddenly, a thunderous voice cut across the din of battle.

"Wait!"

A giant shadow fell across Lu and the Emperor, who whirled around in surprise.

Standing on the quarterdeck of the ship was an

enormous man, who seemed at least seven feet tall. His resolute eyes, piercing pits of molten steel set against his russet-brown face, glared out on the world with open defiance of the enemy that swarmed the deck.

"Who…" Lu asked incredulously. Then, his eyes filled with wonder as they recognized a sixteen-pointed star emblazoned on the man's breastplate.

"He's a friend," he whispered to Zhao, who wordlessly nodded in response.

"Never mind that. Don't jump. Go to the port side and climb down instead. We're waiting for you. I'll hold them off," the mysterious warrior boomed as he entered a fighting stance and brandished his gleaming sword at the oncoming enemy horde.

Lu wordlessly nodded, then led Zhao by the hand across the deck to the opposite railing. As they apprehensively peered over it, to their surprise, they saw not water, but the deck of a smaller catamaran ship that had lashed itself to the imperial flagship. Needing no further bidding, they began to descend, even as the Mongol forces licked their way across the deck like an all-consuming fire.

The warrior that stood in their way roared out a fierce battle-cry, in a language they had never heard before.

"T'vrae'ia Va'a'kau'lua!"

Lu only caught a glimpse of him charging headlong at the enemy, his sword whistling through the air and hacking through the apparently-inferior Mongol weapons, his free fist sending yet more enemy soldiers toppling to the deck in defeated heaps. Then, he and the boy emperor began to climb downward to their salvation.

Zhang Shijie's junk continued to beat its way toward the imperial junk, but he knew his task was fruitless. The giant warship was sinking fast, and its decks were swarming with Mongol troops. The air filled with the cries of Chinese soldiers and court officials as they were mercilessly hacked apart by the enemy.

His heart feeling like it was made of lead, Zhang turned to the man at the ship's control station.

"Make for the mouth of the bay. We're too late. Our only chance now is to get to Dowager Yang on the mainland and tell her the dynasty is lost, unless she can find another relative to appoint."

To his surprise, the man didn't listen. Instead, his eyes stared into the distance, his mouth opening in shock. Zhang whirled around, following the man's gaze.

From behind the sinking wreckage of the flagship emerged another vessel -- a catamaran with two large sails in the shapes of inverted triangles. The ship shot across the bay with shocking speed, quickly clearing the mess of the battle. Zhang suddenly realized he recognized the ship's configuration. He snapped into action, pointing at the receding vessel and turning to the man at the tiller.

"Follow that ship!"

The man needed no second bidding. Zhang's squadron hauled about and left the battle behind, doing its best to keep up with the catamaran. Pulling out a spyglass, Zhang focused on the flag fluttering bravely from the ship's mainmast.

In its upper left corner was a sixteen-pointed star, from which emanated thirty-two rays in red, white, and blue, separated by thin gold stripes.

Aboard the strange catamaran, Zhao Bing huddled together with Prime Minister Lu, looking up in a mixture of wonder and fear at the hulking warrior who stood over them. After holding off the Mongol soldiers so they could make good their escape, he had jumped at the last possible minute from the junk's quarterdeck down to this ship, landing with a thunderous thud. Now, the fast, sleek vessel darted away from the burning Chinese fleet, seeming to fly over the water at tremendous speed. Suddenly, Zhao Bing's eyes widened with joy as the doors to the deckhouse at the center of the ship flew open and a woman hurled herself across the deck, relief writ large on her delicate face as her sumptuous yellow silk robes billowed in the breeze behind her.

"Mother!" the young Emperor exclaimed, wrenching himself free of Lu's grip to run to meet the woman, who wrapped him in a tight embrace, tears streaming down her face.

"I'm so glad you're safe!" Dowager Yang sobbed, her tears containing a mixture of relief at her son's survival and grief for the death of her country.

Suddenly, a joyous grin spread across the young boy's face as two pugs trundled out of the deckhouse of the ship, ran over to him, and began to cover him in kisses.

"Wangcai! Tangtang! You're safe!" Zhao exclaimed in wonder.

"We managed to evacuate them, along with many of our most important treasures and technologies. This is a temporary retreat, not a permanent one," Dowager Yang said. "Someday, we shall return, and China will be free again."

After a few loving moments, the two walked over to the railing of the strange ship and stared wistfully as the green shores of China receded into the distance, almost as if it were a dream disappearing into the mists of memory. A single tear ran down Emperor Zhao's face.

"I tried," the boy whispered, his small voice quavering with emotion.

"There, there," the indomitable warrior soothed in a surprisingly tender tone. "Once, my country faced a similar situation to yours. All seemed lost – but it wasn't, because the flame of freedom burned on in one heart." He knelt down and pointed at the young Emperor's chest. "That fire burns in you now. As long as you still believe, there is hope for China." The man's eyes flicked up to the masthead. Zhao Bing's heart leapt as he beheld not just the unfamiliar flag of the mysterious ship, but also the imperial standard of the Song Dynasty, flapping defiantly in the gathering breeze.

"Who are you?" the boy asked tremulously.

The man, who had appeared so frightening on the imperial flagship, now seemed gentle and fatherly. Zhao Bing could tell from his eyes that this was a kind person. He snapped into an odd salute, placing a fist over his heart, then extending his arm, with an open palm, toward the boy.

"My name is Hezekiah. We're going to take you and somewhere safe, far across the sea, to a country called Wil'iah."

PART I

1283–1286

CHAPTER ONE

THE RANGER OF WIL'IAH

Principality of Ekron, southern Australia, 1283 AD

*P*anic gripped Medea as the braying of the dingoes sounded closer and closer. She bit her lip to stifle a curse as she nearly tripped on a rock, barely catching her balance. Wincing as the iron leg-cuff that symbolized her slave status chafed against her ankle, she stole a quick glance behind her, her pupils dilating with alarm as they were met by the diffused glow of distant torches. She felt a hand grip her upper arm, and whipped her head back around to see Iphigenia, one of her fellow escapees, silently urging her to continue on.

"We're almost there!" hissed the shadowy form beside her, a man from the Dhirari Nation, one of the constituent countries of the kingdom to which she was escaping. Wildly gesticulating to the group of seven women who ran barefoot across the desert, he pointed to a series of boulders, about a thousand meters ahead, that seemed to be in too straight of a line to be naturally placed. "We just have to make it that far!"

Medea squinted, trying to resolve details of the desert floor on this dark, moonless night. While the stars illuminated their brilliant tableaux in a million points of light overhead, it was not enough for her to clearly see where she was going. Her breath caught in her throat as she heard a shout behind her, much closer than she expected. Shivering in the bitter cold of the night, she willed herself onward, heedless of the sharp pains of the rocks as they dug into her bare soles.

Involuntarily, she screamed as an arrow whizzed by her ear, missing it by under an inch.

"Fool!" hissed Iphigenia, her sharp features and raven-black hair barely visible in the gloom. "You will be the death of us all!" Despite her vehemence, Iphigenia herself flinched as another viciously-barbed arrow buried itself in the hard-packed ground next to her running feet.

"There they are!" A cruel voice sounded, only about two hundred meters behind. "Master Ajax wants them alive!"

Suddenly, Iphigenia let out a strangled cry as she tripped and fell flat on her face. Forgetting her own safety and the sting of her insult, Medea reversed course and ran back to help. Gently lifting Iphigenia by the forearm, Medea was about to whisper to her not to be afraid, when a large, hairy hand brusquely grabbed her by the shoulder.

"Going somewhere?" Flaring torchlight illuminated the

silver-flecked leer of a Frouzean guard missing many of his teeth.

Medea worked her jaw, but no sound came out. She could hear the rest of her compatriots running ahead of her, but, with a sinking feeling, she realized they weren't going to make it.

She flinched as a dingo, domesticated by her pursuers as an attack dog, emerged from the darkness to growl at her, the torchlight reflecting from the cruelly-spiked studs of its collar and the drool dripping from its bared fangs.

"Not now, not yet. This one's too valuable," sneered the guard at the beast, his hulking frame blocking out an alarming number of the stars that defiantly blazed against the blackness above.

"You don't understand!" Iphigenia cried out. "I wa—"

Suddenly, both the guard and Medea's heads jerked up as a strange thumping sound filled the air. Medea's eyes barely registered the dizzying movement of a strange flying object, before she heard a sickening crack. The once-menacing guard crumpled to the floor like a rag doll. The thumping sound receded again, and the dingo was left frantically barking at an amorphous shape advancing from where the sound had come.

The dingo charged to meet the mysterious shadow, but its braying suddenly stopped as Medea heard an unintelligible, soothing voice sound in the darkness. With a start, she realized the voice was speaking in a language she couldn't understand, but she recognized its strange staccato cadence. Squinting to make out what was going on, she realized that the dingo had rolled over in the dirt, its tongue lolling out in an uncharacteristic expression of joy, apparently calmed by the exhortations of her mysterious rescuer. Encouraged by this unexpected development, Medea tentatively stepped forward. The vague shape next to the happy dingo resolved into a thick cloak, its colors expertly designed to blend in with the desert. The mysterious hooded figure stood up from its crouching position to reveal a commanding height, and Medea stopped, fear gripping her once again.

With a one-handed flourish, the figure threw back the hood to reveal large, inquisitive eyes set in a kind, squarish face. From the darkness of his features, Medea realized with a sigh of relief that this man wasn't a Frouzean like her pursuers. In his other hand, he held a strange, curved piece of wood—the Aboriginal people had a word for it, but Medea couldn't remember what it was – only that it was a weapon that would always return to the thrower. Medea strained to listen as more commotion in the distance indicated that the other Frouzean slave-catchers were similarly dispatched.

"Well, that was a near one, wasn't it?" The man spoke in perfectly-accented Frouzean. Medea picked up the torch that the guard had dropped, thanking the goddess that there had been no nearby vegetation to spread the fire. Holding it up to study her rescuer, she noticed that pinned to his desert robes was a blue and white six-pointed star, with a red circle inscribed, inside of which was a gold eight-pointed star. Her breath caught as she recognized the symbol.

"Yes, you are among friends," the man said, his eyes twinkling in the torchlight as he was joined by three other dark shapes, fresh from dispatching the other pursuers. Medea realized with a start that he wasn't very old – his boyish face looked like it couldn't be more than twenty-five.

Striding over to Iphigenia, who still lay splayed on the floor in apparent shock, he reached out a hand and gently pulled her up. "Are you all right?" He asked.

Even in the dim torchlight, Iphigenia was visibly flustered as her cheeks filled with color and she batted her eyelashes. "Well…yes, thank you, kind sir," she said with uncharacteristic sweetness. Medea rolled her eyes, grateful for the cover of night.

"Where are the others?" Medea asked, remembering her compatriots with alarm.

"They have crossed the border safely, led by their Dhirari Exodus Road guide," another voice said, "and the remaining slave catchers have been rendered unconscious." Medea's eyes widened in surprise as she realized this person was a woman. A dark shape emerged from the gloom and threw off its hood to reveal a sharp, angular face and frizzy hair barely restrained in a bun.

The woman walked over to Medea and pulled her in for a comforting hug. "You don't have to be afraid anymore," she said, her soothing tones backed with unmistakable steel.

"We'd best get going. We don't know if there are any more slave-catchers in the vicinity," the leader of the group said, releasing Iphigenia from his helpful grip.

"What about him? Is he…dead?" Medea asked, tentatively motioning to the guard.

"Oh, him?" the man asked. "No, he's just in for a good night's sleep. He'll be fine in the morning. Maybe that smack on the head will make him reconsider his evil ways."

"Shouldn't we finish him off now, while we have the chance?" asked the woman who had hugged Medea.

"Sixth Commandment, Deborah," the man gently chided.

"You and that Sixth Commandment," she sighed.

Pointing again to the boulders marking the border, the man said, "It isn't far now." He made a strange snickering noise to the dingo, who happily jumped up, tail wagging.

With that, the man began striding purposefully toward the rocks, with his compatriots, the dingo, and the escaped slaves following.

As Medea passed between the two largest boulders, a gust of wind hit her face. Normally, desert winds at night were biting and cruel, but this one felt…different – invigorating, encouraging, and gentle. Even the stars seemed to burn a bit brighter overhead. The man who had rescued them turned back and placed a fist over his heart before unclenching it and extending his open hand to the two escaped slaves.

"Tamino ben'Gershom, Knight Commander of the King's Rangers of the Order of the Flame of Zebulon, at your service. Welcome to Wil'iah."

CHAPTER TWO

TRUKANAMOA

On and on the little party passed through the trackless desert, insignificant specks against the vast carpet of desolation that passed in all directions as far as the eye could see. Medea, astride the camel that she had been lent by the rescue party, couldn't fathom how her mysterious saviors could possibly navigate through this featureless wilderness of bitter nighttime cold and scorching mid-day heat, but forward they forged on to an uncertain destination. Even less clear was how they would possibly have enough water to get wherever they were going. In the small hours of one morning, as the faintest glow began to brush the painterly canvas of the eastern sky, the last drop in her canteen ran out.

Dread coursed through Medea's veins as she helplessly shook the vessel. Iphigenia flashed her a dirty look that wordlessly said, "Don't remind me."

Medea squinted in the predawn gloom at the leaders of the rescue party, their camels huddled together in close conference. Her untrained ears could barely hear a muttered song from the Dhirari guide that floated like a whisper through the star-studded night. He had been singing like this for the whole trip, although Medea couldn't imagine why.

Two hours later, as the malevolent, lidless sun inexorably rose to blast the earth with its days, the leader of the party, Tamino, called a halt. Medea's eyes widened in wonder as they focused on a well standing in the middle of the cracked ground before them. She leapt off the camel and ran toward it, joining the rest of the escaped slaves while Tamino drew miraculous water with a bucket and filled the canteens. Medea desperately gulped the water down before refilling yet again, thanking her gods that this water existed – or was it a dream, a mirage of the endless, merciless wasteland?

"How is this possible?" She gasped at Tamino.

In answer, the corners of his large, brown eyes crinkled into well-worn smile lines as a bright, easy grin carved deep dimples into his kind, steadfast face. He motioned to the Dhirari guide.

"The song tells him the way. His people have navigated across the whole continent in this manner for a thousand generations. Its words will always lead us to what we need, right when we need it," he responded. "Shortly, its sweet notes will speed us on to our destination."

Countless miles of starkly beautiful landscape marched by as they journeyed north, the sun tracing a great arc over their heads too many times for Medea to track. However, gradually, the endless flats around them began to change. A thin, dark line appeared in the distance, growing gradually but perceptibly larger as the camels staggered forward. As they pitched their tents one day, Deborah, the woman who had aided their rescue, said cheerfully, "Almost there! We'll arrive tomorrow morning." Medea's heart leapt at the news, but she didn't know what was in store for her at their enigmatic destination.

That night, the dark line loomed ever larger, a threatening black void against the brilliant jewels that sprayed across the sky. With a shock, Medea realized that the muted thump of camel hooves against sand had given way to a crisp clop as they impacted a paved road. Slavery in the court of Ekron had not exactly given Medea a thorough education in geography, so she spurred her camel forward and asked Deborah, "Where are we?"

"Those are the Tjoritja Mountains ahead," she replied proudly. "Very soon, we will reach Trukanamoa."

Trukanamoa? The legendary fortress-capital in the desert? A thrill raced down Medea's spine at the thought of the great city. In the days of her servitude tales of its splendor and might had held the darkness at bay, as had whispered stories of the brave and noble people who defended it. Yet, as the legends clandestinely whispered through the oppressive halls of the palace of Ekron, she had scarcely believed such a place could truly be real.

As the great rays of the sun blazed over the eastern horizon to bathe the rust-colored mountains in light, all of her doubts melted away. The perfectly-paved road before them ran by a river, ramrod-straight, toward a gap in the mountains. Standing squarely in the midst of the gap, illuminated by the pink sunrise, a massive castle glowed in the distance. Its three concentric walls looked like they were made of light itself, studded with steadfast towers that proudly dared any enemy to try to force the gap. From the highest of the twelve towers that formed the innermost ring of the fortification, a giant flag flapped in the morning breeze – a great sixteen-pointed star blazing with the reflected radiance of the russet-gold sunlight, and thirty-two red, white, and blue rays that boldly burst in all directions from its center. On either side of the proud structure soared the mountains, either side of the gap crowned with another castle perched precariously against the sheer rock face, its commanding keep standing sentinel over the desert below. Incredibly, impossibly, this was not the extent of the mighty fortress before her, for yet another set of walls rose half-completed before the castle. The urgent ringing of hammers and chisels floated over the clear air toward them.

"Trukanamoa, capital of the faithful kingdom and fortress of freedom," Tamino said, his voice quavering with pride. "I haven't seen it myself in almost a year."

As the little group neared the great castle, they passed through the two walls under construction in front of it. Medea marveled that, at its base, the tapering read wall was at least sixty feet thick, comprised of densely-packed earthen layer capped on either end by massive sandstone blocks. She noticed Iphigenia inspecting the half-completed defenses with interest.

"Who is this built to stop?" She marveled. Nothing in Ekron's arsenal, or anything in the old empire, could make so much as a scratch.

To her surprise, a look of foreboding crossed Tamino's face. "Unfortunately, there is a world beyond this island continent of ours – and an implacable enemy who will stop at nothing to rule the whole world. When his gaze inevitably reaches our shores, we will be ready."

Medea suppressed a shiver.

However, Tamino seemed to shake off the ominous sense of doom and returned to his normal earnest, cheerful demeanor. "Not to worry, ma'am, that problem is almost five thousand miles away. Let us rejoice in your newfound freedom."

Both the road and the river split in front of the castle, the river filling a deep moat that surrounded the outermost curtain wall tower. On either side, walls stretched from the castle to the edges of the mountain gap, with massive gatehouses standing guard over the road as it passed through to the city beyond. As the party approached the gap, Tamino called up to the guards atop the barbican in the strange tongue of the Wil'iahns. In response, a blast of sound hit Medea's ears as a dozen conch shells wailed in welcome, and the drawbridge of the gate creaked down to admit them entry. An iron portcullis noiselessly withdrew into the stone mass above, revealing an iron-studded gate emblazoned with the star of Wil'iah that opened to welcome them to the city, the doors stretching forward almost like the comforting arms of a warm embrace. As they stepped over the drawbridge, Medea noticed Iphigenia staring at the machicolations above – threatening, yawning gaps in the overhang where murderous missiles could pour down in the event of an attack. To Medea's surprise, once inside the gatehouse, they encountered another gate; Iphigenia's eyes flicked over to the arrow-loops that lay in wait on either side to envelop attackers in a deadly crossfire. The second gate swung open, only to reveal a third – and a fourth – and a fifth! The gatehouse's deadly tunnel seemed to stretch into infinity, but, finally the seventh gate parted to reveal a vast vista stretching into the distance – and Medea's heart leapt into her throat.

A soaring cathedral towered over them, its countless

spires and mountainous dome seeming to reach the heavens themselves. The clear, heart-strengthening tones of a bell wafted down from the highest of the pinnacles as Medea looked beyond the church to a vast garden that stretched far into the distance, where another tower stood nearly three miles away, crowned with a leaping flame. Medea's though jumped back to her rescuer's first introduction. "Is that --?"

"Yes," Tamino smiled. "THE Flame of Zebulon, kept continually burning for nearly two thousand years – even in the days of our captivity."

Medea turned to watch as a woman hurried over to them from an official-looking, but rather small, building to their left, crowned with a gold cupola. The statuesque woman seemed to float over the ground to them with regal dignity, her eyes flecks of smoldering coal set in a sharp-featured face framed with a barely-controlled mane of frizzy, iron gray hair. A diadem crowned her brow, from which sprouted an enormous, burnished spike.

Tamino snapped into a salute, which Medea clumsily tried to imitate. However, the woman's august features, to Medea's surprise, broke into a wide smile.

"Oh, stop it," she said as she rushed forward to envelop Tamino in a steely hug. Medea's eyebrows arched as she exchanged surprised glances with Iphigenia.

"It's good to see you, Mother," Tamino said warmly.

"Mother?" mouthed Medea at Iphigenia.

"These are the latest guests to arrive via the Exodus Road," Tamino said to the woman as he swept his outstretched hand to indicate the escapees. He then pointed at the woman. "It is my pleasure to introduce you to Her Faithfulness Adirah, Queen of Wil'iah, the legendary 'Lioness of Zebulon.'"

"If she's the queen, that makes you --" Iphigenia

stammered.

"Never mind that," Tamino hastily interjected. "Deborah, I believe these folks have an appointment with the Exodus Office."

"Yes, sir, right away," the warrior snapped into a salute and then turned to the refugees. "Follow me."

For her part, Adirah pulled her son in for another hug, her heart swelling relief that he had returned from the dangerous border regions unscathed.

"How are the Marches?" she asked, wincing slightly, for she already knew the answer.

"Well, the wreck of the old empire is as unstable as ever," Tamino replied, "but we're managing to keep order on our side of the border. I'm glad we're able to help some escape across." Tamino's eyes suddenly lit up as another figure raced across the square.

"Jessica!" He said jubilantly, his face lighting up in recognition. "You're back here as well?" he asked as he pulled his sister into a bear hug.

"Well, it is the end of the training year," Jessica said as Tamino pulled back to get a good look at her face. Her eyes, two blazing flames set below bladelike eyebrows, seemed to bore right through everyone she looked at. The formidable outcropping of her chiseled face wordlessly defied all comers with the stately ferocity of a lioness, an impression reinforced by the intractably voluminous hair that framed it. She continued, "Regrettably, Jeremiah is still at sea."

"You both made it back just in time," Adirah said, her voice suddenly deadly serious. "The situation across the sea continues to deteriorate. The time for action fast approaches, so your father has called an emergency meeting with Ephraim-Manasseh. Their delegation is supposed to arrive later today."

Adirah gave her son a quizzical smile as a hint of color filled his cheeks.

"Is the whole royal family coming for the state visit?" he asked, clearly trying to mask a mysterious emotion.

"Last I heard, yes. Why?"

"Well, if we are receiving such esteemed guests, I'd best get ready," he evaded before dashing off to the palace across the square.

✳ ✳ ✳

Two short hours later, fanfare floated up from the gates as a carriage, escorted by twenty horsemen, swept through and proceeded on the road around the Castle and the Grand Cathedral, finally coming to a stop in front of the palace. Emblazoned on its doors was a quartered crest charged with a bull and a bush. The royal party of the United Kingdom of Ephraim and Manasseh, an allied country to the north of Wil'iah, had arrived. The heroic figure of Wil'iah's King Hezekiah stood alongside his family in front of the palace to greet them.

Gamaliel, the ever-jovial king of Manasseh, alighted from the carriage, joined by his wife Sheerah, the war queen of Ephraim, whose famous defiance of Frouzea's might had touched off the war that ultimately ended the old empire's tyranny. Next came their son Gideon, a mighty warrior.

Last out of the carriage was the Princess Avora'tru'ivi. Her twinkling, liquid eyes were twin stars set against her heart-shaped, fine-boned face, framed by magnificent lustrous cascades of sable hair interwoven with small jewels and beads that glittered like the impossibly brilliant night sky over the deserts of Kati-Thanda. The princess somehow managed to balance an air of essential sweetness with an aura of danger, much like her mother. Her brown eyes twinkled with mirth, but also betrayed a sharpness that indicated that her joviality was not synonymous with pure pacifism; she was a gentle trade wind breeze that could whip into a typhoon at any moment. Adirah noticed Tamino, now dressed in a spotless blue and white dress uniform, stand up a little bit straighter and clear his throat with marked awkwardness.

Avora'tru'ivi stepped up to King Hezekiah and Queen Adirah, dipping her head and placing a fist over her heart in the traditional gesture of respect. "Your Majesties," she said. Her voice was at once ethereal and earthy, simultaneously a tinkling chime in a gentle summer breeze and a sonorous sentry-bell, heavy with emotion. She then turned to Tamino and repeated the gesture, though this time, she locked her eyes directly with the prince's.

Tamino himself bowed and placed a fist over his heart, though he did not break from her gaze. He cleared his throat again and said, "Princess."

Avora'tru'ivi next turned to Princess Jessica and prepared to dip her head yet again, but Jessica said, "Oh, enough already!" and ran forward to warmly embrace her Manassite counterpart. "I am so glad you're here! It has been too long! We have so much to discuss."

At this, Hezekiah broke into a wide smile, and stepped forward to give Gamaliel a similar embrace. Laughing, he said, "I think we are all way beyond the introductions. Come inside quickly; we have a wonderful feast prepared!"

CHAPTER THREE

A FLAME AGAINST THE DARKNESS

*T*he dining room of the palace was surprisingly unadorned. Its ceiling, crafted of rich woods, was in the shape of a pavilion interior, an homage to the tents of the Zebulite and Aboriginal resistance that had overthrown the original Frouzean Empire and created the Kingdom of Wil'iah. Set at the center of the roof was a single crystal rendition of the Star of Wil'iah, the national emblem, lit from within by a candle. Painted around it were stars representing the night sky on the night that the Vow of Wil'iah, Hezekiah's promise to create a free nation, was taken. A raised, aromatic eucalyptus wood table ran down the length of the room, around which were arranged plush divans covered with rare Chinese silk in geometric patterns. The table was garnished with waratah flowers in many colors. Incongruous next to this happy decoration, tacked to one wall was a massive map of Asia and the South Pacific, prepared with the help of the Chinese bureaucrats rescued from the Song Dynasty. A vast swath of the map was stained with the red of the Yuan Dynasty and its affiliated Mongol Khanates, while most of what remained was colored pink for its vassals. A brave shade of bright blue marked Wil'iah, Ephraim-Manasseh, and a precious few other nations that had made the bold decision to defy the seemingly inexorable might of Kublai Khan. Hezekiah effortlessly commanded the attention of all at the table.

Spread on the table was a sumptuous assortment of foods. While the cuisine of the Judgate of Tjoritja, the province that included the capital city of Trukanamoa, was not as renowned as the bountiful seafood menus of Wil'iah's prosperous eastern provinces, the royal cook staff had prepared a suitable meal. Silver platters piled high with gracefully-arranged desert fruits and vegetables, a main course of rotisserie chicken and roasted beef seasoned with Indonesian spices, and a dessert consisting of whipped goat's cream sprinkled with sweet desert fruits awaited the diners. A multitude of beverages were available including fresh spring water, cow's milk, and several varieties of tea imported from Java. The table settings included the Imperial fine bone porcelain that had been rescued from China four years prior as it fell to the Mongol Empire.

Adirah, dressed in a finely-embroidered silk tunic with a gold headdress trimmed in pearls, hissed in Hezekiah's ear, "Where is Tamino?"

The king whispered back, "Something about washing his face to get rid of more dirt from his travel. I don't understand. I don't think anybody here cares."

Queen Adirah stole a glance at Princess Avora'tru'ivi

and gave a slight, knowing smile.

Just then, Tamino arrived at the door, breathless and somewhat flushed, as if he had been running. His cape swished behind him and caught on the door hinge, causing the prince to sigh in exasperation and bend down to tug it free.

"Sorry I'm --- late." He said, stopping in his tracks with a catch of his voice as he saw Princess Avora'tru'ivi sitting on her divan. His eyes grew wider and an extra depth of color filled his cheeks, as the corners of his mouth quivered.

Queen Adirah gently laughed. "That's quite alright. A place is prepared for you!"

Realizing with some trepidation that his seat was right across from the princess, Tamino nervously sat down. The light from the torchieres surrounding the table reflected off the gold and silver Star of Wil'iah emblazoned on his hauberk.

Italereme, king of the Arrernte Nation, the local Aboriginal people, turned to him. "Tamino, my boy! I hear you have been on all sorts of adventures in the border Judgates!" he said, using the Wil'iahn term for a province.

Seeming to shake himself from whatever had occupied his thoughts, the prince smiled and recounted some of his adventures from his time in Wiluna, Anangu, and Kati-Thanda.

Italereme chuckled. "And is there a future queen of Wil'iah somewhere in those judgates?"

Tamino's eyebrows arched, registering a mixture of surprise and embarrassment. He regarded the napkin in his lap and nervously cleared his throat, opening his mouth to respond.

Princess Jessica interjected. "Well, Italereme, tell me-how is the water level in the watering holes of the Tjoritja

Mountains these days?" She hazarded a quick dart of her eyes to her brother, who gave her a grateful smile, and at Avora'tru'ivi, who was slightly but noticeably blushing. Jessica prepared a new set of dry, procedural questions about local food supplies, tax policy, and military preparation to ask Italereme before he meddled any more in her sibling's personal life.

The thunderous voice of Hezekiah suddenly sounded, instantly commanding everyone's attention. "Alright, it's time to discuss the business at hand. As we all know, four years ago, China fell to the Mongols. My friends, it seems the hour has come when Kublai Khan is no longer satisfied with this conquest. Even now, our spies tell us he is preparing to move against Dai Viet. Our foreign minister, Lu Xiufu, will explain the situation." The king swept a massive hand to welcome the former Song minister, who now served his adopted country. Lu cleared his throat and began to point at various places on the map with a long stick.

"The Khmer Empire has agreed to pay tribute to the Khan, but Champa has tenaciously resisted. King Inrdravarman and Prince Harijit retreated from the capital and instead have waged guerilla warfare against the Mongols. The Mongol general Sogetu has been forced to retreat. Dai Viet has for some time now been in an unsteady tributary state to the Mongols, but now the Mongols have demanded passage through Dai Viet to launch a larger invasion of Champa."

"All of these countries are so far away. Why are we concerned? Isn't it best if we just keep our heads down and avoid drawing attention to ourselves?" asked Gideon.

Queen Sheerah pointed at the collection of islands to the south of Champa and Dai Viet.

"If Dai Viet and Champa both fall to the Mongols,

Indonesia is clearly next. According to our intelligence, the Singhasari Kingdom on Java is currently expanding, but they are likely not strong enough to defeat a Mongol invasion. And if they fall," Sheerah gave her compatriots at the table a knowing look, "Only a very narrow strip of water will defend us from the largest empire on Earth."

Tamino cleared his throat. "Last I heard, the population of China alone was in excess of seventy million. That's nearly twenty times Wil'iah's population."

Hezekiah sat back.

"Dai Viet was able to repulse the Mongols once before, in 1258, but that victory was so costly that they accepted vassal status anyway. At that point, Kublai Khan had yet to conquer China. Now, it is highly doubtful that Dai Viet could succeed again. We have to make a decision. Do we intervene, do nothing and face certain war at a later date, or try to negotiate with the Mongols?"

Lu Xiufu interjected. "It's worth noting that we have not spent the last four years idly watching these events unfold. Admiral Zhang Shijie, my compatriot in the failed defense of the Song Dynasty, has been hard at work modernizing Wil'iah's armed forces with the best of Chinese technology to face the Mongol threat. We have learned from the mistakes that we made in the defense of my homeland. If anybody knows how to fight the Mongols, it's Zhang. He even spent some time serving in their army before he defected to the Song, many years ago."

"I'd like to take a moment to acknowledge the changes that Zhang's technology has brought to Wil'iah's army and navy," Jessica added. "Let's just say I love gunpowder. Our forces are now miles ahead of the Frouzean principalities, which has helped us keep our borders much safer, as I'm sure my dear brother can attest."

Tamino soberly nodded, but then looked askance as Gideon opened his mouth to ask a question.

"I heard that the Mongols have been known to offer generous negotiating terms, but any country that dares to fight them is instantly and mercilessly crushed. In fact, they often slaughter the whole populations of cities that defy them. Surely we don't want to suffer the same fate?" Gideon's question earned him a surprisingly sharp, exasperated look from his sister.

"Why would the Mongols negotiate with us? We have nothing to offer them," Adirah asked.

Avora'tru'ivi nervously cleared her throat.

"If I learned one thing from my mother," she said, smiling at Sheerah, "It's that we never negotiate with the enemy. I think the answer is obvious. We must form a large alliance to defeat the Mongols." Gideon gave his sister an incredulous look, which the Princess simply responded to with a sweet smile.

Hezekiah stroked his chin. "King Kertanegara of Singhasari has formed an alliance with Champa already and has continually refused Mongol demands for tribute. Perhaps the groundwork for such an alliance is already being laid. If we can persuade Dai Viet to refuse the Mongols access to their lands, Champa may be saved. Together, we all might be strong enough to hold off the Mongols. Japan and Dai Viet have already proved that they are not invincible."

"What about Japan?" asked Tamino. "Should we not consider an alliance with them as well?"

Lu responded, "Since the fall of China, the East China Sea and the trade routes to Japan have not been safe for our ships, and we have not had any contact with Japan. News of their miraculous victory over the Mongol fleet came only from second-hand sources, which made the outlandish claim that a typhoon destroyed the entire Mongol fleet. Whether or not this is true, Japan is out of our reach for the moment."

"The first step to building our alliance is to unify our continent against the Mongol threat. Kublai Khan's vultures have yet to reach this far south," Hezekiah continued, "but they will undoubtedly come with their characteristic demands for tribute. I can say with confidence that Wil'iah will render no such obeisance. It is my request today that the United Kingdom of Ephraim and Manasseh make the same commitment. No separate submittal."

Sheerah grinned. "Surely you remember what happened the last time somebody demanded tribute from me?"

Adirah laughed. "History will not soon forget the smashing of the idols."

"Are we sure this is wise? This seems like tweaking the tail of a tiger that has yet to notice us," Gideon said.

"The tiger will notice us eventually. We need to seize the moment and build this alliance now, while we have a chance of defeating it. If we wait until we are alone, then we will be dinner," retorted Avora'tru'ivi.

"That settles it then. We must dispatch ambassadors to Issachar to gain their support, and," Hezekiah winced, "Pelesetania."

Sheerah pounded her fist on the table. "Manasseh does not recognize Pelesetania. The only reason we haven't taken our western provinces back from them is the three hundred thousand troops that Prince Jason holds at the ready."

"Those are three hundred thousand troops that we do not want aiming their spears at our backs while we try to defeat the Mongols. I find Pelesetania as distasteful as you, and I am confident that someday Manasseh will win back her west, but in the meantime we need to work together. Khan is as much a threat to Jason as he is to us. Surely he will recognize that. I don't ask you to extend diplomatic recognition, but we need to at least open communication with him. The rest of the old Frouzean Empire, or what's left of it, would hardly be of any use – or be any threat – to our alliance. The five principalities, and to a lesser degree Tanitania, are failed states too busy fighting each other to muster any sort of wherewithal. I doubt they even know about the Mongols, but Pelesetania has managed to maintain a modicum of strength," Hezekiah responded.

"We must also dispatch a diplomatic mission to Singhasari, Champa, and Dai Viet immediately to bring them into our alliance," said Adirah.

"I will go," volunteered Tamino. Adirah's eyes flashed dangerously to her son, betraying nervousness.

"Tamino, this is a hazardous mission. You could be captured by the Mongols. Perhaps it would make more sense to send a more experienced member of the Order."

Tamino flushed slightly. "Mother, I have just completed my five years as a ranger conducting dangerous operations on the border. I think I am up to this task. And," he added with a gentle smile, "I think our offer will be more convincing if it comes from the prince."

Adirah sighed. "Very well. We will prepare the Ava'ivi to sail for Singhasari at once. Your mission is to persuade King Kertanegara to expand his alliance with Champa to include his neighbors to the south. After that, you are proceed to Champa, find King Inrdravarman and Prince Harijit, and recruit them to our cause. Lastly, you must go to Dai Viet and convince the Tran Court not to permit Mongol troops to transit their country."

Tamino nodded. "What about the Khmer Empire and the Pagan Empire of Burma?"

Hezekiah frowned. "Both of those have already sworn obeisance to Khan, and the Pagan Empire is descending into chaos. I think visiting the Khmers might be worth it, but I will leave it to your judgement on the ground regarding Burma." He then turned to the rest of the party. "We must also solidify our alliances on our own continent."

A slightly tremulous voice sounded in response.

"I will go."

The heads all swiveled to Avora'tru'ivi, who smiled sweetly from her chair at the table. Adirah grinned, but Gamaliel's eyebrows furrowed.

"Sweetheart," he said, "Pelesetania especially is a dangerous proposition. I can't let you go there."

Gideon sat up a bit straighter in his chair, brushing a wayward strand of hair out of his eye.

"Sister, it is my place as the crown prince to conduct this mission. It would be highly irregular for the princess of Manasseh to conduct such a diplomatic mission alone. I have misgivings about this plan, but I should be the one to carry it out."

"Tamino wants to serve his country," the princess responded, taking a moment to beam at the prince of Wil'iah, who suddenly became very interested in a bush pear on his plate. "I want to serve mine. This is a special opportunity for me to learn more about the diplomatic arts." Her voice was filled with more force than she thought she really had.

"But—" her father attempted to interject.

"Gamaliel, she can do it," interrupted Sheerah.

"She doesn't have to go alone," added Princess Jessica. "I can go with her. I too would like to learn more about diplomacy. This way, both of our nations can be represented. And, as you know, I can take care of myself."

With a sudden fluid motion, she unsheathed her dagger and hurled it at the wall, burying it perfectly between two stones.

"I told you! Not in the house!" Adirah chided.

"I see no problem with this plan," Hezekiah chuckled. "The princesses will visit Issachar first. I have no doubt they will accept our plan. As for Pelesetania, it remains to be seen, but I suspect Prince Jason might listen to reason. His much-flaunted three hundred thousand soldiers won't do much alone against Khan's hordes. As for the independent Aboriginal Nations, we already have a mutual defense treaty with Pilbara, Tunuvivi, and the Murri Confederacy. The only one we have a shaky relationship with is the Yonlgu. They will be their last stop on the way home."

"I hate to bring this up," interjected Adirah, "but what about Hosania?"

Gamaliel and Sheerah suddenly both glowered with dark expressions.

"We are not on speaking terms with them, ever since they tried to take over our country and sabotage our church. I should think you would be the same. After all, it is largely due to their actions that Zebulon fell in the first place." Gamaliel growled.

Tamino interposed, "My last visit to the Dark Kingdom didn't give me the impression they were interested in cooperation." He suddenly got a faraway look in his eyes, then hazarded a quick glance at Avora'tru'ivi, who blushed as she remembered the adventure they had shared in Hosania as children.

Hezekiah nodded. "We have to have some standards."

"Well, it seems as though everyone has their action plans," Adirah said.

"When we have finished assembling the alliance, we will

all meet up at Shechem to make our plans. Your capital is closer to the action than any of our ports," Hezekiah said to the Manassite delegation.

"I think it's time to brush up on my Vietnamese," Tamino smiled as he rose from his chair.

"Did I say you were dismissed?" Adirah waggled a single finger at him.

Tamino turned several shades of red and immediately sat down.

"My apologies. I am unused to ceremony after five years at the border."

Adirah grinned.

"I take it you are also unused to dessert?" The queen clapped her hands, and several waiters came into the room, their platters piled high with delicious treats and confections. The queen looked at her companions at the table.

"What are you waiting for? Eat!"

CHAPTER FOUR

IN THE GARDENS OF THE ELYSIUM

The magnificent feast finished, Princess Avora'tru'ivi hurried down a corridor of the palace, her heart pounding as she realized the enormity of the task she had taken on. Retiring to her quarters in the guest house at the rear of the palace, she took a moment to enjoy her surroundings, trying to calm her nerves. Her corner room was beautifully built out of whitewashed marble, with ceiling beams of expensive foreign hardwood intricately carved with geometric patterns, stunningly-blue tiled floors, and hand-knotted carpets hanging on the walls. On one side was a bow window with three elegant ogive arches, each covered by a hand-carved alabaster screen with a pattern of stars, through which breathed a gentle breeze that carried with it the scents of the garden outside. Avora'tru'ivi moved over to a basin in the center of the bow window, noting the variety of multicolored boronia flowers floating in the sweet spring water. Coming face to face with her reflection in a mirror set over it, she looked deeply into her own eyes, watching as fear and determination wrestled within them.

"You will do whatever you need to do for Manasseh," she whispered to herself, balling her hand into a fist for emphasis. She tried to narrow her eyes in an encouraging, resolute expression, but the brown, liquid pools that stared back at her in the mirror betrayed none of the bravado that she had portrayed when she volunteered for the dangerous mission.

You're a decent actress, she thought, *but do you have the courage that you need to march into the teeth of your enemy?*

Deciding that she needed to take a walk to clear her mind, Avora'tru'ivi exchanged the somewhat stuffy finery of the evening for a more freely-flowing set of white desert robes, embroidered with gold thread and a variety of colored beads. The princess opened the fragrant eucalyptus double doors that led to the courtyard garden and stepped outside. It was a glorious, nearly cloudless night studded with thousands of stars; the princess felt her heart leap as a faint wisp of cloud, high in the heavens, floated away to reveal the five blazing lights of the Southern Cross.

Dear Mother, Give me strength, she thought.

The garden was beautifully lit by the gentle glow of the full moon. She took in the scene; at the center of the garden stood a three-tiered fountain, with its playful cascades of sweet-scented water; around it was arrayed a riot of flowers both native and exotic. Some had come all the way from far Pacific islands and even from China and India, while others were the more familiar boronias and waratahs of her native land.

Flanked on either side by smaller fountains was a small side gate; the princess quietly opened it and stepped out into a small but neatly paved street that led to the much more grand public Elysium Botanical Gardens that fronted the palace. The gardens had been planted to provide a green space for the city's residents and to commemorate the sacrifices of those who gave their lives to win the kingdom's independence from the Frouzean Empire less than twenty years before. After quietly walking down the street, she beheld the gardens in their full nighttime grandeur. An interesting mixture of the wild and the orderly, there was a definite overall symmetry to the design, but within it, paths and streams meandered as if they had minds of their own. Within the gardens was one of the greatest assemblages of foliage in this part of the world. Beside nearly every plant found in the continent were fragrant flowers and towering trees imported from all corners of the known world. The gardens were dotted throughout with monuments dedicated to war heroes of the kingdom. The princess, with no specific destination in mind, began to wander through the gardens. This was her first time visiting the newly-completed city of Trukanamoa, and she wanted to take it all in.

At length, she found herself face-to-face with a grand block of sandstone carved into the shape of Solomon's temple, atop which burned a flame whose warm, defiant glow lent a golden tinge to the surrounding foliage. Unlike the Wil'iahn script of most of the monuments she had seen, this one was written in the ancient Hebrew language that was still used in some circles as a commemorative, liturgical, and academic tongue. She began to read it aloud, and her voice caught in her throat as she realized who it was for.

In eternal memory of a man whose singular courage
And disregard for fear and danger
Lit the way to freedom for an entire people
And set alight once again the ancient fire that burns in all of us.
In loving memory of Joshua VII Vreva'maua'ahava,
Rightful King of the Faithful Kingdom of Ephraim
Who defied the might of Frouzee and was so treacherously slain in
return
We are forever in his debt.

A single tear slid down the princess' face as she reached out to stroke the rough sandstone of her uncle's monument. She bowed her head in solemn silence, silence which was suddenly broken by a gentle voice behind her.

"I come here frequently when I am home."

The princess whirled her head around to behold Prince Tamino, standing a little ways off, his kindly features set in relief by the leaping flames of the monument. The princess, with no small amount of alarm, felt her heart do a small somersault as her childhood friend drew near.

"I understand why," she said. "I am incredibly touched to see that this is here."

The prince bowed his head. "We keep that flame burning at all times, no matter the weather. We will never forget his courage." His voice was warm and gentle, embracing her spirit like the dulcet tones of a cello on a brisk autumn day.

Avora'tru'ivi tried to do her best to elegantly wipe way the tears that continued to leak out of her eyes. "We all have so much to learn from him."

"Allow me," said Tamino as he withdrew a soft white cloth from a pocket and proffered it to the princess, who thanked him with a nod and began furiously dabbing at her tears.

"Would you like to walk with me for a little while?" He asked, as the moon mixed with the blazing fire in his large, dark eyes. "You have much to tell me, for it has been far too long!"

"Why should I ever forgo the chance to share a garden stroll with the brave ranger of Wil'iah?" she asked with a playful smile.

The prince let off a chortle. "Don't believe everything you hear about my exploits. The achievements of the King's Rangers of the Order of the Flame of Zebulon tend to get…embellished with each retelling. Most of the time, I was delivering mail."

"An important duty, no doubt. Imagine what regular communication must mean to those people," Avora'tru'ivi responded encouragingly.

"Indeed, indeed. We had some excitement here and there with the occasional Frouzean bandit or property dispute, but it was for the most part uneventful. To tell the truth, I most enjoyed the opportunity to get to know more of the citizens of this new Kingdom. I lived with them, ate with them, worked with them, and helped them build their homesteads and villages. After all, I am their servant, so it is best if I become acquainted to their needs."

The princess' heart was warmed to hear him speak so tenderly of people which other, lesser men might see as subjects. "And that's why I lov--- uh, hold you and your family in such high regard. Always looking out for everyone above yourselves." *You'd better watch your tongue*, she thought. At this, the prince stopped abruptly and flashed a glance at her. Even in the darkness, she noticed a tremor shake his lanky frame. He looked as if he desperately wanted to say something, but then seemed to cancel it and kept walking, approaching the great church that fronted the gardens on their southern end.

"Well, Princess, so far as I believe, that is what Wil'iah is all about. A nation where nobody is forgotten, nobody is left alone in the darkness, nobody is rendered defenseless when the forces of darkness come knocking. Where the light of Truth is accessible to all, where the brave banners of the faithful always fly high, where honor and decency are courageously upheld, and where law is the ruler, not the might of some petulant strongman. Where people regardless of their circumstance or background can come together to build something greater, grander, and nobler than could be imagined by themselves. Some call it an impossible dream. Some call it an empty hope told to children at night to steel their hearts against a cruel world. But look around, Your Highness. None of this would be here if your nation hadn't kept the flame alive in the dark days when we were enslaved by Frouzea, or if you hadn't leapt to our aid when my parents finally rose to overthrow the Empire."

Tamino suddenly stopped and held out his arm, pointing to the hulking castle that loomed in the background, its concentric ramparts and lofty towers seeming to glow with the reflected light of the moon and its entourage of stars.

"There stands our greatest fortress, steadfast and defiant."

He next turned and regarded the enormous Church of the Everlasting Victory, whose cascading semi-domes climbed skyward like peaks on a mountain. The largest known dome in the world crowned its summit, its burnished, gilded surface warming the cool glow of the moon as it seemed to suffuse the air with its own brilliance. Surrounding the soaring pile of domes were no fewer than sixteen identical bell towers, each crowned with a lantern inside of which blazed a thousand candles.

"Our most treasured symbol of hope – our prayer in stone."

As Avora'tru'ivi's wondering eyes passed over the unmatched splendor of the church, they were drawn to the next jewel of Trukanamoa. A mirror-like circular pool, which almost perfectly reflected the constellations that stood sentinel over the city, surrounded seven pointed domes that seemed to rise, as if by magic, from the water. Formed from soaring ogive arches, the domes were tenderly and indirectly lit by a multitude of small lanterns that floated in exquisite boats on the pool. The prince's gentle voice described this new spectacle.

"My heart leaps at this soaring symbol of freedom, the Palaces of the Council of Uluru, the legislature where all have a voice- where the true power in the Kingdom of Wil'iah resides, with its people."

Tamino then turned and swept his hand over the magnificent carpet of flowers and monuments that stretched into the vast distance behind them, with the Tower of the Flame of Zebulon standing proudly at its northern terminus atop a hill.

"Here it stands. It is not an impossible fantasy, not a vain hope. Wil'iah is real, thanks to the courage of our parents' generation, who fought to make the dream a reality." Suddenly, the prince's brows furrowed as a cloud seemed to pass over his face. "Yet even now dark forces are gathering, for the light of Wil'iah and her allies has grown too strong for them to bear. Someday I must face the responsibility of tending our flame against this growing night. I am worried, Princess, that I may not have the strength to do it. Our light has persisted, through fallen kingdoms, marauding empires, and perilous journeys across impassible mountains and endless oceans, for forty-two generations since my ancestor David." He turned to her, an expression of profound concern writ large on his face. "What if it ends with me?"

Avora'tru'ivi earnestly looked into his eyes and gently placed her hands on his arms, which perceptibly tensed at her touch. "Listen to me, Tamino. I fully understand how you must feel. Both your parents and my parents are larger-than-life figures in our respective nations. They are still with us, and yet they are the stuff of legends. Every day I wonder to myself, 'will I be able to live up to the legacy of the war queen of Ephraim? Would I have had the courage to roust myself from mourning my murdered brother to smash the pagan idols of Frouzee, even though it meant war and likely death? I wonder if I would be able to have the determination of Uncle Joshua that is so appropriately commemorated by that memorial. I'm not sure if I even have the courage to merely go to Pelesetania on a diplomatic visit and face Prince Jason. I wish with all of my heart to have the fortitude and the strength to defend my dear country. For, though our nation has made its share of mistakes, we are not without honor."

Tamino's eyebrows arched in surprise. "Of all the people I would suspect to lack courage, you are not one of them. After all, who was it who singlehandedly resolved, as a twelve year old nonetheless, to rescue the Scroll of St. Thomas from the clutches of Hosania?" The pair began to walk again, meandering back into the gardens.

Avora'tru'ivi cast her eyes at the ground, the nervous tremor creeping back into her voice. "Sometimes I wonder if I was that same person. There are days that I feel so helpless. I fear that the people of Manasseh are starting to forget who we are, the role we play in our people's eternal resistance against the forces of darkness. In the years since the sacrifices of our parents' generation, I fear we have grown too comfortable." A hint of bitterness now began to permeate her tones. "Even my own brother is more interested in merriment than military preparation. I love him, but I question his priorities. Perhaps there will be a time for jollity, but it is not now, not as the clouds of darkness close in on our light."

Tamino sighed. "Peace is my fondest wish. I would see this kingdom, now a resolute and honorable place, but a stern one, filled with light and music." He pointed across the gardens to an empty field that spread itself next to the forbidding-looking Palace of Justice. "Just over there, someday I hope to build a great opera house, a palace for our artistic traditions to stand alongside our fortresses and courts. But I know it is not time for that yet. Now is a time to stand," Avora'tru'ivi noticed his brow furrow with clear apprehension, "but I don't stand with the stature of the giants of the past, or even of the present. Wil'iah needs a larger-than-life hero like my father if we are to stand up to the Mongols. But all it will have is me."

Just as he said this, the pair came to another monument. Carved into its carefully-polished surface was a rendition of Wil'iah's thirty-two-rayed battle flag, below which were inscribed two words.

Never forget.

A strange warmth filled Avora'tru'ivi's heart as she remembered why she didn't have to be afraid. She gently took Tamino's hand, noticing that he involuntarily drew an intake of breath as he flinched at her touch, but then returned the gesture with a warm squeeze.

"Do you know what this monument is trying to tell you? Every time my heart is filled with doubt, the thought always comes to me that we are given everything we need to face any particular situation by the unending beneficence of our almighty Father-Mother. It isn't up to us to defend Wil'iah. It isn't up to us to defend Manasseh. God is our defense."

Tamino inhaled deeply. "Yes. Yes, I know. I have heard the same message. The ultimate defense of Wil'iah lies not with our force of arms, nor with great heroes or heroines. I only hope that I will be able to see this clearly when the time comes."

The princess leaned in closer and moved her hands to Tamino's shoulders. "But know this, mighty prince of Wil'iah. I have grown up with you. We have been fast friends from birth. I have watched you grow into who you are today. There is nobody I trust better to guide your Kingdom forward into the next age. You are strong. You are brave. You are valiant. You have everything you need to keep your people safe, just as I have what I need to defend mine."

The princess withdrew her hands and, espying a red waratah flower, bent down to pick it. She gently cradled it with both hands and presented it to Tamino. "And understand, Tamino, that in this you are not alone. Wil'iah is great, and mighty, and a light to us all, but she is not without friends. Together, we will face whatever comes. Together, we will tend the fire, and the Flame of Zebulon shall endure. As we both go on our respective missions to build this alliance and defy the tide of darkness, take this flower as a sign of my friendship- my favor, if you will. If it wilts, know that what it represents shall not fail. Our friendship is forever. Everywhere you go on this quest for our freedom, I will be with you."

Tamino grasped the flower with both hands and held it up to his breast pocket. "Then I shall treasure this symbol, and keep it safe here, close to my heart."

Even in the pale light of the moon, Avora'tru'ivi could

see that the prince visibly flushed, and wondered if she was doing the same. The two leaned closer together, their breaths almost mingling in the still desert air.

"Princess, I –" Whatever Tamino was going to say was interrupted by the boom of the great bell in the towering cupola atop the great dome of the Church of the Everlasting Victory. It crashed out its message eleven more times.

The prince started. "My goodness, it's later than I realized. It has been wrong of me to keep you up so late. Allow me to walk you back to the palace." The prince turned, but hesitated, drew a deep breath, then, "Thank you, again, for strengthening my heart. I now see why I was guided to take this walk tonight."

CHAPTER FIVE

THE CIRCLE

Principality of Gath, southeastern Australia

*T*he Bazaar of Gath was a teeming, seething morass of bedlam, as swirling colors competed with a cacophony of sound for dominance of the air. Unwashed children dodged unsteady carts laden with pottery, grapes, jugs of wine, and other local handicrafts that lurched in the rutted, unpaved streets, splashing mud and dung on their surroundings. The air today was stiflingly hot; none of the customary breezes blew in from the nearby sea to set the flags and sails of the ships crowding into the harbor aflutter. The oppressive heat did nothing to dampen the overwhelming sound of squealing pigs, the braying of the emaciated donkeys pulling the carts, the ominous crack of whips, and the reedy voices of shopkeepers attempting to hock their wares.

Through the chaos threaded a striking-looking woman with raven-black hair, wearing a simple white shift and a gold band around her right arm. Doing her best to avoid the various catcalls and wolf-whistles that seemed to greet her every move, she fought her way to an extravagant tent that was finely embroidered with gold filigree. She reached out to open the flaps, when a giant hand grasped her forearm.

The woman looked up to see the colossal form of a soldier of the prince leering down at her, his wolf-like eyes offset by an unkempt beard.

"Now, why's a nice girl like you going into a place like that?"

"I am here on official business for my masters," she said through gritted teeth.

"And what kind of business would your master be in that he would need anything from there?"

The woman twisted her lips into a sly smile. "My masters wish to achieve fulfill many objectives. Sometimes the objects of their aims require...persuasion."

"Then surely your masters wouldn't mind if you came home a bit late today?" The soldier gave the woman what she supposed was intended as a charming grin, but the effect was sickening. She yanked her arm from his grip.

"I really must be going. The Circle doesn't like to be kept waiting."

A look of muted terror briefly crossed the soldier's face as he began backing away. Nonetheless, he recovered quickly.

"It's a shame your masters don't let you have any fun," he smirked before turning away to pursue his next victim.

The woman rolled her eyes and pulled open the tent, her nostrils instantly assaulted by a barrage of bizarre scents.

A gaunt woman stood up at her entrance, a strangely vacant look in her eyes. Her long, narrow face was framed by stringy, iron-gray hair that looked like it hadn't been washed in recent memory. Behind her was a rack filled with bottles of all sizes and colors. The air was thick with the haze of cloying incense.

"Yes, sweetie, what can I do for you today?" the woman wheezed.

"You know what I'm here for."

"More of the same, I gather?" The woman turned to the rack behind her and selected seven bottles before putting them on the counter.

"You heard me."

"That's Bathsheba's Breath, the Caress of Jezebel, the Kiss of Ildico, the Fire of Nineveh, the Spirit of Gomorrah, the Revenge of Lilith, and the Veil of Salome. Your master's appetites must be ravenous."

"I live only to serve. I know not the specifics of the master's plans."

The thin woman nodded. "That will be fifty."

"Your prices have increased."

"I'm just trying to keep pace with inflation. Besides, I lost a cargo last week when an Ekronite pirate ship burned it."

"Take your money. I'm not interested in your woes."

As she exited the tent with the basket under her arm, the slave girl shielded her eyes against the sun with her free hand. Her gaze focused on the distant acropolis of Gath, once the center of her known world. A contrast from the squalor of the market, the complex was surrounded by thick walls and crowned with a complex of temples and a massive palace- or at least it once had been. Now, sections of wall had caved in, leaving piles of rubble; other sections had been disassembled more deliberately by marble scavengers who hoped to sell the valuable stone on underground markets. The once-proud columns of the temples were chipped and cracked, and some of them had toppled over completely, causing several roof cave-ins. The once brightly-painted buildings had peeled and faded into a sickly grayish-white that was streaked with dirt and residual marks from the flames of a dozen lootings.

"Someday," she whispered to herself under her breath as she began to make her way toward the acropolis, looking down in a vain attempt to keep her sandaled feet from stepping into the raw sewage that ran through the fetid streets. She passed out of the bazaar into the slum that ran right up to the base of the once-glorious acropolis, the mud-brick homes stacked atop one another in a nonsensical jumble. She winced as the contents of a chamber pot fell directly in front of her from a second story window. Jerking her head up to the window, she was greeted by the annoyed face of an old woman, who yelled down.

"Watch where you're going, idiot!"

In response, she raised a fist and shook it skyward before continuing on, flinching at the bark of a dingo chained to a post with a studded collar. Suddenly, she felt a hand on her shoulder, and turned around to see a very unstable middle-aged man with bloodshot eyes lurch toward her. He kissed her, filling her nostrils with the stench of stale wine. Grimacing in disgust, she shoved the tottering man away, who fell face-down in the mud with an audible squelch. Hurrying forward faster, she made her way through the confusing maze of streets to a giant crack running up the base of the acropolis. Looking behind her to make sure nobody was watching, she ducked inside.

She knew the unlit passageway by heart, so she picked her way through the darkness rapidly, her eyes eventually picking up the diffused glow of a distant torch. Eventually, this glow resolved itself into a flame that illuminated a wet, rough-hewn set of stairs that ascended into an uncertain light. She climbed, emerging into the ruins of one of the acropolis' temples, this one dedicated to the goddess Astarte, the mother goddess of the Philistine people and of love and war. The building was in atrocious condition. She noticed a group of men in red hoods huddled in the corner, whispering excitedly. She approached them, set the basket on the floor, then lay prostrate on the floor, her nose touching the dirty marble and her hands outstretched towards the hooded figures.

"Ah yes, Iphigenia, I see you have brought the ingredients we need," said one of the men. However, when he looked in the basket, he drew in his breath with disgust.

"You forgot the Whiff of Baghdad! Imbecile!" He aimed a sharp kick at Iphigenia's ribcage, knocking the wind out of her lungs.

"You never asked for it. It's not included in the usual order," Iphigenia hissed through gritted teeth. She didn't have much dignity as a slave of The Circle, but she prided herself on a steel-trap memory.

The priest advanced toward her, his strangely vacant eyes not matching the contorted sneer of his chapped mouth.

"Well, look at this! Backtalk! I would think you'd be more grateful. After all," he said, passing his dead eyes over her in an unsettling leer, "you're getting a bit long in the tooth. Your skills with our elixirs have been valuable, but every tool outlives its usefulness. If you were the chosen one, we would have known by now."

Her mouth quavering in a mixture of pain, humiliation, and fury, Iphigenia scuttled out of the room. However, her progress slowed as her ears caught snippets of the conversation of the hooded men.

"Kublai Khan…." "Dai Viet…" "our continent is next…" "Wil'iah is going to fight…"

Knowing that the ruined temple offered many places to clandestinely listen to a conversation, Iphigenia turned around and approached the circle of figures again, hiding herself behind a strategically placed urn.

"All of our hopes have failed us. Our dream of reviving the empire is dashed. The incarnation of Frouzee, of Astarte, that we have prayed for, that we have invested so much effort searching for worthy candidates for, has not materialized. And, now, with the hordes of the Great Khan massing on the horizon, the days of our much-reduced people may be numbered."

"What if Wil'iah is able to defeat them?"

"Fool! Wil'iah is a weak and wretched nation. They couldn't hope to win a single battle against the Khan. I look forward to watching our hated enemy burn to the ground. But I dread the day when we are next."

"Only the gods can save us now."

"They certainly haven't seemed interested in our pleas."

"Then we must redouble our efforts. I know it is the gods' will that the old empire be restored. Perhaps this expected invasion is an opportunity."

An opportunity.

Iphigenia looked down at the gold armband, the symbol of her servitude, then cast a glance at the enormous statue of Astarte that dominated the room, her head crowned with two enormous horns and a five-pointed pentagram – the symbol of the lost Empire of Frouzea.

She recognized a chance for survival, but she didn't

CHAPTER SIX

TRUJUSTAKANOA

Trujustakanoa, Wil'iah, northwest Australia

$\mathcal{T}$rujustakanoa, Wil'iah's greatest city in the west, stood resolutely on the southern shores of Marduwarra Sound, the vast natural harbor on Wil'iah's northwest coast. While Trukanamoa, built recently during the reign of Hezekiah, was the picture of serene, ordered splendor, Trujustakanoa's storied, winding streets were filled to the bursting with the intrigues and mysteries of a thousand years. The bustling metropolis was the busiest port on the continent's west coast, and the gateway for Wil'iahns to trade with all of Asia- at least it had been. In the days since the Mongol's conquest of China, trade had died down significantly, as China herself was no longer a trading option, and the surrounding waters were not safe. All too many merchant ships sat idle at the wharfs.

However, one rather important ship was anything but inactive. A double-hulled warship meticulously painted in a dignified royal blue and embellished with gilded stars, the ship calmly pulled at the ropes tying her to the circular quay that hosted the nucleus of Wil'iah's formidable Western Fleet. Connecting the twin hulls was a large wooden platform crowned with intimidating battlements and two proud masts. Though the sails were furled, flags flapped bravely from the masts' peak. One was the royal standard of Wil'iah. The other was the flag of the admiral of the Western Fleet.

"Good to see you again, old girl," Tamino said as he espied the name boldly painted on the ship's stern- *Ava'ivi*, "Justice" in the Wil'iahn vernacular language. As he walked up the gangplank, another familiar face greeted him.

"And it's good to see you, Admiral," Tamino said as he snapped into a military salute.

Zhang Shijie stepped out of the shadows. His face had changed much since the fateful day of his rescue four years before. Now, he had more gray hair, and carelines crossed his visage.

"Welcome aboard, Your Faithfulness."

"I've never seen the *Ava'ivi* looking so splendid."

"She's received a full refit with some of the new tricks we brought from China. As I'm sure you know, she is serving as the model for the large numbers of Galor'ivi–type cruisers we're currently building. She's perfect for such an important mission."

"Yes, indeed, Admiral. Now may be our chance to finally begin to roll back the darkness that has overtaken your country."

Zhang shook his head. "Wil'iah is my country now."

Tamino swept his hand over the impressive ship.

"Well, Admiral, if you don't mind, I'd like a tour of the old girl's new capabilities."

A sly smile crept up at the corners of the admiral's mouth.

"Of course."

Tamino nodded to the cannons that resolutely pointed out in all directions on the *Ava'ivi's* platform – eight to a side and two facing fore and aft.

"These are bigger than I remember. I thought the guns that you brought from China were handheld."

Zhang chuckled. "They were. This new concept of firearms is still in its infancy, but, when your adopted country is facing a nearly invincible enemy, and you are graced with a seemingly inexhaustible defense budget, what do you do? You innovate. The basic principles were sound. We just needed to experiment with the metallurgy to make larger weapons. These are mark IV naval guns, firing a nine-pound solid shot. I can assure you that Kublai Khan has nothing like this."

Tamino nervously looked at the new, untried weapons.

"Do we know they work?"

Zhang replied, "Well, they've been extensively tested in both land and sea conditions, but just in case, the Ava'ivi has a few more daggers up her sleeves." He pointed to four castle-like bastions that jutted out from the corners of the ship's deck platform, on which large objects lay wrapped in canvas. "She has four 'crouching tiger trebuchets,' a more compact catapult design that we brought over from China, mounted on rotary platforms. They are capable of firing incendiary shot, including 'thunder crash bombs.'" He then pointed to a series of swiveling hexagonal objects mounted on the merlons that divided the ship's gun emplacements from each other. "Those are fire arrow launchers. Each one contains sixteen arrows and can be reloaded," a sudden conspiratorial gleam filled his eyes as he led Tamino toward the bows of the ship, "but that's not this ship's deadliest weapon."

"Oh?"

Zhang walked over to a box-like object secreted in between the two bow guns and unwrapped its canvas covering, revealing a chest on wheels, with a strange tube-like object affixed to its top.

"This," he said proudly, "is a fierce-fire oil cabinet."

"A what?"

"Well, for the less-dramatically-inclined, it is a double-piston naphtha flamethrower."

"I see," Tamino said as he grimly looked at the vicious weapon.

"Of course, all of this is just the beginning," Zhang said, gesturing to another vessel docked further down the quay. This ship, half again as long as the *Ava'ivi*, had a fully-enclosed gun deck and two ornately-carved dragon heads on its twin bows.

"Is that the *Elah*?" Tamino asked hesitantly.

"Indeed, the first prototype of our new *trungabrang*-type battleships," Zhang said, his voice filled with delight. We have nearly forty in commission now, or in the final stages of fitting out. She encapsulates everything we know about ship construction, including all of China's ancient wisdom-watertight compartments, heavier buloke ironwood scantlings, you name it. She's also more heavily armed – thirty-two mark V naval guns firing a 12-pound shot, thirty crouching tiger trebuchets, thirty fire-arrow launchers, and four oil cabinets."

Tamino whistled in wonder.

Zhang continued excitedly. "As you can see, we have three of these ships on station so far – that's *the Lion of Judah* and *Reliance* over in the distance -- and the rest are working up with the Eastern Fleet and should be here shortly, hopefully by the time we get back."

Tamino nodded grimly. "I wish this weren't the case, but I have a bad feeling we're going to have to take advantage of that fact." Nonetheless, he shook away the dark look that had crossed his face. "Is the *Ava'ivi* fit for sea?"

Zhang nodded. "She's as ready as she'll ever be."

Tamino smiled. "Well, then, what are we waiting for? Singhasari, here we come!"

A conch shell sounded behind them, and the *Ava'ivi's* crew swarmed to their posts. The two inverted triangular sails unfurled and instantly billowed in the morning breeze. Above them, behind the mainmast, the royal standard of Wil'iah snapped in the wind. After the lines were cast off, the *Ava'ivi* nimbly nosed away from the pier and began to head out towards open water, the sparkling sound before them, and, beyond that, the Indian Ocean.

CHAPTER SEVEN

THE *SHECHEM*

Gulf of Manasseh, off the northern coast of Australia

The *Shechem*, flagship of the Royal Navy of Ephraim and Manasseh, languidly cut its way through the sun-dappled waters of the Gulf of Manasseh, its two large sails gently billowing in the warm breeze. Princess Avora'tru'ivi peered over the side rail, delighting in the myriad shades of blue that the ocean reflected from a cloudless sky. Another shadow joined hers on the water, and Avora'tru'ivi looked up to see Princess Jessica.

"How do you really feel about negotiating with Pelesetania?" she asked.

"Well, to be honest, I'm not thrilled. But I am fully willing to serve my country, no matter how distasteful the task."

"Frankly, I don't think we should be negotiating at all. That state is illegitimate, and we both know it. Someday, I'm sure Manasseh will take back her western provinces from Pelesetania. Hopefully, that day will be soon. I'm honestly not sure why we have even allowed that former Frouzean outpost to persist on your occupied territory."

"Our stance so far has avoided bloodshed," Avora'tru'ivi responded. "It's my hope that we can honor that precedent."

"Perhaps," Jessica said doubtfully, as she cast a baleful stare in the opposite direction, to the east, where, far beyond the horizon, another threatening peninsula lay.

"At least my father has the good sense not to try negotiating with Hosania," she continued.

Avora'tru'ivi suppressed a shudder, thinking back to her last harrowing experience in the Dark Kingdom.

"I know what you mean, but really, are they any worse than Pelesetania? At least they are a Christian nation."

Jessica scoffed. "You should know better than anyone else that there is no Christ in their version of Christianity."

"We may not agree with them on everything—"

"Do we agree on anything? They caused a civil war, tried to turn back centuries of progress, caused my country to be plunged into twenty years of slavery, and then had the unmitigated gall to steal the Scroll of St. Thomas from the Mother Church! They're lucky we don't gather our forces now and smite them!"

"Jessica, that isn't necessary. We got the scroll back, and the crimes of the past won't be solved with more bloodshed. I agree that they would be an... unreliable partner in the alliance."

"Yes, it's thanks to you that we have the scroll back, but we'd better watch them carefully to make sure they don't stab us in the back again."

Avora'tru'ivi returned her gaze to the water, her cheeks slightly flushing with color. "I had help with the scroll."

Jessica gave her a significant look.

"Yes, you did, didn't you? My brother talks about that adventure that you two had all the time. It's hard to believe that was thirteen years ago."

Avora'tru'ivi looked into the distance, a wistful look filling her eyes.

"I'm glad I have such a good friend." Worry wormed its way into her mind as she thought of Tamino sailing off to unknown dangers in Asia, but she swatted it away with a wordless prayer.

Stay safe, Tamino.

CHAPTER EIGHT

IPHIGENIA'S GAMBLE

Gath

*I*phigenia sat upright in her cot, beads of sweat refusing to evaporate in the stifling air. It was time. She gingerly slipped out from under the diaphanous sheet, her bare feet touching the uneven stone pavers. She had almost made it to the door when a voice hissed in the stillness of the dormitory.

"Where are you going?" Briseis, one of Iphigenia's fellow slaves to the Circle, rubbed sleep from her eyes.

"It doesn't concern you. Go back to sleep."

"But, it's past curfew. You could be whipped, or

sacrificed. You and I are both getting too old to serve the purpose for which we were chosen. When I was taken as a candidate, my parents were told that the prophecy said She would choose one of us as a vessel by the time we were twenty. We're both past our expiration dates. I don't have to remind you that not all of those bones in the temple are from livestock."

"Never mind that, go back to bed," Iphigenia said, advancing toward Briseis.

"I don't want them to hurt you."

"Hush," Iphigenia said, reaching up her sleeve for a glass vial she had secreted under the gold armband. She passed the vial under Briseis' nose. The other woman's eyes crossed, and she toppled back into bed.

"That's right, go back to sleep. Don't worry. I'm going to get us both out of here – by giving them exactly what they want," Iphigenia hissed at the unconscious form of the only thing resembling a friend that she had, then turned around and exited the dormitory.

Threading her way through dimly-lit, decrepit passageways, she came to the storehouse where the various potions and fumes of The Circle were kept. Finally finding the red bottle that she needed, Iphigenia next rummaged around in the corner of the storehouse for a package she had secreted there earlier that day, after a visit to the bazaar. She pulled out two ivory horns, stroking them with a satisfied grin on her face, a grin that belied the nervous churn that filled her stomach as she tried to convince herself that her scheme would work.

"All hail Astarte," she whispered.

CHAPTER NINE

SINGHASARI

The Kingdom of Singhasari, Java

*T*he *Ava'ivi* cruised with unhurried elegance into the Singhasari port of Surabaya, navigating its way through a harbor teeming with ships of all sizes. Although, at eighty cubits in length, the *Ava'ivi* was among the largest ships in the Wil'iahn fleet, she was dwarfed by some of the jongs in the harbor. These huge Javanese cargo vessels towered over the water, their triangular sails seeming to fill the sky. As the flagship, the *Ava'ivi* also had special diplomatic duties, and her deckhouse was much more luxuriously appointed than the ones on her fellow ships in the navy.

Tamino emerged from the deckhouse to admire the giant ships that surrounded his own vessel.

After docking and disembarking, Tamino and his small travel party approached the Singhasari palace with a mixture of nervousness and curiosity. The building was low-slung and partially sunken into the ground, with a lowered courtyard a level below the primary ground level. The walls of the courtyard were punctuated at regular intervals by grand, ornately carved sandstone gates that towered over the party, while the rest the buildings were crowned with carefully-woven rattan roofs.

After announcing themselves to the guards and declaring their request for an audience with the king, Tamino and his entourage were escorted into the throne room. King Kertanegara sat at the end of the hallway on a great throne with a tall, circular blue back. He seemed to be covered in gold, with an elaborate crown, a large necklace, a breastplate, and sleeves all made from the precious material. Tamino was struck by the intricacy of the metalwork; a thousand chaotic, swirling patterns seemed to flow between the peaks of the crown. Standing next to him was a stern-looking man who Tamino surmised was Raden Wijaya, the chief general of Singhasari's armies. Four graceful women in shimmering red dresses surrounded Kertanegara's throne, further wrapped with glittering gold sashes, and crowned with golden headdresses that reminded Tamino of mountains, or perhaps Buddhist stupa temples. The youngest of the women looked to be about eight, while the eldest seemed to be roughly Tamino's age.

"His Excellency Crown Prince Tamino of Wil'iah!" announced the guard. Tamino immediately rendered the civilian salute, dipping his head in respect, putting a fist to his heart, then opening his palm and extending it to

Kertanegara in a gesture of openness. The king nodded his head.

"Greetings, Your Excellency," he said. "Long have we valued our trade relationship with your country. It is a pleasure to meet you in person."

"The pleasure is all mine."

"What brings you all the way here? You are far from home."

"Your Highness can be assured that he is not the only one who has analyzed the Mongol threat. Though at the moment it seems to us to be remote, we know that it is only a matter of time before the baleful eye of the Great Khan is turned across the sea, to both of us."

The king gravely nodded. "Indeed. We have already received his messengers asking us for tribute. So far, we have been able to rebuff his attempts, but the situation grows more serious every day."

"Surely you have heard of the Khan's designs on Dai Viet and Champa?"

"You Wil'iahns are certainly well-informed, for a people so remote. I take it you know of our new alliance with Champa?"

Tamino smiled. "That is indeed the true subject of my visit. It is clear to Wil'iah that none of our countries is independently strong enough to resist a determined attack by the forces of the Great Khan. But, together, we might be able to do it. We see your alliance with Champa as an important first step to implementing a much larger plan."

Kertanegara nodded. "Perhaps you are suggesting a wider alliance?"

"Your Highness is most perceptive. A formal alliance between the nations of our continent, Singhasari, Dai Viet, and Champa could muster forces significant enough to give Kublai Khan pause. Together, we could contain his advances to their current extent, although we see no hope of liberating China at this time."

"What are the terms of your alliance?"

"Our plan is very simple. All of our nations will sign a mutual defense agreement and form a league. We will share intelligence and military technology with each other. If one of us is attacked, the others will all come to its aid. We will also work to form an independent trading association to reduce the Mongol stranglehold on the trade routes. In turn, no member of the league will make a separate peace with the Mongols nor enter into a tributary or vassalship arrangement."

"Seeing as we have no intention of doing so, I will think on your offer," Kertanegara responded as he looked the prince of Wil'iah up and down. "Your reputation and the reputation of your nation proceeds you, Your Excellency. The Wil'iahns are known as a just and honorable people, and your military prowess is unquestionable. In all of our dealings with your people, we have never once encountered fraud or criminal intent. I see a bright future of cooperation between our nations. I would like to see us become closer."

Kertanegara rose from the throne and motioned for the four women to step forward.

"Allow me to introduce my daughters, the four princesses of Singhasari, Tribhuwaneswari, Prajnapara-mitha, Narendra Duhita, and, my youngest, Gayatri Rajapatni."

Tamino nodded respectfully.

"Your Majesties."

"Tribhuwaneswari will show you around our palace grounds while my ministers consider this offer of alliance." Kertanegara gave the eldest of the daughters a significant look. She gracefully stepped over to Tamino and bowed deeply.

"No need for that, Your Highness. In my country, we bow only to God."

The youngest of the four daughters giggled, earning her a sharp glance from her father.

Tamino and Tribhuwaneswari stepped out the throne hall and proceeded to walk the grounds of the palace, admiring the profusion of tropical plants and colorful plumage of the birds that swooped in and out of the trees, tweeting incessantly.

"I have never seen so much greenery in my life," Tamino marveled.

"Oh? Is yours a desert country?"

"By and large, yes, although our eastern provinces are more temperate."

"Tell me, Prince, what is your country like?"

"I don't know how to describe it. It is magnificent and desolate at the same time. It can burn with heat or freeze with cold. It is a land of mighty fortresses and great churches, and a land of empty deserts and small villages. But undergirding it all is the Truth. It is home."

"Do you think I would enjoy it?"

"Perhaps. It is not as warm and tropical as this place, but it has a beauty all its own. Your family should visit sometime. We would be happy to welcome you."

"Indeed. I should like to meet your wives."

Tamino stopped and laughed. "Our policies regarding that are...somewhat different."

"What do you mean?" the princess cocked her head, her ornate earrings tinkling in the wind as she looked up at Tamino with large, dark eyes.

"When I marry, it will only be once."

"When!?" the princess looked him up and down. "You must be younger than I thought. You come across as very mature."

Tamino struggled with rising embarrassment as he realized where the princess was probably steering this conversation.

"I was born in the Year of our Lord 1258, twenty-five years ago."

"And nobody married you?"

Tamino nervously cleared his throat. "It is not uncommon for people in my country to marry later than is usual in this part of the world. I recently completed five years of service as a ranger on the southern border."

"Oh, was that required to be…eligible?"

"Well, no…but service to my country came first. There was no time for other pursuits."

"And now?"

"Uh, well…"

The princess advanced towards Tamino and touched the now-wilted waratah flower pinned to his tabard.

"What's this? Why wear a dead flower?"

"It was given to me by… a very special friend." Tamino's heart filled with warmth as he thought of Avora'tru'ivi. He took a deep breath; all this talk of marriage made him finally admit to himself that he couldn't imagine his life without her.

Tribhuwaneswari noticed a wistful, faraway look fill Tamino's eyes. She let go of the flower and retreated.

"I see. I wish you the best of luck with the assembly of this alliance. I too wish to be free of the Mongol threat." She fluidly whirled around, her flowing sleeves catching the wind, before seeming to float over the grass as she made her way back to the palace with grace and dignity.

Tamino found himself suddenly alone – or so he thought.

"Tread carefully." A voice sounded behind him.

Tamino turned around to find himself face-to-face with Raden Wijaya, the general. Tamino nodded in respect.

"I'm not sure what you mean."

"King Kertanegara regrettably has no sons. When he dies, it will be my duty to carry this kingdom forward."

"I see."

"I will not tolerate rival claimants to the throne."

"I have no designs on your inheritance."

"Whatever Kertanegara may think, if you want this alliance, you'd better not have designs on anything else." The general's eyes involuntarily turned toward where Princess Tribhuwaneswari had made her elegant exit.

"General, I came here with one purpose and one purpose only- to seek a military alliance against Kublai Khan. I'm sure you understand that such an arrangement would be in both of our interests."

"I also understand how these arrangements are often sealed."

"In Wil'iah, we do not use our hearts as bargaining chips."

"A noble sentiment, perhaps, but these are unusual times."

"Even if they were bargaining chips, mine has already been cashed in."

Raden Wijaya's eyes narrowed as he too noticed the flower incongruously pinned next to Tamino's ranger badge.

"Very well. I bid you a good day. Long may the alliance between our nations endure."

A few hours later, Tamino arrived in the banquet hall.

Kertanegara sat at the head of the tables, flanked on either side by his daughters. He motioned for Tamino to sit across from him.

"Welcome to the banquet hall, Your Excellency. I trust that the food will be to your liking."

Tamino smiled. "Indeed, it will be a welcome departure from desert rations," he said as his eyes passed over golden platters overloaded with fish and tropical fruits.

As they began to eat, Kertanegara continued speaking.

"My ministers have carefully considered your offer. We see no reason why it would not be advantageous for us to expand our existing alliance with Champa more broadly. Kublai Khan's hand is mighty, but it will stretch beyond its limits if it reaches for our islands. I only regret that we cannot forge even closer bonds of fellowship," he said, leaning forward. Tamino stole a glance at Tribhuwaneswari, who averted her eyes to avoid making contact. Fighting a pang of guilt, he responded,

"I see a bright future of military and economic cooperation between Wil'iah and Singhasari. All told, I think this is a good arrangement for our nations while also honoring…prior commitments."

Kertanegara nodded gravely. "Perhaps. Commitments can shift and alter as much as the tide. If you change your mind—"

Tamino pursed his lips and bowed his head. "I don't see that happening, but I thank you for your hospitality and friendship."

"Very well," Kertanegara raised his goblet.

"To the alliance!"

CHAPTER TEN

THE PRINCE OF PELESETANIA

Principality of Pelesetania, northwestern Australia

"**W**ake up. We're here," Jessica hissed into Avora'tru'ivi's ear. The Manassite princess mumbled something in her sleep. She groggily rubbed her eyes and brushed a bushy bunch of hair out of her face, then stood bolt upright.

"Oh! We're here! You mean we're in Pelesetania!"

"No, we're in Israel," Jessica responded sarcastically.

"Really?"

"Of course not. You'd better get yourself dressed. We're going to be expected topside in less than half an hour."

A short time later, both princesses emerged from a hatch onto the deck of the Manassite warship. A Polynesian-style voyaging vessel similar to the long-distance ships of the Wil'iahn fleet, the *Shechem* had two hulls flanked on either side by a large outrigger. A multi-deck platform connected the two hulls, its upper deck crowned with wooden crenellated battlements. Glistening black cannons of Chinese design yawned out between the openings. Two masts carried distinctive crab claw-shaped sails emblazoned with the sign of the three arrows, Manasseh's military emblem. Fluttering at the masthead was a flag of truce and Avora'tru'ivi's royal standard, depicting a rampant bull.

As they sailed past the acropolis that guarded the entrance to the harbor, Avora'tru'ivi studied its dirt-streaked walls. They had once been whitewashed in the imperial Frouzean style; in a bygone era, the city had been the spear point of Frouzee's efforts to conquer and hold the northern coast of the continent. Perched above the frowning ramparts were a series of temples to various Philistine deities, as well as a long, colonnaded palace. Although quite grand and beautiful when new, the temples' colorful paint was now flaking in places, and the roof of one of the lesser temples had caved in. Protected by a breakwater below the acropolis lay the war fleet of Pelesetania, better-kept than the buildings. Dozens of galleys gleamed in the sun, brightly painted as if to mask the fact that their technology lagged several generations behind the *Shechem* and the similar vessels in the Royal Wil'iahn Navy. Stretching beyond the naval harbor was the civilian port, a riot of color as junks from Asia and local pearl boats darted in and out, often barely missing each other.

The *Shechem* steered towards a long jetty, which currently also hosted a large jong flying the emblem of Singhasari. Avora'tru'ivi's heart leapt a bit- perhaps there was hope for an alliance after all.

A small pilot boat flying the flag of Pelesetania approached them. As it grew closer, Avora'tru'ivi could make out a portly but pompous-looking man standing with one leg on the forepeak, resplendent in golden armor and a flowing crimson cape, his head crowned with the hated feathered helmet characteristic of Philistine soldiers. In one hand he held a tall pole crowned with a disc and two horns, a long-recognized symbol of imperial Frouzea.

"Who goes there?" he yelled when he was in earshot.

Avora'tru'ivi's heralds lined the rails of the ship and gave out a blast on twelve conch shells. Then, one of them stepped forward to address his Pelestanian counterpart.

"Her Majesty Avora'tru'ivi, Princess of Manasseh, and Her Faithfulness Jessica, Princess of Wil'iah, favor you with their presence! We come in peace to treat with His Excellency Prince Jason!"

"Prince Jason is available by appointment only," sneered the herald.

"Surely personages as important as the princesses require no appointment."

"The prince makes no exceptions," the herald looked the princesses, who had appeared at the rail, up and down, "even for you."

"Very well then," Jessica interjected in a purposefully flippant tone, "If Jason isn't interested in hearing our plan to save his country from the Mongol hordes, I suppose we'd be happy to return to our own countries--" She cast a baleful glance at the crumbling walls of the fortress. "—where we pay much more attention to maintenance." With that, she spun on her heel and walked away, Avora'tru'ivi following.

"That was rude!" She whispered.

"Perhaps. Pelesetania is not known for its courtesy. I have found that sometimes people respond best to their own language," Jessica hissed.

"I don't think Tamino would have been rude."

"Tamino isn't here."

Suddenly, the ship began to swing toward the dock. Avora'tru'ivi ran over to the captain, who stood directing the crews working the *Shechem's* twin tillers.

"What's happening?" the princess asked.

"We have been granted permission to dock. Apparently Prince Jason might have a gap in his afternoon schedule."

Avora'tru'ivi stole a glance at Jessica, who smiled triumphantly.

A short while later, the princesses and their entourage stood facing two enormous bronze doors set atop a majestic staircase that ascended from a tiled square. Flanking the doors on either side were large braziers filled with licking flames -- and hulking soldiers clad in the traditional armor of the Homeric Guard, the much-feared elite fighting force of the bygone Frouzean Empire.

They're still holding on to the past, Avora'tru'ivi thought. But the grandeur was only an echo. Her discerning eye noticed spots of corrosion on the armor, stains on the cloth, and none-to-carefully manicured beards. One of the guards, breaking protocol, locked eyes with Avora'tru'ivi and leered, giving off a wolf whistle. The princess quailed, unused to this kind of harassment.

Jessica stepped in front of Avora'tru'ivi and bared her teeth with an audible growl, placing her hand on the hilt of the sword strapped to her belt for emphasis.

"Not another noise out of you," she hissed.

The guard looked like he had been physically struck,

then stood up a little straighter and looked directly out to the square, becoming as still as a statue.

Jessica nodded with some satisfaction, then turned to face the doors. Her chief herald rapped on them with a long pole.

The doors ponderously swung inward, creaking and groaning from an obvious lack of lubrication. As the princesses stepped through them, Avora'tru'ivi's eyes strained to adjust to the darkness as she tried to see who had opened the doors. Her gaze was met with the frightened eyes of an indigenous boy who was chained to the door.

Feeling like she was going to be sick, Avora'tru'ivi mustered the most reassuring smile she could manage and directed it at the young slave. His eyes widened in surprise as he noticed that both he and the princess shared the same dark skin tone. She leaned down and whispered to him her best Frouzean,

"Why are you here?"

"They...took me," he responded in broken Frouzean, his voice barely a wisp in the wind.

Jessica, noticing the exchange, locked eyes with the boy and gave him an encouraging look, doing her best to impart to him a modicum of strength and dignity, even as she boiled with fury. She pulled Avora'tru'ivi aside and whispered to her.

"That boy was kidnapped!?"

"It would appear that our 'friend' Prince Jason is indulging in state-sponsored abduction," Avora'tru'ivi said grimly.

"I won't stand for this. We should leave now."

"Your father told us to meet with Jason. Maybe we can exact some diplomatic concessions to free him and whomever else has been taken."

Jessica gave her counterpart a doubtful look, but wordlessly agreed to proceed. The two princesses then turned to face the long hall before them.

The hallway was lined on either side by columns that had long ago been stained the crimson of the empire, but had now faded to an almost salmon-like color. Dust motes flickered through the shaft of light that entered through the lone skylight set in the center of the roof. A frayed red carpet rolled out before them towards the dais at the far end of the hall. Barely visible in the distant gloom was a gold recliner, on which luxuriated a rather slovenly-looking man clad in an ill-fitting toga. Several women surrounded him, attempting to combat the stifling heat in the room with enormous fans made from peacock feathers- no doubt imported at great expense from India.

One of the Pelesetanian heralds stepped forward to introduce them, his reedy voice echoing through the nearly-empty hall.

"Her Majesty Avora'tru'ivi, Princess of Manasseh, and her Excellency Jessica, Princess of Wil'iah, here to pay respects to your esteemed personage."

"We'll see about that," hissed Jessica under her breath. Avora'tru'ivi placed a staying hand on her friend's arm.

This announcement was greeted with an at-first indiscernible sound that Avora'tru'ivi quickly realized, with no small amount of shock, was flatulence.

"Come on in, girls. What do you want?" the man on the recliner yawned.

"This is insulting," whispered Jessica as she stepped forward.

As the princesses approached the dais, Avora'tru'ivi studied the prince of her country's nemesis. He looked like he hadn't shaved in about a week, and from the smell, had gone even longer without a bath- unless he had been bathing in wine. The prince's bloodshot eyes were set in a roundish face with drooping jowls, crowned with a feathered helmet that perched unsteadily on a mass of unruly, oily black hair. It seemed to cost him significant effort to hoist himself into a vertical seating position as he regarded the princesses, a half-empty wine bottle loosely held in one corpulent hand. Avora'tru'ivi caught an unsettling glimmer in his eye as he regarded her, but, remembering her training, drew herself to her full height and refused to be intimidated.

"I never thought I would see the day when the proud princesses of the Peoples of the Dirt would come crawling to me," he slurred.

Jessica instinctively raised her hand as if to slap him, only standing down at a warning glance from Avora'tru'ivi.

"We are not crawling. We are here to help you," Avora'tru'ivi responded, attempting her best soothing tone despite the prince's use of racial epithets.

"I don't need your help," Jason brayed, even as he looked Avora'tru'ivi up and down.

"I'll let you decide that. However, surely you have been following the events in Asia as closely as we have."

"What? Are you talking about Kublai Khan? That's a world away from here. He would never attack us here."

"The Mongol Empire's ambition knows no bounds. Their empire stretches all the way to the Mediterranean. They are moving now against Southeast Asia, and there's no reason to believe our continent isn't next if they succeed."

Jessica interjected. "Last I checked, the population of Pelesetania was under a million. You can hardly expect to defend yourself against the entirety of the known world alone."

Jason sneered at her. "My armies are widely feared.

Kublai Khan knows better than to attack me. The glory of the empire lives on here."

Jessica snorted. "I certainly don't know anyone who is afraid of your armies."

Avora'tru'ivi shot her a warning glance.

Jason chuckled. "Just ask your pretty friend here. There's a reason why Manasseh hasn't even tried to take back their western provinces." A wolfish spark seemed to ignite in his bloodshot eyes.

Avora'tru'ivi realized she had to rein in the conversation before it spiraled out of control.

"Listen, Jason, we understand how proud of your country and your armies you are. It is clear from the grandeur of these buildings that the empire lives on here. But all of this is threatened by the Great Khan. Now is the time for us to put past differences aside and work together to defend this continent. How do you want to be remembered- as a hard-headed prince who led his people to ruin through stubbornness, or as a shrewd statesman who knew when to make an alliance when it was offered?"

Jason looked at her with renewed interest. "Alright, I'll listen. What exactly are you proposing?"

"Wil'iah and Manasseh are assembling an international league to contain Mongol growth in the region. Our goal is to keep them from capturing Southeast Asia and Indonesia, and, by extension keep them from attacking us. This alliance will be based on mutual defense and respect. If one of the partners is attacked, all will come to its aid. There will be additional benefits including special trade relationships as we seek to compete with the Mongols economically. However, all participants must abide by a code of ethics, including respect of the sovereignty of other nations and their peoples," she said, casting a pointed stare over her shoulder at the Aboriginal boy chained to the door.

"What's in it for me?" asked Jason as he vainly tried to suppress a belch.

"Well, avoidance of destruction and ruin, for one."

"What's keeping me from simply making a deal with Kublai Khan? It seems to be working for the Khmers." Avora'tru'ivi noticed his face flush as he leered at her; she hoped it was the copious amounts of alcohol he evidently consumed.

"And lose the independence of your proud principality? You would become nothing but the Khan's puppet, a plaything for the court of Xanadu."

These words clearly hit home as Jason sat more upright, his eyes seeming to ignite with the spark of some idea – an idea that Avora'tru'ivi was pretty sure she wasn't going to like. His nostrils flared as he began to breathe more heavily. "I will consider your offer. But I have a few conditions."

"Name them, and we will consider them."

"I am not stupid. I have long realized that I am surrounded by potentially hostile nations. My principality is the last bastion of Philistine culture in the north. It is clear to me that the empire isn't coming back. I recognize that it is time for me to make more stable arrangements. If I join your league, Manasseh, Ephraim, Issachar, and Wil'iah must promise never to make war on Pelesetania. Manasseh must recognize the sovereignty of Pelesetania and relinquish any claim she makes over our territories. Along with this diplomatic recognition must come free trade as well as safe transit through Wil'iah for traders from Pelesetania bound for former Frouzean territories in the south."

Jessica sharply took in her breath. "You ask for much."

Jason grinned. "I am not finished. Look around," he said, swinging a chubby hand around to regard the hall.

"This place could use some redecoration. I'm sure you can tell that Pelesetania requires a woman's touch, and I am without heirs- at least any legitimate ones," he smirked.

"I don't follow," Jessica retorted.

Jason suddenly locked his inflamed eyes with Avora'tru'ivi. "You know, there's a very old trick for resolving diplomatic difficulties between neighboring countries. There would be no better way to heal the rift between Manasseh and Pelesetania. I'll make you a deal. I will join your alliance if you marry me."

Avora'tru'ivi's stomach dropped to the floor.

"This is outrageous!" hissed Jessica as she whirled around and prepared to purposefully stride out the door. Avora'tru'ivi hesitated for a moment, then turned to follow, insult playing openly across her face.

"Come, now, Princess, I can't believe you'd so flippantly reject me. Everyone knows that girls like you secretly want bad men like me."

"In that case, you are seriously misinformed," she spat at Jason over her shoulder.

Jason passed gas again, but then called after the princess.

"You know, I'd think about this more carefully, honey. Let me rephrase my terms. You can marry me, or I will join in a different alliance- with Kublai Khan. You've heard the expression- who you can't defeat, you ally with. Besides, I would think you would be grateful to find such an eligible husband as myself. It's no secret that Manasseh wants their western provinces back. Becoming my wife, or at least one of them, will certainly go a long way toward making that some sort of reality. Think about it. You'd either get me, a ridiculously attractive husband, or you will get a beachhead for your worst enemy right on your doorstep."

Jessica scoffed, rolled her eyes, and kept walking.

However, Jason's threat hit home on Avora'tru'ivi, who halted her progress. She winced, then she called after her friend.

"Wait!"

She then turned to Jason, fighting the urge to vomit as she forced out her next words.

"Your proposal deserves due consideration. Your logic is sound. I will think on it. Can you give me a moment?"

"What!?" Jessica stopped in mid-step.

"I love my country more than I love myself," Avora'tru'ivi said, then pointedly stared at Jason, "or you."

"I'll be waiting, honey!" called out the prince in response, earning another hiss from Jessica.

With that, the princesses ducked behind a column.

Jessica took both of Avora'tru'ivi's shoulders and shook her.

"What are you doing!?"

"He made it pretty clear. If we don't get married, he will help Kublai Khan destroy Manasseh – and Wil'iah. He's put us in a position where we might need his help. If I marry him, I can secure that help and avoid giving Khan a beachhead."

"We don't need him that much! In fact, we don't need him at all! If he's going to threaten us that way, I'd just as leave invade this rotten country and wipe it off the map!"

"Come now, Jessica, that is hardly a Christian thought."

"Not any less than considering becoming some sort of pagan bride!"

"Listen, Jessica, I love my country, and I will do anything to defend it. We cannot afford for Kublai Khan to get a beachhead in Australia. If Pelesetania doesn't join our alliance or even worse, makes a deal with Khan, I will have much bigger problems than a disagreeable husband."

"No, you are the one who needs to listen. This is a

ridiculous proposal, and I don't think you should consider it for one second. There are other answers. Even if the Mongols manage to make a deal with Pelesetania, we can cut it off from China using our seapower, and defend ourselves on land if need be."

"Yes, and then thousands of brave men and women will die because I could not stomach an unappealing marriage. If I am truly to be the princess of my people, I cannot afford to be that selfish," she said, her voice filled with reluctance.

"I don't believe this. Nobody expects you to enter an arranged marriage. And I'm sure those brave men and women would gladly lay their lives on the line rather than see you suffer this fate. Listen to me. I've known you for your whole life. I know you're braver than this. I know you're stronger than this. Think back on your nation's history. What happened the last time some Philistine thug tried to force a princess of Ephraim to do his will, under veiled threats of violence?"

Images flashed before Avora'tru'ivi's mind's eye of her mother, Sheerah, bravely picking up a sledgehammer and smashing the idols of Dagon and Baal, knowing full well it meant an invasion from Frouzea. To that day, it remained one of the most celebrated moments in Ephraim's long history. She knew what she had to do.

Avora'tru'ivi stood up a bit straighter, pushed her shoulders back, forced her chin up, and re-emerged from behind the pillar.

"Ah, beautiful, I see you've reached a decision! Come, let's have some fun!" Jason beckoned.

Instead, Avora'tru'ivi opened her mouth to address the foul prince.

"We appreciate the time you took out of your purportedly very full schedule to meet with us regarding a potential alliance against the Mongol Empire. We have duly considered the conditions that you set forth and have determined that they are unacceptable. Furthermore, our visit here has uncovered illegal human trafficking activity occurring within your borders with state sanction and approval. Such activities are antithetical to the principles of our proposed alliance and will not be tolerated. Our league hereby relays to you the following demands:

"All slaves taken from the Yolngu Nation and other Aboriginal states must be returned at once. All Aboriginal citizens living within the borders of Pelesetania must be granted citizenship status and property rights following the system pioneered in Wil'iah. Women must be similarly afforded citizenship. Pelesetania will pay an annual tribute to Yolngu to an amount double that which they have taken in raids. Border regions with Manasseh must be demilitarized except in the event of alliance activity."

Avora'tru'ivi then paused for emphasis, and squarely faced the prince, a slight smile gracing her otherwise steely features.

"Lastly, I cannot accept your 'offer' of marriage. If you are truly concerned about your lack of a legitimate heir, as you stated, perhaps you can marry one of your many concubines and raise one of your reported one-hundred twenty children to legitimacy."

With that, she spun on her heel and strode purposefully toward the door, Princess Jessica following after delivering one final bare-teethed snarl at Jason.

As Avora'tru'ivi and Jessica approached the door, Jessica called a halt, a conspiratorial glimmer igniting in her fierce brown eye. Avora'tru'ivi instantly understood her intentions, a wide smile breaking across her features. Jessica walked over to the Aboriginal boy and drew her sword. The boy's eyes widened in fear, but the terror quickly changed to wonder as the princess brought the Pilbara steel weapon slamming down on the chain. The poorly-made link shattered, and Jessica gently took the boy by the wrist and whispered in his ear,

"You're coming with us. Our next destination is your home."

"What do you think you're doing!?" yelled one of Jason's guards as he stepped towards the princesses and the boy.

"Oh, yes, please, *do* try to stop me," Jessica said, raising the point of her sword to the man's gut. "I'm willing to guess your armor is no better-made than that chain." Then, flashing a dangerous grin at Avora'tru'ivi, she lunged forward. "I suppose there's only one way to find out!"

The guard turned and ran. The doors slammed shut with thunderous finality.

"WHAT!!?" Jason hurled the wine bottle onto the floor, earning a wince from the herald as it shattered into a hundred pieces.

"Is something the matter, your highness?"

"That witch! She'll be sorry! Yes, she'll be really sorry! Just wait…just wait…" Jason suddenly focused on the distressed herald.

"Well don't just stand there! Get me more wine, NOW!!!"

CHAPTER ELEVEN

ALL HAIL ASTARTE

Gath

Leaping torchlight haltingly lit the musty temple of Astarte, which was otherwise dark except for a single shaft of light that filtered in through a dirty skylight and illuminated a cracked marble altar stained the color of dried blood, its front upturned into two horns. The once-gleaming, tiled floor was littered with rubble, scraps of cloth, and the decomposed carcasses of a variety of livestock animals.

At the end of the long, colonnaded hall facing the decrepit altar, a bronze door ponderously groaned with protest as five hooded figures strained to push it open. Their faces shrouded in darkness, the figures picked their way forward among the rubble and bones, each carrying a foul-smelling basket.

The five figures gathered around the altar, each of them hypnotically mumbling an unintelligible chant as they opened the baskets and emptied their putrid contents onto the altar. Dozens of fish carcasses tumbled out onto the horned slab, making slippery slapping sounds as their lifeless bodies impacted the bloodstained marble.

The central figure threw back its hood to reveal a bald head covered in minute wrinkles, with two vacant eyes set in an age-spotted forehead. The man opened his chapped mouth and began to speak in a quavering, raspy voice.

"Hear our cry, o eternal goddess of love and war! Hear our prayer, o great Astarte! For we are cast down, we have fallen from greatness, and we need you to descend from your exalted place in the heavens once more to lead our people to victory! We are surrounded by enemies, and there is no courage or valor left in our nation to resist. Gone is the splendor of our golden age of the great Frouzee, our cherished incarnation to this world of your unending majesty! And now, an enemy more great and terrible than we could have imagined will shortly come knocking at our gates! We call upon your eternal power, your breathtaking beauty, and your undying majesty! Hear our cry, and accept our offerings unto you, great Astarte, great Frouzee!"

As his voice's last wheezes echoed through the dank room, the oppressive, suffocating silence began to reassert itself over the temple chamber. The five figures ceased their chanting and held their breath as one of the fish slipped off the altar and fell to the floor with a squelch.

Suddenly, a crack of thunder shook the room as an

enormous, putrid cloud of red smoke rose from the altar. The high priest's eyes filled with a maniacal awe as his lips trembled and his hands shook. Gradually, the smoke began to diffuse into the poorly-lit sanctum, revealing a shadowy form that resolved itself into the shape of a woman. With a fluid, confident motion, she stepped forward out of the smoke, revealing a luridly-painted face crowned with two ivory horns flanking a gold crescent.

"It's *good* to be back," she said, the words thickly dripping from her scarlet mouth.

Words failed the priest as he fruitlessly worked his mouth.

One of the other priests narrowed his eyes as he focused on the mysterious woman's face.

"Iphigenia? Is that you?"

The woman threw back her head and let out a braying, full-throated laugh that reverberated around the dismal hall.

"Fool! This body is no longer Iphigenia, for I have judged her, and she was worthy to be my vessel on this miserable Earth, for as long as I deign to tread on it! After all, this is what I instructed your order to do, isn't it? Did you not scour the empire to find young girls who might be appropriate vessels for the return of your eternal goddess and take them here, to this decrepit temple?

Her accuser sputtered, "Well, yes."

"And did not Iphigenia meet your criteria? Many have passed through this wreck of a temple before, but I have judged her, and *only* her, worthy to be my vessel."

"Yes, she was…promising at first, but I thought her time had passed! She was beginning to outlive her usefulness!"

"Fools! Goddesses such as I can use anybody they want!" The woman's contralto voice thundered through the temple. "Now, this body is no longer to be called Iphigenia, for your prayers have been answered. I am Delilah, Second Incarnation to Earth of the Eternal Goddess Astarte and Frouzee of the Frouzean Empire! I have returned to save my people from the enemies that now beset them! Your prayers have been answered, and now is our chance to take back control from the petty princes that have ruined my empire!"

The ancient head priest still looked doubtful, but then one of the younger ones tentatively nudged him.

"It seems that our prayers have indeed been answered," he said, briefly making eye contact with "Delilah" and giving her the slightest of winks. "After all, weren't we daily hoping for someone to assume the mantle of our eternal empress?"

A smile crept up the corners of Delilah's face.

"Now, what is the proper response to the appearance of a goddess who condescends to grace your miserable souls with her presence?"

The priests all nervously looked at each other.

"*On. Your. Knees.*"

The five priests gingerly knelt on the ground, wincing as rubble dug into their kneecaps.

"Is this how you thank a goddess for descending from her perfectly good heavens to your aid? I have half a mind to leave again."

The lead priest, who was only just now beginning to recover his faculties from the shock of Delilah's appearance, seemed to make a decision, and called out.

"All hail Astarte!" With that, he bent his head down and kissed the floor. His four companions followed his lead.

"That's better," the woman said as she surveyed the room, pursing her scarlet lips in disapproval.

"This place looks terrible. It seems we have an empire

to take back."

CHAPTER TWELVE

THE DANCER IN THE DARKNESS

Champa, southeast Asia

The *Ava'ivi* gently cruised along the shore of Champa, in Southeast Asia. Tamino and Admiral Zhang stood at the rail, watching the jungle shoreline go by.

"This is not going to be like the last visit," the admiral said to Tamino. "Champa is at war, and King Inrdravarman is in hiding high in the mountains."

Tamino nodded. "The only way to find him is through our local OFZ cell. I know where to find them. Fortunately, that was covered in my training."

The admiral regarded him gravely. "We will have to take

you in close to shore in the cover of darkness and drop you off in a dinghy. You'll have to land on the beach alone and make your way into the interior."

Tamino patted the captain on the shoulder. "If I'm not back in a month, you know what to do."

That night, the *Ava'ivi* came close inshore, all of her running lamps extinguished. Tamino, in a one-person canoe, lowered over the side, clad in a camouflaged cloak that lay over the uniform of a Mongol soldier, a disguise completed by heavy makeup and moustache appliques. He immediately made for the nearby beach with strong, consistent strokes of the paddle. As the canoe struck bottom, Tamino leapt out and dragged it up the beach, hiding it under the abundant mangrove foliage that fronted the edge of the beach to the left. Listening carefully for any movement, he began to pick his way through the dense forest toward the coastal road that his silk map (designed specifically not to make noise) had told him fronted the shore.

He spent two hours surreptitiously creeping along the roadside, occasionally ducking down into a ditch to avoid being seen by Mongol patrols. Every so often, he thought he heard rustling in the underbrush behind him, but every time he went to investigate, there was nothing there.

At length, Tamino arrived at a village, whose location matched the one circled in red ink on his map. He immediately headed for the local tea house, wincing as he heard the sounds of uproarious carousing emanating from the normally-demure establishment.

Pushing open the double doors, he stepped inside

to be greeted by a cacophony of chaos. Mongol soldiers drank huge tankards of foaming liquid, singing braying songs and occasionally fighting each other, while others played tabletop games or even staggered about, attempting an approximation of a "dance." At the center of the tea house was a stage. Tamino knew that this was where he needed to be. He quickly made his way over to a miraculously-empty table. A rather frightened-looking waitress, clearly a terrorized member of the local village population, came over to him and began to speak Mongolian.

"What can I get you?" she asked.

Attempting his best imitation of a brusque Mongol solider using the language he'd worked hard to perfect, Tamino growled, "Wulong, please."

The waitress looked surprised. "Regular wulong? Or do you want the Friday Night Special?"

Tamino wasn't sure what the "Friday Night Special" was, but based on his surroundings, he probably didn't want to know.

"Just the regular, thank you."

The waitress gave him an odd sidelong glance, then scuttled back into the kitchen. She emerged a short time later with a large porcelain pot that was chipped in several places. She shakily poured the tea, wincing at each outburst from the Mongols.

"Are you sure that's all that you want?" she asked.

"That will be fine, thank you."

Tamino began to gingerly sip the tea, taking in the surroundings and waiting for his cue.

"Well, look at this sissy, drinking his tea," slurred a Mongol soldier as he staggered toward Tamino.

The prince rolled his eyes.

I was hoping this wouldn't happen.

94

"Can't stomach anything else, sweetheart?"

Tamino deliberately tried to ignore the solider, but this last attempt to avoid a confrontation failed.

The soldier swatted the teacup out of Tamino's hand. It flew across the room and hit the floor, shattering into a million pieces as the tea flew everywhere.

Tamino stood up, reaching his full commanding height. Looking down on the solider, he simply responded with his best Mongolian accent,

"You know, you're going to have to pay for that."

The Mongol soldier growled and swung a fist wildly at Tamino, who deftly avoided the blow.

"Can't take a punch, *sister?*" jeered the soldier as he swung again. This time, Tamino caught the man's fist in his hand and used it to push the already unsteady man off-balance; he ended up in a heap on the floor. Tamino sat back down and tried to ignore him, but the effort was in vain. The soldier got back up off the floor and tried again.

Tamino evaded the attack once again, but this time, he swung in response, internally wincing at the need for violence. His fist connected with the soldier's chest with such force that he was thrown into a nearby table, ending up once again in a mound, this time unconscious.

"Anybody else?" Tamino growled at the other Mongol soldiers who had begun to take interest in the exchange. Rather than engaging, though, the nearest one nodded in respect and went back to guzzling a tankard of rice wine.

Suddenly, movement caught Tamino's eye as a riot of multicolored silks appeared on the stage. A dancer began to make fluid movements, flinging sashes and strands from her brightly-dyed costume in all directions. Some of the Mongol soldiers took notice and began whistling disrespectfully. After a few minutes, the dancer began to work her way around the room with a basket in which she hoped to collect coins from the soldiers; but for every time a Chinese coin clinked into the basket, a soldier would rudely spit instead.

Finally, the dancer reached Tamino. He dug into his utility bag and withdrew a medallion emblazoned with a six-pointed star inscribed with an eight-pointed star. He locked eyes with the dancer and gave her a knowing look, before dropping the large medallion into the basket with a dramatic flourish. The dancer stole a glance at the medallion, her eyes growing large. She gave Tamino an almost imperceptible nod before flouncing on to the next soldier in the room.

The dancer, having collected her haul for now, ran backstage, but not before once again locking eyes with Tamino and subtly motioning for him to go outside. He called the waitress over; she scurried toward him, her eyes widening in concern at the sight of the shattered teacup.

"Was the tea not to your liking?"

"On the contrary, it was delightful. This should cover the cost of replacing the cup. I would stay to clean up, but I have to go." Tamino handed her several Chinese coins.

"You're not like the others, are you?" she asked quietly.

Tamino didn't answer. He merely bowed his head, pushed the chair in, and walked out of the tearoom.

As he exited the outer door and walked beneath the eves of the tearoom, a hand shot out from behind a column and grabbed him by the collar, dragging him into the shadows.

"You'd best be careful. It would be a shame if fire burned down this teahouse." A voice hissed.

Tamino froze. "Such a flame would burn forever," he replied calmly with the pass-phrase, relief washing over him as the hand relaxed and released his collar. As he turned around, he discerned the dancer in the darkness.

"Why are you here?" she hissed.

"I bring urgent news from Trukanamoa. I must see Indravarman. I've been told you know how to find him."

"It had better be important. That's not an easy trip."

"Would I be here if it wasn't important?"

"Very well. Come with me."

The dancer, now clad in a more demure set of robes that looked more like something a normal villager would wear, led Tamino out by the hand into the street, giggling coquettishly. A few older women from the village regarded the scene with an under-the-breath "tsk-tsk," but on the whole, nobody seemed to pay much attention to them. After weaving their way through several teeming streets, they arrived at a house on the outskirts of the village.

Dropping her flirtatious charade, the dancer pulled Tamino inside, giving one more wary glance outside before shutting the door.

"My name is Minh, Associate of the Order of the Flame of Zebulon, at your service," she said, rendering the traditional Wil'iahn military salute, an incongruous sight when paired with her slight frame and Champan village dress.

"Benaiah ben'Gershom, Knight Commander, at your service," Tamino replied with his assumed identity for the mission.

"I take it you're not really a Mongol," she said as she studied his makeup.

"I'm afraid not."

"Why are you trying to see the king?"

"Wil'iah is working to assemble a large alliance to defend the region against Mongol aggression. I was sent to give the king vital tactical information and to recruit Champa to join the league. Do you know how to find him?"

"No, but I know someone who does. You'd best get your sleep now. We will leave at dawn."

CHAPTER THIRTEEN

THE YOLNGU

Yolngu Confederacy, northwestern Australia

In the gathering evening, the *Shechem* rode at anchor as the princesses went ashore in a small dinghy to meet with a chieftain of the Yolngu, the rescued Aboriginal boy from Jason's court in tow. One of several powerful indigenous Australian nations, along with the Pilbara Confederacy and the Kingdom of the Murri on the East Coast, the Yolngu dared to resist the depredations of Pelesetania. They were known to be a mysterious but honorable people with a strong sense of family, with whom Manasseh maintained an uneasy peace. Avora'tru'ivi had attempted to understand more about their culture before the mission, but she still did not completely understand the nation's "moiety" system, whereby everything in the land was divided between two overarching family groups, the Dhuwa and Yarritja. It was her understanding, for example, that a child of the Dhuwa must marry a child of the Yarritja. Furthermore, the culture included avoidance relationships- while sons-in-law held their mothers-in-law in high regard, they did not touch or make eye contact with them. Such were the ways of many of the original inhabitants of the continent; different as they were, Wil'iah had proved that cooperation was possible, so she decided she was going to let Jessica take the lead in this round of negotiations.

As the dinghy brushed against the sand and the princesses stepped ashore, a stern guard appeared out of the evening gloom and called on them to halt, hefting a spear.

"What do you want?"

Avora'tru'ivi struggled to remember which dialect of the Yolngu Matha, the language of these people, she needed to use.

"We would like to speak with the leader of the Marrakulu."

"Why?"

"We need to discuss an issue of grave import to your nation's secur--," Avora'tru'ivi began to say, but before she could finish, the rescued boy darted out from behind Jessica and ran over to the guard, a wide, beaming grin across his face.

"Uncle!" he yelled out jubilantly.

The guard nearly dropped his spear with shock, then ran forward to embrace the boy. However, suspicion quickly clouded his face, and he turned back to the princesses, leveling the spear at Avora'tru'ivi.

"What is the meaning of this!? Why did you have him?"

"We rescued him from the clutches of Prince Jason," Jessica responded hastily. "One of our goals here was to bring him home."

The guard's features softened.

"Very well. I and my clan thank you for this. I will take you to see the king."

The princesses were escorted to a campfire set in the center of the village, which was decorated throughout with strings of pearls recovered by the Yolngu's skillful divers. Sitting in by the fire was a severe-looking man who rose and introduced himself as the king of the local Dhuwa group, a clan called the Marrakulu. When he saw the young boy joyfully clinging onto his uncle, the king stood up, a grin breaking over his face.

"What, besides returning my grandson to us, brings you to our village on a nice evening like this?" he asked the princesses. Various citizens of the village, their interest piqued by the disturbance, began to emerge from the houses. When they caught sight of the boy, they began to rejoice, hugging him and showering him with affection.

A smile played over Jessica's sharp features as she responded, "We assume that the threat in the north needs no introduction."

The chieftain nodded gravely. "We have heard from our Makassan trader friends that a great enemy looms in the distant lands. Even the Baijini have fallen to its terror, or so we've been told. We haven't heard from them in years."

"Baijini?" Avora'tru'ivi asked.

"Chinese traders," Jessica explained.

"Yes, in older days the Baijini would regularly come to our shores to trade for pearls and trepan, dried sea cucumber, but we haven't heard from them in over five years. According to the Makassan traders, the Baijini's country was overtaken by this threat around that time. Our subsequent communication with Wil'iah has confirmed their demise," he said, nodding to Jessica.

"Then you are aware that Australia may be next?" Avora'tru'ivi asked.

The chieftain nodded, his eyes filled with concern. "What the Baijini could not contain, we cannot hope to."

"We think there is a chance, if we work together," said Jessica.

The man regarded her and Avora'tru'ivi with a contemplative but quizzical expression.

"Very well. What do you propose?"

"The only way for our individual, small nations to resist the seemingly overwhelming might of the Great Khan is to band together. We propose a grand league of nations, stretching from Australia to Asia, that will leap to each other's' mutual defense. Including the Yolngu in the protective embrace of this alliance is a top priority for us."

"Who else is in this alliance?" The Yolngu king asked.

"Well, as of right now, Wil'iah, Issachar, and Ephraim-Manasseh are the founding members. Prince Tamino of Wil'iah is on a trip to try to recruit Champa, Dai Viet, and Singhasari to our cause. We attempted to recruit Pelesetania" – the king's eyes narrowed in disgust – "but such an alliance proved too distasteful for us to conclude," Jessica finished hastily.

The Yolngu chieftain suddenly pounded his fist on the ground.

"I'm shocked you even considered it. Those thugs are thieves, conquerors, and murderers. Even now they raid over our border, stealing our children to serve as slaves in their debauched courts. We will never work with them. But," he said, motioning to the boy now being tightly squeezed by an old woman, "I see you have already discovered this."

Avora'tru'ivi gritted her teeth. "What Pelesetania is doing is reprehensible. I only regret we could not rescue more of the children."

Jessica grimaced. "If it weren't for the greater threat of the world's largest empire at the gates, we'd wipe them off the map without hesitation. Someday soon, our fleets will rain destruction on Jason's decrepit palace! Nonetheless, Wil'iah will immediately begin infiltration efforts to rescue as many of the slaves as possible. We're well-practiced at this, as anyone who has walked the Exodus Road can attest."

A smile played at the corners of the elder's face. "Well, it seems you have a spark of the old Wil'iahn fire in you after all." He seemed to think for a moment, then continued. "You both seem like nice ladies. Whatever differences our peoples have had in the past, I think we can put them aside now to face the threat in the north together, as long as you don't cooperate with any of those Philistine thugs. After Frouzea destroyed the Kingdom of Zebulon and conquered Australia, enslaving us in the process, Aboriginal people and the Children of Zebulon fought hand-in-hand to overthrow the Frouzeans and ultimately together created the Kingdom of Wil'iah. The Marrakulu will honor that legacy and stand together with you to face the Great Khan. Our armies may not be anywhere near as strong as Pelesetania's vaunted three hundred thousand, but I know we stand on the right side. As long as you stay true to this, I am willing to advocate for this alliance with the other clans. The Yolngu may not have the great cannons that your fleets boast, but we are a brave people and will fight as mightily as anyone for our freedom. You won't regret this decision."

Avora'tru'ivi looked at the sky, noticing a bright star blazing in the heavens. She could have sworn it hadn't been there before.

"No, I don't think I will."

CHAPTER FOURTEEN

ENTER DELILAH

Gath

The new palace of Gath, built some distance from the crumbling acropolis, loomed over Temur Khan and his retinue. The grandson of Kublai Khan, the Mongol dignitary had been sent to investigate the various Philistine city-states that the Great Khan vaguely knew existed far to the south, not far from the reputed Kingdom of Wil'iah, which the Mongols knew had provided assistance to the Song Dynasty in its death throes. The voyage had been arduous, but Temur's ocean-going junks had managed to make the trip. According to various reports that had reached Khan's palace at Xanadu, these Philistine principalities had once been a powerful empire. Temur Khan had trouble believing it now. He held his nose as the stench of raw sewage flowing, even in front of the palace, assaulted his nostrils. Narrowing his eyes, he took a closer look at the superficially-impressive building. Unlike the buildings on the derelict acropolis, this palace was built out of clearly unseasoned wood that was beginning to conspicuously split with age. Impressively-sized columns supported the palace roof, but their faded finish betrayed a lack of maintenance.

These people will probably be pliable, but I'm not sure they will have much tribute to offer. This trip will hardly be worth it, he thought to himself.

He was jerked out of his thoughts as a callous voice called out from the ramparts flanking the palace's main gate.

"What do you want!?"

Temur discerned a guard dressed in a ridiculously-outré feathered helmet and clad in multicolored armor.

In response, the heralds behind Temur blasted three long blasts on their horns, and then one of them stepped forward, hefting aloft the standard of the almighty Mongol Empire.

"You stand in the presence of the Prince Temur Khan of the Mongol Empire! You would show respect!"

A look of pure terror suddenly crossed the guard's face, and he obsequiously genuflected to the Mongol retinue.

"Why yes, of course, come in, come in," he crooned.

Temur grinned.

"I don't mind if we do."

Temur stepped through the doors and followed the guard into a long colonnaded hallway, hung with red banners emblazoned with the swastika-like emblem of the

Principality of Gath, a long-forgotten symbol that had been lifted from an ancient coin brought along when the Philistine people had fled Assyrian invaders, and, pursuing rumors that their ancient Israelite enemies had done the same, eventually ended up here, in this forgotten continent on the edge of the world.

At the end of the room, dimly lit by a skylight open to the elements, stood a large stone throne, decadently trimmed with all the trappings of empire- emu and cassowary plumes, precious jewels, and haphazardly-placed ropes of pearls. The man sitting on the throne looked to be about sixty years of age, and had clearly once been a mighty warrior, but now sat in a derelict heap upon the throne, his voluminous beard flecked with foam and spittle as he gulped an enormous tankard of wine. Flanking him on either side were two men whom Temur surmised were his sons, based on their highly-ornate, burnished gold armor. Both wore the same ridiculous feathered helmet that the guards displayed and were statuesque and well-built, clearly in their prime, unlike their father. The taller, and presumably older, of the two, was too busy exaggeratedly kissing what appeared to be a slave girl to notice Temur's entrance. The other, with a sly, jealous gleam in his eye, seemed at least to be paying attention to the proceedings.

"We have a ... guest," squawked the guard nervously. The man on the throne briefly paused, then continued quaffing his wine. After an inordinate amount of imbibing, he slammed the tankard down on the ground, shattering the earthenware vessel into several hundred pieces. Two slave girls rushed forward to begin sweeping up the pieces with practiced ease, as if this were a regular occurrence.

"What?" the man belched, trying to focus his bloodshot eyes on Temur and his impressive retinue. When his eyes focused on the Mongol battle-standard, however, he suddenly pushed himself back into the throne as if attempting escape, a look of shocked horror crossing his face. His amorous son, himself noticing the standard in his peripheral vision, suddenly forgot his desires and let the unwilling object of his affections unceremoniously drop to the floor in a bedraggled heap. The other son rolled his eyes.

"How...how did you find us?" the occupant of the throne huffed.

Temur stepped forward, cleared his throat, and smirked before answering the question.

"I bring the greetings of Kublai Khan, the Great Khan of all the Mongol Empire, and now Emperor of all of China, on both sides of the Yangzi, Carrier of the Mandate of Heaven and ruler over Cathay and Manji, Supreme Leader of the known world. It has come to the attention of the Great Khan through the confessions of certain Chinese merchants, and the depredations of the detestable kingdom known as Wil'iah, which assisted the weakling Southern Song in their last gasps against us, that another continent existed to the south, a continent whose resources are of interest to the Khan. I congratulate you; you weren't easy to find. It took many interrogations of many merchants to find anything approaching a map of how to get here. But came we did, and it is our great pleasure to inform you that the Khan has selected your Principality to receive the honor of vassalship."

"WHAT!" roared the man on the throne. "You stand in the presence of Ajax the Great of Gath, and my sons Achilles and Ajax the Lesser," he said as he motioned to his two sons, who grimaced in unison, "and you dare to offer me vassalship!?"

"Consider our offer carefully. It doesn't much matter to

us who you are. Your principality isn't terribly impressive. Remember who you are dealing with. The Great Khan's inexorable might just crushed China, once considered the most invincible nation in the world. You are an insect. We can find you useful, or we can smash you in an instant."

"You had enough trouble finding us," Ajax countered. "I doubt you could get a fleet down here. I don't think your ships are really capable of that kind of long-distance travel. Based on what we've heard, most Chinese ships are suited to river operations."

"Well, we made it here, didn't we? Besides, the Great Khan has recently embarked on a massive naval expansion program that will give us true ocean-going capability. Granted, this will take time, and we have other nations to visit with our generous offers first, but in seven years' time, we will be back, and then you will have to make your choice."

"And exactly what choice is that?" Ajax growled.

"You can become a tributary state to the Great Khan, or we will destroy you and all of your people."

"And what price will the tribute be?"

"A thousand of what you refer to as "talents" of silver, or its equivalent value in other goods, on an annual basis. When we return in seven years, we expect seven years' worth of payment."

Ajax pounded his fist on the arm of his throne. "That is outrageous!"

Temur smiled cruelly. "That is our price."

※ ※ ※

An excitedly-murmuring crowd gathered in front of a raised dais, often used by the prince for public announcements. Two free-standing standards of the Principality of Gath languidly swayed in the stifling, still air, signifying that an announcement was about to be made.

"Did you hear? My friend Chryseis told me. A strange man came to the palace today. He said he was the prince of an empire so vast that it cannot be imagined. He demanded tribute, and threatened invasion if Ajax did not comply," one woman said excitedly to another.

"What did Ajax do?"

"Naturally, he refused the tribute at first, but then, the emissary made it clear just how powerful his forces were. He said that he would send hundreds of warships to exact the tribute."

"Then wha—"

At the blast of five trumpets from the ramparts of the palace behind, a single herald stepped forward between the standards and unrolled a scroll, clearing his throat.

"Citizens of Gath! By now, since this court leaks like a decrepit merchant ship, you have heard that we received a visitor yesterday. He was Temur Khan, envoy of the Mongol Empire. For those of you who don't know, the Mongol Empire has swept over the whole of the known world, crushing all resistance in its path. Even China has fallen to its fury."

A gasp ran through the crowd.

"Khan demanded that we pay him an annual tribute, and threatened to send hundreds of warships if we did not comply," he continued. To this end, the prince has decided to levy a special tax for the deliverance of Gath. Each family shall pay a seventy-five percent duty on their annual earnings from the last year. Those families unable to pay shall yield up a child for national service."

A rumble of anger swept through the assembled mass of humanity.

"You mean we're rolling over to the Mongols?" One man yelled.

"How is anyone supposed to pay a seventy-five percent tax?" wailed a woman in anguish as she held a young boy tightly in her clutches.

"This never would have happened under Frouzee, in the good old days when we were an empire ourselves," growled a grizzled old man.

"Citizens!" The herald squeaked, his normally-confident and suave voice beginning to quaver, "These measures are necessary for the salvation of our great city."

Suddenly, a reedy but authoritative voice cut through the clamor of the crowd as a man clad in blood-red robes ascended to the dais.

"Our city was once great, but now it's a pitiful ruin. Our greatness departed with the last Frouzee."

A voice from the crowd answered the statement of the priest. "Yeah, Frouzee would never have let this happen!"

"And just *who* are you?" sneered the herald at the priest, his bravado betrayed by the nervous darting of his eyes.

"I am the high priest of The Circle. The time has come to return Gath to its true faith. It is once again time to call upon Frouzee, upon our eternal Empress and Goddess Astarte."

"Nonsense," said the Herald. "Frouzee died nearly thirty years ago. She was powerless to keep her empire from crumbling. You and your 'Circle' are a ridiculous cult, hanging on to the past with desperation. Everyone knows that."

"The empire only collapsed because her people failed to properly worship her. We have a chance at redemption. She promised she would return in another incarnation to our people, if only we had enough faith," responded the priest.

"I remember Frouzee! I remember when we were great!" a voice yelled from the crowd.

The priest smiled. "Yes, yes, we all remember, don't we? Once, our empire ruled this entire continent. Our armies were the terror of the world. All the mudfaces were our slaves. We lived in luxury. Our economy boomed. All found employment. All of this glory occurred under Frouzee. Look at us now," he intoned, sweeping his hand around the crumbling city for emphasis. "We are a ruin, a mere fragment of what was. Our empire has fractured into pitiful splinters, of which this one is the most pathetic. This is not due to the great Frouzee, our precious incarnation of the goddess Astarte. This is due to the neglect of the prince, Ajax, a sniveling, petulant weakling who is content to snack on grapes while his nation falls to ruin. There is only one solution," the priest continued as he turned back to the populace, his eyes filled with a maniacal glee.

"All hail Frouzee!" he yelled.

"All hail Frouzee," came an emotion-filled voice from the square.

"Citizens! You must trust the leadership of your prince!" yelled the herald.

The priest silenced him with an imperious, withering look. "That's quite enough out of *you*." Turning to the audience, he raised his voice again.

"We were once a great empire! We can be again, if only we have enough faith!!" He raised his hand and pointed to the rear of the square, where a large object was covered in a crimson sheet. Two acolytes of the Circle, dressed in the same robes as the high priest, yanked the sheet off with a flourish. A gasp ran through the crowd as it beheld an enormous wooden altar inscribed with the symbols of the goddess Astarte and the inverted pentagram of the empire.

"The goddess Astarte will indeed descend to earth once

again as a new Frouzee and deliver us from the Mongols, if we show the proper gratitude! Here is our one chance to save our nation from the stupid leaders who have destroyed it, and restore our empire! All hail Frouzee! All hail Astarte!"

This time, a notably stronger response came from the assembled crowd.

"All hail Frouzee!"

The priest continued the call-and-response exercise, each time raising his voice higher and higher with increasingly fanatical delight. Each time, the voices from the square swelled, until a deafening chant filled the square. The herald tried to sneak away, but two acolytes of the Circle rose out of the crowd near the dais and arrested his progress.

The priest produced a medallion from his robes in the shape of the pentagram of the empire.

"Remember who you are! Remember your birthright! Remember that you are the finest creations of the gods, born to rule over all men! All hail Frouzee!"

"ALL HAIL FROUZEE!"

"Now, how do we bring her back? You know what to do!!" The priest yelled as the acolytes withdrew gleaming stone knives from their sleeves.

Individual members of the crowd began moving toward the altar, leading livestock with them and surrendering a myriad of goats, sheep, donkeys, and even cattle to the Acolytes. Soon, the enormous wooden pool that surrounded the altar was filled with blood.

"Very good!" yelled the priest. Now, we must all beg for Astarte's forgiveness and help together!"

As if in a trance, virtually the entire crowd hurled themselves prostrate onto the ground, their arms outstretched to the altar.

"All hail Astarte!!" screamed the high priest, hefting aloft a scepter crowned with two horns and a gold disk.

"All hail Astarte!!" responded the crowd.

"She can't hear you!"

"ALL HAIL ASTARTE!!!!"

A rumbling sound shook through the courtyard as five great blasts split the air. An enormous plume of foul-smelling red smoke rose from the altar, its color filling the wide, fanatical eyes of the high priest. The worshippers in the crowd tentatively lifted their heads, their mouths trembling with awe at the towering cloud.

As the smoke began to clear, a form became discernable. As the afternoon sun's rays penetrated the putrid fumes, they revealed a woman clad in a form-fitting dress of scale armor painted in a red-black pattern resembling the diamond pattern on a snake. Her face was framed with an enormous headdress in the shape of a rearing cobra's hood, which was crowned with two long bull's horns and a central sun-disk rendered in 24-carat gold. A huge, flared collar surrounded her headdress and was embroidered with a horse, a bull, a sphinx, a lion, and a dove, the symbols of Astarte. Around her neck hung a medallion emblazoned with the imperial pentagram, its five points representing the five city-states of Gath, Gaza, Ekron, Ashkelon, and Ashdod. Her face was luridly painted with kohl and red eyeshadow, giving her eyes a serpentine quality.

"It's good to be back," she said, the corners of her mouth turning in a twisted smile.

"It...It can't be..." whispered the herald, his mouth agape, as he struggled against the acolytes that held him in an iron grip.

The priest backhanded him across the face, his bejeweled ring carving a gash into the herald's cheek.

"Insolent fool! Is this how you greet our salvation?"

The woman addressed the crowd.

"I see you've missed me!" She crooned as she swept her eyes over the decaying city. She clucked disapprovingly. "This place looks terrible."

"Is it…is it really you?" a dirt-streaked man in the front row of the audience entreated.

"How could you ever doubt? I am Delilah, second incarnation to Earth of the goddess Astarte and eternal empress of the Frouzean Empire! I see it is time to take our glorious empire back! Too long have you languished in misery and weakness. Once you were the terror of the world. And, now that I have returned, you shall be again!"

At this, the crowd let out a jubilant shout.

The herald, recovering from the blow from the priest, tried to regain control of the situation.

"Citizens! We have no proof that this woman is who she says she is! You must trust the authority of the crown."

Delilah regarded the crowd, then narrowed her eyes at the distant herald.

"Bring him to me."

The crowd surged forward to grab the protesting herald, who squirmed as he was dragged across the square to the altar. He found himself face-to-face with the "goddess," who leaned into the herald's face, her snake-like eyes narrowing in disgust.

"Look at them. They love me," she said. "Why don't you go scurrying to your master, and tell him that, if he's smart, he will submit to the authority of the eternal empress."

"Is that a threat!?" the herald scoffed.

Delilah extended her index finger, revealing an impossibly sharp nail, which she pressed into the herald's puffed-out chest, drawing a small bead of blood.

"Why, yes!"

CHAPTER FIFTEEN

THE JUNGLES OF CHAMPA

Interior of Champa, Southeast Asia

Minh led Tamino on a barely-discernable track through the dense Cham jungle. Around them, exotic birds filled the steaming, humid air with song. At length, they found a clearing and decided to pause for a water break, Tamino passing Minh a large, camouflaged canteen.

"How did you enter the service of the order?" he asked.

Minh took a long swig from the canteen. "My father's friend escaped the Song Dynasty in its final days. He served alongside the expeditionary forces from Wil'iah. From everything he told us, they were a brave and decent people.

They seemed to be strangely set apart from the surrounding world. They carried a certain sense of …honor wherever they went. So, I guess you could say I grew up hearing stories about Wil'iah."

"Then what happened?"

"Well, two years ago, my village was attacked by a Mongol raiding party. I was carried off as a 'prize.' I was so scared that I couldn't even move. But, as if by some miracle, a mysterious figure emerged from the jungle to attack the raiding party and rescue me, along with several of my friends."

"A knight of the Order?"

Minh nodded as she passed the canteen back to Tamino. "The very same. That day, I realized that knight was part of something far larger. I never knew his real name, but I begged him to let me join his order as Champa attempted to throw off the dreaded Mongol invasion. This was early in the period where Wil'iah was beginning to set up intelligence networks in Champa, and he deemed me useful. So, here I am."

"Well, Wil'iah thanks you for your service," Tamino replied as he took a swig from the canteen.

Minh studied him intently, a quizzical expression on her face.

"My turn to ask questions. Who is she?"

"I'm afraid I don't know what you mean."

"Somebody gave you that pressed flower, and I'm guessing it wasn't your mother."

Studying her compatriot, she realized that her comment had instantly transported him to another place. An involuntary smile crept at the corners of his mouth as his eyes seemed to focus on a point a thousand miles away.

"A treasured friend, the most gracious, loving, and virtuous woman in all the world," he sighed, then suddenly looked sheepishly at her. "No offense intended to present company, of course," he said, his cheeks flushing with additional color.

"None taken. How do you know her?"

"We have been friends since we were children. When we were both young, we had a great adventure whereby we rescued the Scroll of St. Thomas from the clutches of the fanatics of Hosania."

"What's she like?"

"When she appears, it is like a star of the heavens has descended to grace us with its presence. She has the sweetness of the most treasured fruit nectar of the islands and the strength of the famed Damascus steel. She is formidable, and wonderful, and just the slightest bit terrifying."

Wow, he's really in love.

"And I assume she knows how you feel?"

"Well…no."

"What!? Then why did she give you that flower?"

"Well, we are very close compatriots. She said it was a symbol of her friendship."

Minh made a soft clucking noise. "Mmm-hmm. Likely story."

The mysterious knight looked at her in surprise. Minh found herself marveling again that his large brown eyes held not the slightest hint of guile – a sharp contrast from the assassins, spies, and thugs she had to deal with on a daily basis.

"Listen, Benaiah—and I know that isn't your real name, by the way— you need to tell her as soon as you get back to Wil'iah. She should be…grateful that someone like you would say such beautiful things about her."

"I don't want to ruin what we already have."

"I don't think that's likely, unless you spend too much

time dithering and she is forced to marry someone else! In this country, many marriages are arranged. Perhaps you would have better luck if you went through her parents."

"Things are different across the sea. She will be able to choose her own destiny."

"Well in that case, you have nothing to worry about. I have another question for you. You and your compatriots in the Order – but especially you – are very different from the 'tough guys' I have to deal with on a daily basis. You're...nice. I don't know how you manage to survive in this world."

To Minh's surprise, rather than answer her, the knight placed a finger to his lips and motioned for her to remain completely still. He cocked his head for a moment, his brows furrowing as he listened intently, to what Minh wasn't sure. Then, with a single fluid motion, he reached to his bandolier, grabbed an odd, v-shaped object, and flung it into the underbrush. Moments later, she heard a strangled cry and a sharp crack. The knight's hand shot skyward and deftly caught the strange object, which he tucked back into the bandolier before charging into the undergrowth.

He returned moments later, dragging the unconscious form of a Mongol tracker.

"My apologies for cutting you off. It appears we had an uninvited traveling companion. To answer your question, nice doesn't mean weak."

CHAPTER SIXTEEN

THE CORRUPTION OF ACHILLES

Gath

Crown Prince Achilles of Gath paced nervously around his chamber in the palace, heedless of the rich tile mosaics that depicted scenes of Frouzean bacchanalia all around him. He was disturbed by the news that a woman claiming to be a reincarnated Frouzee had appeared to take the throne- the throne that one day was supposed to be his. Suddenly, he thought he heard a strange creaking sound behind him. He whirled around with his hand instinctively reaching for the short sword strapped to his belt, then instantly stopped.

Standing in front of him was a woman outrageously outfitted with a snake-like headdress. She exactly matched the description of the "goddess" from the square.

"You. How did you get in here?" Achilles growled, eyeing the locked door to the chamber.

"Goddesses don't need doors," replied the woman, her face slightly lit by an unsettling smile. She began to pace toward him in a fluid, almost feline action. Achilles merely responded by imperiously raising his chin.

"Well," she said as she looked him up and down, "I was starting to worry that there was no greatness left in Frouzea, that there were no more heroes to be my champion." She reached out and grabbed his muscular upper arm. "But what a *specimen,*" she purred.

"What do you want," Achilles snarled.

"What does any woman want? A big, strong man to fight for me," she crooned, raising a hand to stroke his beard.

"Why would I fight for you? If my reports are to be believed, you have donned this ridiculous disguise to usurp my father's throne and seize control of Gath." Achilles' eyes followed her hand as it moved from his beard to his shoulder. He thought he felt a strange prick as one of her blood-red nails passed over it, but he thought nothing of it.

"Gath? Why, you set your sights too low. Someone of your...*prowess* could go much farther than just this city."

"I don't follow," said Achilles as his face began to oddly flush and his breathing began to quicken.

Delilah leaned in to whisper in his ear. "Listen, Achilles. You and I both know that your father has not done right by Gath. He has run this place into ruin. Look around. The acropolis lies abandoned, crumbling. The streets are filled with excrement. We have no goods to offer our trade partners save cheap, poor-quality wine. *Wil'iah* is the pre-eminent military power on the continent. Is this really the legacy you want your family to leave?" Achilles' nostrils flared as his heart began to beat faster.

"My father has done his best in a bad set of circumstances. If you are who you say you are, then much of Gath's present condition is your fault," he said, but he found that his thoughts were increasingly clouded. Was it just him, or was everything in the room beginning to take on a pink tinge?

"No, the old empire fell because of an incompetent and faithless generation that failed me. But I'm back now. And we get to write the next page of history – together."

Achilles found himself taking a second look at the supposed "goddess." What had seemed ridiculous before now seemed...intoxicating.

"Your father has proved his ineptitude through years of mismanagement. Gath needs a man to step forward and seize leadership. And not just Gath. *Frouzea* needs you. You have a greater destiny, Achilles of Gath. After all, if you weren't fated to be a legendary hero, the gods would not have given you such...*gifts,*" she said, looking him up and down admiringly.

"What...what do you propose?" Achilles asked breathlessly.

"It's your turn, Achilles of Gath. Seize the day. Seize the throne. Seize *me.*"

Achilles didn't need any more convincing. He lunged forward and kissed Delilah.

"Tonight we strike," she whispered huskily as she ran her fingers through his hair. "Together, we will go to the king's chambers. Then, as he lies in his usual drunken stupor, we will smother him with his own pillow."

"Smother..." Achilles looked for a second like he was

rethinking his loyalties, but then he visibly shook, and went back to kissing Delilah.

"Such a death will leave no trace. To the rest of the world, it will appear that his drunkenness finally caught up with him. It will only reinforce the general air of uselessness that he has already created. And then," she locked her gaze with his clouded, befuddled eyes, "*Long live the king.*"

CHAPTER SEVENTEEN

JAYA INDRAVARMAN

Interior of Champa, Southeast Asia

*J*amino and Minh continued to pick their way through the jungles of Champa, warily watching for any sign that they were being followed. At length, they came to an odd clearing with a distinctively-shaped tree standing at its center. Minh stopped and held up a hand.

"This is where the transfer happens."

"Transfer?"

"Do you really think your order would be so stupid as to have an operative who knew exactly how to get to Indravarman from the coast? This is as far as I go. We're supposed to meet someone else here."

Tamino nodded. "Smart. That makes sense."

Minh began to pace around the clearing, making a series of bird calls that had enough of a pattern that they could be recognized – if you knew what to listen for.

After a minute, a rustling in the tree above betrayed another presence. Tamino instinctively reached for his boomerang, but paused as he realized this was likely Minh's contact.

A Cham man dropped out of the tree into the clearing with deft precision, then snapped into a salute at Minh, who nodded in reply.

"Yes?" he asked.

"This man needs to see Indravarman."

"On what authority?"

Minh dug into her knapsack and withdrew the medallion inscribed with the Order's symbol that Tamino had dropped in her tips dish. The soldier's eyes widened with recognition.

"You've come a long way."

Tamino smiled reassuringly. "If this goes the way I expect, a lot more of us are going to be making the trip."

The guide looked skeptically at Minh, who simply smiled back.

"You can believe him." She turned to Tamino. "Well, this is as far as I go. For the brief time we've had together, it's been a pleasure serving with you."

Tamino snapped into the Wil'iahn salute. "Likewise."

"Champa thanks you for what you are trying to do." Minh turned back toward the way she had come, but then paused and threw her head back over her shoulder.

"And Benaiah—"

"Yes?"

"If things don't work out with your 'angel' back home,

you know where to find me."

With that, Minh strode back out of the clearing, noiselessly disappearing into the jungle. Tamino watched her leave, a quizzical expression on his face. He then turned to the guide and motioned for them to move forward.

Tamino and his new friend strode noiselessly through the dense jungle, every attempt by Tamino to make conversation meeting terse, one-word responses. The man seemed to be constantly wary, his eyes flicking at the slightest sound from the underbrush. Tamino found himself wincing at each flutter of a bird or snap of a branch. Although the man gave no specific sign of real alarm, Tamino couldn't shake the feeling that they were being watched.

This is your training getting the better of you, he though. False alarms never helped anybody.

Suddenly, Tamino noticed an unnatural movement in the canopy above. This was no false alarm. He instantly reached for the boomerang, but his companion whirled around with a belaying motion.

Almost noiselessly, a dozen perfectly-camouflaged soldiers dropped out of the trees on long vines, instantly surrounding Tamino and the Cham operative. One fighter, clearly the leader, stepped forward and saluted Tamino's taciturn companion, but then his eyes fell on Tamino – and his Mongol disguise.

"We have been betrayed!" he hissed, his eyes flashing dangerously. His fellow soldiers all drew wickedly-sharp swords.

"No, you don't understand! He's—"

The protestations of Tamino's guide were instantly cut off by an abrupt hand motion from the Cham captain.

"I trusted you. But to bring a *Mongol* into this, our most

secret place of strength? This is unbelievable." He snapped at the soldiers. "Tie them up and take them away!"

At least they aren't going to kill us right now, Tamino thought as he obligingly surrendered his weapons and allowed his hands to be tied. *Surely we'll be able to sort out this misunderstanding.*

The soldiers blindfolded Tamino and the guide and shoved them forward with brusque prods of their sword handles, leading them through an essentially-nonexistent track through the jungle. At length, the Cham captain kicked Tamino into the center of a clearing and ripped off the blindfold. Tamino looked around and was surprised to see what appeared to be a mobile command center, here in the jungle. The man standing in front of him was none other than Jaya Indravarman V himself, King of Champa, whom Tamino recognized from a diplomatic function long ago. Even in the dire situation, Tamino's heart made a small leap as he realized he had, against the odds, found the elusive leader.

"This Mongol scum was conspiring with this traitor to betray our location to the enemy! I shall be glad to kill them for you," the captain sneered.

Deliberately modulating his voice to take on a calming tone, Tamino protested. "This is a mistake, your Majesty. I am not a Mongol."

"You certainly look like one."

"My companion here is a known agent of your armies. Surely you trust him," Tamino soothed, gesturing toward the guide with an open palm.

Indravarman studied Tamino more closely. "Your accent doesn't sound Mongol."

"That's because I'm not. Untie me, and I will show you who I really am."

"Why should I trust you?"

"Because," Tamino said in his still-imperfect Cham before switching back to his native tongue, "*Va'tua ma brang ba brang'goa iva moa zi'a Tru'ivi!*"

"Untie him at once!" Indravarman barked at the shocked captain, who fumbled about for a knife to cut the bonds.

As soon as he was free, Tamino ripped off the false Mongol moustache and eyebrows, wincing slightly, before also removing the wig.

Indravarman looked like he had been hit by a rickshaw.

"Tamino!? What on this green earth are you doing here?" His eyes suddenly narrowed at the soldier who had threatened the prince's life.

"On your knees, now, soldier! Do you realize what you have just done?"

"No, no," Tamino interjected, "In my country, we bow only to God."

"I---I don't understand," stammered the soldier.

"You are standing in the presence of the crown prince of Wil'iah!"

"What!?!" exclaimed the guide. "You said your name was Benaiah ben'Gershom!"

"Well, I can't just go throwing about my real identity, now can I? Besides, Benaiah is my middle name, and Gershom was my father's assumed identity before he emerged from obscurity to lead our people to freedom."

Indravarman laughed. "Well, now that that's all cleared up, what was so urgent that you came all the way here?"

Tamino smiled. "Champa's courageous struggle against the hordes of the Great Khan has not gone unnoticed. The time has come for freedom-loving nations everywhere to join arms in determined resistance to the so-called unstoppable threat. We are assembling a grand alliance, and Champa is the tip of the spear, should you choose to join us."

Indravarman's eyes narrowed. "Who else is in this alliance?"

"Wil'iah's steadfast friend, the United Kingdom of Ephraim-Manasseh, and my previous stop, Singhasari. My next destination is Dai Viet."

"And what are the terms?"

"An attack on one is an attack on all. No separate peace with Kublai Khan. No tribute, no concessions, no surrender."

Indravarman stepped forward and extended an open hand.

"Champa has always been proud to call Wil'iah a friend. You have yourself an ally."

CHAPTER EIGHTEEN

NOT A DRACHMA

Gath

A crowd once again gathered in front of the royal
palace of Gath, an excited murmuring filling the courtyard.
Heralds and criers had run all over town that morning,
loudly trumpeting that there would be a major royal
announcement that day.

The murmuring instantly died down as the blasts of five
trumpets split the air, and two standard-bearers holding
aloft the vertical banners of the prince of Gath stepped out
onto the balcony, preceded by a herald.

"Citizens of Gath!" he squeaked in a high-pitched voice

that didn't match his ponderous girth, "A great tragedy has befallen our nation!"

The murmuring returned as speculation rippled through the assembled masses, but it was cut off almost as soon as it had begun by another fanfare from the trumpets.

Achilles of Gath swaggered out onto the balcony, clad from head to toe in entirely black armor, with a mournful expression plastered on his face that didn't quite reach his eyes. Ajax the Lesser, his younger brother, followed slightly behind. Forcing his voice to crack as though he had been weeping, Achilles addressed the crowd.

"Last night, my father, Ajax the Great of Gath, passed into the underworld."

A shocked gasp blew through the square.

"As many of you know, he had an unfortunately excessive affection for the drink. It finally overcame him. So, now, in this hour of despair, I must step forward to succeed him. It is my hope that, with the newfound help that has descended from the Heavens, I will lead our nation to greatness—nay, our empire to greatness!"

At this last surprising assertion, Achilles thrust his huge fist skyward, earning a lusty cheer from the still-shocked audience.

"For too many years we have been content to be a vestigial remnant of our former glory, an island of strength in a sea of chaos. For too long we have been content to call ourselves merely citizens of Gath, when, in fact, we are race chosen to lead an empire- and not just any empire- the greatest in the world!"

"Take it back!" someone yelled from the crowd.

"Yes, yes, take it back indeed. And, just in time, our goddess has descended from the heavens to join me in this great effort to retake Gath's greatness and restore our empire!"

"Frouzee!" yelled the crowd in unison.

A strange creaking sound filled the air as the floor opened beside Achilles and a figure began to rise from the gaping hole, slowly rotating to face the crowd as it did so. First, two horns appeared. Then, a gold pentagram inscribed within a burnished disk; then, an obsidian carved cobra in strike position, its eyes two flaming rubies; next, a crimson headdress in the shape of a cobra's hood. And finally, the smirking, painted face of the Frouzee Delilah, a visage greeted with a rapturous ovation from the assembled rabble below.

"*All hail Frouzee! All hail Astarte!*" they yelled in unison.

Delilah stepped off her platform and sidled over to Achilles, before theatrically kissing him. As a deafening cheer arose from the crowd, a jealous gleam filled Ajax the Lesser's eyes.

"Henceforth you will no more call yourselves citizens of Gath," Delilah crooned. "You will refer to yourselves by your rightful and proper name- imperial citizens of Frouzea! Our revolution starts here, but it will not end until all of the lands that once trembled under the shadow of our flag rue the day they defied us!"

Delilah basked in the roar of approval that met her words.

"And we will begin by cleaning up the absolute mess strewn about all around us. First, we will restore the acropolis. Secondly," she said, giving the audience a significant look, "Prince Ajax's seventy-five percent tax to fund tribute to the Mongols is hereby immediately cancelled. Instead, we will seize the riches of the wealthy upper class that has reclined in comfortable mansions while you break your backs in labor, and use their funds to build our armies! We will lay down the utmost for our defense, but not a drachma for tribute!"

At this announcement, a deafening rumble rose from the square as the crowd jubilantly accepted the tax cut.

A smile played at the edges of Delilah's crimson mouth.

"However, even I will not be able to defend our empire alone. We need soldiers for our armies. Where are the faithful sons of Frouzea? Where are my adored Adonises? I call on you, the men of Frouzea, to answer me plea and join me. Those examples that I find appealing will be permitted to join the Homeric Guard, our most elite military unit, which will be restored to its former formidable fearsomeness!

Almost immediately, men began fighting their way through the crowd toward her, salivating at the chance to be recognized in such a way.

"I will serve my Frouzee!" one of them yelled, a wild, hungry look in his eye.

Delilah, filling with self-satisfaction, allowed herself a grin.

"And, while taxes are summarily cancelled, goddesses always enjoy symbols of gratitude. The court of Frouzee will gladly receive any gifts that you can spare as voluntary tokens of affection for me. We will apply the proceeds toward our common defense! We will show the world what Frouzeans can do when working together!"

Another delirious cheer rose from the crowd.

"Well, what are you waiting for? Get to work!"

With that, Delilah spun on her heel and strode back into the palace, silently exulting in the endless homage that poured from the square directly into her soul. Achilles followed, slightly behind, like an obedient dog. Ajax watched them go, then followed, splitting off to head to his own apartments.

"I trust you have prepared reasonably luxurious

accommodations for me?" Delilah said to Achilles imperiously.

"Just you wait," he grinned.

After navigating a warren of passageways, the two leaders arrived at a set of bronze double doors. Two rather disheveled-looking soldiers stood guard, wry sneers on their faces.

"Another one for the collection?" one of them asked.

"What did you say?" Delilah replied, the steel in her voice unmistakable.

"Gods, no!" Achilles replied hastily. "If you know what's good for you, you will kiss the floor. You stand in the presence of a goddess."

The two guards looked at each other warily, then rendered the appropriate obeisance.

"I'll deal with you two later. Now, open the doors." Delilah snapped.

The two men hastily hoisted themselves to their feet and opened the doors.

A pool of water, filled with frolicking women, dominated the scene that confronted Delilah. Screeching cockatoos and cockatiels swooped through the air and perched domineeringly as colorful clouds of budgerigars wheeled about. Even more women luxuriated around the pool's edge, languidly fanning themselves with feather plumes.

One of them noticed the open doors and the two new guests, and then a crowd of suddenly animated women raced to the entrance, giggling coquettishly at Achilles.

Delilah's eyes narrowed as she noticed gold armbands on every single one.

"What is this?" she hissed at Achilles.

"They…keep me entertained." He said, his face an odd combination of self-satisfaction and sheepishness.

Putting on an air of distinct disapproval, Delilah regarded the semicircle of women. One particularly observant woman, however, noticed that the disgust didn't reach her eyes- which instead telegraphed concern.

Delilah turned and gave Achilles an inscrutable stare for a moment. Then, in a sudden flash of movement, she slapped him hard across the face.

"Goddesses don't share their champions. *I* will provide all of the entertainment now."

Achilles winced as he held a hand to his stinging cheek, while Delilah turned to the women.

"You are free to go. Guards, remove the armbands as they leave."

"Now, wait just a seco—"Achilles' protest was instantly cut off by a withering stare from Delilah.

"Don't test me. Would you rather I turn my affections elsewhere? That brother of yours is nearly as *delicious* as you."

Achilles balled his fist for a moment, looking as though he might strike the "goddess." But, clearly thinking better of it, he brusquely nodded at the women, who streamed out the door. The last one to leave turned for a split second back to Delilah, a look of gratitude plainly written in her piercing blue eyes.

Delilah didn't respond. Instead, she strode further into the room, noticing another set of double doors.

"That had better not be another harem," she sneered.

Achilles hastily shook his head.

"No, that is my sparring room. After all, this doesn't come for free," he said, waving a hand over his impressive musculature.

"I've seen better, in the good old days," Delilah said dismissively as she strode toward the doors and yanked them open.

A single wooden post stood in the center of a circular room lined with two rows of crimson bleachers. A large mound lay at its base, which Delilah initially mistook for a rock – until it moved.

The stirring form hosted itself up onto two enormous, stout legs. Standing before Delilah was a hulking giant of a man that made Achilles look like a middleweight. Delilah realized with shock that he must be well over seven feet tall. But, titanic though he was, he was restrained- both of his legs were in shackles, a thick chain wound around his midsection and terminated at an iron ring in the post, and both hands were fettered to the top of the pole. The man was covered in bruises and streaked with blood. His stringy, matted hair framed a blocky face dominated by a split lip, a broken nose, and a black eye. When the man's one good eye focused on Achilles, he let out a guttural yell and surged forward, his seemingly inexorable progress abruptly stopped by the chains.

Suppressing the urge to retch, Delilah coldly turned to Achilles.

"Would you care to explain this?"

"Well, any good warrior needs a sparring partner."

"'Partner' is the biggest stretch since Wil'iah claimed to be an actual country."

Delilah turned back to the wretched sight before her.

"What is his name?"

"He doesn't have one. We're not entirely sure he's completely human. He appears to be at least part mudface."

"If that were true, it would certainly be distasteful. Nonetheless, if we are to reconquer the empire, an asset like this cannot go to waste. This man will no longer be your sparring 'partner.' Instead, he will be my personal guard and manservant." Delilah turned away from the titan

CHAPTER NINETEEN

DAI VIET

Thang Long, Dai Viet, Southeast Asia

The serenity of the Tran court of Dai Viet was instantly shattered as the two gilded, studded doors to the throne room flew open, slamming against the walls. Tran Tranh Tong, the retired emperor and Tran Nanh Tong, the sitting emperor, both sat bolt upright in their thrones, fear written plainly on their faces. General Hung Dao, commander of Dai Viet's forces, stood next to the thrones, a scowl drawn across his face.

Framed in the brusquely-opened doors were the hulking forms of two Mongol generals, Toghon and

Sogetu, the latter recently back from his failed expedition against Champa. However, given his fearsome demeanor, one would never have guessed that he had been beaten.

"Your...excellencies. How may I help you?" Nanh Tong asked hesitantly.

"Spare me your pleasantries, Tran," growled Toghon. "As you are aware, the Great Khan is engaged in a war of conquest with the Kingdom of Champa, and their dishonorable guerilla tactics have so far denied us our rightful victory." Sogetu snorted in derision at the last phrase.

"Yes...we have been following the course of that war closely, although I can assure you that we have held true to our tributary relations—"

"If you expect me to believe that you have rendered no assistance to Champa, you must think me an idiot," Toghon sneered. "All the same, your past duplicity is irrelevant. You have an opportunity to win our forgiveness."

Hung Dao stepped forward and placed a staying hand on Nanh Tong's shoulder.

"Be careful what you agree to," he whispered.

"I don't remember asking for you to speak," Toghon yelled.

"You stand before the throne of Dai Viet, not before the occupied throne of China. I don't need your permission to speak," retorted the general.

"Watch your tongue, if you want to keep it," interjected Sogetu.

Nanh Tong gave Hung Dao a withering look, then turned back to Toghon.

"What do you propose?"

"Dai Viet will allow the armies of the Great Khan to pass through without molestation, or her people will face the consequences."

"You must understand, Toghon, that, while we have not acted to assist them, the Cham people are our friends. This is a difficult request to accept."

"We call this a 'choice' only nominally," said Toghon as he drew his sword and menacingly stroked the blade. He then approached the throne and leaned his bearded countenance right into Nanh Tong's face, his foul breath filling the emperor's nostrils.

"You of course, could choose to defy us, which will mean certain death for you and for your people."

"Nothing is certain. Surely you remember what happened the last time you tried to invade our country?" Hung Dao interjected.

Toghon tore himself away from the emperor and rounded on the general, looming over him as his voice dripped with derision.

"That was before we conquered China. If the mightiest nation on earth couldn't contain us, do you really think your measly country could? Go sit down in your proper place, General."

Walking back over to the emperor, Toghon cleared his throat and repeated his "request."

"Now, *Emperor*, it appears you have a 'decision' to make. Our soldiers will go through Dai Viet to Champa regardless of what the next sentence out of your pitiful mouth is. You can either make this journey easy for your people- or fatal."

Tranh Tong's lips trembled as he struggled to form his reply.

"Dai Viet will—"

"—Not allow any such invasion to violate her sovereignty, and neither will her allies!"

All the heads in the room instantly whirled around to

identify the source of the unexpected interjection. To everyone's surprise, a brown-faced man wearing a white and blue uniform stood square in the middle of the throne room.

"And you are?" sneered Toghon.

"Never mind who I am. The important thing is that your wave of conquest has come to an end."

Tranh Tong squinted at the sixteen-pointed star emblazoned on the mysterious visitor's chest.

"I've seen that symbol before, but not for a long time. Are you from—"

"Wil'iah. Your eyes do not deceive you. Crown Prince Tamino, at your service." Tamino rendered the military salute to both Nanh Tong and his retired father.

"Wil-*what?*" Toghon sneered.

Tamino didn't answer him. Instead, he looked directly at Nanh Tong.

"Listen, Emperor. Dai Viet is a proud nation with a proud history. You are one of only three countries to successfully repel an invasion by the Mongols. You don't have to roll over so easily now. Champa needs you to resist. But, more importantly, your people need you to resist."

"What are these 'allies' you speak of?" asked the emperor.

"Wil'iah has not ignored the Mongol threat. In response, we have assembled an alliance of nations to defy the supposed might of the 'Great Khan.' If you join us, we are, together, strong enough to shatter the myth of their invincibility. Remember who you are, Emperor! You are the heir to the legendary Tran Dynasty, the terror of Kublai Khan!"

"This is outrageous!" snapped the Toghon, who next turned to Tamino.

"Listen, princeling," he said, his lips curling derisively.

142

"You may think yourself wise and powerful, assembling this pitiful 'alliance' against us. But your upstart country will pay the price for its arrogance. When you are on your knees, your cities are laid waste, and your armies are held in subjection, you will understand what it means to defy the omnipotence of the Great Khan!"

Tamino stared back levelly, his eyes backed with steel. "Only one power can claim omnipotence, and it is most certainly not the Great Khan. Should your forces, in their unending folly, attempt a landing on our shores, it is the Khan which shall learn a lesson in humility. Our nation's ultimate defense is beyond anything you could imagine."

"The Great Khan will hear of your insolence!"

"Good."

Tamino advanced toward the ambassador.

"In fact, I can give you an exact script. You can tell your Khan that the Faithful Kingdom of Wil'iah will never pay the Mongol Empire, nor its holdings in occupied China, a single shekel in tribute, nor will we comply with any of their imperious demands. In his bullishness, the Khan has overstretched his hand. Furthermore, the assembled league that has united its banners against you will never surrender."

Toghon drew his sword again and waved it in Tamino's face.

"I have half a mind to kill you right now, boy!"

Tamino swallowed hard as his eyes widened in a mixture of surprise and fear, but then he visibly gathered himself and stood up about half an inch straighter.

"Go ahead and try!" he replied, placing his hand on his own hilt for emphasis.

"NOT IN MY THRONE ROOM!" boomed the emperor with surprising forcefulness, suddenly commanding everyone's attention.

"You *do* have a choice, Emperor!" yelled Tamino at Nanh Tong. "And I think you know what you need to do!"

"Choose carefully," hissed Toghon through gritted teeth.

"Dai Viet has indeed made a choice," Nanh Tong spoke solemnly. "Forces of the Great Khan will not be permitted to pass through our territories in order to attack Champa. If you choose to punitively strike in response, we will defend ourselves accordingly."

Toghon spat on the ground, then whirled around to leave the throne room, motioning for Sogetu to follow. Before exiting the room, he paused, sneering at the Emperor.

"You'll regret this, fool!"

General Hung Dao called out in response.

"We'll see, won't we?"

The doors slammed shut with a ringing crash, and the throne room was momentarily left in silence.

Tamino nodded his head and saluted the emperor once again.

"I applaud you on your decision. Today is a proud day for Dai Viet."

"Perhaps. But I fear it may be the day we have sealed our own destruction," replied Nanh Tong.

"Not if we prepare properly," interjected Hung Dao. "Your Highness, I propose that we immediately send 15,000 troops to reinforce Champa. In the meantime, the court must make preparations to evacuate to a more secure location. Our climate and our terrain are the weaknesses of the Khan's forces. We must burn the villages and crops that would otherwise sustain them during their invasion."

"Scorched-earth tactics are expensive," remarked the Emperor.

"Losing the war would be more so," Hung Dao replied.

"And what of this alliance?" Tranh Tong added, addressing Tamino.

"Our league has sworn to make no separate peace with the Mongols until this menace is ended. If any of us is attacked, the rest will jump to the defense. Singhasari, Champa, Ephraim-Manasseh, and Wil'iah presently comprise the league."

"Well, given the high-spirited decisions made tonight," replied Tranh Tong, "I suppose you can add Dai Viet to the list."

"It will be an honor to fly our flag alongside yours," said Tamino. "Given our conversation with the esteemed Mongol ambassadors, it appears that an invasion isn't far away. I will return to Wil'iah at once and prepare our fleets."

The emperor nodded gravely.

"In that case, we will look to the south for our salvation."

CHAPTER TWENTY

SALOME

Gath

Briseis, Iphigenia's friend from the Circle dormitory, scurried through the warren of passageways of the palace of Gath, finally coming to the former harem. The two tall guards gave her nods and unsettling leers before opening the doors to admit her. Briseis' attention was instantly, raptly drawn to a giant four-post canopy bed in the center of the room, its drawn, diaphanous pink curtains revealing an unmistakable silhouette.

"Who is it?" a contralto voice crooned.

"It's me."

With a fluid pull on a silk cord, the curtain raised, revealing Delilah sprawled luxuriously across a silk blanket, taking in the vast empty expanse of the former harem. The great frolicking pool's water was now languidly still; the stiflingly hot air in the crimson room hung like an oppressively wet blanket. She stole a relieved glance at her arm, which still bore the tan line where the gold slave band had once wrapped like a boa constrictor, then smiled as she surveyed her new dominion, almost in disbelief at the sheer audacity of her plan and its seemingly-impossible success.

All mine, she thought triumphantly, but doubt gnawed at her nonetheless. How long could she really keep this charade going? The people of Gath had proved more pliable than her wildest dreams could have anticipated, but she was fairly certain at least one of the priests of the Circle was well aware of her real motives and identity. All the same, she reveled in the adoration of the people and the luxurious treatment she was experiencing – things she had never experienced before, and things she was not willing to give up.

Audacity got you here. Audacity will carry you through, she thought as she shook off her doubts and turned to face her only confidante.

"Ah, Briseis, my most loyal subject. How can you help me?" Delilah crooned.

Briseis seemed to bristle at being called a subject by her friend, and stole into the room, racing across the floor with startled leaps that reminded Delilah of a panicked gazelle. The woman got uncomfortably close to Delilah, about to whisper into her ear, when another loud knock sounded at the door.

"WHAT??" yelled Delilah.

The doors timidly opened, to reveal a procession of servants dressed in flamboyantly-colored silks and bejeweled veils.

"We bring gifts from a grateful nation," the lead servant squeaked, before genuflecting and opening a silver box filled to the bursting with fire opals. Another servant manhandled a gilded rack draped in nearly endless strings of pearls. Yet another hefted a rolled-up silk carpet.

"How nice! Go ahead and add them to the pile." Delilah languidly raised her little finger to point out an enormous, sparkling heap of treasure that had accumulated in the corner of the room. As soon as the servants had added their contributions, they kissed the floor, and scuttled back out of their room, the thud of the doors lending a certain satisfying finality to the proceedings.

Briseis opened her mouth, about to say something, when another knock sounded at the doors.

"Yes?" Delilah smiled.

The doors timidly opened to admit a raven-haired woman carrying a platter overflowing with delicacies from the kitchens. The woman moved as fast as she could with the platter, placed it on an end table, and threw herself prostrate at Delilah's feet.

"And you are?"

"Salome, your Worship. You probably don't remember me, for your thoughts are filled with items of infinitely greater importance than me. But you saved my life and delivered me from the most wretched servitude in the harem of Achilles. For that I owe you my everything. I pledge my life to your service. I will bring you anything you wish. I will do anything you want."

Briseis rolled her eyes at the saccharine performance.

"Very well, Salome, there is always room in the heart of a goddess for her loyal children. I will elevate you to the status of my handmaid. Run along, darling, to the imperial costumer and get yourself some proper clothes."

Salome hauled herself up from the floor and briefly made eye contact with Briseis, whose blood ran cold as she realized that Salome's piercing blue eyes were filled with none of the innocent awe that had been pasted over her voice. Salome flounced back out of the room, leaving the doors to close with another satisfying thud.

Briseis leaned back in.

"What are you doing!?"

"I don't know what you mean, darling."

"This is insane! Nobody is seriously going to believe this...this goddess story!"

"Oh, but they do, darling. Look around. All my people love me. It's amazing what happens when you tell people what they want to hear. Make them feel good about themselves, and suddenly they would give up anything for you. And I've got that scrumptious oaf Achilles wrapped around my finger." Delilah's voice was filled with more confidence than she really felt.

"What next? What happens when they find out that you're not really a goddess?"

Delilah feigned shock, then placed a long-nailed finger on Briseis' trembling lips, suppressing her own shudder at the thought of being discovered. She internally steeled herself. The only recourse was to go forward, to continue the ruse in more and more dramatic ways. She hissed to her confidante.

"They never will, dear, because, if you value either one of our lives, you will keep those lips shut."

CHAPTER TWENTY-ONE

ON THE LOGGIA

Shechem, Kingdom of Manasseh, north-central Australia

The citadel of Shechem, capital of Manasseh, bedecked with battle-flags of the constituent nations of the league, was an especially splendid sight as it welcomed the returning envoys from their missions to assemble the coalition. The *Ava'ivi*, which had conveyed delegates from Dai Viet, Champa, and Singhasari bearing the seals of their respective kings, rode at anchor alongside the *Shechem*, which had brought similar greetings from Issachar, Yolngu, and the other local allied nations of Tunivivi and, Pilbara.

On one of the long outdoor colonnades which ran behind the ramparts of the citadel, Avora'tru'ivi and Jessica walked side-by-side, their ornate diplomatic finery catching the clear sunlight and reflecting a thousand flecks of gold onto the polished columns.

"Well, I'm proud of you, Avora'tru'ivi. I know this mission felt like a stretch for you," Jessica said.

"I'm glad I finally had the opportunity to serve my country in a meaningful way. As we've mentioned, I've spent way too much time cooped up in this palace."

"I think we both learned a lot. And," Jessica gave her friend a significant look, "I think you made the right decision regarding…certain offers."

Avora'tru'ivi grimaced. "I find that man revolting. I will tell you right now, in that case, given the choice between marriage and a convent, I'm going to the convent. My heart is reserved for one alone."

※ ※ ※

Tamino similarly strolled along the loggia, lost in his thoughts. Had he been too bold in incurring the wrath of the Mongols? Were thousands of Wil'iahns about to lose their lives because of his mistake? After the accords were signed here in Shechem, he would have to proceed immediately to Trujustakanoa to muster the Western Fleet to come to the aid of Dai Viet. Suddenly, his heart leapt as he heard familiar voices- his sister and…Avora'tru'ivi. Tamino shook himself from his concerned thoughts and prepared to step out of the shadow into the light.

"—given the choice between marriage and a convent, I'm going to the convent. My heart is reserved for one alone."

Tamino's blood ran cold. Stopping dead in his tracks, he struggled to regain his composure. Taking a deep breath, he gathered himself and prepared to face the women.

As Avora'tru'ivi and Jessica continued on their stroll, they were surprised and delighted when Tamino stepped out from behind a column and greeted them with a smile.

"Tamino! You made it back!" Avora'tru'ivi ran forward to give her friend a hug. He noticeably tensed, but returned the gesture before also embracing his sister.

"I'm sure you have all kinds of stories to tell, Tamino!" Jessica said.

Tamino smiled, although, curiously, Jessica noticed that it didn't reach his eyes.

"Yes, there were many adventures. I'm sure you can say the same." He then turned to Avora'tru'ivi and gently placed his hands on her shoulder.

"Princess," Tamino said, with a curt nod, "I want you to know that I am very proud of you. I support your choices unreservedly and completely. It is an honor to call myself your friend."

With that, he straightened and said, "I must go prepare for the treaty signing. I will see you then." He spun on his heel and continued walking down the colonnade.

Avora'tru'ivi turned to Jessica.

"What was that all about?"

"I don't know. He can be difficult to figure out sometimes."

Later that evening, an excited hubbub filled the great hall of the citadel of Shechem. On the raised dais fronting the chamber, a long table stood, backed by the assembled flags of the nations of the league. A row of stern-faced dignitaries sat at the table, passing a roll of parchment down the line with a black swan-quill pen. Finally, the pen reached King Gamaliel and Queen Sheerah, who jointly signed for Ephraim-Manasseh. However, the monarchs yielded their speech time to Avora'tru'ivi, who instead graced the audience with a determined, yet, sweet, smile.

"For many decades, the world has cowered in terror at the word 'Mongol.' For too long, their forces have swept over nation after nation, crushing any resistance. They believe they are destined to rule the whole world." Suddenly balling her fingers into a fist, she continued, "That ends today!"

A hearty cheer rang up from the audience.

"Today, the free nations of Asia and the Pacific join arms in resolve and friendship to form an unshakeable alliance. Together, we will resist this tide of conquest and turn it back! Each of us individually cannot hope to stand against the hordes of the Great Khan, but together, we shall prevail! As princess of the United Kingdom of Ephraim and Manasseh, it is my great privilege to join with all of the dignitaries here to declare the official formation of the League of Shechem, the world's best hope for freedom!"

As a deafening cheer filled the great hall, Avora'tru'ivi's eyes met Tamino's. In them, she saw a strange mixture of pride and sadness, before the prince looked away.

CHAPTER TWENTY-TWO

RUNNING ON TIME

Gath

A grizzled old woman staggered through the streets of Gath with her daughter, the latter carrying a large basket piled high with bread on her head, both of them moving their eyes from surprising sight to surprising sight.

A team of soldiers in perfectly-polished armor of the Homeric Guard stood sentinel on a nearby street corner, carefully surveying the goings-on and overseeing a group of slaves as they shoveled away at the heaps of excrement, human and otherwise, that had become such a fixture of life in the city that nobody noticed it anymore- at least until it was gone. Every few minutes, a full wheelbarrow of the foul substance would be pushed away, leaving bare pavement that hadn't seen the sun in years.

The old woman raised a wrinkled, sun-spotted hand to her brow and squinted into the distance. Scaffolding surrounded the three great temples of Dagon, Baal, and Astarte that crowned the once-deserted acropolis. The complex now teemed with activity as thousands of figures crawled over it like an anthill, dragging polished marble blocks into place, clearing rubble, and repainting the elaborate bas-reliefs carved into the entablatures of the buildings. At the center of the acropolis stood a tall triumphal column, which had originally been erected in the year 1223 to commemorate the destruction of the old Kingdom of Zebulon. It had stood ignored for decades, but now, the old woman's heart leapt as she beheld an enormous red and black banner flapping from its capital – not the flag of the prince of the much-reduced Principality of Gath, but the battle-standard of the Frouzean Empire.

She was startled from her reverie as a stagecoach clattered down the street, drawn by two black horses with red feather plumes and bearing the seal of the empire on its doors. The woman turned to her daughter.

"I hear that those are actually running on time now."

The younger woman gently patted the basket on her head.

"And, thanks to the tax cut, we can actually afford to eat."

"I had my doubts about this 'goddess,' but now…" the older woman replied.

Her daughter smiled.

"All hail Frouzee."

Across the street, two shadowy figures lurked in a darkened alleyway between two fetid row-houses.

"We'd best get back to the Hidden Fortress," one of them said. "The Order's going to want to hear about this."

"You're absolutely right," came the whispered response. "However, don't forget His Faithfulness' policy- we won't interfere with any people's right to self-determination. We cannot influence what happens in this place, so long as it doesn't touch us. That said, we can certainly watch every move that this 'goddess' makes."

"This is the time for action. This is the moment that has made us shiver in terror for over three decades – the moment we have waited for in subtle dread – the empire has returned."

"Don't start shivering just yet – Gath is far from reconquering the rest of her empire, but we must watch. And, if it comes to war, we'll be ready."

CHAPTER TWENTY-THREE

THE BATTLE OF BIEN DONG

Gulf of Tonkin, Southeast Asia

Hundreds of crab claw-shaped sails crowded the waves like the brandished weapons of a crustacean army as Tamino leaned out over the *Ava'ivi's* side, hanging onto the foremast's shrouds with one hand as he shielded his eyes from the glare with the other. The long, dark green line of the Dai Viet shoreline stretched out as far as he could see in either direction. Based on the charts that General Hung Dao had provided, the fleet had nearly reached its destination. He stole a glance at the fleet behind him. Some forty *trungabrang* battleships, with *Elah, Lion of Judah,*

Reliance, *Michmach*, and *Council of Uluru* in the lead, stretched out in a formidable line behind him, their proud dragon-headed bows daring all comers. The line was flanked on either side by two lines of twenty-five *galor'ivi* cruisers about one hundred twenty feet in length, essentially scaled-down versions of the battleships based on the *Ava'ivi's* design but incorporating improvements such as watertight compartments. Surrounding this main portion of the fleet's striking power was a cloud of *shaluas*, single-masted, single-hulled, exceptionally fast and maneuverable ships designed for scouting and hit-and-run missions. Bringing up the rear was the secondary battleline of one hundred fifty *tua'ivis*, light cruisers about ninety feet in length and essentially miniature versions of the Ava'ivi. In all the fleet of some four hundred fifty warships was the largest naval force ever to put to sea under the Wil'iahn flag, which snapped bravely above Tamino's head.

As his head swiveled to the view ahead of the flagship, it was greeted only by empty sea.

Where are they? He thought. The allied fleets were supposed to rendezvous here. Of course, given the vast distances involved, anything could have happened.

Suddenly, a cry floated down from the crow's nest atop the foremast.

"Sail, off the starboard bow!"

Tamino, and most of the rest of the deck crew, raced to the starboard rail, squinting at a white speck barely visible on the horizon. As the minutes ticked on, Tamino grew increasingly nervous. Was this the allied fleet, or the Mongol Navy he had hoped to pre-empt?

Finally, he turned to the crew on the quarterdeck and hollered, "Beat to Quarters!"

The threatening, insistent thunder of the drum shook the *Ava'ivi's* planks as her sailors raced to their stations, tying down and stowing anything not needed for battle. Gun crews clambered around their weapons, loading them with practiced ease, before the ominous black cylinders creaked out of the crenellated battlements surrounding the ship's weapons platform.

A series of flags ran up the *Ava'ivi's* mainmast, signaling the other ships in the fleet to clear for action and turn towards the approaching ships. In a few minutes, the fleet had precisely executed the maneuver and stood at the ready, their guns bared in defiance of whatever approached.

As the fleet inexorably approached, Tamino's stomach churned while he waited for the lookout to make a positive identification. Suddenly, all the tension melted away as the voice called once again from on high.

"It's a jong, sir, a big one!"

The *Ava'ivi's* deck erupted into cheers as an enormous ship hauled into view, proudly flying the ensign of Singhasari. The vessel was pointed at both ends and was equipped with rudders on both sides, and seven masts with lateen sails. A square platform jutted over the bowsprit, with another one over the sternpost, and a long deckhouse stretched over nearly the entire length of the hull. As it pulled alongside, the *Ava'ivi's* crew manned the rails and gave off three hearty cheers, with an answering cheer emanating from the Singhasari flagship. Gradually, the rest of the allied fleet lumbered into view. There were roughly fifty of the powerful jongs, as well as an assortment of about two hundred smaller ships – *malangbangs* and *kelulus*.

The arrival of the Singhasari fleet was gratifying, but there was still no sign of the Manassite force.

Tamino was about to signal to the Singhasari flagship for a conference when the lookout shouted once again.

"Sail, off the larboard bow! It's a junk, sir!"

Tamino raced back to the *Ava'ivi's* bows, and, sure enough, a junk plunged through the waves toward the allied fleet. Fortunately, from this distance, it didn't look like a Mongol vessel, but Tamino ordered the bow chaser guns primed just in case.

As the new vessel gradually rolled into view, Tamino breathed a sigh of relief as he beheld the ensign of Dai Viet flapping in the breeze. A few minutes later, the vessel hauled itself alongside the *Ava'ivi*, signaling that it was bearing an important message.

Steeling himself for what might be bad news, Tamino hoped that the fleet wasn't too late. He signaled the Singhasari flagship to send its admiral across in a boat, so he could also be updated. Simultaneously, the *Ava'ivi* signaled the *Elah* to send over Admiral Zhang. Two sailors hurled a rope ladder down the *Ava'ivi's* side to the smaller junk, and helped the messenger clamber aboard. In a few moments, Tamino, Zhang Shijie, and the Singhasari admiral crowded around the messenger in the deckhouse of the Wil'iahn flagship, Hung Dao's chart of the Dai Viet coast spread out before them.

"We gathered our fleet as fast as we could," Tamino said, his voice filling with concern. "Please tell us we aren't too late. Has Dai Viet fallen?"

"No," gasped the messenger. "The Mongols, under Toghon and Sogetu, did in fact invade, but we abandoned the capital of Thang Long to their advance and made for the jungle, where we engaged in our specialty- guerilla warfare. The Mongols attempted a pincer movement on the royal family, but they escaped, and the Mongol forces rejoined. That's when Hung Dao struck. Sogetu was killed, and Toghon was defeated by Prime Minister Quang Khai's army at Chuong Duong. Now, Toghon is fleeing down the Red River, whose mouth is not far from here, but the

Mongol fleet is coming up to rescue him."

Zhang Shijie gravely nodded. "We have a chance to stop him, if we can cut off the Mongol army from their navy. Do you know anything of the composition of the Mongol fleet?"

"Based on our intelligence sources," the messenger answered, "the fleet is led by the Kipchak admiral Sidor, with over nine hundred ships. They're mere hours away."

Tamino suppressed a grimace as he realized his force was heavily outnumbered.

"Very well, we'll simply have to outthink them," Admiral Zhang said as he studied the mouth of the Red River on the chart. "We'll place the battleships, and the largest of the Singhasari jongs, across the mouth of the river to block their progress, in a line-ahead formation, with the flagship at the center. The cruisers, *malangbangs* and *kelulus* will cover the battleships' flanks, while the *shaluas* launch hit-and-run attacks with their oil cabinets, winnowing down the outsides of the Mongol fleet as it approaches."

"What if the battleships are overwhelmed?" the Singhasari admiral asked.

"It is essential that the Mongol fleet not be allowed to reach Toghon," Zhang replied. "If we have to, we'll sink our own ships in the channel to block their way."

Tamino grimly nodded. "Let's hope it doesn't come to that. Let's not forget that our fleet is better equipped, better trained, and has better morale than the enemy, most of whom are unwilling conscripts. We're fighting for something."

After the allied commanders returned to their ships, the fleet worked its way up the coast in magnificent array, until the mouth of the Red River yawned at them to the west. In the distance, angry plumes of smoke rose from where the Dai Viet army stood locked in a death struggle with Toghon's ground forces. The allied fleet deployed in a roughly crescent-shaped formation in front of the mouth of the river, with the battleships at the center forming a single resolute line per Zhang's suggestions. The Chinese-Wil'iahn admiral flew his flag from the *Elah*, several ships in line behind the *Ava'ivi*, which stood dead center.

The intervening hours seemed like days as the fleet's crew waited in agonizing silence. Tamino walked the decks of the flagship, checking and rechecking that everything was ready, until he felt he would go out of his mind. Still no enemy fleet came.

Finally, the voice of the lookout pierced the air, filling Tamino's senses with a mixture of anticipation and dread.

"Sail, off the starboard beam! Make that two…no, three…many sails. Junks."

"That'll be them," Tamino said with a calm he didn't really feel, and, once again, the coxswain beat to quarters. A series of signal flags ran up the *Ava'ivi's* mast, in the special code devised by the League of Shechem and conveyed to all ships in the fleet.

TODAY, WE STAND TOGETHER.

The allied fleet burst into motion as the various squadrons began carrying out their assigned tasks. The *shaluas* raced off to bite the heels of the enemy, their single crab-claw shaped sails disappearing into the distance as they skimmed across the water with effortless grace. Gradually, the lead junk lumbered into view, and Tamino found his breath catching in his throat. The enormous vessel had four masts and lofty castles on its bow and stern that towered over the low-slung *Ava'ivi*.

"Almost in range, almost," Tamino whispered to himself as the huge ship inexorably bore down on him. Finally, raised his arm and then brought it swinging down.

The *Ava'ivi* shook as her cannons roared in defiance of the enemy flagship, great spumes of flame erupting from her blue-painted battlements. White plumes of water flared up from the frothy sea ahead of the junk, but to the prince's satisfaction, debris shot skyward from the Mongol vessel as at least two of the *Ava'ivi's* salvos found their mark. In response, the Mongol vessel's trebuchets let off an enormous volley of incendiary projectiles, which fell vainly about forty feet in front of the Wil'iahn flagship.

"Prepare another volley!" Tamino yelled to the gun crews, who were already frantically heeding the order before it had even been given. A few moments later, another coordinated broadside thundered forth from the *Ava'ivi*, but this time, shrieks filled the air as one of the guns exploded, sending iron shrapnel flying across the flagship's deck.

I knew we needed to test those things more, Tamino scornfully thought as the Mongol warship continued its advance, despite the multitude of gaping holes that now yawned from its forecastle.

"Ready trebuchets!" Tamino yelled to the corner weapons platforms. The crews gingerly loaded iron shells with long fuses into the trebuchets, then lit the fuses, wincing slightly.

"Fire!"

The two starboard trebuchets flung their projectiles at the approaching Mongol flagship, both hitting home. Earsplitting explosions reverberated through the sky as the "thunder crash bombs" found their marks.

In response, the Mongol ships' own trebuchets let off another volley, sending its own deadly fusillade of bombs arcing through the air. Tamino nervously watched their progress as they began to plummet toward the *Ava'ivi*.

God save this ship, he thought.

CHAPTER TWENTY-FOUR

THE FALL OF GAZA

Principality of Gaza, southeastern Australia

A thunderous rumble split the air as the corner tower of the citadel of Gaza came crashing down, the fluttering battle-standard of Gath's neighbor principality descending with it.

"Good! I see the sappers did their work," Delilah said as she surveyed the scene from a safe distance, luxuriating in a sedan chair as Gazan arrows fruitlessly buried themselves in the ground about 100 feet short of her. Salome sycophantically fanned her with emu plumes.

"Shouldn't be long now," Achilles murmured in

agreement, resplendent in golden battle armor.

As the dust cleared, hundreds of Gathite soldiers streamed through the jagged, yawning hole in the once-resolute wall, even as giant boulders from siege trebuchets slammed into the portions that were still intact. Smoke from a dozen fires belched from the battered fortress as its brave defenders tried to fight an increasingly hopeless battle. Delilah watched the violence for about half an hour more, a strange smile ever so slightly curving up at the ends of her mouth. Every so often, her eyes would flick to the other main tower of the citadel, whose flag still snapped defiantly in the breeze, and the smile would briefly turn to a grimace. However, she quickly grew bored of the spectacle, and turned her attention to Briseis, who stood ready to attend to her.

"Darling, in my pavilion is a large glass lantern. Please bring it to me – but be careful not to open it."

Briseis returned a few moments later, shaking in terror as her trembling hands proffered the lantern to the empress. Inside the glass vessel was an enormous, hairy spider.

"*Wha*--what is this?" Briseis stammered.

"A prime specimen of the latest batch," Delilah crooned. She raised a long nail and tapped the glass. In response, the spider reared up on its hind legs, exposing half-inch, wickedly curved fangs. Briseis recoiled in horror and nearly dropped the lantern.

"Latest *batch?* You're breeding these things!? If this is what I think it is, do you know how dangerous these creatures are? They eat *birds!*"

"Sometimes my people need to be *convinced* of the necessity for loyalty to me. This occasionally requires theatrical demonstrations," Delilah replied.

She looked away for a moment, surveying the vast army

encampment behind her. She smiled with satisfaction at the giant battle-flag of the Frouzean Empire that rather presumptuously flapped overhead, a stretch considering that less than one fifth of the former Empire currently owed fealty to it. She was snapped from her reverie by the huge, bejeweled hand of Achilles on her shoulder.

"Finally," he said.

Delilah turned to see the standard of Gaza slowly lowering itself down the pole.

"Alright, it's time to go," she said, snapping her fingers at the fawning servants who languidly fanned themselves around her, completely ignoring the disturbed look on Briseis' face as she returned the spider to Delilah's pavilion.

"Come on, what are you waiting for!? Not even Wil'iahns are so pathetic!"

The servants suppressed grimaces and hefted the poles of the sedan chairs on their shoulders, carefully carrying it through the carnage that splayed across the path to the ruined walls of the citadel. Once inside, Delilah was greeted with the sight of about two hundred bedraggled Gazan soldiers marching toward her with their hands over their heads, many of their tunics torn and bloodstained.

Delilah surveyed the prisoners with a sly grin.

"Well, you put up more of a fight than I expected. The empire will need more men like you. I, in my unending beneficence, are prepared to offer you clemency, if you acknowledge me as your goddess."

Two of the prisoners looked askance at each other.

"Make up your minds quickly. Goddesses don't like to be kept waiting. I'm sure you all know the alternative." Delilah smiled at the two prisoners and motioned to one of the Homeric guards that flanked her to her right. His two massive hands pulled a single thread taut with an audible snap as he leered at the prisoners.

One of the prisoners hesitantly spoke.

"All hail Frouzee." He said as he lowered himself to the ground and kissed the floor. His companions, seeing the apparent logic of his decision, followed suit, all mumbling their homage to the "eternal empress."

"I can't hear you," Delilah responded.

"ALL HAIL FROUZEE!" desperately yelled the prisoners.

"That's better. Where is Prince Patroclus?" she said.

One of the soldiers from her army stepped forward, his gravelly voice cutting through the rubble.

"He was found hiding in his bathroom."

"How wretched. Bring him to me."

A short time later, two Homeric Guards hauled a short, stocky man, wild-eyed in terror, before the empress.

"Well, Prince Patroclus of Gaza, in the flesh. How...disappointing. Based on the pedigrees I've seen in Gath, I was expecting something a bit more impressive."

"Go to Hades!" Yelled Patroclus with a surprising amount of force considering the indignity of the circumstances surrounding his surrender.

"Well," Delilah crooned, "Strong words from a scared little boy found hiding behind a toilet. I take it you don't acknowledge me as your eternal empress and goddess?"

"You're no goddess," he responded.

"More's the pity." Delilah turned to Achilles. "I think it's time we sent a ... message to Ashdod, Ashkelon, and Ekron. They must know what it means to defy me. Bring me a piece of parchment and a camel."

"What? Why?"

"Goddesses don't owe you explanations," she said. "Just do it, and quickly. I don't like to be kept waiting."

Delilah loomed over Patroclus, whose terrified eyes focused on the hissing cobra atop her snake headdress.

Delilah withdrew a hand into her voluminous sleeve and squeezed a bulb. Two jets of liquid spit out of the cobra's delicately-carved fangs, landing directly on Patroclus' face. The prince immediately began shrieking. One of the Homeric guards began to advance toward him, once again drawing a string taut as a wicked grin spread across his bearded face.

Turning from the pitiful display, Delilah addressed the captured soldiers.

"Welcome to the empire."

CHAPTER TWENTY-FIVE

STRIKE ONE JUNK!

Gulf of Tonkin, Southeast Asia

Avora'tru'ivi gripped the shrouds of the *Shechem* with whitened knuckles, gritting her teeth as the ship pitched up and down in the waves. She hazarded a glance behind her at the decks, strewn with debris and soaking wet from the storm they had just passed through. Scanning the horizon, she was relieved to see that the rest of her squadron was fully accounted for. But something else gnawed at her. They were late. The tropical storm that had struck the fleet had likely delayed their arrival at Dai Viet by several hours, possibly as much as a whole day. And those were not hours that they could afford. Shaking herself in an attempt to combat her nervousness, Avora'tru'ivi picked her way to the deckhouse and ducked inside. There, she came face to face with Captain Machir, who commanded Manasseh's flagship.

"How badly were we delayed?" she asked.

"Well, it may not be as bad as we thought, but we'll likely be a few hours late."

"And what do we know of the tactical situation?"

"Not much, Your Highness. As you already know, the Mongols were expected to launch both a land and sea-based assault on Dai Viet. Our contingent is supposed to join the Wil'iahn fleet, as well as allied ships from Singhasari, in the defense of their coastline. But we don't know how many Mongol ships will be there."

Avora'tru'ivi grimly nodded, then went back outside to the railing. For what felt like an eternity, she watched the seemingly infinite ocean recede before her. No matter how much the Shechem plunged through the waves, there were always more. The very air itself was pregnant with anticipation. She found herself involuntarily gripping her saber every so often as the hours rolled by.

Suddenly, she thought she heard a roll of thunder, even though there wasn't a cloud in the sky. Instantly perking up, she tried to scan the horizon, but saw nothing. Then, a voice from the crows' nest pierced the tense silence.

"Sail, off the larboard bow!"

The sound of a snare drum instantly split the air, and the wide platform that connected the *Schechem's* twin hulls became a riot of activity as sailors beat to quarters, stowing anything that didn't need to be on deck and taking the large canvas covers off of the catapults and cannon that surrounded the platform on all sides. Avora'tru'ivi's heart involuntarily leapt as the small pennant that normally flew at the masthead was struck, and an enormous battle-ensign of the United Kingdom of Ephraim-Manasseh was unfurled in its place, snapping instantly in the gathering breeze.

Captain Machir stepped out of the deckhouse in full dress uniform, a glittering cutlass at his waist.

"Your Highness, I understand that you wish to be part of these proceedings, but I really must insist that it would be safer for you in one of the hulls."

"Your attempt at humor is not amusing," the princess responded icily.

Giving up his attempt at gallantry almost as soon as he had begun it, the captain instead gave her an admiring nod and set about ensuring that the ship was ready for battle. On the aftmost of the her two masts, a series of signal flags ran up, instructing the other ships in the fleet to move into an arrow-shaped line abreast formation. The *Shechem* cooperatively tacked onto her new heading; Avora'tru'ivi marveled at the ship's responsiveness. Suddenly, her stomach filled with tension as she caught her first glimpse, on the horizon, of their destination. All she could see were flecks of white signifying distant sails, but crashing reports echoed back across the open water. Once again, she found herself gripping the railing.

We're too late. The battle has already started.

However, the fast Manassite ships, paragons of Polynesian design and seamanship, closed the distance quickly. More and more of the scene became visible, and it wasn't good.

Avora'tru'ivi's heart vaulted into her mouth as she realized that the allied fleet was badly outnumbered, and the battle had degenerated into a chaotic melee, all semblance of tactics and maneuvering lost to the wind— and with it the advantage of the Wil'iahn ships' similar

Polynesian design. The mass of ships stretched as far as the eye could see on either side. Avora'tru'ivi winced as, to her left, a blinding flash engulfed a Wil'iahn catamaran. When the smoke cleared, its shattered remains were already sinking, its battle-flag still defiantly waving from its remaining mast. To her right, another Wil'iahn ship, which she recognized as the battleship *Lion of Judah*, was surrounded by five Mongol junks. Despite the tenseness of the situation, the ship was giving a decent account of herself, her thirty-two guns spitting defiant flame as her fire-arrow launchers rained their incendiary missiles on her opponents. A great tongue of flame erupted from one of her dragon mouths, setting the junk across her bows ablaze. Another junk was careening out of control, completely dismasted.

"Well, there's nothing else to do but join in. Large-scale fleet maneuvers will be useless," Machir said grimly.

Avora'tru'ivi nodded. "Signal the fleet to engage the enemy at will," she said through gritted teeth.

A new set of signal flags ran up the *Shechem's* mainmast, and Avora'tru'ivi noticed the *Ramoth-Gilead*, the ship nearest their portside, instantly break formation in response, her forward guns spitting flame and her catapults flinging red-hot projectiles as she leapt forward. Similarly, the *Schechem's* own forward battery roared to life, its earsplitting challenge to the Mongols simultaneously filling Avora'tru'ivi with pride and dread. To their starboard side, the warships *Gideon* and *Joshua* placed themselves on headings that would take them to the embattled *Lion of Judah*. Breathing a sigh of relief, Avora'tru'ivi now focused on the situation ahead. Two large Mongol junks, their forward and aft sections crowned with enormous fighting castles bristling with weapons, had broken off from the main fight and were headed directly for the Manassite flagship.

"Run out the port and starboard batteries. We'll try to run between them," Machir said.

"Won't that just allow us to be pummeled by both ships? We're more maneuverable; we should take advantage of that," Avora'tru'ivi responded.

The captain looked peeved by her interruption, but seemed to reconsider, and then nodded with a look of surprise on his face. "You're right, we could cross in front of both of their bows and rake them." He turned back to the two crews manning the ship's twin tillers on the quarterdecks of her hulls. "Hard a-starboard!"

The swift ship quickly responded to the crews as they heaved on the massive wooden tillers. The ship wore around, presenting her broadside to the first of the Mongol junks, which was just within range.

"Fire!" Machir yelled.

The *Shechem* shook as her entire broadside fired almost simultaneously, and the great catapults placed on turntables on her weapons platform added their own, much-larger projectiles to the volley. The *Shechem's* third type of weapon, a battery of ballistae mounted at the corners of the platform, fired fuming fire-lances at the enemy ship. The Mongol ship was instantly engulfed in a cloud of debris as the projectiles hit home. While the enemy ship's ox-hide coverings protected it from flaming arrows and other conventional incendiary weapons, they did nothing against the powerful, advanced guns carried by the allied fleet. Avora'tru'ivi watched with satisfaction as the junk's foremast came crashing down, but then had to duck as a return volley from the ships' forward batteries slammed into the *Shechem*, sending deadly splinters flying.

The fight continued this way for several minutes, the maneuverable Manassite flagship weaving in and out of

Mongol formations and dealing damage with her powerful weapons. However, this didn't come without cost. A Mongol projectile managed to fell the mainmast, which severely reduced the *Shechem's* maneuverability. Just then, Avora'tru'ivi looked out over the starboard railing, and a cold fear gripped her as another vessel loomed up against them. But this one was different. Piled high with flammable wood, it didn't appear to have anyone on it.

"Fireship!" she yelled! Crewmen rushed to the railing and frantically tried to stave off the fireship, which was going to detonate at any moment, with long poles. Behind them, additional crews worked to jury-rig another sail.

"Can we sink it with the guns?" Avora'tru'ivi asked Machir. The taciturn captain shook his head.

"If we fire now, we could risk detonating the ship."

Suddenly, another cry came from the port side. Two ships, decked over so as to be completely enclosed, came alongside, flaming arrows flying out of loops and ports on their sides. The oar-powered ships were bereft of sails.

"The guns can do something to those, though," Machir said. He ordered one of the portside guns jacked up so that it was depressed to an extremely low elevation. A thunderous report shook the air as the weapon sent a cannonball crashing through the roof of one of the enemy ships, which instantly began to sink.

Unfortunately, this didn't solve the problem of the fireship, which continued to bear down on the Shechem.

"Out oars!" Machir shouted, and a forest of long paddles suddenly nosed their way out of ports on the *Schechem's* sides. The ship began to inch forward, helped by the remaining sail on the foremast. Avora'tru'ivi gave a cheer at this development, which turned to a cry of alarm as a shadow fell across the deck.

A giant Mongol junk, bigger than any she had seen, was

bearing down on the portside, trying to reinforce the remaining "turtle ship." A massive drawbridge extended down from its bow, with the clear intention of a boarding attempt. A frantic volley of the *Schechem's* batteries did nothing to slow it down.

Suddenly, hope was unfurled once again as the jury-rigged mainmast sail caught the wind, and the *Shechem* shot forward. The giant Mongol junk passed behind them, and, too late, Avora'tru'ivi realized they were going to be raked.

"Everybody down!" she yelled as a furious hailstorm of projectiles rained down on them from the Mongol Junk. One of the tillers splintered into a thousand pieces, and, once again, the *Shechem* was out of control.

As luck (or something else) would have it, that was the last volley the Mongol battleship ever fired.

Her captain had been so preoccupied with raking the *Shechem* that he failed to notice the fireship bearing down on him, which had been meant for the Manassite flagship.

An earsplitting detonation rent the air as the enormous stockpile of explosives aboard the fireship detonated. The enormous junk disappeared in a cloud of ugly black smoke. When the ringing in her ears subsided and the smoke began to clear, Avora'tru'ivi saw the shattered remnants of the ship slipping below the waves.

Aboard the *Shechem*, damage control crews were already hard at work installing a new starboard tiller. Fortunately, the *Shechem* could still maneuver, however clumsily, with just one tiller, and the steered away from the wreckage of the enemy battleship.

"Strike one junk!" Avora'tru'ivi yelled as she pumped her fist into the air. But, before her jubilant shout could die on the wind, her joy turned instantly to fear.

Two passing ships separated, clearing the view ahead. In the distance was a blue-painted warship, the naval ensign of Wil'iah bravely fluttering at its remaining masthead. Even amongst the chaos, the ship was instantly recognizable- the *Ava'ivi*. And it was not alone. Four large junks surrounded it, and her deck was swarming with Mongols. For the hundredth time that day, the princess's heart leapt to her throat.

Tamino.

On the *Ava'ivi's* weapons platform, Tamino and a cadre of knights frantically hacked and swung at the veritable forest of pikes and cutlasses that assaulted them from all sides. The open deck of the Wil'iahn flagship had degenerated into an utter melee, soldiers from both sides dropping like flies as arrows furrowed down from the Mongol junk's castles. Tamino ducked behind his large shield as he swung his Pilbara steel blade wildly, managing to stave off yet another Mongol attacker, but minute by minute, step by step, his party was forced back toward the railing. Before him, the shattered deckhouse was a smoldering ruin. There was simply nowhere to go.

Out of the corner of his eye, Tamino caught a flash of color – his ship's flag, still snapping resolutely in the wind, a blaze of open defiance against the annihilation that pressed in on all sides.

If it ends this way, at least it was in the service of the innocent. We will go home with honor, he thought.

"Let's show them what Wil'iahns are made of!" he shouted to his demoralized compatriots as he rallied his strength and began to advance again. But this burst of hope was short lived, as, once again, they were driven back towards the railing, and, beyond it, the angry sea.

God, I know you are our true defense, Tamino attempted to pray through the din.

Suddenly, a seeming whirlwind struck the ship as everything changed in an instant. A thunderous broadside shook the air from somewhere beyond the mass of Mongol boarders, and one of the enemy junks caught fire and was forced to disengage. The triumphant jeers of the Mongols turned into panicked shouts as some new force hit them from behind. The Mongols began to press forward again, but this time, it was in an attempt to escape, not an attempt to destroy. Bemusedly, Tamino leveled his saber and shield once more and charged forward, heartened by the unexpected turn of events.

Just then, the horde of enemies before him parted like the Red Sea, and Tamino let out an involuntary gasp.

Charging forward, in full battle-array, her hair billowing like a battle-flag in the wind and her eyes filled with a fearful fire, was Avora'tru'ivi, her saber a blinding flash as it scythed back and forth like the out-of-control blades of a windmill. As she advanced inexorably forward, terrified Mongol soldiers pushed and shoved to get out of the way.

She'll make one terrifying nun, Tamino thought, his heart filling with admiration.

As the unstoppable force known as the princess of Manasseh finally reached him, the frightening smolder faded from her eyes, replaced with tearful relief. The saber that had whistled through the air with the fury of a typhoon clattered to the deck.

"Thank God you're alive," she said simply, and leaped forward to engulf Tamino in an intense bear hug, which, to his unending surprise, suddenly turned into a rapturous kiss. Instinctively, Tamino found himself kissing her back, before the nagging reminder of her vow pierced his thoughts. Recoiling in horror at his own indiscretion,

Tamino stepped back, his face filled with shame.

"I—I can't do this to you!" he said in anguish.

Avora'tru'ivi looked like she had been struck, but then her eyes narrowed as she focused on the waratah flower still resolutely pinned over Tamino's heart. A mixture of confusion and exasperation filled her eyes.

"You—you are so confusing!" she yelled.

Tamino didn't have the opportunity to answer. Their moment had given the Mongols time to regroup, and the melee resumed, the tide of battle sweeping the prince and princess away from each other. All across the dramatic tableaux of the *Ava'ivi's* deck, allied and Mongol soldiers hacked and swung at each other, but, eventually, the allies won the day, particularly after reinforcements arrived in the form of the Wil'iahn battleship *Reliance*, which crashed through the Mongol blockade and sank a junk before sending her own boarding party to the flagship's rescue. All around them, similar battles played out on countless other warships. The Manassite fleet may have been late to the battle, but it made up for it with the ferocity of its assault. Soon, the Mongols were in open retreat, the allied forces too exhausted and damaged to pursue.

As the last group of Mongol soldiers found themselves cornered on the quarterdeck of the *Ava'ivi's* port hull, Tamino looked around, anxiously scanning for the princess. Finally, his eye caught a flash of color- the flag of Ephraim-Manasseh fading into the distance as the *Shechem* sailed away.

CHAPTER TWENTY-SIX

THE CAPITULATION OF ASHKELON

Former Frouzean Principality of Ashkelon, southeast Australia

"She did *what?*" King Minos of Ashkelon sat bolt upright on the throne. The informant who stood before him had kept him well supplied about Ashkelon's regional rivals Gaza and Ashdod over the years. Now, he looked like he had seen a ghost. Perhaps he had.

"You heard me. She brought down the walls of Gaza, captured Patroclus, blinded him with asp venom, and had him strangled with a single thread in front of his subjects. This grisly task completed, she stuffed a threatening note in his mouth, sewed up his remains in a camel and

179

delivered said camel to Ashdod as a 'present.'"

"Where did she even think to do something like that?"

"According to the merchants in India that we sometimes deal with, the Arabs did a similar thing to an envoy of the Sassanid Empire."

Minos suppressed a retch. "What did this morbid missive say?"

"'Nobody defies a goddess."

"And Ashdod's response?"

The informant solemnly lowered its head. "Ashdod is now the third state of the restored Frouzean Empire."

Minos ordinarily would have been pleased to see Ashdod thus humiliated, but as he thought on his own tenuous position, the principality's plight suddenly didn't seem very funny.

The informant stepped forward, quickly cast his eyes around the room, and began to whisper in Minos' ear.

"I'd best be very careful, if I were you. I know how mortifying it would be to submit to Delilah's authority, but it is becoming increasingly clear that the woman is unstable. Unfortunately, she has the public entirely sold on her purported identity as a "goddess." It's amazing what a few puffs of red smoke and some acts of sheer barbarism can accomplish."

Minos nodded.

"In the meantime, you have the opportunity to secure a prestigious position in this new empire, for however long it lasts," the informant continued. "If you go along with her now, you will survive to pick up the pieces when the show is over. Follow her instructions to the letter and bide your time until this entire charade comes crashing down." The informant withdrew and began to walk out of the room.

"Where are you going?" asked Minos.

"You still need ears on the outside. Heed my words," the informant said, looking Minos up and down, "*Prince.*"

✳ ✳ ✳

Below the aloof and commanding battlements of the citadel of Ashkelon, similar news was licking through the dusty, chaotic streets like an uncontained wildfire.

"Gath has reconquered Gaza, and now Ashdod has surrendered to them as well!" came a terrified whisper.

"Yes, but they march not under the emblem of Gath – they fly the battle-standard of the empire!" came an excited reply.

"I heard that the goddess Astarte, Frouzee herself, has returned, just as we were promised! The time has come for us to take back our country! Enough with these petty princes!" hissed an old woman.

"When was the last time *you* were proud to be Frouzean? She speaks of us as the people destined by the gods to rule the world!"

"There's a chance for us to reclaim our greatness!"

Above the street, a washerwoman threw open the shutters to her decrepit second-floor room, hefting a roll of red-colored material. She untied a series of knots, and the cloth unrolled to reveal a giant black pentagram inscribed in a white circle, set against a wide red stripe flanked by white and black stripes. A chorus of hearty cheers greeted the appearance of the flag of the Frouzean Empire.

"I've been keeping this against the day when I could display it proudly again!" the woman wailed out window. "All hail Frouzee!"

Across the street, two sets of eyes peered out from the

inky blackness of a junk-filled alley.

"Did you see that?" one of the murky figures hissed.

"I never thought I'd live to see that again. I wish I hadn't."

"We need to report back to the Order about this disturbing development immediately. We must depart for Verwonnah at once."

"We're already fighting a war, possibly an endless one, against the largest empire on Earth. We can scarcely afford a second war on another front."

"Hopefully it won't come to that, but if it does, we'll have a war on our hands whether we can afford it or not. We'd best be ready. Don't worry, His Faithfulness has been preparing for this for thirty-five years."

CHAPTER TWENTY-SEVEN

THE VICTORY PARADE

Shechem, Kingdom of Manasseh, 1285 AD

*T*he broad avenue leading from the harbor to the Citadel of Shechem was a riot of colors and sounds as the throngs of citizens welcomed the victorious fleet home. As each allied warship entered into the harbor, the mastheads festooned with ensigns and pennants, their guns roared a thunderous salute to the citadel, whose own batteries responded in turn. The *Shechem* and the *Ava'ivi*, as the flagships, took the central docks flanking the avenue, looking battered but triumphant as enormous battle-flags waved from their sternposts. Tamino and Avora'tru'ivi each led mounted groups of officers down the gangplanks and looked solemnly forward as the victory parade proceeded up the avenue, pelted with flowers from the adoring citizenry as they feted the alliance's triumph. Lines of trumpeters blared their instruments with jubilant fanfares all along the avenue.

A woman in the audience excitedly explained the situation to her friend. "The Mongols attacked Dai Viet like they promised, but the Imperial Family escaped Thang Long and burned all of the villages, so the Mongols had nothing to eat. When the general Sogetu's troops got bogged down in Champa's jungles, they went north to attack Dai Viet, but they were attacked by Champa's army and Sogetu was killed! Then Dai Viet defeated Toghon's forces, and when he tried to escape, our fleets destroyed the Mongol Navy!"

While decorum and military tradition required that they both look straight ahead, their faces virtually emotionless masks, Tamino stole a glance at Avora'tru'ivi, fruitlessly trying to read her face. He was still trying to make sense of what had happened on the quarterdeck of the *Ava'ivi*.

Avora'tru'ivi could feel his eyes searching her, and darted her eyes sideways, trying to use her peripheral vision to analyze the situation without breaking her apparent forward concentration. Tamino noticed her movement and abruptly snapped his head back forward, swallowing hard.

What is he doing? The question gnawed at Avora'tru'ivi, who was equally confused by the events on the Wil'iahn flagship. Curiosity finally overcoming her better judgement, Avora'tru'ivi hazarded a more directed glance at her friend. Sure enough, the waratah flower was still there, pinned right over his heart.

*Why keep it, if…*Avora'tru'ivi thought she knew him

pretty well, but his actions lately hadn't been making much sense.

For his part, Tamino suddenly felt like he was being watched. Trying to maintain the illusion of stoic fortitude, he slowly turned his head to the side, where, to his alarm, his eyes met Avora'tru'ivi's. He tried to force himself to look forward again, but he simply couldn't do it.

Avora'tru'ivi felt an electric jolt course through her as she met his eyes, but she took the opportunity to study them. Adding to her confusion, she could detect clear affection, but also sadness, and even anguish.

He said "I can't do this to you." What could that mean?

Forcing her attention back forward, Avora'tru'ivi's eyes took in the row of flags representing all of the constituent nations of the League of Shechem. Suddenly, a horrible thought wormed its way into her mind.

You know all too well how these alliances are often sealed. You experienced it yourself with Prince Jason. What if the only way for Tamino to convince one of these countries to join the league was…both Singhasari and Dai Viet have eligible princesses roughly our age.

Avora'tru'ivi swallowed hard as her eyes welled with tears, which she fought to force back down.

I suppose he knew he had to do his duty. Freedom must come first. Her face set itself into a stony, resolute expression.

Tamino noticed her face harden as he glanced sideways yet again, his heart sinking. At length, the procession reached the gates of the Citadel, and the Wil'iahn and Manassite groups parted ways. Tamino had to fight with all of his might to avoid giving her a longing backward glance as her train receded into the distance.

CHAPTER TWENTY-EIGHT

THE LAST LINK

Gath, Frouzean Empire

Delilah, clad in a dress of tropical fish scales, luxuriated on a recliner that floated in a pool of water, filled with fragrant flower petals and sedated, docile albino crocodiles. Before her stretched the unmatched splendor of the colonnaded Opal Throne Room of the restored Old Palace of Gath, the magnificent imperial palace that crowned the acropolis. Frescoes on the walls depicting Philistine victories over the Israelites were framed by magnificent crimson columns that stretched up to a ceiling decorated in red, black, and white geometric patterns, lit indirectly by a trench of blazing oil that stretched all the way around the room's perimeter. Any part of the walls not covered in frescoes were studded with blazing fire opals that glittered like thousands of iridescent stars. Before the elevated throne platform stood a red and black carpet that had been painstakingly crafted by artisans in the court. Golden plates overflowing with grapes surrounded the carpet. Women giggled as they flounced around the "eternal empress," throwing plump grapes in each other's mouths while some of them fanned Delilah with enormous plumes plucked from subtropical birds.

The sudden crash of a gong rang through the room.

"What is it?" Delilah asked languidly as she stretched on the recliner. Salome, who sat nearby in attendance, perked up at the sound of the gong.

"His excellency, Prince Theseus of Ekron, has arrived to parley with you!" Shouted a herald.

"Ah yes, the evening's entertainment. Send him in!" Delilah flashed a wicked smile at Heracles, who smirked in response.

The doors opened to admit a tall, handsome man, who strode into the room with great apparent confidence, although a quick glance into his eyes betrayed fear.

A pity. He's cute. Well, I guess I have to make some sacrifices, she thought to herself.

The two heralds of Ekron that flanked him to either side raised silver trumpets and gave off a fanfare. One of them then stepped forward.

"His Excellency Theseus III, Prince of the Principality of Ekron and defender of the Eternal Temple of Dagon."

"Ah yes, I've been expecting you to come crawling to me at some point," Delilah yawned as one of the "tame" crocodiles raised its head from the water and hissed at the prince.

Theseus stood a bit straighter, umbrage writ large on his face. "I have come to offer you an alliance. Is this how you show your respect?"

Heracles cleared his throat. "You stand in the presence of a goddess. It is you who should show respect. Where is your sense of propriety?"

Delilah sat up on the recliner. "Goddesses don't need alliances. But they expect respect."

Theseus sneered. "As far as I am concerned, you are a mere consort to a prince of a state equal to my own. I owe you no such obeisance."

Delilah smirked. "How interesting. Ekron is known for its weakness and its treachery, but not for its insolence. I guess I have to add to my list of...*unsavory* impressions of your principality." She suddenly cocked her head as if in thought. "Actually, I mean MY principality! I am the second incarnation to Earth of the goddess Astarte, the Frouzee prophesied to unite our people and restore them to greatness. You, and you alone, are all that stands in my way. And you are insignificant next to my omnipotence!"

Theseus took a deep breath, then steeled himself to continue the "negotiations."

"Your Highness—"

"That's 'Your Worship' to you!"

"—surely you can be reasonable. If it is, as we surmise, your intention to make war upon the Kingdom of Wil'iah, then Ekron will gladly join you in arms. We will even offer you attractive trade concessions. But we are a proud and independent state."

Just then, Briseis hurried into the throne room, a mixture of anxiety and curiosity playing across her face.

Delilah sneered. "I'm not sure what you have to be proud of. As I recall, Ekron was the only Frouzean state to make a separate peace with Wil'iah in the last war. You even let their queen escape. As I see it, you are in no position to demand anything. Now, if you value your vaunted status as prince of Ekron, you will submit to my authority, or there will be consequences. Be a good boy and kneel!"

Theseus glared at her. "Ekron will never submit to you! I will never kneel!"

Delilah gave a wicked smile and a knowing look to the Homeric Guards that flanked the carpet.

"Oh, yes, you will!"

At a nod from Delilah, the guards yanked the carpet from beneath Theseus with a great flourish. The prince and his heralds crumpled face-down onto the floor, which they failed to notice was hinged.

"That's better! However, the goddess Astarte does not quickly forget slights on her person. I'm afraid negotiations have concluded." She gave a nod to a woman to her right, who pulled a giant, jewel-encrusted lever.

The hinged floor dropped open, and Theseus and his heralds fell into a pit whose floor was an oddly squirming blanket. From its depths, Theseus looked up at her in horror.

"Yes, Goliath bird-eating spiders. Named for our national hero. I've kept them nice and hungry for a special occasion like this. Enjoy dinner!"

With that, she clapped her hands, and the slave released the lever, sending the doors swinging back up. Delilah turned to the guards.

"When my darlings have had their fill, you know what to do."

Briseis recoiled in horror, her hand involuntarily shooting up to cover her mouth. She rushed over to Delilah and hissed urgently into her ear.

"Was that really necessary?"

"Briseis, darling, in order to rule an empire, one must be authoritative. Goddesses don't allow for any competition."

"But that's the third person you've killed!"

"Just think how many lives we will save from the Mongols by building a strong empire. I don't have to remind you that their next visit, when they will demand tribute and threaten us with their armies, draws nearer and nearer. We must unite the empire by then if we are to stand up to them. And don't forget," Delilah hissed, her eyes suddenly displaying a spark of fear, "that lives closer to home depend on our empire's success."

Briseis' eyes narrowed as she suddenly focused on the gold armbands that gripped the arms of all of the women surrounding Delilah.

"Wait," she said, a note of alarm creeping into her voice, "I thought you abolished slavery."

A strange light filled Delilah's eyes, deranged and remorseful all at once. She opened her mouth and laughed, a harsh, braying sound. "It was a nice idea while it lasted. However, to be a true empire, to maintain the proper appearance of dominion and power to cow our enemies, I'm afraid they're still necessary. I keep them well treated. In fact, to serve me as my slaves is the highest privilege possible! It is the natural state of things, for a mortal to be a slave to a goddess!"

CHAPTER TWENTY-NINE

A CONFESSION

Citadel of Shechem, Kingdom of Manasseh

*J*amino stared out at the sunrise that stretched its dramatic tableaux across the heavens. "Please don't take her from me, dear Father. She is noble indeed to wish to serve you in such a way, but that only makes me love her more. I have always been your faithful servant and I ever shall continue to be, but please, please don't do this. That would be too cruel for you to place such an angel on Earth, and to make in me a heart capable of loving her so truly, and so deeply, and yet deny such a heart." Now tears flowed unbidden from his tightly shut eyes. "I promise that if you do not take her, I will be an utterly devoted and faithful servant to her all the days of my life. I vow to be worthy of such an angel."

He stood on the balcony for several moments, his eyes closed in prayer, as the clouds turned pink all around him. "Nevertheless, not my will, but thine, be done. If it be your judgement that she can best serve the cause of good in such a manner, I will not interfere. I trust you, always."

Just then, Tamino heard a knock at the door. Quickly wiping the tears with his sleeve, he turned and purposefully strode to it, opening the door to reveal the intense face and magnificent mane of Princess Jessica.

"We need to talk," she said, forcing herself through the door.

I guess I don't have much of a choice, he thought.

"What is going on with you? You've been acting very strangely ever since you got back from Dai Viet, and, frankly, you were acting odd before you left. You know, I like to think I know you pretty well, but I feel like you are some sort of stranger now. What on Earth happened?"

Tamino looked at the floor. "Its…personal. Don't worry about me. I'll be fine."

A suspicious gleam entered Jessica's piercing eyes. "Come to think of it, Avora'tru'ivi's been acting pretty odd since the expeditionary force returned as well. Was the battle more…eventful than either of you are letting on?"

Tamino recoiled. "I don't know what you are talking about."

Jessica laughed. "You have many virtues, brother, but skill at deception is not one of them. I can read you like a book. Come on, out with it."

Tamino backed up toward an overstuffed silk sofa that lay against the wall, with a tapestry depicting St. Thomas' arrival in Manasseh hanging above.

"Out with what?"

"Alright, do you want me to spell it out for you? You love her, and she loves you. I don't know why this is so difficult."

Tamino's eyes flashed to his sister in surprise. "You know about that?"

"Anyone with a functioning pair of eyes knows about that."

Tamino sank into the couch cushion and sheepishly inspected the finely-embroidered pattern.

"Well, you're right. I do love her, but I can't—or at least I thought I can't. Now I don't know what to believe."

"And just why can't you?"

"Because she has promised herself to God! For me to love her is to trample on her holy vow- and that is inexcusable! I told her this on the ship when she rescued me and kissed me—which I do not understand, by the way, if she has pledged herself to service, which is, of course, a noble and laudable goal that I cannot tempt her away from—but then she seemed upset with me, and then, of course, we had to return to the batt—"

"What on earth are you talking about?" Jessica interrupted her brother's incoherent babbling.

"I would think you would know."

"What holy vow? What service?"

"Please don't mock me. She told you she was going to the convent."

Jessica recoiled in surprise. "I honestly don't remember her ever saying that. Where did you hear such a thing?"

"I promise I didn't intend to eavesdrop. I overheard your conversation by the unhappiest of accidents."

"What conversation?"

"She told you that given the choice between marriage and a convent, she would choose the convent. It was a statement that at once devastated me and filled me with admiration. How could I presume, with my earthly, mortal love, to sully such a valorous commitment?"

Hearing no response, Tamino looked up to see his sister silently convulsing with laughter. An extra depth of color filled his cheeks.

"Jessica, this is serious!"

Jessica fought to regain her composure, hitting the table, waving a hand in front of her face, and having to tamp down several aftershocks of laughter before she could finally form a coherent sentence.

"Clearly you missed the context of our conversation. That will teach you to eavesdrop!" she jokingly chastised, waving a single finger at her brother. "Avora'tru'ivi was not referring to marriage in general. She was referring to a very specific, very distasteful proposal that she received during our diplomatic mission."

Tamino's normally-flat eyebrows arched in surprise. "What? From whom?"

Jessica snorted. "Prince Jason."

Tamino suddenly stood bolt upright, his hand involuntarily going to his hip, where his sword usually hung.

"HE asked her to marry him?" he said, his nostrils flaring.

"Don't worry, she said no," Jessica laughed.

Tamino's brow knit as he seemed to think for a minute. "I suppose he actually had a point. That would have secured good relations between Manasseh and Pelesetania…but I just can't imagine…"

"Oh come on, we don't need him. Avora'tru'ivi knows that. But that wasn't the real reason why she didn't marry him. It was because she wants to marry someone else."

Tamino looked around the room as if searching for the

object of the princess's purported affections. "I wouldn't dare hope…"

"Yes, YOU! I love you, Tamino, but you can be really dense sometimes. She gave you a flower as her sign of undying affection, for heaven's sake!"

A look of relief, joy, and wonder crossed the prince's kind features.

"But now, you're acting all strange, you haven't talked to Avora'tru'ivi in days, and she probably thinks you want her to become a nun! What are you waiting for? You'd better get your act together, *now!*"

Tamino rushed forward, grabbed his sister into a great bear hug, and planted a kiss on her cheek.

"I love you."

"Yes, I love you, too. Now GO!"

Tamino hurriedly gathered a few items, then ran out the door, slamming it behind him in his haste.

Jessica shook her head.

"Honestly!"

CHAPTER THIRTY

TAMINO'S REQUEST

Sheerah, War Queen of Ephraim, sat at her toilette, brushing her iron-gray hair and adjusting her ceremonial armor in preparation for the morning's state breakfast. She quietly hummed an ancient Ephrite hymn, appreciating the beams of the morning sun that filtered in through the multicolored glass of the chamber. Suddenly, she heard a knock at the door.

"Yes?"

The door noiselessly opened to reveal one of her guards, her hand grasping a burnished spear. "Your Majesty, the Crown Prince Tamino requests to speak with you at your earliest convenience."

"Ah," the queen smiled. "Of course. Send him into my

sitting room. I will be there in a moment."

The guard placed a fist over her heart, pivoted on one leg, and marched out of the room.

A moment later, the queen emerged into the sitting room that adjoined her apartments. Octagonal in shape, the room was sumptuously outfitted with finely-embroidered cushions and luxuriant carpets on four of the walls, each carpet painstakingly woven to depict an important moment from the history of Ephraim. Three of the other panels had screens that led to a balcony that surrounded the room, while the fourth led to her other rooms. In the middle of the room, Prince Tamino awkwardly paced about with his hands clasped behind his back. When his eyes caught the glint of Sheerah's armor, he started and whipped his head around to meet her. Eyes widening, he rather clumsily bowed.

"Oh, come now, my friend, there is no need for that here," laughed the queen.

"I trust that the queen is in good health?" he said, resuming his pacing about the room.

What is going on? Thought the queen.

"Yes, of course, never better! What brings you to my apartments on this beautiful morning?"

The prince stopped to regard one of the carpets that displayed Joshua leading the Israelites against the city of Jericho. He seemed to gather himself, stood up straight (which noticeably increased his height by several inches), then whirled around to face the queen. Sheerah was surprised to see that his face betrayed an earnest pleading mixed with acute anxiety. He paused a moment, then his words came tumbling out like a waterfall back in Shiloh.

"There is only one way to say this, so I am just going to say it. I am hopelessly in love with your daughter, and have been for as long as I can remember. It is my dearest wish to marry her, but, as much as it would throw me into despair not to, I will not do so without your permission."

Sheerah's face lit up in a mixture of surprise and delight. With a radiant smile, she stepped forward to place her hands on the prince's shoulders.

"Well, it's about time! Dearest Tamino, you are like a son to me already. The princess can marry anyone she likes. If she should choose a Philistine, I would have my reservations, but I would not interfere with her choices. As it stands, I could not think of anyone that would make me happier than you. You absolutely have my blessing." She pulled the prince in for a tight hug. After a moment, she pulled back to see elation writ large on Tamino's face. Then, his eyebrows narrowed again, and he asked,

"I know that His Highness the king is away. While tradition only requires your permission, I would wish to ask him as well."

Sheerah laughed again. "If Gamaliel has a problem with this arrangement, he will answer to me. That would earn him a right good smack, and, trust me, while I may be advancing in years, a smack from the war queen of Ephraim can still make any man think twice before defying me. And, besides," she said with a conspiratorial smile, "This isn't really a surprise to anybody."

Tamino's face registered surprise.

"Trust me, we all saw this one coming. I don't think she has ever seriously considered anyone else."

The prince gave her a grateful smile as he docked his head in respect. "I thank you for your support, Your Majesty. It is my fond hope that it will not be long before I can call you Mother."

"I look forward to that day. Go in peace, valiant prince of the Faithful Kingdom."

CHAPTER THIRTY-ONE

THE DAGGER

*A*fter leaving the queen's apartments, Tamino returned to his guest accommodations and replaced his royal finery with a simple set of traveler's robes. Slipping the deep hood over his face, he exited the citadel and began to wind his way through Shechem's ancient streets. While Trukanamoa was a new city, built only a few decades prior and designed with a central masterplan, Shechem was a bewildering pile of intrigue and mystery, a warren of impossibly narrow alleys and exotic bazaars filled with outlandish wares from all around the world. At length, Tamino came to an aged building displaying a sign of an anvil. Taking a deep breath, Tamino stepped inside and removed the hood.

A kindly old man stood behind a counter, wearing a blacksmith's apron. "Can I help you?" he said brightly, before his eyebrows narrowed slightly. "You look familiar."

"I seem to have one of those faces," Tamino evaded.

"I see," the old man said with a twinkle in his eye that made Tamino wonder if his paper-thin disguise was actually working. "What can I do for you today?"

"I need to forge an engagement dagger, out of the finest materials you have." Tamino withdrew a bag of gold shekels from his utility bag and plunked it on the table.

"Who's the lucky lady?"

"I'm the one who's lucky."

The old blacksmith chuckled. "It would save you some trouble to get a premade one. I have a nice selection."

Tamino shook his head. "She warrants a custom one. I know how to do it."

The blacksmith looked him up and down. "I suppose you would. You a knight?"

"Something like that."

"Very well," the old man said, stepping out from behind the counter. "Follow me. I keep a private smithy for projects like this. If you give me the hilt specifications, I can do that for you while you make the blade."

For the next fifteen hours, Tamino hammered away at the glowing ingot of Pilbara steel, beads of sweat standing out on his brow, which furrowed with concentration. Finally, after what seemed like a week to him, he held a glittering blade in front of his face, his eyes reflecting in the blade of the weapon. Returning to the main room of the smithy, Tamino realized with a start that night had already fallen, but the stalwart blacksmith was still here.

"Thank you for staying late to help me," Tamino said.

"Well, this is a special project," the man said with a

wink. He stepped over to the counter and returned, preferring a magnificent hilt on a silk pillow. The handle was made from solid jade and crowned with a pommel stone of solid opal encrusted with pearls. The golden cross guards were each finished with an enormous, glittering diamond.

Tamino let out a sigh. "It's beautiful."

"As is, no doubt, the soul that will receive it," the smith said. "Alright, let's get that blade installed."

The final piece of the work done, the smith put the dagger in finely-embroidered scabbard emblazoned with the emblem of the three arrows.

Tamino slid the bag of coins over to the smith. "Keep the change- all of it."

As Tamino exited the smithy, he paused at the door and turned back. "Thank you for this beautiful dagger. This is exactly what I was hoping for."

The smith winked.

"It was an honor, Your Faithfulness."

CHAPTER THIRTY-TWO

ONE ALONE

*A*vora'tru'ivi stood on the balcony of her apartments in the citadel of Shechem, imploringly looking at the Milky Way, which stretched its brilliant curtain across the cloudless sky. The light of the Southern Cross, which blazed triumphantly overhead, twinkled in a single tear that slid down her cheek as a gentle breeze swayed the gossamer curtains behind her.

"God, what should I do?" she pleaded, gripping the polished marble railing for support.

I can hardly fault him for putting his country's, and really the world's, best interests first. I even almost did the same myself, she thought. *That is a noble sentiment.* She shuddered as she thought back to her anguished declaration on the decks of the *Ava'ivi*.

Now I haven't heard from him in over four days. I must have lost him.

Just then, a whistling sound filled the air. Casting her eyes about to find its source, Avora'tru'ivi sighted an arrow arcing up towards the balcony, its ballistic trajectory bringing it to a gentle, clattering landing on the tiled floor.

Her eyebrows narrowing quizzically, Avora'tru'ivi knelt down to pick up the arrow, which she noticed lacked a head. Tied to the shaft was a note, which she gingerly opened.

Meet me by the Scroll of St. Thomas in fifteen minutes, if you would please.

-T

Pinned to the top of the note was a petal from a red waratah flower.

What is this? She asked herself. *He wants me to meet him in a church?* Suddenly, her stomach fell as the import of the flower petal hit her. Was he giving her back her favor?

Deciding that these questions could only be answered by confronting the situation head-on, Avora'tru'ivi gathered herself, wiped her eyes, and put on her slippers. Leaving the comforting confines of her apartments, she worked her way through the warren of splendidly-tiled passageways, trying not to notice the puffy eyes that greeted her in the mirrors that lined the halls. Finally reaching the ground level of the royal apartments, she stepped through the open gate and came face-to-face with the Mother Church of Shechem. The ancient domed structure soared resolutely into the night, its burnished dome reflecting the diffused radiance of the Milky Way. To her surprise, a warm glow spilled out onto the surrounding pavement from the intricate stained-glass windows. Finding a side door ajar, the princess slipped into the edifice and immediately headed for an ornately-carved limestone staircase that descended into the catacombs of the cathedral. She knew this route by heart.

After passing through several vaulted hallways, she came to a great rotunda supported by twelve polished columns with engaged statues of the apostles and warmly lit by oil lamps. In the dead center of the rotunda stood a great stone plinth, on which rested an ornately-filigreed scroll protected by a crystal box whose facets reflected the brilliance of the lamps in all directions, projecting a kaleidoscope of colors on the surrounding walls. Her breath involuntarily caught in her throat as her eyes focused on a figure standing next to it.

"Thank you for coming here on such short notice," Tamino said softly, his voice betraying an unmistakable mixture of earnestness and apprehension.

Avora'tru'ivi held up the note and pointed at the flower petal.

"Do you have something to say to me?"

"A thousand words would not suffice," the prince responded, his voice trembling with emotion. Avora'tru'ivi's still-reddened eyes widened in surprise as he seemed to steel himself, took a deep breath, and dropped to one knee. With a shaking hand, he reached to a scabbard strapped to his bandolier and drew a brilliant bejeweled dagger, pausing for the smallest of moments to let its impeccably polished surface reflect the light of the lamps before laying on the glass-like floor, its hilt pointing directly at the princess.

Avora'tru'ivi worked her mouth, but no words came at first, until she finally managed to force out a question.

"Wh--what are you doing?"

Tamino locked eyes with her, his gaze a strange mixture of tenderness and desperation.

"Twelve years ago, the forces of darkness tried to steal this great light from your people," he said, motioning to the glittering scroll. "And they very nearly had the victory- but for the courage and determination of someone whom I can only describe as an angel on Earth. On that day which began in darkness and ended in hope, I had the privilege of joining my best friend in a bold and seemingly impossible quest to recover this treasure and set right the wrong dealt to Manasseh. During that whole fantastical journey, a spark ignited that has since gently grown into a blazing fire whose singular brilliance outshines the sun. I love you, Princess Avora'tru'ivi of Manasseh, with every fiber of my being. It is you which warms my heart, you who carried me over the farthest seas, you who gave me the determination to return from each and every battle. I have always loved you, for as long as I can remember. No word written by all the learned poets of antiquity can describe it. There have been so many times that I wanted to tell you, but when I thought you were going to a convent, I pleaded with the Lord not to take you from me, for I don't know how I could live without such an angel as you."

Convent? What convent?

Avora'tru'ivi shook with pent-up emotion, the fountain of tears that she had managed to stanch once again overflowing.

"I—I don't understand. You didn't betroth yourself to some other princess?"

Tamino's eyes widened in shock as his brows furrowed together.

"What? Of course not! I couldn't fault you for committing yourself to God, but if I marry, it will either be you – or no one."

Tamino placed a hand on the blade of the dagger and gently pushed it toward the princess, the finely-worked weapon making a sweet bell-like sound as it scraped across the fastidiously polished floor.

"Princess, I vow with everything I am to always defend the honor and grace of the most wonderful woman in all the world, you. I promise to cherish your kindness, your love, your omnibenevolence, to the end of the world and beyond. I pledge to love you for eternity, to ever be your faithful servant, and to thank God continually for having the incredible care for me to bestow on me such a privilege. Would you do me the unspeakable honor of joining swords with me, marrying me, and together building the Faithful Kingdom into a shining beacon of hope for all the world? Will you join me on this journey, as we seek to uphold and defend truth, justice, and love here in God's Far Garden and in lands near and far? Will you allow me to love and cherish you for all eternity?"

A smile as wide as the Tanami desert broke across Avora'tru'ivi's face as she ran forward, pulled him into a tight embrace, and kissed him on the mouth, her hand digging into the hair on the back of his head. Tamino's eyes closed, his shoulders slumping with palpable relief as he held her close. Then, almost as soon as it had begun, it was over, as Avora'tru'ivi recoiled and laughed.

"Where on Earth did you get this convent idea from?"

Tamino sheepishly inspected the finely-tiled floor. "I…accidentally overheard you talking to Princess Jessica on the loggia. You said to her that 'given the choice between marriage and a convent, I choose the convent. My heart is reserved for One Alone.' While I now understand that you were referring to a marriage proposal that Prince Jason apparently offered to you, my immediate assumption was that you were making plans to go to the convent. After all, you did say your heart was reserved for 'one alone.'"

Avora'tru'ivi pretended to tear her hair out with exasperation and gently chided, "Of course you would think that! But I suppose that's why I love you. While I do dearly love our almighty Father-Mother, I have no such intentions – but I did lock my heart away for 'one alone.' It was *you*. It was always you."

Now it was Tamino's turn to cry. A shudder of joy shook him from his core outward.

"Always?"

Avora'tru'ivi's large, dark eyes darted over to the scroll that stood above them. "One awful day, I stood, shaking in terror, as I realized it was all up to me to save my country's greatest treasure. I was afraid and I thought I was alone." She squeezed Tamino's hand. "But I wasn't. Unbeknownst to me, I was entertaining angels unawares- in this case, in the form of a cherished friend, who was there when I needed him the most. Together, we saved the Scroll of St. Thomas, and from then forward, I knew we could do anything together. In the ensuing years, I watched you grow into the most gentle, most kind, most courageous, most chivalrous, and most valiant man in the world. Our stories and legends speak of true love, one of the most powerful forces in the world, a great gift from our Father-Mother. I didn't have to look very far to find it. I don't just love you with all my heart, you are my heart, Galbi."

Galbi. My heart.

Tamino raised his free hand and wiped away a thin rivulet of water that coursed its way down his face, which looked like it was about to break from the smile that splayed across it. He flicked his eyes to the dagger which still lay on the floor.

"You know, you still haven't actually answered my question."

Avora'tru'ivi playfully slapped his hand in feigned vexation, then reached down to her finely-woven belt, withdrawing her own dagger, its hilt encrusted with rubies, diamonds, and fire opals. She reached down and crossed its shining blade with the dagger on the floor, before gently placing her hand over his.

"I promise to stand with you on the shores of this land from now to eternity. I vow to build with you the dream of Jeremiah, and to show the whole world what it means to be faithful and free. I pledge to love you, my Galbi, with my whole being, even as I always have. I promise to marry you and joyfully shall be faithful to you as long as I draw breath, and ever after I cease to."

Tamino reached across and wordlessly pulled the princess into another embrace. This time, their foreheads touched and their breath mingled in the traditional honi of their ancestors. They held like this for many moments, heedless of the passage of time. Finally, Tamino whispered,

"Whatever comes our way, we can do it."

CHAPTER THIRTY-THREE

AN ANNOUNCEMENT

*T*he Great Hall of the Court of Shechem was filled to the brim with excited guests, all bedecked in the greatest finery of the kingdom, and many other lands besides. Dignitaries had come for the victory celebration from across the League of Shechem, and even from farther beyond. The room was a riot of color. In one corner was the delegation from Singhasari, their golden headdresses and richly-embroidered garments reflecting the lights that bravely blazed from the chandeliers. In another corner were the iridescent, flowing robes of the delegation from the Tran Dynasty. The room was decorated specially for the occasion with a riot of flowers brought from many places in the alliance, and the flags of members of the league hung proudly from the rafters. At the head of the room hung a captured Mongol flag, below which burned one candle for each ship lost during the battle.

The crowd fell silent as the Princess Avora'tru'ivi appeared on the dais, resplendent in the traditional Manassite celebratory dress. She wore over her forehead an elaborately-beaded gold headdress dotted with jewels and pearls; from it hung additional strands of pearls punctuated by twelve medallions inscribed with the emblems of the twelve tribes. She was joined a moment later by Prince Tamino, who garbed himself in a more demure white and blue Wil'iahn formal uniform, on which was emblazoned the Star of Wil'iah.

The prince cleared his throat, then addressed the audience.

"My friends, we are gathered here today to celebrate the victory of freedom over tyranny. Today the so-called unstoppable tide of Mongol conquest looks a little bit less inevitable, thanks to the courage and resolve of all of the nations in our precious little League of Shechem. The waves of Khan's ambition have broken upon our resolute rocks, and free people across the Pacific have raised their swords to say, "Thus far, and no farther!" I do not for a moment believe that the threat to our freedom has permanently passed. The Mongol Fleets will return, but we will be ready for them. I know that, personally, I have faith that the Almighty God of Israel shall protect us against this scourge, and the flame of freedom shall not pass from the Earth!"

At this, there came an especially jubilant cheer from the Wil'iahn, and Ephrite-Manassite delegations.

The prince continued. "But today, we will not burden our hearts with such matters. Today is a day for joy and singing. Today the esteemed princess," he bowed his head to Avora'tru'ivi, "and I have a special announcement to make."

One of the queen's guard turned to whisper to her compatriot in the audience. "I knew it. We're building more battleships."

Tamino opened his mouth, but it was the princess who next spoke. Grabbing Tamino's hand and pulling it high over both their heads, she addressed the gathered dignitaries.

"We are getting married!"

A gasp from the crowd was followed by applause and cheers, especially from the Wil'iahns and the Manassites. Tamino pulled the princess in for a hug, which redoubled the cheers. The prince cleared his throat, and the crowd fell silent.

"The princess and I have loved each other for a very long time. We have not set a date yet, but rest assured that you will all be notified when we do. In the meantime, please celebrate the great victory of our alliance of freedom!"

CHAPTER THIRTY-FOUR

ON TO TANITANIA

Gath, Frouzean Empire

*D*elilah and Achilles looked admiringly at a map of the reconstituted Frouzean Empire, now encompassing all five Principalities plus the outlying, formerly lawless territories of Outer Frouzea and Nullarbor, as well as the island of Ithaca to the south.

"Well, my darling genius, I never thought we would get this far," Achilles said as he roughly kissed the "eternal empress."

"It seems you have a limited imagination," Delilah

purred.

"Only about some things," Achilles huskily responded as he caressed her arm. Delilah internally cringed, but her painted face didn't betray her disgust.

Suddenly, they were rudely interrupted as the doors to the map room were flung open by another figure, a muscular, bearded man slightly shorter than Achilles. His eyes focused on Delilah and ignited with a spark of what could only have been jealousy as his nostrils flared like a bull.

"Ah, yes, my baby brother, come in!" Achilles boomed. "We've been expecting you. Come, see the new extent of our domain!" Ajax the Lesser clenched his jaw as a dark look crossed his face in response to his brother's patronizing tone.

"Only for now," Delilah crooned.

"What do you mean, darling?" Achilles asked.

Delilah swept her hand over another splotch on the map to the west, this one purple.

"We haven't actually gotten the whole Empire back yet. The Mongols will be back in just three years. We need to present the strongest possible front when they arrive. There remains Tanitania, that disloyal, dissolute collection of breakaway provinces. I have not forgotten their betrayal."

"But Tanitania is a powerful nation, much better-organized than our rival principalities," Achilles questioned.

"Which is why a frontal assault is not the right strategy here," Delilah responded. "Instead, you and I are going to pay their new king, Hasdrubal, a visit!"

"I see. Subtlety will succeed where force of arms will fail."

"Precisely!" Delilah clapped her hands together. She

then turned to Ajax, who flushed again as she locked eyes with him. "Ajax, in the meantime, while we are away, I will turn over the running of the empire to you. If you don't disappoint me, you will be rewarded."

Ajax sharply took in a breath, his chest puffing out.

Achilles laughed. "Yes, brother, don't disappoint our goddess here, or else there will be even more reasons to call you Ajax the Lesser!" He guffawed with laughter and tromped out of the room. Ajax responded by almost involuntarily shooting his hand to the short sword buckled to his hip. Delilah swept forward and placed a staying hand on his well-muscled forearm, Ajax flinching at the touch. Delilah placed her lips to his ear and hissed,

"Don't worry. You'll get your turn."

CHAPTER THIRTY-FIVE

THE GAUNTLET

New Carthage, Lower Tanitania, southwestern Australia

asdrubal, King of Upper and Lower Tanitania, sprawled across his throne, his brawny presence instantly commanding the throne room which stretched into the distance. Its impeccably polished floor reflected an image of polished wood columns with solid gold capitals, between which were luxuriously draped great bolts of precious Tyrian purple cloth. The secret to its manufacture had been carried across the sea in Hanno the Navigator's ships some seventeen hundred years prior on the Carthaginian people's flight to the east, and, to this day, only Tanitania had the knowledge necessary to produce this treasure of the lost Empire of Carthage. Lining the throne room were two lines of perfectly-groomed guards, their burnished breastplates only adding to the brilliance of the room. To the uneducated visitor, it would seem like this was an empire that had stood on its own for centuries; in fact, Tanitania had been brutally subjugated less than fifty years prior by the original Frouzean Empire, only regaining its independence when the empire collapsed due to the Wil'iahn revolt. All the same, Tanitania was a nation of incredible wealth, with the continent's highest grain production, greatest stands of trees, and largest gold reserves.

The silent splendor was shattered as a herald at the doors to the room slammed his staff against the floor, sending a ringing sound through the air.

"Your majesty has a visitor! She has not identified herself nor shown her face, but from the magnificence of her sedan chair and the extent of her entourage, she is a woman of great prestige!"

Hasdrubal sat up a bit straighter in the throne as he huskily cleared his throat. "By all means, send her in."

His eyes narrowed as the doors opened and he saw two columns of men dressed in what he recognized as the uniform of the Homeric Guard, the once-legendary elite fighting force of the Frouzean Empire. Behind them, on a litter carried by a dozen slaves, was a sedan chair with silk curtains festooned with peacock feathers and gold tassels. The slaves set the sedan chair on the ground.

Suddenly, a flash of light blinded Hasdrubal, and everyone else in the room, as a thunderous crack filled the air and a plume of red smoke rose from the chair. When it cleared, the chair was in shambles. In the midst of the ruins, a woman stood with a sly smile on her face. To

Hasdrubal's infinite surprise, she was a spitting image of Tanit, the patron goddess of his empire.

A hulking man with broad features swaggered up from behind the woman and proffered a scroll.

"You stand in the presence of the Eternal Goddess Tanit, patron saint of the Imperial Provinces of Upper and Lower Tanitania and their territories of Arboria and Aurania, now descended to earth to rule once again over men, Eternal Empress of the Principalities of Gath, Gaza, Ashdod, Ashkelon, and Ekron, Dominator of the territoriess of Nullarbor and Outer Frouzea, Mistress of the Island of Ithaca and by her own Grace and Worship Eternal Frouzee of the Frouzean Empire."

"What is *this*?" Hasdrubal thundered in return. "The Frouzean Empire, so-called, collapsed thirty-five years ago, and my family was forced to pick up the pieces. You can call yourself whatever you want, but you are no goddess, no matter how impressive your light show is."

The man with the scroll turned red and sputtered in anger, but the woman simply raised a hand to stay him.

"The Frouzean Empire, including the four provinces which you now count as your kingdom, lost its way when it forgot who the real power was in this world and stopped worshipping me. However, I have grown tired of sighing over the foibles of mortals and have chosen to descend back to this miserable world to lead us once again to greatness." She began advancing towards Hasdrubal.

"In fact, I would like to personally congratulate you on your recent accession to the throne, Hasdrubal." The woman looked approvingly around the impressive throne room. "It's clear that the line of the Barcas has not sunken to the same depths that their Philistine counterparts did in my absence. Truly, you have proven yourself worthy of my favor."

Hasdrubal narrowed his eyes again. "Your favor is noted and appreciated, but I fail to understand the authority from which it comes. The last I heard, the fragments of the Frouzean Empire were busy fighting each other as their splendid buildings fell to ruin."

"Your sources did not fail you—until now. I am back. The Frouzean Empire has been restored, and just in time. For surely you are aware of the threat that faces us all?"

"You speak of Wil'iah?"

"Ha! I speak of no mudfaces! I speak of a power so great and so terrible that only a goddess could face it down. I speak of the forces of the Great Khan, the inexorable tide that has swept the north and now casts its baleful eye to us."

Hasdrubal's eyebrows knit in concern. "We have followed the reports of the Mongol's movements. The loss of China was...distressing."

"And do not your sacred texts say that, in the time of the Children of Dido's greatest need, their mother goddess Tanit would step down from her celestial throne to their salvation? Well, here I am!"

"Our texts did not indicate that she would come to us as a Philistine empress."

"Oh Hasdrubal, your conceptions of deity are too limited! Our peoples were once one, thousands of years ago, and were united once again in living memory, just four short decades ago."

"'Unity' is hardly a concept that applies here. Our kingdom was brought under the knuckle of Frouzee when her armies marched across the Nullarbor to slaughter our brave soldiers at Kalgoorlie. We did not join the Empire by choice."

"That was then, this was now. This throne room is indeed magnificent, but you need to cast your eye even farther, Hasdrubal. When I chose to come down from Heaven, my choice was to reunite our peoples in friendship and love, not domination, for only together can we defeat the enemy who threatens us all."

"What exactly are you proposing?"

"You have the chance to rule it all, alongside me, as the heroic champion of your Goddess. But there is a rival claimant. As splendid as you are," she said, looking him up and down, "A prince of the Philistines, Achilles of Gath, is equally worthy. If we are to be one people, we must have one ruler."

"Where is this Achilles?"

"Right here!" a voice boomed from the entrance to the throne room.

Achilles of Gath strutted in, with his head held at an imperious angle and his barrel-like chest thrust out proudly. The lines of Homeric guards parting before him, he marched up to Hasdrubal, then stopped in front of the throne, his legs spread apart in a commanding stance. After pausing a moment, with a dramatic flourish he removed his right glove and held it in front of his face. Then, after looking around the room and meeting the eyes of Hasdrubal's retinue, he hurled the glove onto the ground. A shocked murmur ran through the entourage.

"Fight me at the sun's apex tomorrow, if you dare!"

"If? This is hardly an open question. A Philistine princeling is no match for a descendant of Hannibal," Hasdrubal spat back.

"We'll see, won't we?" the woman smiled. "Whoever wins this fight will win the throne of the whole united empire...and *me*."

Hasdrubal stood from his throne and stepped down, stooping to pick up the glove. He then moved to within a few inches of Achilles' face and sneered into it. The

Philistine prince responded with his own unyielding gaze.

In a flash of movement, Hasdrubal lifted the glove and backhanded Achilles with it across the face, before dropping it to the floor and grinding it with his heel. Then, he stomped back up to the throne and sat once again.

His face a tableau of rage, Achilles instinctively reached for his short sword, but his hand was stayed by the woman, who crooned, "Soon enough, soon enough."

"I will see you tomorrow," Achilles simply said to Hasdrubal before spinning on his heel, getting in a flourish of his crimson cape. Hasdrubal called out after his receding figure.

"Enjoy your last twenty four hours."

CHAPTER THIRTY-SIX

THE DUEL FOR THE EMPIRE

*T*he next morning, Delilah delightedly preened Achilles as he stood resplendent in the finest battle armor Gath had to offer, a perfect complement to the extravagant surroundings of the tent. The "eternal empress" cooed as she adjusted the straps and belts on her consort's assemblage and handed him a polished weapon. Finally, she flounced back to her vanity and put on a special lipstick that she had prepared just for the occasion. This last task completed, she pranced back over to her champion and passionately kissed him, Achilles responding enthusiastically.

"I won't fail you," he said as he kissed her face in three dozen places.

"Oh, I know you won't," Delilah said with a smile. "I've made arrangements that ensure a favorable outcome."

※ ※ ※

The Great Circus of Tanitania was a riot of purple as all of the city's gentry, and a good portion of its numerous riffraff, crowded the bleachers, anxiously awaiting the most exciting fight to ever happen in the giant stadium. At the head of the structure stood an enormous gate flanked by statues of war elephants, between which was hung an enormous Tanitanian flag inscribed with the Sign of Tanit, the symbol of the Tanitanian nation. The excited murmur of the crowd instantly died as a jubilant fanfare from a dozen silver trumpets split the air.

"His Royal Highness Hasdrubal, King of Upper and Lower Tanitania and the Imperial Provinces of Arboria and Aurania, Conqueror of all!" sang a white-robed chorus.

Hasdrubal, clad in full parade armor and hefting an enormous burnished shield, his head crowned with an enormous helmet flanked with two giant horsehair plumes, swaggered out from between the two war elephants, holding his arms out as he basked in the jubilant cheer of the crowd.

At the opposite end of the stadium was a notably less grand gate, flanked by small engaged statues of the legendary general Hannibal Barca and Carthage's founder, Dido. From between the statues stepped Achilles, similarly resplendent in his imperial regalia.

"Prince Achilles of Gath!" the chorus derisively sang. Achilles was assaulted by a loud cacophony of boos and jeers from the audience, which hurled food rubbish in his general direction and patriotically waved Tanitanian flags.

A moment of doubt crossing his normally overconfident features, Achilles looked up at Delilah's royal box. The empress was resplendent in a white gown intended to call to mind the features of the goddess Tanit. Achilles didn't appreciate her disguise as a Tanitanian goddess, but he realized the pretense was needed if they were to win the support of the Tanitanian populace once Hasdrubal's blood drained into the ground. Noticing his pause, Delilah blew him a kiss and waved.

Achilles turned to squarely face Hasdrubal and hefted his own round shield, inscribed with the pentagram of the Empire.

A priest stepped forward into the middle of the circus and cried in a loud voice.

"Today Achilles of Gath challenges Hasdrubal of Upper and Lower Tanitania, Arboria, and Aurania to single combat, to the death. To the victor will go both the entirety of the former lands of the Frouzean Empire, and the affections of the damsel Delilah, the incarnation to Earth of the goddesses Tanit and Astarte. Will either of you offer the other quarter or mercy?"

"No quarter!" both men yelled. Hasdrubal spat on the ground. In response, Achilles made a shockingly vulgar gesture, earning more jeers from the crowd.

"Very well," the priest said. With that, he brought a mallet crashing down on a huge gong, its ring reverberating through the Circus. The two men charged at each other and immediately began to seek out weaknesses in the other's defenses. They twirled about, jabbing and thrusting with their long spears, but always each one blocked the other's attack, spear striking shield with a bell-like ring. On and on they whirled, their spears seeming almost like the blades of windmills. The crowd sat on the edge of their seats, salivating at the entertainment and the spectacle. But, gradually, it became clear that Achilles, the younger and more virile of the two, was getting the upper hand. Finally, Achilles managed to catch Hasdrubal's spear between his shield and his thickset arm, and wrenched it out of the king's grip. He dramatically, derisively snapped the spear over his knee before throwing the pieces to the side and letting out a guttural yell. Hasdrubal backed away, his eyes filling with panic as Achilles bore down on him with his enormous spear pointed directly at the King's heart. Hasdrubal fumbled to draw his short sword from his belt. Suddenly, Achilles stopped short, a note of triumph writ large on his face.

"You warrant something more exciting than merely being run through," he said as he threw the spear to the side and drew his own sword. "I can't make this too easy. I want your slow death to entertain my people."

Not a moment later, the two men were at it again, their swords flashing in the overhead sun as they hacked and jabbed at each other, each cheating death by mere millimeters.

Delilah leaned forward in her chair, watching the two men wail on each other with piqued interest. Briseis came forward and whispered into her ear.

"When is it going to happen? How do you know you won't also be affected?"

"Just watch, darling," Delilah crooned. "And don't worry about me. I took the antidote last night."

"What? When is what going to happen? Why am I always the last to know everything?" Salome whined. Briseis rolled her eyes.

Delilah's eyes narrowed as she noticed Achilles begin to breathe more heavily than usual, sweat running down his face in great rivulets that soaked his beard. She clenched her fist in anticipation.

Soon.

With a mighty heave of effort, Achilles suddenly cast aside his shield and swung his sword with both hands, knocking Hasdrubal's blade flying. An old grandmother screamed as the sword buried itself, point-first, in the bleachers behind her, missing her by an inch.

Hasdrubal was knocked over by the force of the blow, leading to a panicked gasp from the crowd. He scrambled to raise his shield in time to block a furious storm of blows from Achilles, who hammered on the shield with his sword like a madman, foam flying from his mouth. The crowd winced at each sickening clang as Hasdrubal's once-resplendent shield became a mangled, dented mess. Still the relentless assault continued, Achilles now bellowing like a bull with each blow. Suddenly, he staggered forward, seeming to lose his balance.

Delilah involuntarily stood up from her chair, a wild look filling her eye.

Achilles' eyes, suddenly bloodshot and bulging, filled with rage and panic as he stumbled and then crashed to the ground. Hasdrubal seized the unexpected opportunity and dove for Achilles' sword hand. The two men rolled in the dirt, wrestling for the blade, but Achilles' grip, despite his sudden incapacitation, proved invincible. While he refused to let go of the sword, the rest of his movements grew increasingly sluggish, until he could barely move. Forgetting the blade, Hasdrubal seized his chance, picked up the mangled shield, and began repeatedly bashing his opponent with a relentless series of sickening crunches.

The crowd erupted into cheers as their king dealt blow after blow to the prince of Gath, his blood mingling with the dirt around him. Soon, Achilles was almost unrecognizable, and still appeared unable to move. Hasdrubal, his chest heaving with effort and uncontrolled animal rage, thrust his arms into the sky in a victory pose, holding the twisted, bloodied shield aloft for all to see. The jubilant crowd responded by showering him with roses.

For her part, Delilah alit from her box and wafted over the field of battle toward the two combatants.

Achilles gasped on the ground, his vision swimming as Delilah rushed over to him and crouched down, gently stroking his cheek. He fought to focus his eyes on her as he went into shock.

"*Why...?*"

"It's simple, Achilles. Only one could win. The Philistines have already accepted me as their empress. Tanitania never would unless their king was the champion." She leaned in to whisper into Achilles' ear as he gasped for air. "You were *magnificent*. But, I don't need you anymore."

A great convulsion shook Achilles' once-powerful, but now-paralyzed, frame as his life left his body. Delilah stretched out two long-nailed fingers and closed the prince's eyelids.

Delilah solemnly rose from the battered corpse and walked over to Hasdrubal, who still stood in his victory pose, his chest heaving as a rivulet of blood ran down his temple. Delilah turned to the assembled crowd of Tanitanians and took his hand, thrusting it into the air. The crowd erupted into an enormous cheer.

"Behold, my brave champion!"

CHAPTER THIRTY-SEVEN

'TIL DEATH DO US PART

A day later, Delilah sat at a bejeweled mirror, dressing herself once again as an image of Tanit, patron goddess of Carthage.

"Briseis, darling, surely you remembered my special wedding lipstick? I'll be so disappointed if I don't get to wear it!"

"Of course, your highness," the handmaid meekly answered, proffering a canister to the Empress. Delilah regarded the cosmetic product for a moment, then tossed it over her shoulder.

"Fool! I was referring to the Kiss of Ildico!"

Briseis' eyes widened. "But…that…"

Delilah flashed a wicked smile. "Of course. How else

am I to win my empire?"

"Well, I thought you were going to rule it together…"

"Goddesses don't share!" Delilah motioned toward the chest of potions that she had brought onboard. "Bring me the antidote first."

"Yes, your highness." Briseis rummaged around in the chest before producing a green bottle and offering it to the empress.

"What? What antidote? What is going on?" Salome inserted herself into the conversation.

"Observe, darling, observe," Delilah simply crooned as Briseis gave her rival a rueful look.

Delilah uncorked the bottle, tossed her head back, and took a sip from it, holding her nose with her other hand.

"Foul, but effective," she said handing the bottle back to Briseis, who next passed her another lipstick canister. Delilah flounced over to a mirror and began meticulously applying the product. "It must be perfect," she said. Once satisfied, she smacked her lips and gave the canister back to her servant.

"After all," Delilah crooned, "I want our first kiss to be one history will never forget."

An hour later, the circus was once again filled with many of the same people who had "graced" its bleachers the day before. Hasdrubal had insisted that no time be wasted in preparing his wedding to Delilah. After, all, he had pointed out, his had been the victory, and to victor would go the spoils without delay.

The circus was decked from foundation to entablature with costly Tyrian purple banners, the cloth alone representing wealth a thousand times greater than most of the attendees would ever see in their lifetimes. Suddenly, they all gasped in unison as a dozen trumpets blared at the elephant gate. The dowry had arrived.

On and on it came. Carts piled high with carpets and pottery, cages filled with exotic animals, sledges piled high with jewels and gold, cadres of frolicking dancing girls, barrels filled with Gath's famous wine and barrows filled to the bursting with fire opals, pearls, and silver ingots. The wealth of an empire was paraded before the wondering populace, as musicians and dancers of the imperial Frouzean court wheeled about, joyously, if discordantly, banging on tambourines, drums, and all manner of other dissonant instruments.

Finally, the crowd quieted down as the main event arrived. Five hundred soldiers of the Homeric guard marched through the gates in perfect formation. Then, between the two enormous sculpted elephants emerged a flesh-and-blood example. The elephant's thunderous steps filled the courtyard, its long ivory tusks caught the morning sun, and it trumpeting call exhilarated the audience, who instantly rose up and cheered.

Atop the elephant, on a gyroscopically-stabilized platform, reclined Delilah, resplendent in her Tanit costume. Briseis and Salome, her bridesmaids, also sat atop the platform, fanning her with giant emu plumes and assortments of peacock feathers.

The elephant rumbled to a halt before a dais, over which stood a priest. On either side of the priest were two large marble staircases that had been dragged into the circus by gangs of sweating slaves. These same slaves now ascended the staircases and gingerly lifted the platform off of the elephant's back, taking great care to keep it level. They then carried it down the stairs, making valiant efforts to make the platform appear as though it was floating, rather than stepping down. Finally, it was set on the ground, leaving Delilah just a bit higher than the altar.

Hasdrubal eagerly stood before the dais, a hungry look

on his face. Delilah looked away and daintily extended a hand down, as though she were expecting someone to take it, or at least to kiss it. Breaking protocol, Hasdrubal leapt forward and did just that, before helping Delilah gracefully alight on the purple carpet that had been spread before her. The two turned to face the priest.

"This is a momentous occasion," the Tanitanian priest said reverently. "Not only has the goddess Tanit chosen to grace us with her presence—" Delilah smiled-- "But she has seen to it that the two halves of our former empire are joined together once again, but this time, not in conquest, anger, and subjection, but in love." Delilah flashed an adoring smile to Hasdrubal, although it by no means reached her eyes.

"Once again we will be a great, united nation, the terror of all the world, as things should be!" shouted the priest, leading to a jubilant shout from the crowd.

"Now, on to the reason why we are all here. I shall be succinct. Do you, Hasdrubal, King of Upper and Lower Tanitania and Arboria and Aurania, soon to be Emperor of the Reunited Empire of Frouzea, take this goddess as your lawfully wedded wife?"

Hasdrubal licked his lips like a dog looking at a piece of ribeye steak. "I do," he said brusquely.

"And do you, Delilah, second incarnation to earth of our beloved mother goddess Tanit and holder of a thousand other titles of equal splendor and brilliance, take this King as your lawfully-wedded husband?"

Delilah's eyes narrowed, giving her face a distinctly serpentine expression.

"I do."

"Very well. In the authority invested in me by, well…" the priest looked over at Delilah, "you, I pronounce you man and wife, and the Empire of Frouzea reunited. All

Hail Frouzee."

Delilah stood on her toes as Hasdrubal bent down to kiss her, the crowd cheering around them. As he pulled back to beam at his new bride, Delilah's mouth twisted into a smile as she addressed her new husband.

"'Till death do us part."

CHAPTER THIRTY-EIGHT

THE WEDDING

Trukanamoa, Wil'iah, 1286 AD

*T*he Cathedral of the Everlasting Victory's gleaming towers, festooned with garlands of desert roses and waratahs, stood tall over the many-splendored gardens of Trukanamoa. Today, their bells pealed with joyful tones, for it was Tamino and Avora'tru'ivi's wedding day. The great church was packed to the brimful with a diverse assemblage of citizenry from around the Kingdom and the known world. Citizens and chieftains came from every constituent nation of the Kingdom; the Judges of all of the Judgates and their entourages mixed with ranchers from

Maranoa, cattle-drovers from Kinipapa, sailors from Marduwarra, pearl-divers from Yaringa, and traders from Tanami. Lords and ladies of the courts of Dai Viet, Champa, and Singhasari were joined by a Yolngu elder. A contingent of Asmat villages from Papua shared a bank of pews with a party from Pilbara.

At the center of the soaring rotunda at the heart of the church was a raised circular channel, surrounded on all sides by the pews reserved for the families of the bride and groom. The interior of the church rang with the thunder of thousands of voices, while the light that streamed in through the church's clerestory windows fell upon a riot of color, representing the garments of the whole of the known world. Suddenly, the entire building shook with the peal of the massive organ, whose pipes permeated the stonework surrounding the rotunda. A blast on the largest pipe, an enormous tube resembling a cannon that stood four stories tall and was nearly ten feet wide, instantly put to silence the excited hubbub of the crowd.

A medley played by the hundreds of bells in the cathedral's seventeen towers opened the ceremony. The sound of a medley of cherished favorites in the Wil'iahn canon, including *Zebulon, Flame of the Desert, The Flame of Zebulon, The Pillar of Fire, The Song of Balthazar, Victory Hymn of the Faithful Kingdom, Battle-Cry of the Eternal Resistance,* and the always-popular *Tear Down the Gates of Hell* was accentuated by the sweet smell of the dozens of varieties of flowers, both native and foreign, that spilled out in huge bunches from priceless porcelain urns strategically placed throughout the church.

After the patriarch of the church led the attendees in singing the *Vow of Wil'iah* and the *Prayer of Gideon,* the national anthem of Manasseh, forty men and forty women stepped forward on the west side of the rotunda and blasted out a fanfare with long silver heralds' trumpets and precious conch shells gathered from the east coast of Ephraim. This marked the beginning of the bridal procession. As the fanfare continued, Prince Gideon of Manasseh entered carrying the tall *tahili* standard, a tall pole carved with images representing the life and lineage of Princess Avora'tru'ivi, inlaid with priceless pearl, exotic hardwoods, and festooned with jewels and tropical flowers. He marched forward and placed the pole in a matching receptacle on the iron ring in the center of the rotunda. Once the *tahili* was placed, signifying the princess' presence in the church, the organ pealed out a joyous fanfare as Avora'tru'ivi appeared, with a dramatic fluff of her headdress, at the far end of a double line of the stern-faced War Queen's Guard, their bright spear points seeming to reflect her radiance. Clad in a dress and headdress of the purest white silk and bedecked in pearls, the princess was a picture of joy as her bright smile greeted the thousands of onlookers. As she began to advance up the line of amazon-like guards, their spears crossing with a dramatic clang behind her as she passed each pair, the Royal 'Uli Choir stepped forward to sing a special chant prepared for the occasion by Prince Tamino.

Hail Avora'tru'ivi, God's oath descended to Earth
Most radiant of stars, brightest of flames
Sweetest of songs and dearest of hearts
How, o Lord on High
Are we thus blessed, are we so favored
By the presence of this most precious of angels?

Hail friend to all of God's creatures great and small
Benefactor of wise and weak, strong and slight
Tender of fires, defender of light

Hail heart of purest gold, voice of sweetest silver
Hail unending beneficence and love
Hail valiant bastion of truth

Hail assembler of alliance and arbitrator of disputes
Hail avenging angel of Bien Dong
Whose fleets hurled back the darkness and turned defeat to victory

Hail brightest lodestar of our hearts
Hail burning ember that warms us when night is long
Let us all hail Avora'tru'ivi, most beloved princess of Manasseh!

As the choir wrapped up the chant, the princess gracefully stepped inside the iron circle, to the deafening cheers of many of the onlookers, which was silenced once again by a blast of the organ's trumpets. At this fanfare, an honor guard of knights of the Order of the Flame of Zebulon, fully-outfitted with burnished parade armor, filed out to take positions flanking the eastern nave of the church. Once in position, they rendered the military salute of Wil'iah in perfect unison, then stood completely still as the trumpeters and shell-blowers stepped once again into the rotunda to play a joyous fanfare as Tamino's brother, Prince Jeremiah, and Princess Jessica entered carrying the *tahili* of Prince Tamino, their carvings depicting the setting desert sun in the border provinces and the tall sails of ships. With the *tahili* placed in the iron circle, the siblings retired to their pew, briefly pausing to favor the patriarch and the 'uli choir with the open-handed civilian salute. Their task completed, the great *Zhunga'ivi* pipe of the organ shook the building once again as a beaming Tamino, outfitted in a gleaming white dress uniform of the King's Rangers of the Order of the Flame of Zebulon emblazoned with a gold

Star of Bethlehem, appeared at the far end of the east nave and began to solemnly march up the line of knights. Each time, as he passed, the knights drew their gleaming swords in precise coordination and crossed them above his head, their clashes accented by the beating of a great drum. As this occurred, the 'uli choir stepped forward again the recite the chant prepared by Avora'tru'ivi for Tamino's entrance.

Behold Tamino, valiant prince of Wil'iah
Heir to David, Ranger of the South
Victor o'er the fleets of Arafura
Defender of the Faithful Kingdom and Steward of God's Far Garden!

Hail bright star of my heart
Blazing flame against the darkness
Assuring warmth to those who shake in fright
Tall and strong, filled with righteous might!

Hail heart of purest light
Hail eyes turned resolutely above
Hail faith imperishable, courage eternal, fidelity undying
Hail steadfast fortress of truth and love

Hail dauntless hope of my heart!
Hail intrepid Truth!
Hail staunch, unflickering flame of my devotion!!
Hail beacon-fire of virtue and honor!

Let us hail together the one who brings us our assurance
The great standard of affirmation that our Dream will endure
Hail Tamino, Crown Prince of Wil'iah, my heart!

As the final strains of the 'uli lingered over the audience, Tamino stepped inside the iron circle and smiled at the princess as the crowd clapped. The room went silent as King Gamaliel of Manasseh and King Hezekiah of Wil'iah rose from their pews bearing porcelain vases filled with fragrant sandal oil, which they solemnly passed to their respective children before rendering the military salute and returning to the pews. The prince and princess poured the oil into the circular channel that surrounded them. Prince Gideon and Princess Jessica next approached their respective siblings with lit torches and passed them; Jessica slightly broke protocol by giving her brother a quick kiss on the cheek. Tamino and Avora'tru'ivi then, in unison, touched the torches to the oil, which immediately leapt to life, becoming a fabulously multi-colored blaze that surrounded them. At this pivotal moment, the organ pealed again, and the onlookers joined together in a rafter-rattling rendition of *The Flame of Zebulon*.

This completed, the patriarch ascended to the dais and, with the 'uli choir as backup, recited a chant describing the history of marriage as a sacred rite among the Zebulite and Manassite people. As the last strains of the 'uli floated over the audience, the patriarch turned to Tamino.

"Do you have a message that you wish to convey to this woman?" he asked with a twinkle in his eye.

Tamino nervously cleared his throat and squared his shoulders, making eye contact with Avora'tru'ivi, who smiled back. Drawing in a deep intake of breath, Tamino began to sing with warm, cello-like tones.

"This I vow, here in the greatest church in Christendom, standing upon the holiest stones in this faithful kingdom, to cherish and defend, to the end of my days, the angelic expression of the Most High known to us as Avora'tru'ivi, Princess of Manasseh. I pledge

my eternal loyalty, my everlasting love, and my undying devotion to your kindness, your strength, your courage, your valor, and your virtue. I promise to cherish you from henceforth even to the end of time, as I have cherished you for as long as I can remember. I swear to defend your honor and your light against all darkness and deceit, for as long as these hands can wield a sword. Today, in the presence of the assembled hosts of the world, I declare my unending gratitude for your unsurpassed effulgence, and, on my knees, I thank the almighty God of Abraham for his beneficence, that an angel so radiant as yourself should happen to appear before me, and that in your heart, as wide and as grand as the sea, there should be a place for me. From today until the hosts of the light assemble at Tel-el-Megiddo, my heart is yours. My sword is at your command. And in each of all of those unending days, I shall pass each moment in endless thanksgiving."

The patriarch next turned to the princess and smiled. "Do you have an answer?"

Avora'tru'ivi's sweet, bell-like voice now filled the soaring golden dome of the great church, almost seeming to emanate from the burnished walls themselves.

"This I vow, as I stand on the stones of this greatest, most valorous of nations, my adopted land, to love and cherish the valiant and honorable man named Tamino ben'Hezekiah, Crown Prince of Wil'iah and Heir to the Throne of David, from henceforth even unto eternity. For, as I have always known, standing before me in this greatest church in all the world is someone who does not just fill my heart to the very overflow, but who is my heart. I will ever treasure your courage, your kindness, your gentleness, your strength, and your noble spirit. I promise to join hands with you, to stand back-to-back, and with you defend the age-old dream of Jeremiah in this Far Garden. I vow to work with you to raise this nation to an ever-higher standard of virtue, and to stand with you against all

enemies at home and abroad. And each and every day, my heart will leap that I have the privilege of fighting the good fight on this earth alongside a light so resolute, a hope so steadfast, a beacon of truth so unwavering, as the man I have loved since first our spirits met together."

The vows completed, the king approached Tamino with the fabled Zrain'de'zhang, the sword that liberated Wil'iah from the Frouzeans and had reportedly descended fully-forged from the heavens, proffered on a silk pillow. Similarly, Sheerah, War Queen of Ephraim, approached her daughter with her famous scimitar, whose bite was the stuff of Frouzean nightmares. They each hefted the famous weapons with a mixture of awe and trepidation; Tamino nervously smiled at his bride-to-be, then backed to the extreme end of the circle. After three beats on the drum and a blast from the great *Zhunga'ivi* pipe, the bride and groom charged at each other and clashed the weapons together three times, each impact sending sparks off of the keen edges of the swords. After the third clash, Tamino heaved a huge sigh of relief. The pair turned back to back and thrust their swords together high in the air while jointly yelling *"Ivrae'ia Va'a'kau'lua!,"* the battle-cry of the Kingdom. Together, they began to sing *The Vow of Wil'iah*, joined by the choir and the congregants.

As the last glorious strains of Wil'iah's most sacred anthem faded, the fire in the circle burned down, and the breath of the organ was exhausted, the patriarch threw his arms open wide and yelled, "By the authority vested in me by the Church of St. Thomas and the laws and statutes of the Faithful Kingdom of Wil'iah, I pronounce you man and wife!"

The entire crowd stood up and cheered, using the opportunity to throw great showers of flower petals into the air. Queen Sheerah and Queen Adirah both ran to the circle, jointly carrying the traditional quilt they had crafted together, which was emblazoned with the symbols of their respective children as well as their united coat of arms. As Tamino and Avora'tru'ivi embraced, their mothers wrapped them tightly in the quilt.

Tamino smiled as he pulled Avora'tru'ivi in for the Honi, the traditional kiss of the Wil'iahn people in which foreheads are touched and breath is shared. All around them, fragrant flower petals and the peal of the church's bells filled the air.

"We did it."

CHAPTER THIRTY-NINE

THE END OF THE CIRCLE

Gath, Frouzean Empire

A crowd gathered once more in the square of Gath, anxiously awaiting the results of the state visit to Tanitania. They didn't have to wait long.

Heracles swaggered out onto the platform, flanked by heralds who blasted their trumpets with a jubilant fanfare.

"It is my honor to present Her Worship Frouzee Delilah!"

The crowd cheered, but, instantly, the jubilation died down into expressions of dismay as Delilah appeared on the dais, dressed all in black, her face streaked with tears.

She sniffled as she spoke. "Prince Achilles, great paragon of our nation's strength, was foolish enough to challenge Hasdrubal of Tanitania to a duel. The whole empire, and my affections, were to be the prize."

The crowd gasped at the thought of such an extravagant bargain.

Now the tears flowed again as Delilah exaggeratedly sobbed. "And, in the ensuing fight, brave Achilles was struck down by Hasdrubal. I had no choice but to marry him…and unite our empires in the process!"

The crowd wasn't sure if it was supposed to cry or cheer. One old woman asked, "Are we under the Tanitanian flag again?"

Delilah raised her chin ever so slightly, a veneer of dominion beginning to assert itself.

"I, of course, resigned myself to a life of wedded bliss with Hasdrubal. After all, he was nearly so handsome as Achilles. But then, when my heart was already filled with grief—" Delilah suppressed a sob, "---tragedy struck again. On my wedding night, Hasdrubal overindulged in the drink – and never woke up."

The crowd gasped again.

"And, broken as I was, wracked with sorrow, I realized I had no choice but to take up the mantle that fate had so cruelly bestowed upon me. My fellow gods Dagon and Baal did indeed agree that the time had come."

"What mantle was that?" a wide-eyed teenager asked.

"DOMINION OVER THE WHOLE EMPIRE, OF COURSE!" Delilah yelled as her face suddenly filled with glee. At this unexpected turn of events, the crowd erupted into patriotic fervor, waving untold thousands of miniature Frouzean flags as they whooped and hollered.

Suddenly, the jubilation was interrupted by a huddled

group of men in red robes that picked their way through the square, the crowd parting before them. Soon, the priests of the Circle came face to face with Delilah.

The leader stepped forward.

"It's time to drop this charade. We all know who you really are!"

Delilah cocked her head quizzically.

"Oh?"

"Your name isn't Delilah, and you are no goddess. You are a slave girl of the Circle. You should be wearing a gold slave-band, not these ridiculous 'funeral clothes.'"

"What a strange way to display gratitude," Delilah said, a look of feigned shock animating her luridly-painted face. "Who was it who restored this empire to greatness and recaptured nearly all of its former territories? Who was it who fulfilled your dreams of reviving Frouzea and bringing to resurgence the terror that once gripped this whole continent? Who? WHO?"

One of the priests whispered, "She has a point," but he was instantly silenced by the leader.

"You are a fraud, Iphigenia! You are no goddess?"

"Such insolence," Delilah sneered. She then turned to the assembled crowd, which milled about nervously, unsure of what to make of the confrontation between two revered authority figures.

"Have your lives improved under my command?"

"Yes!"

"Are you grateful?"

"*Yes!*"

"Now, what is the traditional way to express gratitude to your Goddess?"

"SACRIFICE!" yelled a fanatical-looking older man from the mob.

A deranged fire lit in Delilah's eyes.

"Why, yes, someone remembers!" She languidly swung her arm out to point at the priests.

"And what better gift than these? Their lives, spent in service to me, can end with the same nobility!"

A look of pure horror crossed the priest's face as the crowd cheered behind him and a thousand torches were thrust into the air.

"Prepare the altar. I will be waiting," Delilah smiled.

A jubilant answer floated up from the mob as the priests were dragged away.

"ALL HAIL FROUZEE!"

PART II

1288–1293

CHAPTER FORTY

THE BATTLE OF BACH DANG

Bach Dang River, Dai Viet, 1288 AD

*T*amino stood at the railing of the *Ava'ivi*, anticipation filling him with tension. The veteran warship rode the waves of the Bach Dang River gently, her sails furled for the time being. But all over her quiet decks, her crew stood at attention, ready to snap into action at a moment's notice. Along with the rest of the fleet, the flagship lay hidden in one of the many branches of the river. All around them lay the silent countryside of Dai Viet. Once again, Wil'iah's staunch ally was under attack, but, this time, they were ready.

Tamino turned to Zhang Shijie, who paced at the railing beside him. The aged admiral's face was lined with concentration.

"Any guesses on when they will get here?"

Zhang snapped his head over to the prince. "Last we heard, Omar Khan's supply fleet was in full retreat, harried by Dai Viet's scout forces." He nodded to the crewman standing next to him.

"Take another sounding."

The crewman dropped a lead over the side of the ship and reported the water's depth. Zhang Shijie pursed his lips.

"Hmmmm. Almost time. In just a few minutes, the spikes will start to show themselves. Then we strike."

Those few minutes seemed like hours as the fleet waited in silent anticipation, the ships' crews creeping around the decks so as not to make the slightest noise. The din of a distant battle carried over on a gathering breeze. Gradually, it seemed not so distant. The reports of thunderous cannon fire sounded closer and closer.

Suddenly, a bright beacon flared to life atop the hill that commanded the confluence of the tributary in which the fleet lay and the main Bach Dang River.

"They've been spotted! *Now!*" yelled the admiral. Almost instantly, the *Ava'ivi's* sails snapped into position, and the nimble ship sprang forward as her crews ran toward their gunnery posts with the most discretion they could muster.

Tamino silently prayed for victory in this final effort to secure Dai Viet's freedom.

Though we face heavy odds, we are not alone.

Trukanamoa, Wil'iah

An excited murmur filled Cathedral Square as the Trukanamoa town crier dramatically unfurled a scroll, pausing for emphasis as he reveled in the rapt attention of the townsfolk.

"Well, what happened?" yelled a curmudgeonly older man.

The crier cleared his throat and began to read.

"As expected, the Mongol invasion fleet, composed of five hundred ships commanded by the fearsome general Omar Khan and Toghon, son of Kublai Khan, invaded our ally Dai Viet. In fulfillment of our obligations as a member of the League of Shechem, the Royal Wil'iahn Navy sent two hundred ships under the command of Admiral Zhang Shijie and Crown Prince Tamino to reinforce the Dai Viet Navy."

The crowd continued to listen excitedly, although murmurs betrayed their nervousness at the situation.

"Dai Viet employed effective scorched-earth tactics against the Mongols, and Toghon's supply fleet was forced to retreat to the Bach Dang River, where our ships and the Dai Viet fleet were waiting. Although we were outnumbered, we had a crucial advantage- knowledge of the tides. Our allies planted stakes in the riverbed, and their scout forces drew the Mongols in. When the tide started to go out, the Mongol ships were trapped by the stakes, and their only escape route was blocked by our battlefleet. The entire Mongol fleet was destroyed, General Omar Khan was captured, and the Mongol army was defeated. Once again, Dai Viet is saved!"

A hearty cheer went out from the crowd as some of them produced Wil'iahn flags and began waving them.

"Where's Prince Tamino now?" a woman asked.

"The crown prince is scheduled to make a triumphal entrance tomorrow morning!" the crier responded, a cheer rising from the crowd in response.

CHAPTER FORTY-ONE

TAMINO'S PROMOTION

*A*vora'tru'ivi paced in one of the cupolas of the Palace of Trukanamoa, nervously scanning the surrounding area for any sign of a returning war party. She tenderly held her protruding stomach even as a nervous fear gripped her heart. She internally kicked herself that she couldn't go on this particular mission. Looking down at her belly, she tried to console herself.

You wouldn't have been particularly helpful like this.

"I just hope he gets back before I'm due," she whispered quietly to herself. "That is, if he comes back at all." She tried to dismiss her last thought as irrational, but she knew all too well how possible it was that her husband wasn't coming back. Mongol fleets were not to be trifled with.

Suddenly, she heard a strange rustling in the tree whose canopy rose level with the cupola. A gentle voice called out from the leaves.

"Thank goodness. I was hoping I'd make it back in time." Avora'tru'ivi broke into a wide smile as Tamino swung out of the tree and into the cupola. The pair hugged each other warmly, although with a certain amount of care, given the princess' condition.

"Two weeks, right?" Tamino said as he peeked at Avora'tru'ivi's rotund midsection.

"Well, two and a half, but who's counting?" she laughed. "What were you doing in a tree? Aren't you supposed to make some big entrance when you win a battle?"

Tamino shook his head. "I don't like the personal sense of glory associated with all of that pomp and circumstance. I was just doing my job."

"And very well, at that," a deep voice boomed, startling both of them.

The enormous form of Hezekiah emerged from the spiral staircase leading to the cupola, leaning slightly on a cane. He gently shook his head at his son.

"You know, I never liked the parades much either. But the public is going to want to see you. Especially now, since I have an important announcement to make."

"What announcement?" asked Tamino.

"Over the last five years, you have repeatedly demonstrated leadership, courage, and integrity as you assembled the league and accomplished the impossible: defeating the 'invincible' Mongols in open battle – multiple times. I think it's time."

"Time…for what?" Tamino asked nervously.

"There comes a time in every man's life when he must

pass the fire to the next generation. I've been watching carefully, and I think you're ready. I've decided to retire."

"Re—retire?" Tamino stammered.

"Yes. Wil'iah needs its king to be in his prime. I'm getting old," Hezekiah laughed as he shook the cane at his son. "I can't swing around ships' shrouds"— he gave a wry smile at the tree next to the cupola—"or trees -- anymore. I seem to be slowing down lately, and this way, I'll be around to provide some guidance to you as you get started. I think it's a better system than waiting for me to go Home, and leaving you to pick up all of the pieces without any help."

Tamino looked alarmed at the suggestion. "I don't think—"

"You know, you've always been a pretty good listener," his father boomed. "Listen to me now. You're ready. We just have to get the Council to approve. I love you." With that, the king turned around and headed back down the spiral staircase.

"Sounds like you're getting a promotion," Avora'tru'ivi smiled.

"Two promotions, apparently, one much more important than the other," Tamino said. "I'm going to be a daddy." Suddenly, a frightened look passed over his face. "I'm going to be a daddy—and become a king at the same time."

The princess chuckled. "Don't worry, Galbi. We can do it. Together."

CHAPTER FORTY-TWO

THE HUMILIATION OF TOGHON

Palace of Xanadu, northern China

Fitful shafts of light dimly forced their way into an enormous, dusty room, faintly illuminating splendid walls of marble and gold. In front of a large stained-glass window, the dark shadow of a despot loomed over the chamber. Kublai Khan sprawled across his throne in his palace of Xanadu, drowning his sorrows in wine, heedless of the unmatched, but fading, splendor of his surroundings. His enormous, corpulent form filled his opulent silk imperial robes to the bursting, while malevolent, bloodshot eyes dominated his round, bearded face.

Another stinging defeat at the hands of that damn Dai Viet, he thought to himself as he flung yet another bottle onto the growing pile in front of him. *And those stupid Wil'iahns.*

Suddenly, his bloodshot eyes jerked up as a gong announced a visitor, his adviser, Liu.

"WHAT!?" roared the Great Khan.

"Your son is here to see you," Liu responded.

"What son!?" Khan bellowed.

"Toghon."

"Toghon is no longer my son, but send him in anyway."

The double doors at the entrance to the throne room were flung open, and Toghon was shoved through by two guards. He instantly sprawled on the floor in a frantic, pitiful show of deference.

"Oh almighty Father, forgive me! I was defeated by the treachery of Dai Viet and her wicked allies!"

"Who do you address as father?" Khan asked. "It certainly can't be me."

A look of shocked horror crossed Toghon's face.

"Once you were my favorite. No more. You have repeatedly proved your worthlessness. You no longer have the right to call yourself my son. In fact, you should be grateful that I'm not going to kill you right now. Instead, you will be banished to Yangzhou for the rest of your miserable days. May they be few. I never want to see you again."

A single tear ran down Toghon's face.

"But, Father!"

"SHUT UP! Take him away!" Khan slurred as he aimed another empty bottle at Toghon. The expertly-flung vessel shattered only an inch away from his ankle. Toghon was dragged by the guards, his bloodstained robes dragging across the highly-polished floor. As soon as he cleared the double doors, they slammed shut with a somber finality.

"Listen, Great One. I know you are taking the death of Empress Chabi very sorely, but perhaps you should reconsider"— Liu was interrupted harshly.

"Is this insolence coming from a mouth of a fool that I hear? I have not been too harsh. All of my lackeys, even my own children, have failed me." Khan looked imploringly skyward. "Will there be anyone who will restore us to our greatness? Will there be anyone to replace dear Chabi?"

CHAPTER FORTY-THREE

THE COUNCIL OF ULURU

Palaces of the Council of Uluru, Trukanamoa, Wil'iah

Tamino swallowed hard as his eyes took in the enormous, billowing domes that towered above him. Here was the true seat of power in Wil'iah, the Palaces of the Council of Uluru, a constant reminder of the sovereignty that Wil'iah's indigenous peoples held over the land, and of the fact that the nation's kings ruled only by their consent. The enormous structure made even Hezekiah, who towered beside him, seem small. His father, noticing the nervous look in Tamino's eyes, gave him a reassuring pat on the back.

"This is just procedural. Don't worry, Tamino. Everyone loves you."

Tamino allowed himself a doubtful sideways glance at his father, who was at least five inches taller, and probably weighed half again as much, although he seemed a bit thinner than Tamino had remembered.

No, everyone loves you.

Despite his doubts, Tamino forced himself to stand up straight.

Don't do it for yourself. Do it for him. Do it for Wil'iah.

With that, Tamino, followed by his father, stepped forward across the causeway that cut across the reflecting pool that surrounded the great building. Ahead of him, two bronze double doors whooshed open as if by magic.

Inside, Tamino found himself marching resolutely down a path that led to a podium in the center of an enormous round room, lined on all sides by concentric rings of dozens of desks. Behind every one sat a stern-faced Aboriginal representative. Tamino tried to read their faces, but the expressions remained inscrutable, a fact aided by the nearly-blinding sunlight that streamed in through the clerestory windows that lined the base of the dome. Between each window stood the flag of one of Wil'iah's constituent Aboriginal nations.

Directly in front of him loomed a raised dais emblazoned with the Star of Wil'iah. Behind it stood a woman resplendent in the dress of the Arrernte Nation, one of the founding members of the Council of Uluru. Allira, the prime minister, raised her hands, and the room was instantly filled with the low drone of didgeridoos, their sound vibrating through Tamino's bones. Then, as suddenly as their voices had sounded, silence reigned.

"State your name," Allira's voice boomed, its resonant timbre shaking Tamino to his core.

"Tamino ben'Hezekiah, Crown Prince of Wil'iah." Tamino snapped into the civilian salute.

"You stand before this council because the current king has nominated you as his successor. As you know, the kings and queens of the House of David rule over Wil'iah by the consent of those they govern, and by the authority of this council. This is the agreement that forged a loose alliance driven by common interest into the mighty nation that stands a shining exemplar today. Do you understand that, despite your pedigree, that this council reserves the right to refuse you the throne?"

"I do."

"Very well. State your platform. What can this council expect to see should you assume the throne?"

Tamino nervously cleared his throat, then began to address the council, its members leaning ominously from their perches.

"Should I be accepted by this esteemed council, I swear that I will do all in my power to defend the dream that built Wil'iah into what it is today. I promise to work earnestly and tirelessly for the benefit of all of her people, Aboriginal and Zebulite alike, and to hold every common interest as my interest. I vow never to abuse my power and to instead exercise the might of the throne of David only for right, and to uphold truth and justice both within the borders of this blessed nation and abroad. I will heed the teachings of our master and do whatever I can to uplift the downtrodden, help the poor and needy, and raise the meek to strength. I promise to fulfill the Vow of Wil'iah with every iota of strength I can muster."

Allira allowed herself the faintest of smiles.

"And what specific policy proposals do you wish to present to us?"

"I wish to further build Wil'iah into a shining beacon of

culture and learning by forging a stronger education system, patronizing the arts, and improving infrastructure. My time in the border provinces has shown me that many improvements can be made in these areas, particularly in literacy and the postal service. I propose that the vernacular Wil'iahn language, which currently has many dialects, be standardized and taught, with the goal of giving the gift of reading to every citizen. At the same time, the indigenous languages that form the fiber of our nation's heritage and continued existence are to be cataloged and taught in our schools. For if we can speak to each other, we can understand each other, and we can move forward together. Furthermore, I will take the steps necessary to continue to protect our nation against the many threats that beset it both at home and abroad. I plan to strengthen the Wil'iahn Navy, continue my father's program of fortress construction across the nation, and continue our brave resistance against the 'Great' Khan."

"And just how do you plan to fulfill that last promise?"

"Wil'iah, partially though my efforts, has assembled a powerful alliance which has repeatedly demonstrated its ability to contain the advances of Kublai Khan. I plan to continue to support this league, and work ultimately for the liberation of China and the defeat of Khan."

"Very well. Do you have anything else to state before we enter the question and answer portion?"

"Only this. I promise you that I will do my utmost to be the best first servant to this council that I can be. I cannot promise that I will in every way live up to the stature of my predecessors," Tamino flicked an eye to his father, "but I will try. And it is my honest belief that, with God's help, Wil'iah can weather any challenge that it faces, and that we can all do it – together."

Allira nodded, then pounded a gavel down on her dais,

formally opening the question and answer session. Tamino was bombarded with every conceivable query, ranging from tax structure and government-bestowed benefits, to postal routes, to fortification design, to diplomacy, to the layout of future monuments in the Elysium gardens. One particularly grizzled representative asked the most ominous question of all- how Tamino would minimize casualties in the event of a devastating land invasion by Mongol forces.

"Our military is actively working on such scenarios. At the moment, the initial plans are secret, but I will do everything in my power to protect each and every one of our citizens, to the last child."

The old representative merely nodded in response, but Tamino could see the doubt in his beady eyes.

After what seemed like at least three hours, but was likely closer to just one, Allira slammed her gavel once more.

"This concludes the question and answer portion. We now allow twelve minutes for deliberations. Council members are welcome to speak among themselves as they come to decisions. We will vote at the conclusion of this period."

The chamber instantly became a nearly deafening cacophony of voices as the representatives turned to one another and excitedly chattered. Tamino fought to keep himself from attempting to eavesdrop, when he felt a powerful hand touch his shoulder.

"Regardless of the outcome of this vote, I'm proud of you," Hezekiah said. "I count my blessings daily that you are my son. And remember, though the throne seems to stand alone, you never are," he flicked his eyes upward.

After the requisite period, Allira rapped the dais with her gavel again.

"Alright, that concludes the deliberation period. Do any delegates require more time to reach a decision?"

The silence that followed was nearly as deafening as conversations that had preceded it.

"Very well. I will proceed down the roll call, by Judgate, starting with Tjoritja. For the Arrernte Nation, I accept this man as our new king," Allira continued.

Tamino involuntarily let out his breath.

Allira continued. "Anmatyerre."

"Accept."

"Alyawarre."

"Accept."

"Wankanguru."

"Accept."

"Pintupi."

"Accept."

The roll of nations went on and on, Tamino's heart leaping with each acceptance, although there were a few denials. Finally, the list came to an end.

Allira smiled. "By a vote of 105 to 3, the council is nearly unanimously decided. Congratulations, Tamino. You will be crowned the second king of Wil'iah in the Church of the Eternal Victory in one month's time, by the authority vested in the Council of Uluru. Long may you reign."

A wide smile broke across Tamino's face as relief washed over him, although he found himself unable to fully process the pronouncement. He immediately rendered the civilian salute, passing his finishing open palm around the whole circumference of the council chamber.

"Esteemed representatives of our nations, I thank you for your confidence. For those who have yet to extend it, I hope I will be able to win your trust. In the meantime, I thank you for your candor and your commitment to the freedom of this nation." He then turned to face Allira squarely.

"T'vrae'ia Va'a'kau'lua!"

A chorus of voices responded.

"T'vrae'ia Va'a'kau'lua!"

CHAPTER FORTY-FIVE

THE CORONATION

*T*he Church of the Eternal Victory was packed to the bursting with well-wishers as its bells pealed a joyous patriotic anthem. Children craned their necks to catch a view of the proceedings from between the heads of their parents and the brightly-colored bunting hung all around the cavernous interior of the church. A moment that came once in a generation, the crowning of the king of Wil'iah, had arrived.

The deafening, excited chatter that filled the volume of the building with anticipation suddenly fell to a whisper as a triumphant fanfare heralded the beginning of the ceremony. Two standard-bearers carrying the *tahili* poles of

Prince Tamino solemnly marched down the center aisle of the east nave towards the great rotunda at the center of the church, followed by The Forty, the king's most elite knights, in full military array, their burnished armor festooned with medals, badges of honor, and brightly-colored ribbons. Finally, behind them, and flanked on either side by Princess Jessica and Prince Jeremiah, Tamino solemnly, slowly marched down the aisle. His steps were accompanied by an *'uli* chant that a single woman wailed out from the choir loft. Her resonant voice described the lineage of the House of David, stretching all the way back to the legendary times of David and Solomon. Each time her song passed to the next generation, the great Jeremiah Bell, rumored to be the largest in the world, boomed in recognition. Forty-two times the bell sounded, until, with perfect timing, Tamino and his procession arrived at the dais that stood resolutely beneath the many-splendored dome. Behind the dais stood the patriarch, with the ancient breastplate of the high priest of Israel, with its twelve jewels, strapped across his chest. Standing behind the priest were King Hezekiah and Queen Adirah, and Princess Avora'tru'ivi, who gently held an infant in her arms. The baby girl held her wide eyes in rapt attention.

The priest held up his arms and addressed the audience.

"Today, we gather in hope, in joy, and in triumph, for, against all the forces arrayed against us from time immemorial, the Flame of Zebulon, that ancient fire that has warmed our hearts against the darkness for untold centuries, persists for another generation. To the clouds that beset us, its warm glow blazes out in a gentle, dauntless defiance. Nobody in all our blessed land, in this Far Garden or abroad, embodies the spirit of the Flame of Zebulon more than Crown Prince Tamino, whose courageous leadership has proven, that despite impossible

servitude to your people?"

Tamino nodded soberly, warmed by the radiant smile that Avora'tru'ivi gave him from behind the dais. He then knelt before the dais.

"I do."

The priest gently placed the crown on his head, then turned to Hezekiah, who removed his sword belt and delivered it to the priest.

"Do you promise to, with the might conferred on you by your omnipotent Father-Mother, defend this kingdom from all enemies foreign and familiar, from all dark forces spiritual and temporal?"

Tamino swallowed hard as his eyes focused on the legendary *Zrain'de'zhang*, the sword of his father.

"I do."

"Then accept the mighty *Zrain'de'zhang*, the great Sword of Light, as the symbol of God's assistance in this mighty struggle."

The priest dramatically drew the sword from its scabbard, its brilliance drawing an audible gasp from the crowd. He dubbed Tamino on both shoulders, then sheathed the weapon and proffered it to the prince, who buckled the belt over his coronation finery.

Next, the priest reverently drew two items from the dais- a signet ring and a long staff.

"Do you accept the wisdom and guidance bestowed upon you, in companionship with your responsibility, by the Almighty?"

"I do."

"Then take this, the signet ring of Solomon, and the great Staff of Aaron, which led our people through the wilderness."

The priest slipped the ring onto Tamino's finger and handed him the staff. As was the custom, Tamino banged the staff onto the polished floor, its reverberating report seeming much louder than the wooden rod should have been capable of creating.

Lastly, the patriarch retrieved an elaborately-filigreed scroll.

"Do you accept the great Law, written here on this scroll as it is in our hearts, which shines as the guiding star of our people? Do you swear to uphold the Ten Commandments and the Pact of Uluru with your dying breath?"

"I do."

The priest conferred the magnificent scroll upon Tamino, who tucked it beneath his right arm. Tamino then turned to the audience stretching before him into the indiscernible vastness of the church. Still kneeling, he began to sing the *Vow of Wil'iah*, which his father had famously originated the night he resolved to free his people from the yoke of Frouzee.

As Tamino finished the last stanza, the crowd erupted into patriotic cheering, but they were silenced by a chiding finger-wave from the patriarch.

"There remains one task."

The patriarch produced a porcelain pot filled with oil. He anointed Tamino's head with it, the slick substance sinking into the prince's black hair.

"Stand," the patriarch said simply.

Tamino rose from his kneeling position. The audience couldn't help but think he looked a bit taller than he had before he had knelt down.

"By the authority vested in me as patriarch of the Church of St. Thomas and keeper of the holy Flame of Zebulon, I pronounce you the second king of Wil'iah, defender of the faith and first servant of the Council of Uluru!"

The applause of the audience had to be restrained for a bit longer, for there was still important work to be done. The priest Continued.

"May the Princess Avora'tru'ivi step forward!"

Avora'tru'ivi, still holding her baby, Princess Judith, stepped out from behind the dais. She solemnly knelt before the patriarch, but not before handing the baby to Tamino, who hastily dropped the Staff of Aaron in order to embrace the child, eliciting some stifled giggles from the audience.

The patriarch cleared his throat. "The esteemed position of queen of Wil'iah is a rank of the highest honor. It is she who stands as the great mother of our country, who nurtures it and defends it, and who guides it forward on the higher path. Do you, Princess Avora'tru'ivi of Wil'iah and of the United Kingdom of Ephraim-Manasseh, daughter of Gamaliel IV and Sheerah, War Queen of Ephraim, accept this most solemn duty?"

"I do," Avora'tru'ivi smiled.

Now Queen Adirah stepped forward.

"It is then my joyous duty to confer upon you the saber of the queen of Wil'iah. May its brilliance rouse hope and courage in our people, and may its bite strike terror into those who would seek to extinguish our light." Adirah unbuckled her own sword belt and offered it to the priest, who similarly unsheathed it and waved it about, its rippling surface catching the light and scattering it in a thousand directions. He then dubbed Avora'tru'ivi, sheathed the saber, and proffered it to her.

"By the authority invested in me, I pronounce you queen of Wil'iah, defender of the faith, mother of her people, and keeper of the Flame of Zebulon!

Avora'tru'ivi turned to face the cheering crowd and yelled the great battle-cry of the women of Wil'iah,

"Shekinah!"

There was one final task to be done. The trumpet of the organ blasted out a peal of patriotic sound- the fanfare of the Council of Uluru. Then, to a rousing, building-shaking accompaniment by the organ, the flags of all of Wil'iah's constituent nations marched solemnly down the aisles and took their positions in a semi-circle behind the dais. Last of them all marched Allira, carrying aloft the original battle-standard of Wil'iah, stitched from spare tent cloth during the darkest early days of the War of the Vow. In each place it passed, it left a reverent awe as people beheld, many of them for the first time, the historic flag of freedom.

Allira finally reached Tamino and Avora'tru'ivi, who stood side-by-side before the dais.

"The Council of Uluru, the voice of the people and the ultimate temporal authority of this kingdom, extends its consent to you to rule this nation as its king and queen, subject to the laws and restrictions laid down in the Pact of Uluru. It is our privilege to join our swords with you as we build this nation into an ever-brighter beacon of truth, justice, and freedom."

With that, she proffered to the flag to Avora'tru'ivi, who beamed in response. Judith, still in the crook of Tamino's arm, happily gurgled her own reply. Allira then turned and swept her arm over the vast assembled audience.

"All rise."

A sound like thunder filled the church as thousands of people rose to their feet, but this was nothing next to the wave of sound that filled every void and space within the proud building.

"God save the king! God save the queen! God save Wil'iah!"

CHAPTER FORTY-FIVE

MILCAH

A short time later, Tamino and Avora'tru'ivi returned to the palace, Tamino gently holding the sleeping Princess Judith in his arms.

"She looks so peaceful," Tamino said wistfully.

"Her life, and our lives, are about to get a lot busier!" Avora'tru'ivi declared brightly. Suddenly, her voice became serious as she looked her husband in the eyes.

"I'm proud of you. I know how you feel about this, and I want to know that we will take every step of this journey together." She bent down to kiss the baby. "You might almost say we have two children to care for now- Judy and Wil'iah."

Tamino smiled, but his eyes betrayed no small amount

of apprehension.

"That's quite the handful…"

"Which is why I figured we could use some help." Avora'tru'ivi walked over to a silk cord and pulled, ringing a small, tinkling bell in the hallway. A few moments later, the knock sounded at the door.

"Come in!" Avora'tru'ivi breezily answered.

The door opened to reveal a tall, gaunt woman with a bony, sunken face, whose long, pointed nose reminded Tamino somewhat of a bird. She held in her hand a large black bag.

"This is Milcah. She was my brother Gideon's governess when he was a boy."

Milcah curtly nodded.

"Alright, if you think this is necessary, I trust your judgement," Tamino said. He kindly regarded the governess. "It's a pleasure to meet you, Milcah."

"Likewise," she said, her voice reassuringly steely. With gawky, long strides, she walked over to peer at the baby in Tamino's arms.

"What a lovely child," she said. "I suppose it's time for her to go to bed."

Tamino sighed, regretting every moment he had to be apart from the baby. "I suppose so." He reluctantly handed Judith over to Milcah, who nodded her head once again and bore the child over to the crib in the corner of the room, gently cooing.

"Sleep, child. Milcah will take care of you."

Tamino, about to step out the door, turned around to face the governess.

"One more thing, Milcah. I'm worried about my father. He never used to need a cane, but he seems to lean on it more and more every day. I'm concerned he isn't taking care of himself. He insists that everything is fine, but I'm not convinced. I'd appreciate it if you'd keep an eye on him as well. Make sure he's eating and sleeping as much as he needs to – he's always been known to deprive himself if he thinks there's work that needs to be done."

Milcah gave him a curt nod.

"Of course. That would be my privilege, Your Faithfulness."

CHAPTER FORTY-SIX

THE TRUE PRIZE

Gath, Frouzean Empire. 1291 AD

Delilah stood on the balcony of the palace of Gath, surveying her newly-expanded demesne. The addition of Tanitania to the Frouzean Empire had restored it to its original size prior to its conquest of Zebulon and the Aboriginal territories in 1223. Briseis walked up to her, clad in a billowy toga.

"Well, Iph—Delilah" Briseis hastily corrected, "I wouldn't believe it, if my wondering eyes didn't see it myself. You really did it. You got everything you wanted."

A faraway look suddenly filled Delilah's eyes. "Not

everything. This is just a stepping stone to the true prize. This is just the beginning."

Briseis' eyes grew wide. "It is? You really don't think we should stop here, at the pinnacle of success?"

Delilah suddenly stopped moving and cocked her head quizzically. "We? Who said anything about *we*? Never mind that. I have a mission for you."

Briseis recoiled, stung by her friend's words. "What is it?"

"You, my darling, are going to go where no Frouzean dares to tread. Only someone as trusted as you could complete this mission. You are going to go to Wil'iah. And there"— Delilah gave a surprisingly wistful sigh, "—you are going to see the true prize."

"True prize?"

"Yes, the true prize. Do you really think we have fully restored the empire? Of course not! I once ruled this whole continent! I must again if I am to defy the Mongols!"

Briseis' eyebrows arched.

"You did?"

Delilah sat back, smiling. "Frouzee did. And that's who I am, remember? Of course you do. Anyway, everything we have accomplished up to this point has lead up to this next achievement -- the reconquest of Wil'iah. Oh, I know what you're thinking, Briseis. Wil'iah is a powerful nation now, a match for our armed forces. That, of course, is why we aren't going to conquer Wil'iah with weapons of war. I will take Wil'iah the way I have taken the rest of my empire."

"You're going to marry the king and then kill him?"

"I don't know what you're talking about, Briseis! To make light of the tragedy that was my wedding night- *how could you?"* Delilah feigned shock and insult. "Sitting on the throne of Wil'iah is the most scrumptious man I have ever laid eyes on – and the moment I did, I resolved that I would have him for myself. When Ashtoreth saw fit to make me her vessel, that became a possibility. Everything I have worked for has led to this moment. All my efforts have been to give me – to give us – a better bargaining position. Between the fact that my armies can protect him from Kublai Khan's hordes and my unequaled, ravishing beauty, the way forward will be clear to Tamino."

Briseis frowned. "I've heard that Wil'iahn men are different."

Delilah's eyes flashed dangerously at her. "All men are the same! The Wil'iahns may hide their true inclinations behind their self-aggrandizing, moralizing masks, but in the end, they are no different. Just like Achilles, just like Hasdrubal, Tamino will fall. And when he does, the continent is ours – and what I deserve will be mine!"

CHAPTER FORTY-SEVEN

AN ENVOY OF DARKNESS

Trukanamoa, Wil'iah

*J*amino sat at his desk in his office in the palace of Trukanamoa, resignedly looking at the enormous pile of mail from all corners of the kingdom that threatened to spill off the polished wooden surface.

One at a time, he thought. For old time's sake, he decided to start with mail from Kati-Thanda. He read through procedural report after procedural report, vainly attempting to suppress yawns. Suddenly, an unusual scroll caught his eye. He pulled it from the pile, and his stomach dropped to the floor as his unbelieving eyes saw the seal that held the scroll together.

In angry red wax was the symbol of the Frouzean Empire.

✳ ✳ ✳

A few short, frantic minutes later, Tamino and Avora'tru'ivi, and stood anxiously at a table in the War Room, deep in the castle of Trukanamoa. Steps rang out as another figure emerged through the doorway- Jeremiah, Tamino's brother. Four years younger than the King, what he lacked in experience he made up for with intensity. Dark, coal-like eyes smoldered under sharp, angular eyebrows, accentuating his sharp features, severe mouth, and close-cropped hair. He grimly regarded the king and queen as Tamino opened the scroll.

We bring the greetings and felicitations, and congratulations to your esteemed personage upon your coronation, of Frouzee Delilah, Eternal Empress of the Reconstituted Empire of Frouzea. As your numerous spies have undoubtedly already informed you, I have been busily putting my country back together. But I assure you that, your inevitable fears to the contrary, the new Frouzea means you no harm. To prove this, I wish to send you an envoy- my handmaiden Briseis, to meet with you and discuss how our two nations can move forward together. I can assure you that she is harmless. If you will accept her presence, she will arrive at the City of Verwonnah on the Kati-Thanda border in one month's time, then proceed to Trukanamoa.
> *Signed*
> *Her Worship Delilah, Second Incarnation to Earth of the Goddess Astarte and Frouzee of the Frouzean Empire, including the Principalities of Gath, Gaza, Ekron, Ashkelon, and Ashdod, the Territories of Outer Frouzea, Ithaca, and Nullarbor, the Provinces*

280

of Arboria, and Aurania, and the Imperial Provinces of Upper and Lower Tanitania.

"Well, the moment we've all been fearing is finally here. The Frouzean Empire is fully renewed." Jeremiah shook his head. "I told you, we should have invaded the first we heard of this 'Delilah' woman and her attempt at empire building. It seems we have gravely underestimated her."

Avora'tru'ivi suppressed a snort. "Her signature is nearly as long as the letter itself."

"Before we jump to conclusions," Tamino interjected, "Don't you think it's the wise thing to do to accept this visitor and see if she truly is genuine? We left Frouzea out of our plans for the League of Shechem because it was a failed, broken state. That isn't true anymore. Maybe this note is sincere."

"She refers to herself as 'Her Worship,'" Avora'tru'ivi said pointedly.

Tamino chuckled. "That much is true. Clearly, Frouzea has not yet gotten over its misguided fascination with all things pagan. Nevertheless, I think it's a good idea to at least hear them out before we let loose the dogs of war. Besides," he said gently, "she's not coming. She's apparently sending a lackey. I know you both believe, deep down, that there is good in everyone. Maybe we can awaken the good in her. Perhaps, even if this mission of theirs begins with deviousness, it can end with new understanding. Perhaps an ancient enemy can be turned into a friend."

Jeremiah rolled his eyes, but before he could object, Tamino continued.

"She will be afforded the same courtesy that any other foreign dignitary would receive. We are clearly instructed by scripture to treat the foreigner as if they were one of our own."

"This is outrageous! I don't think she should even be allowed to set foot on our soil! I have made my position clear. When the Frouzean Empire began to reconstitute itself, we should have invaded immediately." Jeremiah retorted.

"Gentlemen, gentlemen," Avora'tru'ivi interjected sweetly, trying to muster a soothing tone. "Galbi may be correct. Is it right for us to immediately assume that the new Frouzea has devious intentions? I instinctively mistrust them too, but perhaps we should not be so quick to judge."

"Mother and Father have told me everything I need to know about Frouzea," said Jeremiah. Turning to his brother, he continued, "If you insist on allowing this envoy of darkness to trespass our ramparts, that is your prerogative as king. But note my objections. I will attend whatever function you put together, as it is my duty as sovereign protector, but I will not promise to be a warm and gracious host. And, whatever you do, don't give her access to any military or tactical information. That includes castle tours, or even a moment's glance at our guns."

Tamino nodded. "She will not be permitted to enter the castle. We will receive her here, at the palace, and she will be escorted to our door and from it by an armed guard. I don't think it is fair to judge a new nation so severely that we won't even speak with it. That said, we will proceed with extreme caution."

As everyone filed out of the room, Tamino suddenly paused, realizing there was another person he needed to consult. A few short minutes later, he found himself facing a rough-hewn wooden door. He knocked gently.

"Come in," said a voice, clearly trying to muster a modicum of strength. Tamino hesitated, then opened the door and stepped through.

Hezekiah sat propped up in bed, eating a rather-unappetizing, mushy looking porridge. Milcah flitted around the bed, gathering dishes.

"Well, look who it is!" Tamino's father said brightly, but Tamino internally winced. He was looking weaker than ever.

"Father, I don't know how to tell you this, but we just received a letter confirming our worst fears. The Frouzean Empire has reconstituted."

Hezekiah sat up a little bit straighter in the bed, a cloud of concern crossing his eyes. "That is...disturbing."

"They wish to send an envoy here to establish a diplomatic relationship. We decided there was no harm in simply talking to them, but I'm not sure if I like where this is headed."

The old King scratched his chin. "I suppose not. History doesn't have to repeat itself. Perhaps there is a chance for reconciliation."

"I hope so. I just don't want to see everything you built destroyed."

Hezekiah managed a weak smile. "You worry too much. Just listen, Tamino. You will be guided to make the necessary decisions. I trust you."

Tamino almost snapped into a military salute before leaving, but instead walked forward and gave the old man a gentle hug. As he turned to leave, he motioned for Milcah to follow.

"What do you think is going on? How bad is it?" he asked.

"I don't understand myself. I can't figure out what's wrong. I don't think his life is in danger, but I don't think it's prudent for him to participate in any diplomatic discussions with Frouzea."

Tamino nodded grimly. "You're probably right."

A tear leaked out of the corner of the nursemaid's eye. "I wish I knew what to do. I feel like I'm failing him."

Tamino gently took Milcah's hand and looked her in the eye.

"Don't worry, Milcah. You're doing your best. We all know that."

"Indeed. Thank you, Your Faithfulness."

CHAPTER FORTY-EIGHT

INTO THE TEETH OF THE ENEMY

Gath, Frouzean Empire

𝓑riseis jumped as a bell rang in her quarters, indicating that her mistress needed her. Rousting herself from bed, she rubbed sleep from her eyes.

"What is it?" Salome asked sleepily.

"I'm sure it doesn't concern you," Briseis said icily as she slipped a robe over her sleeping clothes and dashed towards Delilah's chambers. To her eternal exasperation, Salome followed.

They entered the chamber to see Delilah reading a scroll, a triumphant expression on her face.

"Ah, Briseis darling, just who I wanted to see."

"You did ring my bell."

"Ah yes, I did, didn't I?" Delilah jubilantly waved the scroll in Briseis' face.

"They took the bait! Start packing your bags, darling."

Briseis smiled, more grimly than she intended to.

Into the teeth of the enemy.

"Are you sure this is a great idea, Your Worship?"

"Darling, this is the culmination of all we have worked for. This is my dream. You'd help me achieve my dream, wouldn't you?"

"Of course, Your Worship."

"I don't understand. Where is she going?" Salome whined petulantly.

A ghastly smile spread across Delilah's face.

"Wil'iah."

"WHAT? Why wasn't I told? Why wasn't I informed?"

Briseis finally snapped. "Because *I* am her trusted confidant."

With that, she strode out of the room, mentally preparing a checklist of items for her upcoming journey.

Salome was left sputtering.

"Who does she think she is!?"

Delilah merely smiled.

CHAPTER FORTY-NINE

BRISEIS GOES TO TRUKANAMOA

Trukanamoa, Wil'iah

Briseis alit from the carriage, trying not to trip on the extravagant gown she had been made to wear for the occasion. She suppressed an involuntary gasp as she beheld the very heart of her nation's hated enemy all around her. To her left soared the stern dome of the Church of the Eternal Victory, and the vast verdant expanse of the Elysium Gardens receded into the distance to her right. However, the building that stood in front of her was surprisingly unassuming. Only three stories tall, it was dwarfed by the surrounding government buildings, and, apart from the covered pavilion on its gold-burnished roof, was almost completely unadorned, its façade consisting only of neatly-whitewashed sandstone.

"*This* is the palace?" She asked the knight who stood sentinel next to her.

"Yes, ma'am." He said.

"Hmpf," she snorted.

The doors to the palace noiselessly swung open to reveal a plump, droll little man flanked on either side by tall knights in full parade armor. With a broad smile on his face, he walked up to Briseis and dipped his head, placing a fist over his heart and then extending an open palm.

"Your excellency," he said, "Welcome to Trukanamoa. We have been expecting you. I am 'Enaua'ivanu, master of the household of the royal palace of Wil'iah. The king and queen are preparing to receive you. Before we show you to your guest rooms, the king would like to have a word with you." He turned back to the entrance and clapped his hands twice. Two lines of six housekeepers marched out of the doors and began to pick up Briseis' multifarious pieces of luggage. The rotund house master spun on his heel and walked back toward the entrance, motioning for Briseis to follow.

Briseis braced herself for a magnificently colonnaded hall, like the throne room in Gath, bedecked with battle-flags and adorned with melodramatic statues. As it was, she was totally unprepared for the sight that greeted her as two intimidating women swept open the iron-studded double doors in perfect unison.

Meeting Briseis' eyes was not an imperious throne room, but a surprisingly cozy office. The room itself was smaller by far than even Delilah's bathroom. There was not a single column in sight; rather, the room was elegantly paneled in Indonesian hardwoods and was gently lit by the leaping flames of a fireplace at its opposite end; above its mantle was a shield that she recognized as the personal coat-of-arms of the king; flanking it were the flag of Wil'iah and the royal standard, and standing on either side of the fireplace were the tahili poles of the king and queen. Commanding the center of the room was a large, finely-carved desk, rather than a domineering throne. Sunk in an easy chair behind the desk was a man who appeared to be furiously writing notes on a scroll of paper. Noticing her entry, he seemed to shake himself from whatever he had been concentrating on, leaned forward, folded his hands together, and looked up earnestly at Briseis.

"Ah yes, the emissary of Frouzea! We've been expecting you. How can I help you today?"

Briseis was taken aback. *This can't be the king,* she thought. Briseis had grown up with terrifying stories of Tamino's father Hezekiah; it was said in Frouzea that his very gaze could slice through stone. In contrast, the kindness of this man's features and the warmth of his voice seemed almost entirely uncharacteristic of the Wil'iah she had been raised to expect.

"Her excellency Briseis, envoy of the Frouzean Empire," announced one of the guards that had admitted her to the office. Briseis detected a note of disgust at her last two words, tinged with something else- was it fear?

I would have added additional titles and honorifics, thought Briseis, her umbrage helping mask some of the anxiety that bubbled up in her stomach.

The man at the desk suddenly shot up out of the chair, revealing a commanding height, and gave her a somewhat sheepish look as he extended his open hand in her direction.

"Forgive me, Your Excellency! I am Tamino ben'Hezekiah, first servant of the Kingdom of Wil'iah and, well, you probably know the rest." Motioning toward an easy chair that stood in front of the desk, he added, "Please, have a seat. I believe we have much to discuss."

Briseis tentatively stepped forward before sinking into the surprisingly comfortable chair. She had been told that Wil'iahns slept on planks of hardwood to maintain discipline. Nervously clearing her throat, Briseis prepared to run through the script that Delilah had drilled into her.

"I bring the greetings and felicitations of Delilah, Second Incarnation to Earth of the Goddess Astarte, Eternal Empress of the Empire of Frouzea, Mistress of the Isles, Dominator of the Principalities of Gath, Gaza, Ashkelon, Ashdod, and Ekron and the territories of Nullarbor, Ithaca, and Outer Frouzea, Brilliant Image of the Goddess Tanit and Heir to Dido, by Divine Right ruler of the Imperial Provinces of the Empire of Carthage and the provinces of Arboria and Aurania, and Sovereign of Palestine, Egypt, Attica, Argolis, Mycenae, Epirus, the Peloponnesus, Macedonia, the Cyclades, Crete, Thrace, Canaan, and Atlantis." Briseis noticed Tamino barely suppress a wry smile as she ran through her Empress' increasingly dubious titles.

"I see," he said.

"She wishes me to convey to you her expressions of friendship and cooperation, and a desire for coordinated activities in the defense of our mutual interests on this continent."

Tamino sat back. "And what might those interests be?"

"The defense of our lands against the Mongol Empire, of course. To this end, Her Worship would like to make an official state visit to this great city at your earliest convenience."

"Surely she understands that cooperation between our nations lacks historical precedence," Tamino replied.

"Naturally. But Her Worship wishes to put the…unpleasantries of the past behind us all. She only wishes for peace," Briseis batted her eyelashes in the "Scheherazade technique" that Delilah had taught her, "and love."

Tamino cleared his throat. "Interesting. I must inform you that, at the moment, the Kingdom of Wil'iah does not extend diplomatic recognition to the 'Empire' of Frouzea in its current form. The circumstances of its restoration are, as I am sure you are aware, somewhat suspicious. However, we are an open-hearted people, and we have no need to hold on to expired hatreds. We will think on your request. In the meantime, you have traveled a great distance to come to our blessed city. You must be famished. We are preparing a great feast for you. I think these topics will be better discussed over a meal."

Briseis winced. She knew from her training that Wil'iahns mostly ate raw meat and bugs. Supposedly it was some sort of character-building exercise. Forcing a smile, she responded.

"Thank you, your Highness. I'm looking forward to it."

"'Enaua'ivanu will show you to your guest rooms while the food is prepared." As he said this, the droll butler arrived at the office and motioned for Briseis to follow. Tamino gave a curt nod and returned to his notes. With a pang of shame, Briseis realized that she had forgotten to peek at what they were. She had probably missed a priceless chance at tactical information.

"We are preparing the finest Tjoritja cuisine for you," Enaua'ivanu said as they made several turns on a dark-paneled hallway lined with the coats of arms of Wil'iah's constituent nations. Briseis winced, wondering what "Tjoritja cuisine" entailed. As she studied the coats-of arms on the walls, she reflected on Wil'iah's confusing political system, in which the indigenous inhabitants of the Kingdom's territories held full property rights and merely allowed Zebulite Wil'iahns to live on their land.

Why don't they just take the land by force? That's what we did. It would make governance much simpler.

After a few moments, they passed out of an archway into a beautiful courtyard overflowing with flowers brought from the four corners of the known world, punctuated by the sweet sound of leaping fountain water. In front of them was a second pavilion set back from the main palace building, its trapezoid-shaped roof reminiscent of a typical home found in one of the South Seas islands.

'Enaua'ivanu led her into the left most of what were apparently two guest suites. Eyeing the bed overflowing with plush cushions and expensive silks and the richly-painted ceiling, Briseis couldn't help but be impressed. This was hardly the hardwood board she had been led to expect. A table in the middle of the room featured an intricately-painted porcelain vase of fresh bird-of-paradise flowers and an assortment of food items; bugs were noticeably absent.

"I will allow you to get yourself situated. Dinner is in two hours. If you need anything, please ring the bell on the wall. We would be more than happy to assist you." The man once again rendered the civilian salute, then ducked out of the room, leaving Briseis alone with her thoughts of surprise at the respectful reception she had received.

I thought they hated us. Why are they being so nice to me?

table piled high with a wide variety of desert culinary specialties- and none of it was raw or crawling.

The woman marched through the entrance, cleared her throat, and announced, "Her excellency Briseis, envoy of the Frouzean Empire."

As Briseis entered the dining room, five people at the table stood to greet her. On the left side of the table stood a commanding, heavyset woman, her broad features seemingly set in a perpetual frown even as she tried to manage a welcoming smile. Next to her stood a tall, broad-shouldered, severe-looking man clad in partial armor. His angular face, widely-flared nostrils, resolutely set mouth, and slightly narrowed eyebrows instantly told her that this man was less than thrilled at her presence as his intense eyes seemed to bore into her.

Tamino stood at the head of the table. Slightly taller than his dour compatriot, he was dressed in a more clearly-civilian assemblage emblazoned with various medals, some of which she had been taught to recognize as the symbols of the Wil'iahn King's Rangers, the crest of the House of David, and the emblem of the League of Shechem – a torch held aloft against the darkness. He also wore a red waratah flower on his left lapel, which struck Briseis as an odd affectation. Unlike the man to the left, his squarish features broke into a wide smile, the corners of his kindly eyes crinkling with mirth. Briseis realized that he even reminded her somewhat of a large, friendly dog.

At the right side of the table stood another woman, whose large eyes betrayed a mixture of sweetness and suspicion. Even so, her long face broke into a radiant smile, her teeth standing out against her bronze skin and voluminous black hair. Next to her stood a dignified, regal Aboriginal woman who seemed to be looking down her nose at Briseis, her withering gaze making the normally self-confident envoy feel quite small.

Tamino spoke first.

"Allow us to welcome you, your Excellency. We have much to speak about this evening." As he rendered the civilian salute, Briseis noted, as she had in the office, that even his voice was warmer than the stereotype she had come to expect of Wil'iahns as stone-cold fanatics. Briefly glancing back at the man standing next to him, though, Briseis wondered if the tropes were in fact rooted in reality.

Tamino continued with his introductions. "It is my privilege to introduce Lady Deborah of Dhirari, Captain of Zebulon," he said, motioning to the intimidating woman to Briseis' left. The king next pointed to the dour man that flanked him. "And Jeremiah, Sovereign Protector." As the King's hand passed to the woman to Briseis' right, his features softened yet more as his smile broadened. "My wife, Avora'tru'ivi, Queen of Wil'iah and Princess of Manasseh." Finally reaching the Aboriginal lady, he concluded, "Her Excellency Allira of the Arrernte Nation and Prime Minister of the Council of Uluru."

"It is my pleasure to make your acquaintances," Briseis responded, trying to remember the Wil'iahn social graces she had learned during her intelligence training.

Tamino sat down at the head of the table, the other Wil'iahns instantly following his lead. Avora'tru'ivi picked up her fork, signaling that all could begin to eat.

"Now," Tamino began, "We are all interested in the reasons for your visit. We've discussed this briefly, but please repeat what you told me so everyone can hear. It is our understanding that the Philistine principalities have once again united into an empire led by a new Frouzee, and that even Tanitania has been brought under its flag, although by somewhat suspicious means."

"King Hasdrubal died in an unfortunate accident,"

Briseis protested. "It was widely known that he had an excessive taste for wine. It finally caught up with him."

A knowing smile crossed the king's face. "Perhaps. Nevertheless, surely Your Excellency can understand that our nation views these developments with some amount of trepidation. We respect the right of the Frouzean and Tanitanian peoples to self-determination, but we are concerned about the long-term aims of this new agglomeration of states."

Briseis feigned shock. "Surely you don't suspect that my eternal empress has designs on Wil'iah?"

"Not having met her, I don't presume to judge," Tamino responded.

"Forgive me, Your Excellency, but I don't have to meet her to have my suspicions," interjected Jeremiah, earning him a dirty look from the queen.

"Back to my original question," recovered Tamino, "Please tell everyone the nature of your visit."

Briseis nervously cleared her throat, and withdrew a small scroll from her pocket. "I come bearing a message from the Goddess Astarte, Eternal Empress of the Principalities of Gath, Gaza, Ekron, Ashkelon, and Ashdod, Dominator of the territories of the Nullarbor, Ithaca, and Outer Frouzea, High Queen of the Imperial Provinces of Upper and Lower Tanitania and the Provinces of Arboria and Aurania, and by historical right Queen of Argolis, Attica, Epirus, Thrace, Asia Minor, Egypt, Canaan, Phoenicia, Carthage, Iberia, Utica, Mycenae, Troy, Achaea, and Atlantis."

Jeremiah barely suppressed a scoff as Tamino responded with the wry smile he had rendered the last time Briseis had rattled off Delilah's titles, Deborah instinctively clenched her fist, Avora'tru'ivi pursed her lips, and Allira crossed her arms.

Briseis cleared her throat again, and continued with her message. "The Frouzee Delilah wishes the warmest greetings and salutations to His Majesty King Tamino of Wil'iah, and her congratulations to his person upon his accession to the throne of that esteemed nation. She desires only for the restored Empire of Frouzea and her neighbor to the north to be bound in close ties of friendship as this continent prepares to defend itself against the menace beyond. She wishes to pay her respects to His Majesty and his family in person, and proposes to make a state visit to the blessed city of Trukanamoa in two months, upon which time she wishes to conclude a pact of mutual cooperation between our nations."

Tamino's compatriots looked thoroughly taken aback. Jeremiah's eyes narrowed.

"Such saccharine sentiments are uncharacteristic of one who bears her titles," he responded. "Surely this offer carries with it conditions."

Briseis feigned grave insult. "True friends demand no conditions, sovereign protector. It is in our best interests to be at peace with our neighbors. Besides, our empire is mighty enough to need nothing from you." She finished rather pointedly.

Queen Avora'tru'ivi spoke next. "I have no need to perpetuate the mistrusts and hatreds of our ancestors." Turning to Tamino, she exchanged a glance with him and continued. "However, I am curious to hear more from you about the nature of the Empress's accession to the throne. The circumstances of her meteoric rise seem too convenient."

Briseis squarely faced the Queen, even as she quailed slightly inside. "The eternal empress commands the respect and adoration of her people. She rules by their consent, not by the whim of princes and kings."

"And what of the four princes or kings who have mysteriously died in the last year?"

Briseis allowed herself to chuckle as she gave the queen a knowing look. "Well, Your Majesty, you know how men can be, always getting themselves into trouble with their lusts and boasts." Hastily turning to regard Tamino and Jeremiah, she bowed her head in respect. "Present company excluded, of course. It is well known that Wil'iahns are…different."

Tamino didn't acknowledge her last statement one way or the other. "In any case, Your Excellency, you may take a message back to your leader. Tell her that we will assent to her visit to our city in two months' time. However, she must come with no more than four guards, and must consent to armed escort at all times while within our borders. She is to report to the border fortress of Vreva'novahi in the nation of Arabana, then proceed on the Capital Road through Kati-Thanda into Tjoritja. She will be received here and afforded the same courtesies we would give any foreign dignitary. She will be permitted to remain here for forty-eight hours. Tell her we have no wish to continue the enmity between our peoples, and it is our fond hope that someday our nations can live in peace. However"— the king suddenly narrowed his eyebrows and pointedly locked eyes with Briseis, "We do not for a moment think that the circumstances that allowed the Empress's rise to power were coincidental. Nor is our hope blinded with naivety. Our nation is fully prepared to defend itself."

Allira nodded in agreement. "The Council of Uluru echoes the king's statements. Your empress is welcome to visit and discuss ways that our nations can put aside their differences. But the peoples of Wil'iah will make no territorial, military, or economic concessions in pursuit of such an end."

"Very well," responded Briseis, "I will relay your assent to the Empress. In the meantime, I should like to take the opportunity to explore the city further. It is rare that someone from my country is permitted to see it. Many are the tales of the wonders hidden behind the staunch walls of Trukanamoa."

"I think that can be arranged," said Tamino, earning himself a sharp look from Jeremiah. "Perhaps after dessert, we can take you on a brief tour of the major monuments of the city. Afterwards, we have a presentation prepared for you."

Jeremiah quickly interjected, "However, I'm afraid anything you see will be restricted to civilian landmarks. I'm sure you can understand why."

What a cold fish, thought Briseis. *He must really hate us.*

CHAPTER FIFTY-ONE

THE WAR MEMORIAL OPERA HOUSE

*L*ater that evening, the king, queen, and Prince Jeremiah, in conjunction with four members of the Judith Corps, the Amazon-like queen's guards, joined Briseis for a stroll around the Elysium Gardens that fronted the palace before a performance at the opera house.

As they emerged from the front gate, Tamino pointed to his right toward the enormous dome rising far in the distance, its burnished tiles reflecting the abundant moonlight.

"That is the Cathedral of the Eternal Victory, the largest church in Christendom," he said, his friendly voice tinged with a note of pride. "It was built by my father. The central dome's diameter is one hundred-forty cubits."

Briseis swallowed hard as she realized the victory the church commemorated was her nation's destruction.

Queen Avora'tru'ivi pointed out a group of seven domes rising majestically from a reflecting pool filled with water lilies. "Those are the palaces of the Council of Uluru, our representative government. We spend much of our time there convincing the council to approve of our plans."

That's stupid. In Frouzea, we just do what we want. How inefficient.

Across the garden from them was a massive block of sandstone that loomed forbiddingly over the steps that led to its entrances. Tamino pointed to it.

"That is the Palace of Justice, home to our nation's highest court. It was built in the High Vrengaic style by my father in a design after Solomon's Temple in Jerusalem. Next to it is the new War of the Vow Memorial Opera House, home to our nation's highest artistic achievements. Actually, while your empress will be here, the Opera will be performing *The Song of Deborah*, one of our most beloved pieces. That building is our end destination this evening. We have a special showcase for you."

Avora'tru'ivi gently squeezed Tamino's arm and jokingly shook her head. "Tamino takes his opera very seriously. You would be hard-pressed to find someone with a more encyclopedic knowledge."

"What is it actually like? In my country, it is said that Wil'iahn opera consists almost entirely of incoherent screeching punctuated by war drums and people waving around weapons."

Tamino gently laughed. "It's a bit more sophisticated than that, although some of our songs can get...energetic."

Jeremiah interjected, *"Especially Tear Down the Gates of Hell!* —a song I'm sure your people aren't terribly fond of."

Avora'tru'ivi gave him a pointed stare as Tamino

tried to interject.

"Tonight's performance is a bit more peaceful. We want to make sure you get an accurate impression of our country," he said, giving his brother a sidelong squint.

After the tour, the balance of which consisted of a meander through the gardens and a visit to the major monuments contained therein, the party arrived at the doors of the opera house. The enormous sandstone building towered over them; Briseis suddenly felt very small for the second time that night.

Settling in to another surprisingly comfortable chair (Briseis was beginning to question her sources about the Wil'iahns' furniture preferences,) she took in the decoration of the interior. Where Tamino's office had been Spartan but comfortable, the Opera House was overwhelming and grand. The ceiling was painted with thousands of gold-leaf stars; at its center was an enormous chandelier of colored glass in the shape of the Star of Wil'iah, inside of which burned a flame. Tamino, seated beside her, leaned in and whispered.

"The stars are painted to represent their arrangement on the night my father took the Vow of Wil'iah, in which he swore to create a free country."

The walls were covered in richly-painted bas-reliefs depicting scenes from what Briseis could only assume was Wil'iahn history. She was ashamed to admit she didn't know much; only that the insolent "people of the dirt" had rebelled against and destroyed the Frouzean Empire, leaving its former principalities destitute. One panel depicted waves splitting apart dramatically while a man raised a staff; another one showed a group of men carrying a mysterious box away from a burning city. The next showed a fleet of double-hulled ships following a blazing star; this was followed by an image of some sort of lean-to structure with a similar looking star above it, with three men kneeling. Other panels showed what she assumed were battle scenes from the war against Frouzea; with an intake of breath, she noticed some of her own national symbols carved into the stone- but not complimentarily.

The chandelier dimmed, indicating that Tamino's mysterious show was about to begin.

A heavyset woman wearing a crown of flowers walked out onto the stage, lifted her hands, and began to chant. Behind her, a group of interpretive dancers were clearly acting out what she was saying with fluid yet powerful movements. The woman's graceful but forceful voice spoke of many things unfamiliar to Briseis; how Abraham had first listened to God and become a faithful servant; how the Children of Israel, including Zebulon, had been delivered from Egypt to the Promised Land, and there came into the original conflict with the Philistines (when Briseis asked Tamino how long ago this had been, she was shocked to learn that David had slain Goliath over 2200 years prior); how the United Monarchy had failed and split into the Kingdoms of Israel and Judah; how Israel fell into decadence and was destroyed at the hands of the Assyrians, banishing the ten lost tribes into the eastern desert, where a brave remnant led by Zebulon tried to restore them to the true path; how Judah persevered under Hezekiah and threw back the Assyrians, but in time fell into the same decay as Israel; how the prophet Jeremiah, seeing the future, was called by God to "build and to plant" by rallying the remnants of Judah and the Ten Lost Tribes and establishing them elsewhere; how Jeremiah delivered the Ark of the Covenant and the riches of Solomon in secret to Eleazar ben'Helon, Captain of Zebulon; how Judah fell to Babylon and Zebulon rescued Jeremiah and the Princess Tea-Tephi from certain destruction in Egypt; how the great remnant fled east on the great *Maka'ivi*, a forty-year journey to a new Promised Land; how they had settled for a long residency on the Mother Island, creating a new culture, before deciding that "God's Far Garden" had not yet been reached; how they embarked on the final journey to arrive in the land they now called home, establishing the Kingdoms of Ephraim, Manasseh, Issachar, and Zebulon – for these tribes had persevered on the great journey where others had lost their resolution and faltered. Thus concluded the first great chapter in the story of Wil'iah.

The woman retreated backstage and was replaced by a regal man who came onstage arrayed in exotic robes that shimmered in a thousand colors; he began to sing the *Song of Casper*, the story of the Zebulite people's long watch for the coming of the Messiah. He told of how a great star appeared in the sky over the royal city of Zebulon (present-day Trujustakanoa), and he embarked on a great journey back to the now-mythical motherland, bearing gold for the great king; how this king turned out to be something infinitely different but infinitely more wonderful than expected; how the people of Zebulon maintained their watch for news of this mysterious savior in the west; how seventy-two years later the Apostle Thomas arrived on their shores with the Good News. At this, "Good King Casper" bowed his head and retreated backstage, to be replaced with a chorus of three women who told the valorous tales of the mighty battles and scholarly triumphs of the late, great Kingdom of Zebulon.

At long last the singers came to the part of the story that Briseis thought she knew. How the enemy Philistine states coalesced into the great Frouzean Empire under Frouzee Jezebel; how it was an unstoppable tide that swept over all of the continent; how Zebulon valiantly resisted, but ultimately was defeated and destroyed; how King

Jehoshaphat and Queen Abigail fought to the bitter end, even as their city was overrun and put to the torch. And here it seemed the story was over, that the forces of evil had prevailed. But it was not so, for in the final moments of Zebulon's freedom, Abigail bore a son that was spirited away in secret to Manasseh to continue the line of David. The story continued; Frouzea brought Issachar and Ephraim to heel and reduced Manasseh to ruin; once again it looked as though the light of freedom was about to go out. Yet again it was not so, for brave Prince Gamaliel of Manasseh swore never to surrender to Frouzea and rallied his nation to continued resistance; in Ephraim, Sheerah, War Queen, seized the throne and smashed the idols of Gath, raising her people to rebellion. In Manasseh, an obscure warrior named Gershom rose up the ranks of Gamaliel's forces, becoming the nation's champion and defender; one night on the moors, a great star ignited in the night and God revealed to Gershom his true identity- he was Hezekiah, heir to the throne of Zebulon and the House of David.

At this, a man clad in gleaming armor emerged onto the stage; in a mellifluous baritone, he began to sing the much-beloved *Vow of Wil'iah*, Hezekiah's emphatic statement of determination to create a new free nation greater than any that had come before; to establish justice and the rule of law throughout the land; to defend the innocent and set alight a defiant flame against the forces of darkness; to prove to all the world that a great state could be built on the values of honesty, decency, fidelity, purity, and courage. As his voice soared and his fist clenched a shining replica of the *Zrain'de'zhang*, the great Sword of Light that had purportedly descended from the heavens to lead the people of Zebulon and their newfound Aboriginal allies to freedom, Briseis even felt her heart stir just a bit.

This caused no small amount of alarm, for this was exactly the story that she had been raised to loathe. But here, in the many-splendored halls of the War Memorial Opera House, with the singer's rousing voice backed by the grand thunder of the organ, with boldly-colored battle-flags hanging all around, with the amiable personage of the king beside her, and with the high-minded words of the Vow of Wil'iah filling her ears, Briseis felt a twinge of doubt. This was not the lawless rabble of "mudfaces" she had been raised to hate. They spoke of freedom, decency, honesty…such words were rarely uttered in Frouzea.

Shaking herself, Briseis fought to regain control. She had a job to do. She was here to assess Wil'iah's defenses, not to swoon over its ideals.

Suddenly, the soaring song was over, and the lights of the theater came back on.

"What about the rest of the story?" Briseis asked the king.

"I think we all know what happened. There is no need to rehearse unpleasantries between our nations. We merely want you to understand why we took the stand that we did. We have never wanted anything but the ability to pursue our ways in peace. We have no wish for continued enmity with your nation, if you will allow us to follow our higher paths unmolested. But, as I am sure you know, we will not hesitate to defend ourselves. You can tell that to your empress, and if she is willing to listen to reason, she is more than welcome to come for a state visit. Know only that our terms will not change. This is the Faithful Kingdom. Here we stand, and we cannot follow any other path."

As they returned across the gardens from the Elysium, Briseis studied the queen more carefully out of the corner of her eye. She was unlike any woman she had seen in Frouzea. She walked with her head held high and her shoulders set back, her towering frame exuding power and authority. She seemed to serve no man explicitly, a concept that was utterly foreign to Briseis. In Frouzea, women were property. Even Briseis, who tonight played the role of an exalted envoy, was sworn to the service of the Frouzee Delilah. Briseis halted for a second.

Come to think of it, Delilah is the only woman I've seen in Frouzea who controls her own destiny. But she is a goddess, not a mortal, she thought, shaking herself from her reverie.

"Is everything alright?" Avora'tru'ivi said, noticing Briseis pause.

"Yes, Your Highness. I stepped on a rock."

The two women, now slightly trailing the rest of the party, arrived back at the guests' suites.

"Please let me know if the accommodations are not to your satisfaction," said the queen. "These things, like artillery, sometimes require a woman's touch." With that, the queen rendered a respectful civilian salute, spun on her heel, and walked back towards the main palace.

Briseis was left in the splendor of her guest suite, alone and somewhat confused. Somehow, she felt different, but she couldn't understand why.

Maybe it's the water. I hear they fill it with toxic minerals to build resistance to poison, she thought before she drifted off to sleep.

CHAPTER FIFTY-TWO

THE COUNSEL OF GIDEON

A few weeks later, Tamino and Avora'tru'ivi sat in overstuffed chairs in the library of the palace, each enjoying books- Tamino was reading a copy of a collection of Chinese Tang Dynasty poems, while Avora'tru'ivi pored over an artillery manual. Judith played on the floor with a wooden castle, built as a rough approximation of Jenolan Castle, which guarded one of the passages through the Blue Mountains in Wil'iah's east.

Suddenly, the idyllic scene was broken by the sound of trumpets announcing an important visitor. Avora'tru'ivi's eyes darted up from her reading in surprise.

"We weren't expecting anybody today," she said.

She and Tamino got up to go to the entrance portico,

but Tamino remembered to ring a small bell. Milcah appeared, seemingly out of nowhere.

"Yes, Your Faithfulness?"

"We have an unexpected visitor. Can you please watch Judith while we attend to this?"

"Of course. Come, child," the birdlike woman cooed at Judith.

Tamino and Avora'tru'ivi emerged beneath the front portico. To their surprise, parked in front of the palace was a gilded carriage with the coat of arms of the United Kingdom of Ephraim and Manasseh emblazoned on the door, which opened to reveal a tall, bearded figure.

"Gideon!" Avora'tru'ivi rushed forward to embrace her brother, but the look on his face instantly put paid to any jollity.

"What is it?" she asked, her brows furrowing in concern.

"Father...he went Home last month. I wanted to tell you in person." Gideon hastily wrapped his sister in a comforting hug.

"What!?" A look of shocked horror clouded the Queen's regal features. Tamino rushed forward, trying to comfort his wife, who quickly dissolved into a puddle of tears. However, to both men's surprise, Avora'tru'ivi quickly regained her composure, although Tamino could tell it was only a veneer.

"I need to spend some time alone. I must prepare for our journey to Manasseh," she said with an unnatural level of equanimity that masked the storm that raged just below the surface. With that, she swept back into the palace, leaving the two men alone outside.

Tamino cleared his throat uncomfortably.

"I suppose this means that you will become the king?"

"I am the eldest," Gideon replied.

"I suppose so. I assume that you will carry on the policies of your father?"

"I will give all of them…careful consideration, but I am beginning to think that perhaps our foreign policy requires more…prudence."

Tamino's head snapped up in surprise.

"What do you mean?"

"We live in a different age than the one your father, and my father, lived in. We are kingdoms trying to survive in an age of empires. We are trees attempting to stand up in a storm. In elder days, so we've been told, some ancient power was there to defend us against our enemies. But, look around, Tamino. Have you seen any chariots of fire lately? Is there any pillar of cloud standing over Trukanamoa? Are there any unusually bright stars in the night sky?

"I am sorry to say, but I fear the days of the Kingdom of Wil'iah are numbered, and ours too, if we continue on our present, defiant course. It was a beautiful dream. And long may it yet live on in the hearts and minds of its people. But your father's dream cannot hope to persist in this era of titans, when our light is as a candle flame against a flood. I wish I didn't have to tell you this, but I honestly believe our best course of action is to reach a negotiated vassalship with the Yuan Dynasty. It would simply be too hard to stand up to them. As they have repeatedly demonstrated, there is no successful resistance to them in the long run. We may delay them for a year, for a decade perhaps, but in the end we will go down in flames. Kingdoms fall to empires. It is the natural way of things.

"Besides, that outcome may be favorable to us. Our nations would benefit from the economic development and military protection brought about by submission to Kublai Khan. The Mongols have been known to be merciful to those who capitulate to their power. We may even be allowed to maintain the Church."

Tamino stiffened, narrowing his eyes at his friend. "A candle against a flood...I find your choice of words interesting. Surely you remember what Isaiah said about times like these?"

Gideon scratched his chin. "I'm afraid my study has grown a bit...lax."

Tamino responded, "When the enemy comes in like a flood, the spirit of the Lord shall raise a standard against him."

"That's just it, Tamino. I believe in my heart of hearts that what we've been taught has some truth in it. But to rely on it when we are facing military catastrophe... it's a fool's errand. We cannot allow our countries' decisions to be driven by bedtime stories told by shepherds long ago, in a distant land."

"It's not just the stores contained in the Books. Everybody knows God delivered Wil'iah from Frouzea. That was only thirty-five years ago."

"My dear friend. People can be persuaded to believe anything if it will allay their fears and stoke their hopes. I'm sure that some people thought they saw or felt something. Perhaps there was even a meteor shower or something. But we simply have no proof that this supposed power that defends Wil'iah truly exists. Think about it. Your father claimed that his sword fell, fully-forged, from the heavens with a message that the time had come to overthrow Frouzea. But he was the only one there when this supposedly happened. Could you think of a better story to rally the disparate forces of the resistance?"

"You wouldn't dare suggest..."

"All I'm saying is that it's a very convenient tale with no evidence to back it up. In any case, I'm not concerned with the past. I'm concerned with the present – a present in which two very large and very powerful empires have set their sights on our kingdoms. The way I see it, we can go down with honor, and thus be extinguished from the earth, or we can do what we can to negotiate the most favorable outcome to us in the short term, and bide our time until these empires inevitably fall. Then, we may have another chance at independence." Placing a hand on the King's shoulder, Gideon looked him in the eye. "Even old Israel and Judah couldn't stand up against Babylon and Assyria, and they were nowhere near as powerful as our adversaries are now. Nobody would blame you, Tamino. In fact, future generations will owe their lives to you if you give up now, before it's too late."

Tamino shook his head. "I understand your concerns, Gideon. We have long been friends, and I respect your opinion. But the time has not come to give up. When my parents vowed to throw off Frouzea and found our dear Faithful Kingdom, they faced worse odds than we face now. And, whether or not the old stories are true, I will never stop believing in our secret defense. As we all know, the storm is coming. But its winds will lift our banners against it."

Gideon gave a curt bow. "It's your decision, Your Faithfulness. I hope you don't come to regret it. In the meantime, we must prepare to go to Manasseh."

Tamino nodded. "My staff will show you to the guest rooms. We'll leave tomorrow."

For his part, Tamino returned to his apartments. After spending some time attempting to comfort Avora'tru'ivi, who responded by giving him a characteristically businesslike set of tasks to prepare for their trip to Manasseh, betraying not the slightest hint of emotion, he exchanged his royal regalia for a drab traveling cloak and smudged his face with trace amounts of dirt. The time had come to exchange the "enlightened" opinions of Gideon for the true feelings of the people.

CHAPTER FIFTY-THREE

THE VOW OF WIL'IAH

*A*pproaching a small inn on the outskirts of Trukanamoa, Tamino ducked inside, conscientiously keeping the hood of his cloak up. He sat down next to a grizzled-looking Arrernte man who sat at a long rough-hewn table, where about a dozen other people plowed into various foods ranging from beef dishes to roasted bush pears. Politely nodding at the man next to him, Tamino began to gingerly eat a boiled cactus, reminding himself that the needles had all fallen out during the cooking process. As he ate, he cocked his head slightly, listening to what the others had to say. Most of the conversation was mundane, focusing on the status of the water table and weather predictions for the coming growing season, as well

314

as the unseasonable warmth of the previous winter. However, the conversation all fell instantly silent when one lady toward the end of the table said, "Did you hear the news? The Frouzean Empire is back."

A heavyset, older man across from her harrumphed. "And just where did you hear that?"

"My sister was in the Old City last week. She said that an envoy came to the palace, who claimed to represent the new Frouzee."

"That's just what we need. Another empire out for our blood," growled another man.

The woman shook her head. "I thought I'd never live to see the day when Frouzea came back."

A young man to Tamino's left ironically laughed. "You must have been kidding yourself. It was always going to come back. It was inevitable."

"What do you think the king is going to do?" asked a younger woman across the table, her eyes nervously scanning the reactions of her tablemates.

The young man responded. "If he was smart, he'd work out some sort of deal. We can't fight two empires at once. It would be absurd to try. Certainly not worth it."

The Arrernte man next to Tamino cleared his throat. "Young man, I think you skipped some history classes. If you knew why we created this country in the first place, you would know that we would never give up trying to save it."

The young man gave the older man a slightly condescending look. "It made sense at the time. An alliance of Zebulites and Indigenous Peoples to fight off a decrepit empire and free themselves from slavery. It was a laudable, noble fight. But it was fight in another age. The world has changed. I just don't think it's worth it anymore."

The heavyset man at the head of the table growled, "You weren't there. I was. If that new Frouzee messes with us, she's messing with a lot more than just our swords and spears."

The young man shook his head. "I've heard all the stories, uncle. It's going to take more than fairy tales to convince me that we should lay down our lives in a hopeless fight. At this point, what are we really fighting for, anyway? I hear that the Mongols give their subjects almost complete freedom."

Trying to change the subject before his tablemates came to blows, the Arrernte man turned to Tamino.

"What about you, mister? What do you think of King Tamino? Do you think he will be able to protect us from Frouzea and the Mongols?"

Tamino smiled back. "I think that remains to be seen. But my opinion doesn't really matter. What do you think of him and his leadership?"

"Well, I've never seen him, but from all accounts he's a good kid. Very nice and polite, and I heard he did some good work as a ranger. I'm sure he will try. But he sure has big shoes to fill."

The doubtful young man interjected. "I don't think anyone will be able to succeed Hezekiah. I don't envy him. If I were inheriting a hopeless cause, I'd probably try to find another job."

Another lady at the table, who had been quiet up until then, spoke up. "I even heard that he may be secretly negotiating with the Frouzeans."

The heavyset older man pounded the table. "The son of Hezekiah would never do that! And if he did, I'd give him a good wallop!"

The young man responded, "I think he should negotiate! I mean, what is the point of all of this? We need to just go along with the tide. Otherwise, we'll be swept away."

Tamino decided this had gone on long enough. He began to slowly hum a familiar tune, so softly that nobody could hear. Steeling himself for a public performance, he stood up, opened his mouth and began to sing the words, quietly at first, but with gradually increasing volume.

This I vow, that we shall ever keep the watch, and set alight the beacon-fires of Truth;
To become as a citadel on the mountain, a strong place that cannot be taken;
To keep the flame burning bright on the hillside, and never under a bushel;
That we shall build here in this desert a faithful kingdom, which shall never fall while true hearts draw breath;
That when the world forgets thee, we shall remember;
That when we are compassed about by darkness, we shall blaze as a defiant light in the night.
That we shall defeat every false way in our hearts, that we might be nearer to thee;
That we shall stand guard over the innocent;
That our nation shall be built on virtue, valor, courage, and chastity.
That ever shall we keep our eyes fixed upon the Star;
That we shall preserve the glory, the memory, of the power from above;
That we shall be just and merciful to all men;
And create a kingdom where all might be free from the whip and chain;
That we shall harm no man except in defense of all that is good and true;
Ever shall we lean on the wings of the Almighty in times of trouble and triumph.

Ever shall we be faithful, ever shall we act valiantly!
This we vow, we, the Faithful Kingdom!'"

As he continued through the *Vow of Wil'iah,* people all throughout the inn began to stop what they were doing and come over to the table to listen. After the first few lines, the grizzled old man and the Arrernte trader both added their voices to the song, which continued to swell as more and more people joined in. By the last lines, the voices had roused themselves into a deafening chorus. Tears twinkled in the eyes of many of the older patrons of the inn, as the old song that had warmed their hearts in ages past filled the air. One older man, who had hobbled into the inn with a cane, now raised it with a bony arm and shook it in the sky like a spear, seemingly forgetting his disability.

As the last note rang through the room, Tamino spoke again. "It sounds like we all need a reminder of what this country is really about. Nearly fifty years ago, a young man stood alone in the desert, trying to understand his place in the world. He knew not that he held a very important place in history, and that, quite soon, his heavenly father would set him forth on a crucial mission. The land he thought was his country was fighting for its last ditch, and his true country had gone down in flames twenty years before. But the ancient fire that had sustained his people down the centuries burned on in his heart. And, that fateful night, he was called to his higher purpose. A great, blazing sword descended from the heavens with a call to ride out of the mists of obscurity to save his people, for he was the true heir to the throne of David and the late, great, faithful Kingdom of Zebulon. That day, he took the famous vow that we all hold close to our hearts. And in ensuing years, his dream of the great, faithful kingdom of the free continued to spread and expand far beyond just the borders of Zebulon. Wil'iah is not a land. It is not a people. It is a dream. A dream that all can aspire to, a dream that holds all in its wide embrace. And as this dream grew from a spark into a raging fire that burned the old Frouzean Empire, and all its wickedness, to the ground, the Zebulite people joined hands and arms with their Aboriginal brothers and sisters in their common struggle for freedom and the higher way. We realized that the dream was for all of us, regardless of creed, language, or nation. And, together, we were stronger than the old Kingdom of Zebulon ever was. This is Wil'iah."

Tamino now climbed up onto the table, as the patrons of the inn crowded around him in rapt attention. "Some people seem to think that this dream isn't worth fighting for anymore, or that it was doomed to failure from the beginning. Some have said that while it was a beautiful idea in olden days, the times have changed, and such a dream needs to be abandoned in favor of something more practical. If you think the odds are against us now, what do you think they were when Hezekiah had but forty men against an empire? And while some may dismiss our history as a collection of optimistic fairy tales, I will always believe that our greatness and our true defense lies not with our force of arms, impressive as they may be. It is our everlasting covenant with the Almighty God of Israel, who, as always, stands behind us, prepared to defend us and lead us on the higher way. That Covenant is just as strong today as it was thirty-five years ago. In the darkest of times, against the most overwhelming of odds, my father never gave up, and neither will I!" Throwing back his hood and opening his cloak to reveal the royal signet pinned to his tunic, Tamino pumped a fist into the air and shouted,

"Ivrae'ia Va'a'kau'lua!"

An audible gasp ran through the crowd as Tamino's

true identity registered with them. The old man and the Arrernte trader immediately, almost involuntarily, snapped into the military salute.

Tamino spoke again over the din of surprised exclamations. "I understand how everyone must feel here. I can confirm that the Frouzean Empire has indeed reconstituted. But, let it be understood, I am making no secret negotiations with them and will make no concessions. Neither will we make any concessions to the Mongols. I know I am not my father, and it will take work to earn your confidence. But please know that I am doing everything I can to defend this country. Wil'iah is a dream worth fighting for." Tamino sent a rather pointed glance at the young man, who now stood rather sheepishly in the corner. "Take heart and be of good courage!"

CHAPTER FIFTY-FOUR

THE ROAD TO RAMOTH-GILEAD

The next morning, Tamino and Avora'tru'ivi sat next to each other in their carriage as it trundled north on the road from Trukanamoa to Ramoth-Gilead. Though Avora'tru'ivi still battled to maintain her veneer of composure, her puffy eyes said otherwise. Tamino placed an arm protectively around his wife.

"Talk to me," he said simply.

"It's not my father that I'm so devastated about. All of us reach the time when we must go Home and man its ramparts. He was surely received there with honor. Although my heart grieves for him, it grieves more for Manasseh. I love my brother, but I fear for the future of the country."

"I wish I didn't have to say that I share your concerns," Tamino said softly. "He indicated last night that he thought it was unwise to continue to defy the Mongols, and that we were both better off making a deal."

Avora'tru'ivi's fist clenched. "How dare he!?"

"He's wrong," Tamino soothed. "I don't care if Wil'iah has to stand alone. We will never surrender to them or any of their allies." He brushed away a tear that leaked out of his wife's eye. "After he visited last night, I went out to find out what the people really think about all of this."

Avora'tru'ivi playfully slapped him on the arm. "I told you to stop sneaking out like that! You're not a ranger anymore!" However, her face was clearly filled with anxious curiosity. "What did they say?"

"They stand completely behind us. Wil'iah, and all of its people, will never surrender."

A smile broke through Avora'tru'ivi's tears, but it died away nearly as quickly as it had appeared. "This coronation is going to be hard. I can't help but think it will feel more like a funeral."

Tamino nodded. "I only hope that Gideon comes to his senses before it's too late." He looked deep into his wife's bloodshot eyes. "You know, sometimes it's a real shame that the eldest comes first in the line of succession."

Avora'tru'ivi quickly looked away. "Oh, come now, Galbi. You know that I respect the laws of my old country. I would never want to usurp my brother."

Tamino gently cupped her chin in his hand and turned her head back to meet his eyes. "I respect your laws too, but that doesn't mean I don't wish they were different. In my eyes, you will always be the queen."

Avora'tru'ivi weakly smiled, then squeezed her husband's hand for support.

"Let's just get through this as quickly as we can. After

all, we have the dreaded state visit of Delilah to look forward to when we return."

CHAPTER FIFTY-FIVE

DELILAH'S STATE VISIT

*f*ar to the south, a sedan chair wended its way along a desert road, borne aloft by staggering slaves. Inside, Delilah reclined, attended by Briseis and Salome, who fanned her with peacock plumes and sprinkled her with water from a bejeweled emu egg.

"I'm afraid I don't understand what we hope to gain from this visit," Salome asked.

"Oh, darling, we will gain everything!"

Briseis cleared her throat. "I was just there. Wil'iah is determined to resist us. They are different from the other countries we have dealt with. Tamino is different from the other men we have encountered. He speaks of a higher way."

Delilah sat up, her eyes flashing dangerously.

"Briseis, in the end, all men are the same. They are all driven by the same things. And, when I sink my claws into his adorable face, he will fall just like all the others. He may speak of a 'higher way', but there is only one true way – that is the way of power, and those who know how to exploit it. We'll see just how long that 'higher way' lasts once he is exposed to my trusty concoction!"

"What if it doesn't work?" Asked Briseis.

"Fool! Has the Caress of Jezebel ever failed to work? And even if, for some reason, my charms fail to persuade him, the facts simply will."

"The facts?"

"Everything we have done has been for the purpose of gaining leverage- a better bargaining position. With a strong empire behind us, our offer will either be too tempting – or the alternative too terrifying – to refuse. We offer him a powerful ally against the greatest empire in the world – or another deadly enemy, and another flank to defend. The choice will be natural. And then, what I deserve will finally be mine." Delilah suddenly focused her eyes on Briseis, who still looked doubtful.

"It's time you had a little faith, Briseis. After all, I am a goddess!"

Briseis winced, but Salome lunged forward, fanning even more vigorously.

"Yes, of course, Your Worship, you are the true goddess! Any man would fall for you!"

A smile crept up Delilah's face.

"Of course he will!"

Several weeks later, Delilah, dressed in a gown made entirely of white albino peacock feathers, with an enormous train covered in pearls and seagull plumes, parted the curtains of her sedan chair to behold the walls of Trukanamoa grimly staring down at her. The imperial cockatoo-feather crown that topped her hair, itself held into two wing-like forms by hidden wire frames, accentuated her features as she disapprovingly looked at the fortress. The place was exactly as she had imagined it from intelligence reports- two mountain ranges, each crested by a high whitewashed wall punctuated at regular intervals by beacon-towers, guarded a gap through which flowed a river. Spanning the river was a great drawbridge anchored by four tall towers; behind the bridge rose the hulking mass of the outer gate of Trukanamoa, flanked on either side by rather forbidding towers and two titanic walls. Standing squarely behind the gate were the three steadfast tiers of the famous Castle of Trukanamoa, whose towers frowned down on the procession. Perched high above the gate on either side of the gap in the mountains were two additional castles known as the East and West Guard. From all of these walls, ominous black cylinders yawned at the procession, which the Frouzee recognized as cannons of Chinese design. The city itself did not look like it was expecting a great diplomatic mission from the greatest empire on earth. Instead, a positively gigantic battle flag flapped defiantly from the highest tower of the main castle.

How cute. They don't trust me. They shouldn't.

Delilah, still luxuriantly splayed on her sedan chair, gave a contemptuous flick of her little finger, intending to call her heralds to blast their trumpets to announce her arrival. However, the slaves didn't seem to notice the miniscule motion. In disgust, Delilah picked up a bush pear from her platter and flung it at the nearest slave, who started in horror and fumbled about for his trumpet.

"Idiots! To think I pay you to do this....Oh, wait, I don't!" Delilah giggled and returned her gaze to the pear platter. She noticed out of the corner of her eye one of the Wil'iahn knights assigned to "escort" duty flinch at her behavior. Disgust was written plainly on his face, but he took no action. The slaves all formed up into a line, their golden collars and bracelets gleaming in the harsh sun of the central deserts. In fact, even in the shade of her tent, it was becoming uncomfortably warm.

Why that old coot Hezekiah chose to build his capital city here, in this Baal-forsaken place, I will never understand.

The slaves gave off three long blasts of their horns, and then Heracles, mounted on the finest charger from the stables of Gath, rode out between their two lines with a large voice trumpet.

"Delilah, Second Incarnation to Earth of the Goddess Astarte, Eternal Empress of the Principalities of Gath, Gaza, Ekron, Ashdod, and Ashkelon, Dominator of the provinces of Arboria, Aurania, and the territories of Ithaca, Nullarbor, and Outer Frouzea, Empress of Upper and Lower Tanitania, Mistress of the Islands, Conqueror of Ilium and Egypt and by right Queen of the Isles of the Aegean, Achaea, Laconia, Argolis, Attica, Thrace, Mycenae, Crete, Rhodes, Atlantis, and Illyria, Chieftess of Canaan, and Perpetual object of Adoration and Worship of the Citizens and Denizens of the Everlasting Empire of Frouzea, bids her greetings to this house!"

A wicked smile worked its way up Delilah's juice-stained cheeks, but disappeared in an instant as a sound like thunder shook the ground. Fires erupted along the top of the outer wall as the guns reported blast after blast. After recovering from her initial shock, Frouzee noticed with some amount of disgust that the Wil'iahn knight nearest her viewing had an oddly satisfied look on his face.

As soon as the thumping cannonade was over, a line of heralds appeared along the wall, each carrying an ornately-carved conch shell. In unison, they all blew, and the outer gate, each door five stories tall, began to ponderously open with a groan. From it emerged a column of mounted knights four wide, each dressed in their finest parade armor. At the head of the column rode a tall man on a magnificent white charger and a woman on a black parade horse.

Delilah beckoned to Heracles, who gamely approached her. She reached into her robes and withdrew a small glass vial containing a single drop of a red liquid.

"This," she hissed, "is one of my favorite secrets. A secret you had better keep, unless you want a kiss...of Ildico."

Heracles visibly shuddered. "What is it," he asked, his voice breaking.

"It is a custom in Wil'iah during diplomatic visits to clasp open hands with visitors, to demonstrate equality and a lack of weapons. This typically takes the form of a receiving line where the chief diplomats, including the royalty, do this with the visitors in turn. You are to take this vial, this secret of mine, and smear it on your right hand. When you shake the hand of King Tamino, who should be first in line, make sure you transfer all of it to him. He will think it is just sweat. He will be wrong."

Heracles arched his eyebrows quizzically. "Poison?"

"Heavens, no! He is much more valuable to us alive than dead." She now reached into her sleeve and withdrew another vial, this one containing another singular drop of a clear liquid. "I will similarly smear his hand with this, the second part of this concoction. The two halves will slowly react, and in six hours' time, he will be madly in love with me."

Heracles pursed his lips jealously and put the vial in his pocket. "And then what?"

Frouzee's mouth curled into a mixture of a smile and a snarl. "And then, Heracles, Wil'iah is ours."

CHAPTER FIFTY-SIX

DINNER WITH EVIL

*T*he dining room of the palace of Trukanamoa filled with activity as the Frouzean delegation took its places along the east side of a long dining table, facing their Wil'iahn counterparts to the west. Delilah, flanked by Briseis and Heracles, stared across the table at Tamino and Avora'tru'ivi, as well as Lady Deborah and Prime Minister Allira, all of whom looked thoroughly uncomfortable.

Tamino awkwardly cleared his throat and was the first to speak.

"Your Excellencies, I regret that more of my family was not here to greet you. My brother was unavailable and my father is…indisposed."

Delilah smiled, but it didn't reach her eyes. "It is an

oversight I am willing to forgive…this time. After all, this is a historic occasion. The first time that the ruling Frouzee of the Frouzean Empire has entered Wil'iah—in friendship. All the same, it's really a shame I couldn't get to see my old friend Hezekiah once again – face to face. It's been too long."

Lady Deborah gave an almost imperceptible grunt, earning her a sharp glance from Tamino. She returned her steely gaze to Delilah, her intense features displaying no sign of the friendship of which Delilah spoke.

"You are correct. This is a most historic, and most unexpected, occasion," Tamino said. "I assure you that, historical prejudices to the contrary," he said, his eyes pointedly darting to Lady Deborah, "Our welcome to you and your retinue is sincere. It is a different world than it was thirty-five years ago, and we have no reason to hold onto past grudges. We must look forward, not backward."

"How *progressive* of you," Delilah responded.

"Well, our highest commandment is to love our neighbor, and, last time I looked at a map, that was you."

Delilah noticed Allira subtly roll her eyes.

Suddenly, a strange growling noise filled the room. Tamino's eyes shot down to his right, and a rare peeved look crossed his face.

"Hush, Samson! This is not how we treat guests!" he hissed. Delilah's eyes followed his to a small pug dog that stood, hackles raised, snarling at the empress.

"What an adorable creature!" Delilah crooned, but her eyes narrowed in a strange form of recognition.

The faintest of smiles crossed Avora'tru'ivi's face, and, when Delilah briefly looked away, Tamino noticed her silently mouth to the pug, *"good boy."*

"Anyway," Tamino hastily motioned to Briseis, "We have heard some inklings of the purpose of your visit from your esteemed colleague."

"Indeed. The purpose of my visit, beyond congratulating you on your recent accession to the throne, is surely not a mystery. But first, allow me to fulfill my primary purpose. Allow me to bestow upon you the acknowledgement of the Frouzean Empire and its associated territories and tributaries of your coronation as the second king of Wil'iah. Stories of your valor and honor have spread beyond your own borders, Your Highness. I see now with my own eyes that the tales of your charm and handsomeness have not been exaggerated either."

Avora'tru'ivi's eyes narrowed as she gripped her dinner knife a bit tighter.

Delilah noticed a hint of embarrassment cross Tamino's face, but he recovered quickly.

"The acknowledgement of your nation is noted and appreciated. And the true purpose of your visit?"

"The threat that looms over all of us needs no introduction."

"Indeed," said Allira. "All of our eyes have of late been cast to the north. It is not a surprise to me that the Frouzean Empire has coalesced once again in response to this threat. We trust that that, and that *only*, was the impetus for its revival."

Delilah smiled again, but her eyes betrayed no mirth. "The threat to us all has inspired my people to return to their faith… but that was always inevitable."

Allira grunted.

"Perhaps."

"We cannot help but mourn the tragic deaths of so many noble princes and kings in the former territories that now belong to the empire," interjected Avora'tru'ivi. "What a terrible set of…coincidences. And for you to lose your husband on your wedding night…my heart breaks for you."

Delilah locked eyes with the queen, seeing in them none of the sympathy that filled her saccharine words.

"Indeed, that was the worst night of my life. To have your heart so filled with love, and to have such love so cruelly dashed—I didn't know if I could go on. But we must go on, mustn't we? There is always another chance," she said, now attempting to significantly lock eyes with Tamino, but he didn't meet her gaze.

"And such a sad fate for Prince Theseus of Ekron! I heard he was killed by...spiders?" Avora'tru'ivi continued.

"You and I both know the saying, 'everything's trying to kill you in this continent.'"

The corners of the Queen's mouth turned up, but the rest of her face was as cold as a stone.

"I have heard from several sources that you have attempted various improvements to the territories presently under your command. Is it true that you have restored the acropolis of Gath?" Tamino asked, attempting a light tone.

"Ah, so you have an appreciation for our architecture?" Delilah smiled.

"Appreciation is a strong word, but I had heard that the acropolis was a complete mess."

"Unfortunately, in my absence, my people let my country fall to ruin. Of course, I suppose that you would prefer it that way," she said, once again locking eyes with the queen, whose eyes narrowed in response.

"Regardless, I hear that the situation for ordinary people has generally improved in Frouzea. It was long a lawless and chaotic place," interjected Allira.

"Yes, it's funny how having a goddess around inspires law and order."

Deborah stifled a cough, which might have been a

laughing fit in disguise.

"I have also heard that you have reduced taxes on your people. It's my understanding that Ajax of Gath tried to levy heavy taxes to pay tribute to the Mongols."

"Indeed. He was weak. We have not eliminated our taxes, but they are going to their proper purposes- the aggrandizement of our empire and the preparations for its defense, not to stuff the pockets of pompous foreign potentates."

"And what of your indigenous populations? Did I hear that you were considering ending the practice of slavery within your borders?" Allira asked significantly.

Delilah's face betrayed no reaction to the entreaty of the Arrernte leader.

"I'm afraid they are still needed."

A black cloud crossed the Prime Minister's face.

"You know, Your Excellency, the current Frouzean Empire doesn't have to repeat the mistakes of the past," said Tamino. "There is a higher way. It was only by failing to walk in it that the old empire fell. You have a chance to write the next chapter of your nation's history differently."

Delilah hesitated, almost indiscernibly, before responding.

"I stand by my decisions in the past. The empire of old did not fall because of anything I did. In fact, I think the blame lies much closer to this room," she said significantly. "But enough of such unpleasant topics. I hear that you and Her Highness have been blessed with a child. I would like to see the child."

Tamino's features softened. "Judith is the light of our lives."

"Unfortunately, she is asleep at the moment, and *won't* be joining us," Avora'tru'ivi interjected, her tones backed with unmistakable steel.

"A shame. Perhaps another time."

The queen didn't respond.

"Well, in any case, as I mentioned, my visit has other purposes as well," Delilah said.

"If you want our military technology to fight the Mongols, you're not getting it," Lady Deborah said flatly.

"Heavens, no!" Delilah feigned insult. "I am not here to discuss anything so base and blasé as fighting. We all know that the continent is threatened. But it is the economic power of the Mongols as much as its military power that concerns us. And believe me, Frouzea needs no instruction on military might from *you*."

Deborah, looking stung, sat up in her chair, making brief eye contact with the queen.

"What do you propose?" Allira asked, her eyes narrowing.

"Well, at the very least, our two countries need to acknowledge that each other exists." Delilah looked pointedly at Tamino. "In that, at least, I agree with His Highness. It is time to put the grudges of the past behind us. Though it is difficult for me, I am prepared, at this crucial juncture in history, to formally extend recognition to the Kingdom of Wil'iah."

"Oh, how *generous*," said Avora'tru'ivi, her voice dripping with sarcasm.

"And, in return?" said Allira.

"We could both profit from a healthy trade relationship. Now that trade with China is not an option for either of us, we need other avenues for revenue."

"Frouzea's chief export is wine, which, as you might be able to guess, is of little interest to us," said Tamino. "But your proposal is interesting. Trade would have to be at specific points. As you are well aware, our mutual border is fortified, and, although we do sincerely appreciate your offer of diplomatic recognition, we have no plans to change that."

Lady Deborah vigorously nodded with a smile.

"We have more to offer than our elixirs," Delilah said. "Surely you know that my personal property, the Province of Aurania, has some of the largest proven gold reserves in the world?"

"We do not lack for gold," interposed the Queen.

"Yes, but can you ever really have enough?" smiled Delilah. "Not to mention, the wheat fields of Lower Tanitania and the forests of Arboria are rich. I don't have to remind you that Wil'iah is mostly a barren desert."

"We are aware of our own limitations. Nevertheless, any long-term diplomatic decisions must be approved by the Council of Uluru," Tamino replied, deferring to Prime Minister Allira.

"We will certainly consider your offer. In trying times such as these, it is perhaps better to move forward together." Allira said.

"Indeed, if we can create a self-sufficient economic zone in this continent, we will be further insulated from the influence of the Great Khan. I hope this is a first step to our nations drawing closer together," Delilah crooned, once again locking eyes with Tamino, who uncomfortably fidgeted in his seat, then looked up with gratitude as he beheld an approaching platter.

"Ah, dessert! Finally. I'm sure you have never tried this before. It is made from heavy whipping cream."

Delilah slyly smiled.

"Truly, the delights of Wil'iah are *many.*"

CHAPTER FIFTY-SEVEN

THE VIXEN OF GATH

*S*everal hours later, Tamino prepared to go to sleep, back in his chambers in the Palace. Opening the gold-leafed book on the night stand to a page labeled "I Samuel 17," he prepared sit down in the large easy chair next to the bed and read. Suddenly, Tamino started at a telltale creak of the floorboards. His eyes darting to the *Zrain'de'zhang* hanging on the wall, he began to creep toward it, careful not to make a sound. Unexpectedly, a demure knock sounded at the door. Warily, Tamino walked toward it, then hesitantly opened it. Standing before him was the Frouzee Delilah, dressed in an outrageous red costume covered in frills, which led to a humongous snake hood-like collar that almost completely enveloped her head. Her hair cascaded down her front in voluminous waves, and, as earlier in the day, her face was adorned with an over-the-top assortment of makeup that made her look almost comical. Tamino tensed and drew himself up to his full height, ready for trouble.

"Your…Excellency. How can I be of assistance?"

"I must speak with you…in private," Frouzee said, presumptuously forcing her way into the chamber. Tamino hesitated a moment, then turned to face her.

Delilah opened her mouth and began to speak in a low, conspiratorial tone. "The balance of power in this part of the world is changing. You yourself have seen the awesome power of Kublai Khan's fleets and armies. His empire is an inexorable tide that each of us alone is powerless to stop."

Tamino laughed. "Ah, now the true purpose of your visit reveals itself. I knew there was a military angle to your visit. Rest assured, his fleets aren't as fearsome as you may have been led to believe. Our navy has proven more than capable of taking care of itself."

Delilah's eyes flashed to him, and she began walking toward him slowly, dramatically extending her legs with each step as her voice steadily rose to an urgent pitch. "This time. Next time will be different. His empire is vast beyond imagination. China alone is more powerful than you could ever hope to be. His authority extends all the way to the land of our forefathers. Neither of our nations is powerful enough to stop him." She had by this point advanced to point-blank range to the king and placed her hand on his chest. Tamino stiffened and took a step back.

"Join me, and together, our nations might be just powerful enough," she purred, dropping her voice to a sultry tone as she continued to advance on the king. Tamino's eyes darted from side to side, realizing that he was being backed into a corner. *Wil'iahns stand their ground,* he thought, drawing himself up to his full height and planting his feet spread slightly apart.

Delilah continued to slink toward him. Suddenly, her arms snapped out, and she placed her hands on his shoulders. "We could be terrific together. I could make you happier than any other woman ever could."

She started to attempt to knead his shoulders. Tamino started in horror, responding, "Ma'am, this is not appropriate."

"You are so tense, so repressed. It is clear that you have never known true pleasure. Let me show you all the arts of India, which I have scrupulously studied- and practiced"

At this, Tamino grabbed her hands and gently but firmly placed them at her sides. "I am not interested in your 'arts,' Indian or otherwise."

Delilah looked hurt, then her voice dropped to a whisper. "Long have I watched you from afar. Long have I loved you in my dreams. You are not like the men I have known. They are all children, animals. You are a man. Together, we could rule not just a continent, but the world!"

Tamino recoiled, his stomach turning. "I must ask you to leave at once. Surely you must know that I am a married man, and I love my wife with all of my heart. There is absolutely nothing that you could offer me that would turn my gaze in the slightest. As for your offer of a military alliance, if it comes to it, Wil'iah can defend herself."

"Avora'tru'ivi? I have seen her. The reports of her beauty and grace are greatly exaggerated. Trust me when I tell you I could make you far happier, and guarantee the safety of your kingdom as well," she said, once gain reaching up to touch his chin while repeatedly squeezing his hand, almost as if she expected some immediate effect. "It's time you came to your senses – *all five of them.*"

Tamino pointedly cast his gaze at the *Zrain'de'zhang* hanging on the wall. Forcing his shoulders back and turning up his head slightly, he responded.

"Get out, while I'm still asking nicely."

Frouzee feigned shock and hurt, even forcing a clearly-fabricated tear from the corner of her eye. "Consider your decisions wisely, O King. I would hate for my affections and that of my Empire to be directed elsewhere – to a man decidedly less charming and handsome than yourself."

She let her gaze linger on him for a second, a strange growl emanating from somewhere in her throat, then she whirled about to exit the chamber. The king called after her.

"God is the only defense Wil'iah needs!"

As the door slammed behind the Frouzean empress, Tamino let out a huge sigh of relief, preparing to return to the Bible that still lay open on the bed. His eyes had just returned to the story of David and Goliath when he heard the side door creak open. Reaching under his pillow for the dagger that was always secreted there, he whipped his head up to behold Avora'tru'ivi standing beside the open door, still in her diplomatic finery from the state dinner.

"Your Faithfulness," he said, immediately dropping the dagger and rising from the bed.

Wordlessly, the queen ran across the room and kissed him full on the mouth, much to his surprise.

After a few moments, she stepped back.

"What was that for?" Tamino asked.

"Galbi. I heard everything."

Tamino's brown face took on a distinctly reddish tinge, not unlike that of the kingdom's soil, and he nervously looked at the floor.

The queen stepped to him once again and gently lifted his head. "I heard everything. And I have never loved you more than I do now."

Tamino gave a weak smile, still shaking slightly from the encounter with the "Vixen of Gath." "Believe me, I meant every word I said. I did not consider her offer for one moment."

"I know, Galbi. I know." The queen exhaled and let out a gentle laugh that sounded like church bells. "But if that *pagh* ever comes near you again, I am not responsible for my actions. She had better leave first thing in the morning. I think you made that clear. And if that woman didn't get the message, I will make it clear."

"Now, dear heart, let's not cause a diplomatic incident. I think we made our stance clear." Tamino allowed himself a grin. "But I do appreciate the ferocity of your objections to her offer."

Avora'tru'ivi smiled. "Of course, Galbi. Always."

Tamino shifted nervously. "Do you think I have made a grave mistake in rejecting her offer of an alliance against the Great Khan?"

Avora'tru'ivi laughed. "Of course not. Do you really think that she would uphold her end of the bargain? She might help us so long as the Mongols are a threat, but as soon as they are defeated, and they will be defeated, she will not hesitate to stab us in the back. Besides, I trust her about as far as I can throw her- which is significantly farther than her corpulent predecessor, I will admit, but still not very far."

"What if she instead allies herself with Khan and they both attack us?"

The queen gently placed her hands on her husband's shoulders and looked deep into his eyes. "Galbi. I married you because you are the kindest, bravest, most valiant man on Earth. I married into this family because I believe with all of my heart in the purpose of this dear country. We are

God's faithful kingdom, a nation that stands for truth, justice, and love in a world that sorely lacks all three. It doesn't matter if one, two, or all of the empires in the world stand against us. We stand with God. I know what is going on behind that kind face of yours. I too struggle to live up to the legacy of the war queen of Ephraim. But neither of us are alone. You are up to this challenge and I am up to this challenge, because our almighty father-mother is up to this challenge. I know that the stories of our parents now seem like remote legends of the distant past, but they are not. The same power is with us now. And good will prevail, just as it always has before."

"Of course it will. But I am not my father, and he is ill at this crucial juncture, and I canno—"

The queen silenced him with a single finger pressed against his lips. "Wil'iah doesn't need Hezekiah anymore. It has something better. It has you."

"But—"

The Queen's eyes lit in a radiant smile as she moved her hand to his cheek. "Do not argue with me, Galbi. Your heart is full of love, and Love will always prevail."

"I love you." The king said, simply.

The queen gave him a quick hug. "I love you, too. Now, what are you reading?" She picked up the Bible and scanned the contents of the page. "Ah yes. Very appropriate."

CHAPTER FIFTY-EIGHT

THE EMPRESS OF CHINA

*B*riseis started as Delilah stormed back into the guest
garters, clearly fuming.

"Start packing. We're leaving!"

"What is it, Your Worship?" Salome asked, throwing
herself prostrate and kissing the floor.

Briseis rolled her eyes.

Delilah tore off the snake headdress and flung it to the
ground.

"It didn't work! It didn't work!"

"What didn't work?" Salome asked.

"HERACLES! Get in here!" Delilah screamed.

Heracles stumbled into the room, yawning as he rubbed
sleep from his eyes. He stopped short as he took in the

343

scene in the guest room.

"What is it, Your Worship?"

"Did you smear the Caress of Jezebel reagent on Tamino's hand like I told you to?"

"Yes, of course, I always follow your orders!"

Delilah paced around the room like a caged animal, her eyes wide with rage. "I just don't understand! He just stood there with that moralizing smirk on his face! There was no sign that he had ever been drugged- none of the telltales! No blushing, no heavy breathing, no salivating! What is WRONG with him!?"

Briseis suppressed an involuntary smile as she realized she'd known it wouldn't work.

"Perhaps Wil'iahns are immune?" she asked quietly.

Delilah suddenly stopped short and focused her inflamed eyes on Briseis.

"WHAT!?" In a rage, she picked up a Chinese flower-print vase and hefted it over her head as if to hurl it a Briseis. Then, seeming to think better of it, she simply flung it to the ground, where it shattered into a million pieces.

"What are we going to do, Your Worship?" entreated Salome sycophantically. "We're running out of time. The Mongols are going to be back soon demanding their tribute!"

Delilah paced around in rage for a few more moments, then seemed to collect herself. However, Briseis could see it was only a veneer. Somewhere within Delilah's eyes, something was broken. When she next spoke, her voice was filled with searing ice.

"It's simple. We implement our...alternative plan. He will pay for his insolence. Nobody rejects a goddess."

"And what 'alternative plan' is that?" Briseis asked, her voice world-weary. "We only have a few months before the

Mongols are supposed to come back. Their seven-year deadline is fast approaching. This was our last chance. We'll soon have an enemy battle-fleet on our doorstep."

Delilah simply smiled.

"You're looking at the next empress of China."

CHAPTER FIFTY-NINE

JASON JOINS THE EMPIRE

Pelesetania, 1292 AD

*P*rince Jason of Pelesetania lounged in his recliner, festooned in a purple silk toga imported at great expense from Tanitania and smelling of pungent wine, which he had recently consumed in vast quantities. Flanking his recliner on either side were six guards clad in the traditional garments of the Frouzean Homeric Guard, pale shadows of the fearsome warriors that had once terrorized the continent.

The musty silence of the room was pierced by two blasts on the long brass trumpets carried by the heralds at the beginning of the room.

Jason languidly raised his bloodshot eyes to the door and let out a large belch. *"Enter!"*

The doors opened to reveal a hulking man who must have been at least seven feet tall, carrying an ornate rolled-up rug.

"What is this?" Jason asked, derision dripping from his slurred speech.

"A gift from the Frouzean Empire!" replied the visitor.

Jason let out another belch and laughed. "What empire?! Frouzee abandoned us long ago."

Without replying, the huge man let one end of the carpet unroll. The carpet splayed out on the floor, to reveal a woman clad in a close-fitting costume made from crocodile skin and crowned with a pair of ivory horns. A necklace of cobra fangs hung around her neck, while her hand gripped a scepter crowned with the heads of a horse, lion, dove, and sphinx.

"Actually, as I recall, it was Pelesetania which abandoned us when the entire army that would become their primary constituency deserted after being beaten by a scared group of Manassite children and old women." She said as she liquidly rose from the floor.

Jason's eyes widened. "And you are?"

The woman's lips curled into a vicious smile. "Be careful how you answer that question. You are merely a prince. You are addressing a goddess!"

Now the hulking man behind her spoke. "You are before Delilah, Second Incarnation to Earth of the Goddess Ashtoreth, Eternal Empress of the Principalities of Gath, Gaza, Ekron, Ashdod, and Ashkelon, Dominator of the Imperial Provinces of Arboria and Aurania and the territories of Ithaca, Nullarbor, and Outer Frouzea, Empress of Upper and Lower Tanitania, Mistress of the

Islands, Conqueror of Ilium and Egypt and by right Queen of the Isles of the Aegean, Achaea, Laconia, Argolis, Attica, Thrace, Mycenae, Crete, Rhodes, Atlantis, and Illyria, Chieftess of Canaan, Empress of Antarctica, and Perpetual object of Adoration and Worship of the Citizens and Denizens of the Everlasting Empire of Frouzea."

Delilah curtly nodded. "Thank you, Heracles."

Jason laughed. "Right, and my grandmother is Cleopatra."

Heracles bared his teeth and clenched his fists. "You will not insult the goddess Astarte in this manner!"

Delilah raised a single finger with an impossibly long nail to silence him. "Perhaps Jason requires … a demonstration."

With that, Delilah banged her scepter down on the floor, the sound ringing down the colonnade. The doors flew open, smashing into the two heralds, who were pinned against the wall. In marched forty men of similar proportions to Heracles, each of them clad in the uniform of the Homeric Guard, just like Jason's spearmen.

Delilah regarded Jason's guards for a moment, then snorted. "I would like to present to you the real Homeric Guard, in contrast to this group of adolescents in costume."

Jason looked much more alert now. "What…what is it that you want?"

Delilah cocked her head back. "Oh, my desires are quite simple. The Frouzean Empire has been restored, and I am its empress and eternal goddess. The Principality of Pelesetania has always been and is now a territory of Frouzea, and as an imperial province, is my personal property. Thank you for taking care of my throne while I was gone." With that, Delilah began to advance towards the recliner, flanked on either side by her guards.

"You-you can't just walk in here and take my country!" stammered Jason.

Delilah turned for a brief moment to look at her guards, then looked at Jason's decidedly less impressive counterparts. "Oh, yes, I most certainly can. But I don't want to. I cannot be in every place at once, unlike that made-up deity the Wil'iahns worship. I need someone to manage the affairs of my property in my stead. That could be you, Jason. I'll even make you a deal."

Jason fidgeted uncomfortably on the recliner. "I'm listening."

Delilah smiled. "A spirit of the night told me that you once proposed to Princess Avora'tru'ivi of Manasseh, who is now the queen of what I'm sure is your least-favorite country."

Jason spat a grape seed on the polished floor. "I was going to marry that witch! But that coward Tamino stole her from me!"

Delilah advanced toward him another step. "If you promise me full cooperation and military support in the empire's upcoming invasion of Wil'iah, then to the victor will go the spoils. We'll be sure to capture her alive for you."

"What about Tamino? I'd like to kill him myself."

Delilah let out a serpentine hiss. "I have my own plans for him."

Jason asked, "Do you have anything else to add to your offer?"

"I thought I was being generous."

"And what if I refuse?"

"I don't see much of a choice for you right now," she said. A single flick by her little finger sent the spear of one of her guards to the throat of the prince. Jason's guards fidgeted, but, eying their forty potential opponents, didn't move.

"I see what you mean. I accept your offer." Jason said in a resigned tone.

"All right then. Now, as my vassal and subject you will pay me the proper respect. You will kneel."

Jason bristled. "The prince of Pelesetania kneels to nobody."

"On the floor, NOW!" The spear pointed at Jason's throat now made contact. Jason nervously swallowed, then slid down from his recliner and knelt on the marble tile.

"Now, what is the proper obeisance to the goddess Astarte?" asked Delilah.

Jason winced.

"I don't feel properly appreciated. Do you know what happens when goddesses don't feel appreciated?"

Jason shuddered, then rendered himself fully prostrate on the ground, finally lowering his head to kiss the floor. Delilah knelt down to pat the back of his head.

"Good boy."

CHAPTER SIXTY

THE TEA PARTY

Trukanamoa, Wil'iah

*T*amino shook his head at the scrolls spread haphazardly on his giant desk. The heavy piece of oaken furniture had been a gift from his father, and its reassuring solidity reminded Tamino of him. A gentle breeze breathed its way through the open window, ruffling some loose paper and setting the battle-flag that hung over his head aflutter.

There simply isn't enough, he thought as he looked at a scroll listing troop reserve totals for each of Wil'iah's twelve judgates. Based on the most recent intelligence reports, the standing army being mobilized by the reconstituted Frouzean Empire numbered in the hundreds of thousands. Wil'iah could only muster a fraction of that number in her regular forces if Frouzea chose to invade.

How could I let this happen? He asked himself, hazarding a glance at the parchment map hastily tacked to the wall. The Frouzean Empire splayed across the bottom of the continent in a malignant red. As all of the stories he had been told as a child of his parents' courageous, thirteen-year struggle against the original empire ran through his head, he involuntarily cringed at the sight of the map.

He was snapped from his reverie by the sound of four church bells, emanating from the Cathedral of the Eternal Victory, which stood just a few hundred meters from the walls of the castle. With a start, he realized that it was time for a very important appointment. Putting the military scroll down, he buckled his sword belt on and pushed in the chair. Hurrying down a sandstone hallway dimly lit by the little light admitted by a row of frowning arrow-loops, he tried to put aside his earlier worries.

After ascending several stories in a spiral staircase, Tamino emerged at the upper levels of one of the tall inner towers of the castle. Above his head was a platform for a massive trebuchet, but one would never guess that fact from the room he entered now. The rough sandstone walls that pervaded the rest of the massive fortress were here replaced with carefully applied plaster, meticulously hand-painted with images of various plants and animals that lived in the kingdom. Kangaroos and wombats gently played together beneath eucalyptus trees while cockatoos and budgerigars swooped overhead. At the center of the room was a low, white-painted table surrounded by a dozen tiny chairs. At the head of the table was a familiar, small face.

"Hello Daddy!" Princess Judith greeted brightly. "You're on time!"

"Always, sweetheart!" Tamino considered the weekly tea service with the princess to be the most important event on his calendar. He carefully rendered the full military salute to the five-year-old, who rose from her chair and greeted her father with a curt nod. Tamino gingerly lowered himself into one of the small chairs, wincing as he thought he heard a crack. To an outsider, he would have cut a comical figure, as his commanding height seemed totally out of proportion with the child-sized furniture.

"What flavors do we have today?" Tamino eyed the tea set, made from the finest bone porcelain, which had been brought with some of the refugees from China twelve years earlier. Its intricate decorations seemed a fantastic echo of the bygone splendor of a lost empire- an empire whose conqueror now had cast his eye on the Faithful Kingdom. Yet the Mongol menace seemed a million miles away in the peaceful innocence of the tearoom.

"We have five flavors today." The princess said, scrunching up her face as she tried to remember them all. "We have jasmine, wulong, Makassar red, pearl plumeria, and the Genghis Khan battle tea."

Tamino started at the last option. "Where did you come up with that?"

"Well, if they are going to be mean to us, we need to know how to stop them. Maybe we can start by drinking their tea," the little princess said.

Tamino chuckled, then widened his eyes as he realized he had broken protocol by not properly honoring the other guests. "Forgive me, your excellencies," he said as he rendered the military salute to the other esteemed visitors – the stuffed wombat, koala, wallaby, kangaroo, dolphin, and cockatoo that were the princess's constant companions. "Please, hostess, do introduce me to our venerated guests!"

Judith sweetly smiled at him. "This is Kertanegara, King of Singhasari," she said, pointing at the kangaroo. Next moving her chubby finger to the koala, she continued, "And this is Tran Anh Hong of Dai Viet." As she continued around the table, Tamino realized that her animal companions were standing in for all of the leaders of the League of Shechem. Amusement mixed with sadness as Tamino wondered if the little princess was growing up too fast. A child's tea party shouldn't be a military conference, he thought. But then again, would I expect anything less from Hezekiah's granddaughter?

After finishing the introductions, Judith politely asked each visiting dignitary which tea they would like, then expertly poured them each a cup, not spilling a drop. Tamino noticed that she seemed to strain a bit to lift the heavy teapot, but her small, determined face didn't betray even a hint of her struggle.

"What do you want, Daddy?" she asked.

"Well, I think I will take your advice and try the Genghis Khan battle tea!" he said.

"Okay Daddy. I didn't like it very much, but maybe you will." She said as she struggled to heft a large teapot.

"Allow me, Your Majesty," Tamino said as he gently took the teapot from her hands and poured some of the dark liquid into his cup. Taking a sip, he winced as the force of the tea hit his mouth.

"Oh my, I think this needs some sugar," he said. If Genghis Khan really drank this before battle, I understand why he conquered most of the world.

After passing him a porcelain plate covered in perfectly-cut sugar cubes, Princess Judith laced her fingers and regarded her guests with surprising sternness.

"Alright. We need to talk about business," she said in a commanding tone. Tamino found himself involuntarily sitting up a little bit straighter. "The Mongols are coming. Are we ready?" she asked. "How many ships do you have?" she inquired of the kangaroo that perched in the chair next to her. After listening with her head cocked for a moment, the princess seemed to find an answer to her own question and recoiled in shock. "Only three hundred! That isn't enough!" She then turned to the koala that sat on her other flank. "And what about Dai Viet?" After waiting again for a few seconds, she nodded. "That's a little better." Suddenly, she locked eyes directly with her father. "And how many ships do WE have, Daddy?"

Playing along, Tamino stroked his chin for a few seconds, realizing his recent study of the military reports was going to come in surprisingly handy during his daughter's tea party.

"Well, Your Majesty, at last count, we have one thousand, two hundred and twenty ships in commission, and we are building three hundred more. Of these, about sixty are the heavy one hundred twenty-cubit *trungabrang* battleships, two-hundred forty are the eighty-cubit *galor'ivi* heavy cruisers, four hundred are smaller, forty cubit *tua'ivi* cruisers, and the rest are light, single-hulled *shaluas*."

"Where is the *Ava'ivi* right now?" Asked Judith. Realizing with no small amount of surprise that she was referring to the veteran flagship of the fleet, Tamino wondered at her impressive grasp of Wil'iahn naval affairs.

"The *Ava'ivi* is docked at the royal shipyards of Balthcutta," said the King. "She recently returned from a trip to Noumea. She is shortly to resume duties as flagship of the Eastern Fleet."

Judith cocked her head again, clearly listening to one of her "visitors." She then brightly "replied," "Oh, that's because everyone knows that girls are strong!"

"I'm sorry, I didn't quite hear. What did his excellency ask?" Tamino inquired.

"Oh, the emperor wanted to know why we think battleships are girls." She matter-of-factly stated.

Tamino had always wondered where the tradition of referring to ships as female had originated. He decided he liked this answer.

"Daddy, how many ships does Kublai Khan have?" This question seemed different from the others – more direct. The king detected a small quaver in his daughter's voice, and a lump formed in his throat as he understood that she was more scared than she was willing to let on.

Nervously clearing his throat, Tamino wasn't sure how to answer the question. He actually didn't know exactly how many ships Kublai Khan had, especially since his last drubbing in Dai Viet.

"Well, Your Majesty, we don't know. We are trying to find out."

Judith regarded him with surprising severity, the seriousness of her round little face almost comical. "Well, that's not okay, Daddy. We need to know."

Tamino wondered if he wasn't doing an adequate job of protecting his daughter from the cruelties of the outside world. A four-year-old shouldn't be worrying about such things. But Tamino also remembered that Avora'tru'ivi resented being sheltered by her parents. Early on, she had insisted that Judith be told the whole, uncompromising truth about the challenges facing the kingdom that she was destined to someday rule. Thinking back on his first unexpected adventure with Avora'tru'ivi when they were children, Tamino remembered that she had seemed unprepared for some of the dangers that they faced. He was glad that Judith wouldn't face the same problems later in her life.

Attempting to cover his own worries about the size of the Mongol fleet by putting on the most soothing tone he could muster, Tamino replied, "There is no need to worry, Your Majesty. We have our best people working on it right now. We will find out, and then we will know how to be ready."

Judith seemed satisfied with the answer, and turned to the cockatoo sitting a couple of chairs to her left.

"That is a pretty dress. I really like the dresses from Champa," she complimented the "princess."

Tamino breathed a small sigh of relief. At least there's still some room in her life for whimsy. He made a mental note to get her a dress from Champa for her next birthday.

Judith beamed, apparently having received a compliment from the "princess of Champa." "Why thank you," she said, spreading her own green-and-white dress out widely for the whole table to see. "I like it, too. Someday, I will get to wear armor like Momma and Daddy! It is too heavy for me now." She turned to Tamino. "Please show them the sword, Daddy."

Tamino stood up from the chair, his limbs creaking a bit from being scrunched up. With a dramatic flourish, he unsheathed the famous Zrain'de'zhang and slashed it about a few times, the legendary weapon catching the afternoon sun and making loud whooshing noises. Judith's eyes lit up when she saw the iconic weapon. Beaming with pride, she turned to speak to the Kangaroo.

"Did you know that God gave that to my grandpa?" She said. "It fell down from heaven. Frouzee is scared of it." Her voice betrayed the same fierce pride and determination that most Wil'iahns had when speaking about the War of the Vow. For Tamino, the conflict was literally a lifetime ago, but it cast a long shadow.

"As well she should be!" Another voice broke into the room as Avora'tru'ivi strode into the room, her diadem catching the afternoon sunlight.

CHAPTER SIXTY-ONE

DELILAH'S DEAL

Gath, Frouzean Empire

Briseis hurried along the passageways of the palace of Gath, her heart pounding with panic. The day everyone had been dreading had finally arrived. The Mongol fleet had appeared off the coast, prepared to exact their tribute from Gath, apparently unaware of the changes in Frouzea's government over the past few years. Luckily for Frouzea, the Mongols had been too busy dealing with Wil'iah and her allies to bother sending any additional diplomatic missions to what they considered a backwater collection of broken-down principalities, beyond the visit they had threatened seven years prior, when they had convinced Ajax the Great to render tribute. Delilah's maneuverings had prepared the empire for this moment, or so Briseis hoped. The Eternal Empress clearly had a plan, although Briseis couldn't fathom what it was at this time – or how she planned to become the empress of China.

Briseis flew down a long, spotless, colonnaded hallway, finally arriving at the set of red double doors that had once led to Achilles' harem. Briseis stopped just short of the doors to catch her breath, earning derisive smirks from the two massive Homeric guards posted on either side. They grudgingly opened the doors to admit Delilah's confidante, whose mouth unwittingly dropped open at the sight that greeted her.

A large alabaster bathtub floated above a bed of hot coals, suspended by two dozen sweating men whom Briseis thought she recognized from the Homeric Guard. Yet more of them marched back and forth from golden tables overloaded with food to the bathtub, where, mostly submerged, Delilah luxuriated. The men popped grapes, lychee, and a dozen other fruits into her mouths as even more of them staged mock fights and wrestling matches on a large silk mat, surrounded by a pool of water filled with albino crocodiles that snapped at the men if they got too close. Delilah giggled excitedly at the scene, fruit juice dribbling down her chin into the pungent solution she had submerged herself in.

Briseis crinkled her nose.

"Is that…butter?"

Delilah languidly turned her head, her eyes focusing on her confidante.

"Ah, Briseis! Yes, I've heard it's a good skin treatment that really gives you the 'goddess glow.'"

Briseis swept her hand around at the dozens of men in

the room.

"And who are all of these?"

"Ah yes, these are my Acolytes from the Bull Pen," Delilah purred.

"The what?"

"Well, I decided that any true goddess deserves to be entertained!" Delilah said, clapping her hands together with an audible squelch of melted butter. "I selected a few of these choice morsels from the Homeric Guard. They now have an even higher office."

"Isn't that what Achilles once said?" Briseis said under her breath, but cursed to herself as she realized she had said it just loudly enough for Delilah to hear.

"*Excuse me*, Briseis?"

"I---I said that you absolutely deserve everything that you receive," Briseis hastily backpedaled.

"Yes, I certainly hope that's what you said! Think, Briseis, think! If I ever get bored of one of these confections, maybe I can give him to you!"

"That's not—" Briseis' protestation was cut off by another voice.

"Oh, how generous!" squealed Salome as she sidled into the room, taking in the scene. "I'd love a snack!"

Briseis had to fight to keep from rolling her eyes.

"Did you come with a specific message for me, Briseis?" Delilah crooned.

"Yes, actually, I did. The Mongol fleet has arrived, right on schedule."

"Ah yes, perfect. Just as I expected. I will prepare to meet them. Tell Heracles to meet them at the docks with a strong contingent of Homeric Guards. We must convince them that an alliance with us is more worthwhile than trying to force us into a tributary arrangement. Are you ready to show them just how splendid your eternal empress is?"

* * *

Temur Khan stood atop the forecastle of his flagship as it glided into the harbor of Gath, a large squadron of warships and treasure junks in tow. His eyebrows furrowed as he surveyed a scene quite different from the one he had seen seven years before. A newly-constructed mole provided docking space for three dozen brightly-painted Frouzean war galleys, each of their decks lined with saluting soldiers. However, these vessels were dwarfed by a positively gigantic quinquerme with three mountainous scarlet lateen sails, covered from ram bow to aftercastle with gold. The vessel rivalled the largest of the Mongol junks in size, and surpassed them all in splendor. Above the docks loomed a forbidding-looking citadel with spotless whitewashed walls, the battlements lined with a row of well-oiled trebuchets. Commanding the entire tableaux was the completely restored acropolis of Gath. The complex was crowned with three temples, the center of which was slightly larger than the other two. Wrapping around the temple complex was an enormous, colonnaded palace. There was no sign of the strewn rubble that had marked the acropolis on his last visit.

A Frouzean pilot boat guided the junk to a dock directly in front of a ramrod-straight road that led to the acropolis, lined on either side by a succession of enormous marble sphinxes. Waiting at the dock was an enormous, hulking warrior in burnished armor and a red feathered helmet, flanked on either side by five hundred soldiers hefting long lances with wickedly-barbed points. On either side of him, standard bearers held aloft enormous red, white, and black banners emblazoned with an upside-down pentagram, a different symbol than the emblem of Gath he had seen before.

It seems there has been a change of government.

As the gangplank slammed down onto the dock, Temur swaggered down, arms folded, a scowl on his face.

"I've come to see Ajax of Gath. It's time for him to pay up," he growled.

The huge warrior facing him merely smiled. "Ajax of Gath is dead. Her Worship now graces the throne." His voice quaked with reverence.

Her Worship?

The soldiers behind the warrior snapped to attention, then began to march down the avenue leading to the acropolis. The warrior motioned for Temur and his entourage to follow. As he passed between the first two of the sphinxes, he was met with the blinding sight of burnished shields suddenly snapping into position all along the two-mile avenue leading to the acropolis that loomed in the distance. Between each sphinx stood twenty more soldiers in perfectly polished armor, stretching virtually as far as the eye could see.

Temur and his attendants continued to march toward the acropolis, but his eyes narrowed as he felt the ground shake with more footsteps than he expected. Turning behind him, he recoiled in surprise as the avenue filled in with yet more troops, completely occupying the growing space between him and the docks.

At length, he arrived at the foot of the acropolis, where a tiled ramp led to the three great temples. Around him, he could now see that the acropolis was also dotted with dozens of lesser temples. The ramp was flanked by two great platforms, on each of which stood five hundred trumpeters that let out deafening fanfares.

The giant warrior graciously bowed his head and

motioned for Temur to proceed. The Mongol prince hesitantly began to walk up the ramp, accompanied by his retinue. Eventually, they reached the summit, where the full scene became apparent. A vast square stretched out before him, tiled with spotless marble. At the very end of the square stood the largest of the temples. Soaring blood-red columns supported a giant entablature, while large statues of a bull, dove, sphinx, and lion flanked the entrance. A sun-like disk made out of pure gold crowned the whole assemblage.

"Her Worship will see you now," the warrior said bluntly.

What on earth? Thought Temur, but he kept it to himself. He ascended the steps to the temple and stepped inside, conscious always of the massive cohort of troops that tromped behind him.

Inside, the temple was completely dark. Temur blinked, trying to adjust his eyes to the dim situation, when somewhere a gong rang. A strange, ethereal chorus reverberated through the darkness.

Oh star of the morning!
Oh star of the evening!
Oh goddess of love!
Oh empress of war!
Oh queen of all the heavens!
Beautiful, inexorable, exalted!
Your illustrious splendor eclipses the sun!
Your fury dominates the waves!
Your radiance shines through all the skies!
We fall at your feet in homage and worship
Of your beauty, your glory, your love!
Oh descend to us, great Astarte!
Goddess and empress of all the earth, the sea, and the heavens!

Suddenly, a great flash of light, attended by a thunderous detonation, filled the room, temporarily blinding Temur. When he recovered his faculties, curtains had parted high in the ceiling to reveal a skylight. A single shaft of light pierced the darkness to illuminate a massive horned throne, upon which sat a woman resplendent in a form-fitting, iridescent blue-green dress covered in hundreds of small sapphires and emeralds. A full array of peacock feathers fanned out from behind her peaked collar. Her striking face was framed by an enormous green cobra-hood headdress, crowned with two horns forming a crescent shape and a gold disk.

What is this? Temur thought.

"Ah yes, Kublai Khan's lackey, come at last," she crooned.

Temur bristled. "I bring the greetings of the Great Khan, ruler of all the world. I would remind you that the time has come for Gath to pay its tribute."

"Ha! Gath! He amuses me!" The illuminated woman's response was suddenly supported by an invisible chorus of derisive laughter that reverberated out of the indiscernible blackness of the temple's interior. "Gath is gone. In its place, the Frouzean Empire has been restored. My people prayed to me, and I deigned to descend from the heavens to lead my people back to greatness. I'm sure you thought you were coming to visit a weakling principality today. You are not." With that, she snapped her fingers, and the curtains parted further to illuminate the whole interior of the temple. The result was blinding. The walls themselves seemed to be made of solid iridescent opal. The sun's light reflected off of the armor of hundreds of soldiers, sending the beams right into Temur's eyes. He squinted, working his mouth to attempt a response.

Suddenly, a strange growling sound cut through the room, and Temur was surprised to focus on an albino crocodile with a studded collar, that lay chained to the floor in front of the strange throne. The "goddess" was also flanked by two brightly-colored birds that Temur recognized as vicious cassowaries, chained to the throne.

Suddenly, another sound interrupted the proceedings as a man was dragged into the throne room by two Homeric guards.

"What's this? Who dares interrupt this important meeting?" the woman on the throne hissed.

One of the guards grunted. "This slave wasn't working fast enough in the armory."

"Ah, that's unfortunate," the woman crooned. "Our weapons manufacturing plants are usually so efficient. More's the pity." She snapped her fingers at a devious-looking woman to her left. "The gong, Salome."

Salome picked up a mallet and struck the gong, its sound reverberating through the giant temple chamber. Two more guards moved to unchain the cassowaries, which instantly rushed forward at the hapless slave, squawking. Their razor-sharp talons made short work of their unwitting victim. Temur felt like he was going to be sick.

"Well," the empress clapped her hands gleefully. "Now that that's over with, I believe we had some business to attend to? Something about Khan paying me tribute?"

Temur bristled. "Pay YOU!? Who do you think you are?"

"That's a good question, princeling. I think I am someone who actually might be in a position to help you. I offer Khan no tribute. But I do offer him information."

"What sort of information?"

"That's for me to know, and Khan to find out, when I

visit him."

"Visit?"

"That is the nice thing for neighboring empires to do, isn't it? A polite visit to exchange information? You have many problems in this region. Problems I may be able to help with. I will come to Xanadu. I'll even bring some housewarming gifts, assuming your fleet is large enough to carry them and my entourage! As for me, I will travel aboard my personal flagship, the *Glory of Astarte.*" Her eyes narrowed contemptuously as she looked the Mongol prince up and down. "Much have we heard about the splendors of Xanadu. I cannot help but think I will be disappointed."

CHAPTER SIXTY-TWO

FROUZEE GOES TO XANADU

Shangdu, Northern China

The forbidding, enormous walls of the Palace of Xanadu loomed over the square, visible reminders of the inexorable might of the Yuan Dynasty. A hundred blue flags emblazoned with the device of the Mongol Empire flapped along its angled, red walls, while great pavilions with the distinctive angled roofs that epitomized Chinese design crowned the entire assemblage. Set in the center of the walls was a great gate. Atop the gate stood a splendid marble platform, on which sat the Great Khan, joined by his Chinese adviser, Liu, and the herald who had ridden

368

ahead of Delilah's entourage to notify the palace of her imminent arrival. Behind them were a line of soldiers and attendants bearing great battle-flags.

Suddenly, the sound of trumpets pierced the air as a line of five hundred buglers mounted on majestic steeds trotted into the square. Liu nervously started.

She's here.

In unison, the five hundred buglers stopped their horses before the gates and yelled together,

"Her Worship Delilah, Second Incarnation to Earth of the Goddess Astarte and Eternal Empress of the Frouzean Empire, Everlasting Object of Adoration of the citizens and Denizens of the Principalities and Provinces of said Empire, Ruler of the Principalities of Gath, Gaza, Ekron, Ashkelon, Ashdod, and Ekron, Dominator of the Territories of Outer Frouzea, Nullarbor, Ithaca, and the Provinces of Arboria, and Aurania, Image of the Goddess Tanit and beloved leader of the Imperial Provinces of upper and lower Tanitania, Sovereign by Historical Right of Canaan, Egypt, Sinai, Iberia, Utica, Cartagena, Mauritania, Tunisia, Carthage, Africa Proconsolaris, Attica, Illyria, Argolis, Achaea, Thrace, Epirus, Crete, Cyprus, the Cyclades, Macedonia, and Asia Minor, Empress of Antarctica and Atlantis and terror of the southern continent, the glorious, the inexorable, the beautiful, has arrived to grace you with her indescribably brilliant presence!" Their final words were punctuated by a thunderous roll of drums.

Liu cleared his throat and yelled out in response, "I trust that said empress has brought with her the tribute we have requested."

An enormous man with a scowling face, resplendent in brilliant armor, but curiously wearing the bands of slaves around his arms, stepped forward between the two centermost heralds.

"Her worship brings so much more."

"And you are?"

"I am Heracles, First Protector of her Worship the Goddess Astarte."

Kublai Khan grunted. "Well, this should be interesting. Send her in."

Liu nodded to the warrior in the square. "She and her retinue may enter."

The great gates of the palace of Xanadu ponderously swung open.

The five hundred horsemen gave five long blasts on their trumpets and retreated to neat lines on either side of the square, which was suddenly filled with movement as dozens of dancers, clad in loosely-fitting toga-like robes, came streaming into the square and fanned out into formation behind Heracles.

"The royal dancers of Gath, handpicked from a young age to serve Her Worship," he bellowed.

The dancers executed a perfectly-practiced routine, accompanied by two dozen tambourine musicians, before running to the sides. This was followed by another blast by the trumpeters as a second dance troupe arrived.

"Her Worship's own Troupe of Gaza, here to perform for you the Dance of the Seven Veils."

The process repeated many times, with dance troupes representing the Principalities of Ashdod, Ashkelon, and Ekron joined by groups from the two imperial provinces of Tanitania and the provinces of Arboria and Aurania. Each of the troupes filled the air with burning incense and cloying perfume that they sprinkled about as they danced; soon, the very air was thick with a thousand scents, which only whipped the audience into further fervor. To the surprise and delight of the rapidly-growing crowd watching in the square, the Auranian dancers were covered from head to toe in fine gold powder. As the last strains of a triumphant fanfare from the trumpeters floated over the square, replaced by a cacophony of sounds created by the various instruments of the dancers, Heracles stepped forward again.

"And now, Her Worship presents gifts, a mere taste of the unmatched splendor of our empire, to demonstrate our friendship. We come not as tributaries but as allies."

Two hundred women came running into the square, holding aloft above their heads billowing streamers of purple cloth, which stretched dozens of feet behind them as they flapped in the gathering breeze.

"Tyrian purple cloth, made only by the master artisans of Tanitania!" yelled Heracles. The initial women were followed by hundreds of slaves bearing five dozen platforms loaded high with bolts of the precious cloth.

Next, slaves staggered into the square bearing five huge chests overflowing with sparkling blue-green jewels.

"Opals from the limitless mines of Outer Frouzea, for your pleasure!" yelled Heracles.

After another blast of the trumpet, a thousand slaves clad from head-to-toe in outrageous costumes made from cockatoo feathers gingerly entered the square carrying golden birdcages.

"A flock of budgerigars, for your enjoyment!"

At another blast from the heralds, the cages were all opened in unison, and the perfectly-trained birds exploded forth into a whirlwind of blues, greens, and yellows. The crowd in gasped and clapped with glee. The seeming avian cyclone twirled about for five minutes, with the air filled with song, before they all descended to roost on the walls of Xanadu.

Next, a hundred women entered the square carrying

larger diamond-encrusted cages.

"Imperial Cockatoos, the noblest birds in the world!"

The doors to the cages flew open, and a hundred pure white birds with impressive feather crowns flapped out, making directly for Kublai Khan, who instinctively covered his eyes as the birds roosted all around him.

Now Heracles stepped forward and raised his voice again.

"Gifts to enrich the famous menagerie of the Great Khan, which is missing the wonders of our continent!"

Into the square marched an orderly line of slaves bearing pallets with large cages bearing all manner of wildlife. A crocodile was followed by five kangaroos, koalas, wallabies, quokkas, cassowaries, little penguins, parrots, emus, venomous snakes, giant bats, monitor lizards, two enormous crocodiles, and even a moa bird and imperial eagle taken from Aotearoa in the days when the empire had ruled that chain of islands.

As the parade of creatures vanished into the gates of Xanadu, Heracles swept his arms to indicate the next round of gifts.

"A selection of handcrafts from our empire to enrich your storehouses!"

A thousand slaves dragged sledges into the square piled high with ornately decorated pottery, intricately-woven carpets, and handmade baskets.

"And now, a special gift from the five principalities!"

Five heralds, bedecked in the colors of the respective principalities of Frouzea, marched forward bearing etched crystal boxes, through which were visible brilliantly-decorated, gold-painted, jewel-encrusted emu eggs.

"These imperial eggs were crafted specifically as gifts for the Great Khan! The artisans have been killed, so their majesty can never be replicated!" The five heralds held the boxes aloft for the adoring crowd to see, the contents being met with a gasp.

"We trust that the Great Khan is a man of good taste. We wish to bestow on him the gift of our wines, the finest in the world!"

Five hundred barrels of wine, held on the trembling backs of yet more slaves, staggered in to the square.

"Each is of a different variety from the proud vineyards of the five principalities!"

Heracles stepped back and threw his arms open wide.

"And now, the greatest splendors of our empire, offered with friendship!"

Five hundred slaves, bearing great platforms piled high with brilliant ingots, marched into the square in orderly lines.

"Five hundred talents of silver, from the bountiful mines of Ekron!"

They were followed by another fanfare of the trumpets, and one hundred and fifty more slaves, this time, bearing golden ingots.

"One hundred fifty talents of Gold. Not even the much-vaunted queen of Sheba could afford to give so much! It is in such abundance that the whole province of Aurania is named for it!"

Liu noticed Kublai Khan's eyes light up at the sight of such splendid riches.

"And now, the glorious might of the Homeric Guard, the universal, inexorable terror of our continent!"

Five hundred members of the legendary elite unit marched in perfect formation into the square, their burnished armor and gleaming spears catching the sun. In the center of the square, they paused and ominously flexed their muscles, an action greeted with some excited squeals from the crowd and a subtle eye-roll from Liu, who had never seen anything so gratuitously blatant.

Suddenly, the entire square fell silent as all of the assembled thousands of slaves, dancers, and soldiers fell prone on the ground, kissing the tiles.

An enormous stone sphinx, bull, lion, and dove were ponderously dragged into the square by a hundred sweating slaves a piece, their surfaces embellished with gold and brilliant jewels that reflected the sun's rays in a thousand directions. Yet their splendor paled in comparison to what came next.

Five hundred slaves arrayed in five columns, their lines flanked by standard-bearers holding aloft the flags of all of the Empire's constituent entities and all of its elite military units and groups of soldiers leading two lines of cows and carrying platters of putrid dead fish, dragged a towering gold altar into the center of the square. Standing some fifty feet tall, it was crowned with two enormous ivory horns and bedecked with a vertical version of the red and black flag of the Frouzean Empire.

Heracles cleared his throat.

"It is time for us to call upon our empress, our goddess, to favor us with her radiant presence!"

Suddenly, the square was a riot of sound and movement as the cows were dragged over to the altar and viciously sacrificed by the Homeric guard as the assembled dance troupes whirled around the altar, shouting and conducting the infamous "immoral rites" that had been described so vividly in Deuteronomy over two thousand years before. Such shocking bacchanalia had not been seen before in all the Mongol Empire. Liu noticed with no small amount of disgust that Kublai Khan eagerly viewed the debauchery; by contrast, Liu himself felt slightly sickened.

As the decadent rituals reached a fever pitch, a sound like a thunderclap split the air, and an enormous plume of red smoke jetted up from the altar and filled the square with its putrid fumes, leaving Kublai Khan doubled over in a retching coughing fit. Liu, his own eyes stinging, staggered over to help him, his face filling with concern. However, both were distracted from their discomfort by an excited murmur that arose from the square as the smoke cleared.

Sitting on a bejeweled throne between the two horns atop the altar was a woman. Blinding golden scales hugged her form from neck to toe, dominated by a breastplate fashioned to look like the sun, with golden rays spreading in all directions. Giant sphinx wings made from gold lamé and white cloisonné spread out behind her, while her head looked down on the proceedings from the center of an enormous gold-leafed disk clearly intended to call to mind the sun, on which was inscribed a pentagram. Rearing from her forehead was an obsidian cobra in strike position. Ropes of pearls lay carelessly strewn around her feet. In one hand she held a four-headed scepter with a horse, lion, sphinx, and dove, crowned with two horns and another gold disk. The entire audience in the square stood transfixed.

With surprise, Liu realized that the level of her platform was similar to that of the throne atop the gate. He began to realize why as the five hundred slaves once again began to drag the altar toward the gate, filing through it as the ponderous structure got closer and closer. Finally, the front surface of the altar was flush with the wall- and about a foot higher. The Frouzee Delilah rose from her throne and gingerly stepped off the platform and onto the wall, coming face-to-face with the Great Khan.

"Well, the Great Khan, in the flesh," she purred as she looked him up and down. "We have much to discuss."

"Aren't you going to kneel?" asked Liu bluntly.

"Goddesses don't kneel, my dear," she said in her distinctive contralto. Without regarding him any further, she stepped forward and leaned into Kublai Khan's face. The emperor began a second coughing fit as another powerful wave of perfume fumes washed over him.

"Welcome to Xanadu, Empress," he sputtered.

"That's better," she said, stroking her cobra scepter. "Now, it is customary, when favored with the presence of someone of such stature as myself, to respond with at least a meal."

CHAPTER SIXTY-THREE

A DINNER OF EMPIRES

*D*elilah and her retinue were escorted by Khan's soldiers to splendid guest quarters in the palace. As soon as the guards had bowed and retreated past the iron-studded doors, Delilah urgently turned to Briseis.

""Bathsheba's Breath. Make it quick."

"But Your Worship--?

"Yes, yes, I personally find him revolting. But an empire from China all the way to the west...now that is quite appetizing."

"You want to marry him?"

"Did I not tell you I would be empress of China? Marriage is but a tool for the wise. Of course, we mustn't be too hasty. He must think it is his idea. I must give the appearance of needing to be persuaded. But all of the pieces are in place. This is almost too convenient. His favorite wife is dead, and his country is worse off for it. And we have already brought with us a suitable dowry." Delilah stood up, a faraway look in her eyes.

"Think, Briseis, think! What better way to ensure that Frouzea is never threatened by the Mongols again? Delilah, Empress of China!"

A few short hours later, the Frouzean entourage found itself facing an enormous table that stretched almost as far as the eye could see, set in a magnificently decorated hall in the Cane Palace of Xanadu, the delicate wicker structure held up by a series of massive golden columns with sculpted dragons wrapped around them. The table was piled high with a bewildering assortment of dumplings, buns, noodles, seafood, meat, and a thousand other foreign delicacies. Delilah glided in, wearing a dress covered in scallop shells and cockatoo feathers, which gave her the appearance of a seaborne dragon. Her close-fitting dress was made of the skins of dozens of brightly-colored sea snakes, while imitation tentacles fanned out behind her, accentuating the fish-head miter that rose imperiously from her head. A sharkskin cape hung from her shoulders, while Briseis and Salome struggled to carry her silk train, which was covered with the skins of exotic foreign asps and native Australian "fear snakes" and stretched over twenty feet behind her. The "eternal empress" gingerly lowered herself onto a finely embroidered chair next to Khan's spot at the head of the table and admired the dinner service, made out of porcelain, jade, and cinnabar. The meal began with a surprising lack of ceremony as Kublai Khan voraciously attacked his plate, the juices of the meat dribbling down his chin and absorbing into his luxuriant beard. Delilah suppressed a grimace, then put on her best approximation of a sympathetic smile.

"It's my understanding you recently lost your wife – at least, one of them."

A faraway look fell across Khan's round features. "She was the light of my life. All the joy in the world has left me. I sit here in my pleasure palace, bereft of happiness."

Delilah managed a somber look. "I too have felt the pangs of grief. I tragically lost my own husband. He was far too young, in the prime of his life, when the scythe of disease so cruelly cut him down." The empress' voice broke. "I never thought I could truly live again," she said, suppressing a sob. "But there is always hope. There is always another chance," she said, suddenly locking with Khan's bloodshot eyes.

"Then we are kindred spirits indeed," Khan replied. "Now, tell me, Empress, just how you accomplished your country's remarkable recovery! I'm ashamed to say that I had not even heard of Frouzea until very recently, yet now you arrive in dazzling display to rival all the splendors of Asia."

"The way I see it, the recovery of great nations requires a woman's touch," Delilah responded, subtly casting her eyes around the room. "And it also requires rooting out corruption," she said, pointedly glancing at Liu, who swallowed uncomfortably. "One of our first steps was to reform the monetary system and rebuild our military. The excesses and personal venality of the various petty princes of my Empire had drained our coffers, not to mention the unscrupulous policies of its ministers. I simply had to take charge and unite our nation around a single goal – the restoration of our empire and the elimination of our enemies…as well as the pursuit of mutually advantageous friendships." A wicked gleam filled her eye.

Khan leaned forward with interest.

"I must say, Delilah, your audacity in coming here in such display is unrivalled in recent memory. I am flattered that you chose to render your empire's tribute in person."

"I offer no tribute to you, Khan. I offer you so much more. I offer you legitimacy."

Khan bristled as he sat bolt upright in his chair.

"How dare—"

"You and I both have the same problem, Khan."

"And what would that be? Overactive appetites?"

Delilah stole a deliberate glance at the Khan's notably protruding belly. "Hmm. Perhaps," she crooned suggestively, "But that is not what I speak of. Your might and your prowess is renowned throughout the world – at least it used to be."

Khan slammed the goblet down on the table, some of the wine spilling out from his vehemence.

"And just what is that supposed to mean?" his bloodshot eyes bored into Delilah.

"Well, to me it's very simple. Once, you were invincible. Even China could not contain you. Now, you aren't."

"Watch your tongue, woman."

"Oh, I don't think I need to remind you that, as of late, your armies have presided over defeat after defeat. What is wrong, Khan? Is the magic gone? Or have you simply run up against a rather…stubborn obstruction?"

"The jungles of Dai Viet proved to be difficult to penetrate, yes."

"I speak of no jungle. In all of your defeats there has been one common factor. One hated nation that I know and loathe, and that you have come to know."

"*Wil'iah.*" Khan spat out the word with disgust.

"Yes, Wil'iah. The so-called "Faithful Kingdom." Faithful, perhaps, to their own interests. I'm surprised at you, Khan. I would have thought that a warlord as mighty as you would have reduced them to red dust by now."

Khan turned red as he sputtered, "They do not stand alone. They have assembled a pitiful alliance, which even now we are gathering the forces to crush."

"I'm not sure how pitiful it really is. The forces you sent to Dai Viet and Champa were not insignificant." Delilah cocked her head, feigning a pensive expression. "You know, I think I know why you have not been able to crush Wil'iah. They are simply too far from you." She looked down and noticed the Khan's wandering hand headed toward her thigh. "In fact, I would say the hand of Khan has overstretched its reach," she said as she swatted it away.

The Khan's eyes bulged in fury.

"Yes, you are too far away, Great Khan," she crooned. Delilah leaned in now, her eyes flashing dangerously. "And, can you truly mount a foreign invasion of such magnitude as the one required to topple Wil'iah if you lack the support of your own people?"

Khan's nostrils flared as he caught a whiff of her perfume. Still, his umbrage rose above the cloying fumes.

"Just what are you suggesting?"

"It is well known that the circumstances of your election were…unorthodox," Delilah sneered. "Your kurultai was held here, in China, not in the lands of your forefathers. It's no secret that the other khanates of the empire pay you only lip service. And even China, the supposed bastion of your power, is not truly yours."

"How dare you?" Khan thundered, but everyone at the table could see an odd glint begin to cloud his eyes as he looked on Delilah with a mixture of fury and growing intrigue.

"You claim to be the emperor of China," Delilah said, "But another lives whose claim is more legitimate." Delilah suddenly rose from the table, abandoning her half-eaten Peking duck, and began to walk toward the door. Briseis and Salome scrambled to their feet to heft the outrageous snakeskin train.

"What!?" Khan bellowed.

"I'm certain you don't advertise this, but the body of Zhao Bing, Emperor of Song China, was never found at the Battle of Yamen." Delilah replied as she continued to advance toward the door, not making eye contact with the khan.

"His ship was destroyed. The only Song scum to survive the battle was that rat, Zhang Shijie."

"That's what Zhang would like to think. I offer you no tribute, but information as someone in a position to help you, out of the blackness of my heart."

Khan now rose from the table, sending a china cup clattering to the ground, where it broke into a thousand pieces.

"What information!?"

Delilah, still advancing toward the door that led to the exit of the banquet hall, stopped and paused for emphasis. She looked back at Khan, the ringlets of her hair flipping coquettishly.

"Zhao Bing, the last emperor of the Song Dynasty and true emperor of China, lives."

Khan nearly collapsed from shock.

"How do you know that?" he demanded.

"Well, it's quite interesting – King Tamino of Wil'iah is in possession of a pug dog, a perfectly contemptible creature. Since it is well known that such a breed was created to serve Chinese emperors, the cur's presence in the court raised my suspicions. I had a source of mine, placed in a position to discover such things, investigate. Zhao Bing is in Wil'iah. Frouzea has a border with Wil'iah over three thousand miles long. Think on these things."

With that, she swept out of the room, followed by Salome and Briseis, both struggling to control the enormous train as it billowed behind the empress. Kublai Khan collapsed back into his protesting chair, his eyes filled with a mixture of alarm and admiration.

CHAPTER SIXTY-FOUR

THE PLEASURE GARDENS OF XANADU

*T*he full moon reflected off the placid waters of the pond that surrounded a mood-altering pavilion set on a picturesque island in the middle of a lake, accessible only by an arched bridge. The moonlight smiled down on the miles of parkland that surrounded the lake, with rolling hills and dark forests, all surrounded by the massive protective walls of the palace. Delilah looked languidly at the surface as small ripples betrayed the location of the carp that frolicked in the still waters. Her "moon goddess" dress, specially made at enormous expense by artisans in Gath, looked back at her, reflected in the placid water. A diaphanous cloak hung about her shoulders, a veil of midnight-blue silk as subtle as a whisper, studded with small diamonds to create the appearance of the night sky. Bunched satin cascaded down her front, woven throughout with dozens of planet-like pearls and star-like sapphires. A great silver disk encompassed her head; set on her forehead was an enormous, mesmerizing moonstone. Suddenly, she heard thunderous, elephantine steps behind her. Kublai Khan huffed and puffed his way over the groaning bridge.

"The poems and sonnets do not lie about the pleasure-gardens of Xanadu," she said.

"My life, and the lives of my wives, are filled with pleasure," he responded.

Delilah smirked. "Perhaps. Perhaps. But I doubt highly that the delights here can compare with the hedonistic splendors of Gath."

"I will wager that they can," Khan said as he reached out to caress Delilah's shoulder, visible beneath the billowing, diaphanous blouse that had replaced her dragon costume. Delilah winced at his touch and tore herself away, gazing once again at the moon.

"Why talk of pleasure when we have more important topics to discuss?" she diverted.

"What more important topic could there be for a woman such as you? Not since Empress Chabi have I met someone with the fire, the vigor, the brilliance, and the beauty as the eternal empress of Frouzea!"

"Ardent words from a man who, not two hours ago, thought me an impudent woman better seen than heard."

"To see you is to see a goddess. To hear you is to hear heaven itself," Khan said as his lungs filled once again with Delilah's perfume. The slightest smile played across the empress' features.

"Is this what you tell all visiting queens? I give you vital military information, and you respond with insipid sweet nothings. Now is the time for action, Khan."

"Indeed it is!" Khan lunged forward and wrapped the squirming empress in a tight embrace. "Marry me, Delilah, goddess of all magnificent splendor! Together, we will rule the world!"

Delilah extricated herself from the Khan's grip and pushed the shocked emperor back, turning her chin up in a haughty sneer.

"I am not looking for a new personal relationship at this time, only a military one. As impressive as your gardens are," she said, sweeping her hand around their splendid surroundings, "I have no need of baubles or playthings to satisfy me, and I have no desire to become yet another addition to your collection. Is this how you repay my generous gift of vital intelligence, with an attempt to turn me into some sort of harem-slave? Begone!"

Khan recoiled, anger kindling in his eyes. But then, he drew in his breath again, and Delilah's cloying fragrances once again invaded his lungs.

"Just think, Delilah, you have already brought a dowry! We could be married without delay!"

Delilah scoffed. "Just because your armies have run roughshod over most – *but not all* – of Asia, just because kingdom after kingdom has fallen to your conquests, doesn't mean you can have whatever you want. I don't need you."

Khan's eyes narrowed as his nostrils flared with rage.

"Then you shall *want* me."

With that, he turned from the Empress and trounced back over the groaning bridge.

As his bulky features receded into the distance, a smile slowly spread across Delilah's sharp features. She suddenly started as a figure emerged from behind a bush on the island.

"You turned him down?"

"Salome! Where did you come from!?"

"Somebody has to keep my goddess safe!" Salome genuflected.

"Never mind that. I have him just where I want him. Don't fret. He'll be back."

CHAPTER SIXTY-FIVE

KHAN'S TERMS

*T*he next morning, Delilah, once again at her toilette, sat up straight as the air was assaulted by a pounding on the doors to the guest house.

"He's back," she purred to Salome, who held out a palette of cosmetics for the empress while Briseis applied kohl to her eyes.

"Of course he is, Your Worship."

"It's time," Delilah said as she rose from the vanity, dressed once more in her trademark snake headdress. She slithered over to the door of the toilette and sidled down the stairs. Heracles stood in front of the doors, his massive arms folded in a gesture of defiance to whatever lay beyond.

"I don't know who it is, Your Worship," he grunted.

"Oh don't worry, I do," she smiled.

"If Khan tries something, I'll gut him like a fish," Heracles growled protectively.

"Oh, this situation calls for much more subtlety than that. I suspect he is back to beg for my hand once again."

Delilah noticed a hint of color fill Heracles' intimidating cheeks.

"And just what do you plan to say to him?" he said.

"We'll see what his terms are, won't we?"

A flicker of a jealous fire flared in Heracles' dark eyes as he yanked the doors open.

"WHAT!?" he bellowed.

Nothing could have prepared him for the sight that greeted him. The broad square in front of the guest quarters was filled with a vast array of gifts of all kinds, presided over by hundreds of soldiers in full parade dress. Exotic animals in cages, finely-carved jade sculptures, chests overflowing with silks, barrows of spices, and treasures plundered from the famed cities of the Silk Road -- Samarkand, Bukhara, Balkh, and Merv -- were strewn about like so many lawn ornaments. Greatest of all was towering tree fashioned completely from silver. Two silver snakes twined their way up the trunk of the tree toward the many silver fruits that hung from its leaves, while four silver lions stood guard over basins at its base. An angel holding a trumpet crowned the whole ostentatious assemblage.

At the center of it all, on a sedan chair carried by groaning slaves, was Kublai Khan. As his eyes caught their first glimpse of Delilah's snake headdress, they filled with an all-consuming fire, and the emperor hauled himself to the ground, approaching the Frouzee.

"You didn't listen to me last night, but maybe you will

listen to me now. These gifts are the merest token of my ardor for you. A woman such as you could make us truly great again, could restore the terrible fire that once bade the entire world tremble at the name, 'Mongol!'"

Delilah haughtily stared down at him.

"Just what is that?" she asked, pointing languidly at the tree.

"That is the most prized treasure of the Mongol Empire, the Silver Tree of Karakorum! It will fulfill all your deepest desires! I offer it to you along with my heart!" Khan raised his hands and clapped. Suddenly, the mechanical angel atop the tree snapped to attention, bringing the trumpet to its lips and emitting a blast of sound. In response, hidden spigots in the leaves of the tree instantly emitted gushing streams of varied alcoholic beverages, while the lions belched fermented mare's milk.

Delilah looked decidedly unimpressed.

"What are your terms?"

"Name them, my goddess!"

Delilah smirked as she languidly extended her hand to Briseis, who hastily handed her a gold-filigreed scroll. Delilah dramatically snapped it open, then began to read.

"If I choose to deign to accept your offer of your hand in marriage, you will comply with the following conditions. The Frouzean Empire, including the principalities, territories, and imperial provinces, shall remain solely my domain, of which I shall remain sole and eternal Empress. Furthermore, you will elevate me to a position above your other wives- not as a mere plaything, but as an equal, a partner and confidante in the creation and running of the greatest empire the world has ever seen. In the course of our conquests of the remaining pitiful, shaking corners of the Earth, you will render to me sole custody of the following territories: Greece, Thrace, Asia Minor, the remainder of the southern continent, Antarctica, Syria, the Levant, Judea, Sinai and Arabia, the former lands of the Roman Imperial Province of Africa Proconsolaris and Iberia, including my ancestral lands of Carthage, the islands of Cyprus, Crete, Sicily, Sardinia, and Corsica, and Egypt stretching as far as the source of the Nile, wherever that may be. In return, I shall be to you a devoted and faithful wife for as long as you shall live. I will help you restore your empire to dominance, just as I have restored mine from the rubble of ruin and humiliation. Together, we will be an unstoppable force such as the world has never seen. I promise you Frouzea's assistance in your own conquest, and the addition to your personal domain, of India, Pagan, Dai Viet, Champa, Singhasari, Japan, the remaining independent portions of Russia, and the far, dark, and mysterious lands of Europe."

Delilah took a deep breath, returned the scroll to Briseis, whose hands trembled at the sheer audacity of the offer, and looked directly at Khan.

"Are those terms acceptable?"

Khan opened his mouth, but, before he could answer, Liu, his adviser, rushed into the scene, red-faced and panting.

"Great Khan! Great Khan! Do not listen to this woman! Her demands—"

Liu's strangled exhortation was instantly cut off as Khan held out a hand to bid him be silent. The entire square fell silent as Khan approached Delilah, still standing authoritatively at the top of the stairs. Then, the crowd gasped as he dropped to one knee.

"In my country, it is customary for the proposer to drop to both knees," Delilah purred.

Heedless of the whispers of shock from the audience, Khan dutifully dropped his other knee.

"I accept your terms. Do you accept my offer?"

Delilah looked around for a moment, as if pondering the question. Then, with great deliberateness, she brought her head down again, so her eyes met Khan's.

"Yes."

The crowd erupted into cheers. Liu raced forward again and tugged on Khan's sleeve.

"O Great Khan, I implore you to reconsider. That woman is not to be trusted. Her actions have left a pattern of death and destruction across all of the known world. Need I remind you that every one of her 'husbands' has mysteriously died soon after marrying her – and she ended up with their territories?"

"I am different. I am the Great Khan. I am untouchable."

"Don't be so sure."

Khan suddenly stood straight up, his eyes inflamed with rage.

"Just who do you think you are, Liu?"

"Yes, just who do you think you are?" Delilah crooned as she seemed to float down the stairs to face the minister.

Liu's eyes narrowed. "Someone who recognizes you and your conniving schemes for what they are."

Delilah feigned a look of shock. "Conniving? Do you really want to speak about conniving, Liu?" Delilah walked up to Khan and began to twist his moustache in her long-nailed fingers before turning back to Liu.

"My sources tell me that you, Liu, have consistently, personally profited off of your economic policies, which have caused out-of-control inflation and left the average Chinese citizen virtually penniless." She reached into a hidden pocket in her bodice and withdrew a wad of paper money, which she threw up into the air and allowed to float down around her. "Look at this. Worthless. Only one person has profited from all of this." Her eyes narrowed as they focused on Liu. *"You."*

Khan's barrel-like chest swelled as he puffed himself up. "Is this true, Liu?"

Liu stammered, searching for a reply as his bowels filled with panic. "Don't listen to her!" He rounded on the empress. "Would you care to explain why your previous husband, in the prime of his life, mysteriously died, on your wedding night, and then you conveniently ended up with sole ownership of all of his territories?"

Delilah dramatically clutched her heart as a black tear ran down her face, the kohl streaking across her cheek.

"You would exploit my tragedy and sorrow to cover your own misdeeds?"

Khan rounded on Liu, his nostrils flared with rage.

"How vile of you, you scheming scum!"

Delilah snapped her fingers at Salome, who emerged from the shadows carrying a folder stuffed with sheets of paper.

"In fact," Delilah sneered, "I even hear that people on the street refer to you as 'Khan's villainous minister." She turned to Khan. "Khan, given the...unusual circumstances of your kurultai, it is absolutely essential that you retain China's loyalty to maintain your...legitimacy. I have here signed affidavits from three dozen important Chinese merchants swearing that this man demanded extra taxes as 'protection,' and promptly pocketed the profits." Khan instantly bristled in response as he furiously turned to Liu.

Delilah crooned on. "And surely this crawling worm's inflationary economic policies have not endeared your administration to them. His corruption is as renowned as my beauty."

Khan grunted in response as Liu sputtered, trying to find words to defend himself.

"In fact, I might almost call his actions treasonous." Her words dripped with venom.

"Now, this is outrageous!" Liu shouted, balling his fist. But he could see that his indignation failed to influence Khan, whose eyes locked on him with a cold fury.

"I assume treason bears the same penalty here that it does in my country?" Delilah purred.

"Death," Khan whispered. He looked almost hesitant for a moment as he regarded the features of what he once thought was his most loyal minister. "The penalty is death. Liu shall be executed at dawn tomorrow."

Delilah straightened, a look of triumph crossing her luridly-painted features.

"Why wait?"

She snapped her arm out, her long-nailed finger outstretched directly at Liu. Somewhere in her billowing sleeve, a mechanism clicked, and a brightly-feathered dart shot out from below Delilah's finger and buried itself in Liu's Adam's apple. The minister was only able to gurgle in shock as he almost instantly began foaming at the mouth and toppled over, spasmodically writhing on the floor for about thirty seconds before he became completely still.

Delilah clasped her hands together with delight before turning back to Khan.

"*Now,*" she smiled sweetly, "I *love* planning weddings!"

CHAPTER SIXTY-SIX

THE WEDDING OF EVIL

*T*he square in front of the Palace of Xanadu once again filled to the bursting with throngs of people anxious to catch a glimpse of their new empress. Suddenly, fireworks exploded in a riot of color, instantly silencing the bystanders.

Through the gate at the entrance to the square marched four elephants in perfect synchronicity. Stretched between them was a silk blanket, on which Delilah luxuriated in traditional Mongol wedding attire, complete with a *boghtagh* headdress resembling an inverted boot. At her appearance, the crowd once again erupted into cheers. At the other end of the square, Kublai Khan appeared astride an exhausted-looking war horse, which barely supported the Emperor's great weight.

As was the custom, the bride and groom circled the entire palace three times, feted with salutary cannon fire each time they passed the main gate as they were bombarded with cheers. Not just the square, but the entire parade route around the castle, was packed with well-wishers, who craned their necks from every window and balcony along the road.

Finally, the elephants and the horse arrived back in front of the gate, which had been filled in with a wooden barrier, again following the Mongolian custom. Kublai Khan alighted from his horse and ordered a great battering ram brought forward to destroy the barrier. It struck three times, each reverberating crash attended by yet more cheers from the audience. At the third blow, the wooden barricade came crashing down, and hundreds of servants streamed out of the opening, unveiling a pure white carpet.

On command, the elephants knelt, and servants brought a cinnabar staircase forward. Delilah gracefully alighted from the silk blanket and swept down the stairs, coming face to face with Khan. Then, together, they walked down the white carpet, at the end of which an elder waited with two large tankards of *airag,* a drink made from fermented mare's milk. Delilah watched in fascinated horror as Khan swallowed his entire allotment in one gulp. She looked uncertainly at the foul-smelling liquid as it was presented to her.

The things I do for my empire, she thought as she held her breath and quaffed it down.

The elder produced a blue scarf, known as a *hadag,* and placed it over a shining goblet that he proffered to the couple. He then began to recite ancient poems concerning love and commitment, the words of which Delilah didn't understand. She didn't really care, but she noticed a tear slide down Kublai Khan's face.

At the close of the poetry, the elder turned to Delilah.

"It is traditional for me to extol your mother's virtues, noting how well she raised you."

"Goddesses don't have mothers. They are mothers – of empires," Delilah crooned in response.

"Very well," the elder nodded. "In that case, I pronounce you man and wife – and you," he said, regarding Delilah, "empress of China and all the lands of the Great Khan!"

Delilah smiled as a list of all of Khan's territories began playing itself in her head. She whispered to herself.

"Oh Frouzee, I have surpassed thee!"

✳ ✳ ✳

The evening's revelry finished, Delilah found herself alone with Kublai Khan. The Mongol Emperor rushed forward to roughly embrace her and plant dozens of kisses on her painted cheeks, licking his lips at the strange taste the makeup left.

"Oh my love, there will be plenty of time for that later. Now, we must talk of the action at hand. To strike our most dearly-hated enemy Wil'iah, you must cross an ocean. But to me, they are on my back doorstep. At any moment, I can attack the very heart of that despised nation. If you want to destroy Wil'iah, you need me," she said, grabbing Khan's marauding hand and bringing it to her cheek.

"You are still across the ocean yourself," he grunted, although Delilah triumphantly noticed him start to blink, as though his eyelids were drawing heavy.

"Ah yes, there is that detail, isn't there? It is plain that you don't understand the Wil'iahns like I do. If you send an invasion fleet, their navy will attack and destroy it. But they have a strict code that they do not attack civilian targets. Now that you have normalized trade relations with me, you can smuggle your troops and weapons into my country with merchant shipments. Wil'iah wouldn't dare attack an unarmed merchant vessel. It is against their misguided sense of honor. Then, when your forces are fully assembled, we strike. I will hand you Wil'iah on a golden platter."

Khan nodded, then frowned. "Won't the Wil'iahns figure it out?"

Delilah shook her head. "Not if we keep our movements discreet. I have decided to add one more bauble to my dowry."

Delilah reached forward to stroke Kublai Khan's impressively pointy beard.

"I have in my personal possession an island that is of limited use to me, but could be of great benefit to you. The natives call it Trouwunna. I call it Ithaca. *You* can call it whatever you like."

Khan grunted in surprise as he fought to keep his eyes open. "You will give me a territory?"

"Yes, yes," she said as she twirled his moustache in her long-nailed fingers. "I will give you the island of Ithaca for you to do with as you please. You can land your troops there. But Wil'iah must not know that I have transferred it to you. We will pretend that it is still under the Frouzean flag so as not to arouse suspicion. After Wil'iah is destroyed, it is ours."

Khan sank onto the bed next to her, yawning. Delilah put up a finger.

"One more thing. I know that your empire sometimes tries to be merciful to its conquered populations. That will not be adequate here. When Wil'iah is conquered, she shall be destroyed – and her people with it. You will be gifted a great, empty nation to settle as you wish."

"How delightfully vicious," Khan grinned.

"I am practiced in many delights," Delilah whispered into his ear. Khan suppressed another yawn as he fell onto his back.

"Soon, Khan, soon. Soon the world will be ours!"

"When do we attack?" Khan wheezed, breathing heavily.

"If my spies are to be believed, Wil'iah's legendary founder, Hezekiah, is on his last legs. He is expected to die in no more than a year. His successor, Tamino, is a weak and cowardly child more interested in art and opera than the business of fighting. When Hezekiah dies, the kingdom will be thrown into chaos."

"And then…" Khan said, his sentence drifting off into a deafening snore.

Delilah smiled.

"And then...we strike!"

When Kublai Khan awoke the next morning, she was gone.

※ ※ ※

Teeming hordes of onlookers crowded the docks and quays of Gath as a giant gilded warship ponderously hauled into the harbor, flanked by two columns of smaller, but still impressive, vessels – and two large Mongol junks. As the *Glory of Astarte* approached the quay that directly faced the grand Imperial Avenue that led straight to the acropolis, excited, nervous speculation spread through the waiting populace, especially once they noticed the bizarre, giant pagoda that had seemingly sprouted from the deck of the ship.

"She took a huge load of treasure to China. She said it wasn't tribute, but it sure looked like it to me."

"Hold your treasonous tongue! Our goddess would never submit to a foreign ruler like that!"

"What do you think will become of us? Are we part of the Mongol Empire now?"

The gossip came to an instant halt as a huge ramp came crashing down to the dock from the bow of the *Glory of Astarte,* accompanied by a thrilling fanfare from the lines of heralds that fronted the low seawall of the docks. A familiar hulking figure stood proud at the top of the ramp.

"Citizens of the Frouzean Empire!" Heracles bellowed. "Her Worship's retinue has returned with treasures from China!"

A hubbub of excitement swept through the crowd.

"First, may I present, back from their first overseas assignment, the Homeric Guard!"

The famed military unit appeared in their full regalia and marched down towards the adoring populace, who pelted them with flowers as the heralds along the dockside blasted out the new *March of the Homeric Guard,* recently commissioned by Delilah for the occasion of her homecoming from China.

"Today is a day of spirit and pride for our empire, the greatest on Earth!" Heracles roared. "For we have returned with our holds full to the bursting with treasures of tribute to the eternal radiance of our goddess, from the Great Khan himself!"

A gasp ran through the crowd as the same hordes of slaves that had carried the riches of Delilah's dowry through the gates of Xanadu now emerged from the depths of her flagship laden with the wares of Khan's favor – treasures of greater value than what Delilah had brought with her to begin with. The cheers of the crowd grew louder and louder as the silks, jade, cinnabar, gold, spices, artifacts, and exotic animals passed up the avenue in glittering array, but nothing prepared them for the vision of a shimmering silver tree, pulled by a team of trained, sedated tigers.

"The Silver Tree of Karakorum, the greatest treasure of the Mongol Empire!" Heracles proudly announced the crown jewel of the parade. "Given freely as a token of appreciation of our glorious goddess!"

A deafening roar of approval rose from the crowd.

"Speaking of our goddess, I'm sure you'd like to see her!" Heracles responded.

The hysterical ovation of the crowd doubled, but it instantly died down to an awed silence as the pagoda atop the imperial flagship began to ponderously inch forward, dragged by four bull elephants. The crowd leaned forward in anguished anticipation as the giant structure slowly worked its way down the ramp, finally coming to a stop on the dock. The audience waited with bated breath.

They didn't have to wait long. The pagoda seemed to disappear in a blinding, thunderous flash of light as hundreds of fireworks detonated all along its length in a glittering display. When the smoke cleared, Delilah stood atop the pagoda, dressed in a scintillating costume designed to resemble an imperial Chinese dragon, complete with iridescent scales and tendrils and a thirty-foot long train that trailed down the side of the pagoda.

Looking as though he might burst with pride, Heracles said, "May I present Her Worship Delilah, Second Incarnation to Earth of the Goddess Astarte and Eternal Empress of the Frouzean Empire, Everlasting Object of Adoration of the citizens and denizens of the Principalities and Provinces of said Empire, Ruler of the Principalities of

Gath, Gaza, Ekron, Ashkelon, and Ashdod, Dominator of the Territories of Outer Frouzea, Nullarbor, and Ithaca and the Provinces of Arboria, and Aurania, Image of the Goddess Tanit and beloved leader of the Imperial Provinces of Upper and Lower Tanitania, Sovereign by Historical Right of Canaan, Egypt, Sinai, Iberia, Utica, Cartagena, Mauritania, Tunisia, Carthage, Africa Proconsolaris, Attica, Illyria, Argolis, Achaea, Thrace, Epirus, Crete, Cyprus, the Cyclades, Macedonia, and Asia Minor, Empress of Antarctica and Atlantis and terror of the southern continent, the glorious, the inexorable, the beautiful – AND" -- the audience leaned forward again, hanging on his every word with intense anticipation – "— Empress of China and ALL the lands of the Mongol Empire, including Cathay and Manji, Dali, Goryeo, Tibet, Gansu, Inner and Outer Mongolia, Manchuria, and Xinjiang, the lands of the Jagadai Khanate, including Khwarzim, Sogdiana, Chaganian, Khuttal, Chach, Orushana, Farghana,, the great cities of Balkh, Merv, Burkhara, and Samarkand, the lands of the Khanate of the Golden Horde, including Russia and Siberia, and the lands of the Ilkhanate, including Persia, Mesopotamia, Armenia, and Azerbaijan! Today our glorious empire is joined in the bonds of love and matrimony with the second-greatest empire on Earth – and together we will be unstoppable!"

The very earth seemed to shake as the audience's stunned silence rapidly turned into frenzied ovation of their empress' triumph. A veritable forest of Frouzean flags sprouted into the air as Delilah's triumphal pagoda was dragged up the avenue toward the acropolis. She was preceded by a procession of the Homeric Guard, now joined by additional military units of the empire, replete with chariots and mobile siege equipment, followed by the parade of her treasures.

Two figures in the crowd, their faces obscured by deep hoods, seemed less than enthusiastic as the seemingly-endless military parade passed before the adoring onlookers.

"I swear I've seen that Homeric guard before," one of them whispered to the other.

"I think they're cycling them back in to make it look like there's more of them than there really are," came the response. "That's an old trick. However, it's not the numbers of troops here that concern me. If she has really concluded an alliance with the Mongols, then I'm afraid the day we've feared has finally, well and truly, arrived. We must make for the Hidden Fortress at once and begin our preparations."

"God save Wil'iah," came the forlorn, hushed reply.

"God, and good planning, will."

CHAPTER SIXTY-SEVEN

THE REDEMPTION OF TOGHON

Yangzhou, Jiangsu Province, China

*T*oghon, Kublai Khan's disgraced son, stewed in his living room in the hovel where he now took up residence in Yangzhou. Disgusted at the situation, he hurled a teacup across the room, which shattered as it hit the wall.

"If only it weren't for that scheming Wil'iah!" He yelled in a rage.

Suddenly, his rant was cut short by the tinkle of a bell at the front door. Toghon brushed his unwashed, greasy black hair out of his face in a vain attempt at respectability, and opened the door, to reveal a modest-looking postman.

"A letter has arrived for you. It's postmarked Xanadu," the postman said as he bowed deeply.

A shocked, hungry look invading Toghon's eyes, he snatched the letter from the postman's outstretched hand.

Dear Toghon,

It's my understanding that you're a man with something to prove. If you want to get in your father's good graces once more, and if you want to finally have your revenge on Wil'iah, I have an opportunity for you. We are in the midst of planning an invasion. I am willing to offer you a command position in this war, in exchange for your loyalty. You must return to Xanadu at once, and from there make preparations to proceed to our muster point on the island of Ithaca.

Your (step)mother,
Delilah.

Toghon hurled the letter aside, whirled around, and began throwing his few remaining possessions into a travel bag.

"Going somewhere?" asked the postman.

"Yes indeed. I have a country to invade."

CHAPTER SIXTY-EIGHT

OFF TO BALTHCUTTA

Trukanamoa, Wil'iah, 1293 AD

*J*amino sat at his desk in Trukanamoa Palace, sorting through the various pieces of mail that had accumulated that morning. Opening a scroll that had been sealed with an emblem displaying a shield supported by two black swans, he scanned the contents for a moment, then called over to Avora'tru'ivi.

"It looks like the White Cathedral in Balthcutta is finally completed! They want us to come dedicate it."

"That's a long way away," Avora'tru'ivi said. Balthcutta was Wil'iah's second-largest city, a port on the east coast, recently built. The newly-completed cathedral was the crown jewel of the city and a symbol of its completion.

"I'm not sure if I should go," Tamino said. "Dad's not doing very well right now, despite Milcah's best efforts. I feel like I'm needed here."

"I know how you feel," Avora'tru'ivi said, "but he would probably want you to go. All the same, you should probably just ask him."

Tamino wordlessly nodded, then walked out of the office. He urgently strode through the halls of the palace, finally reaching a chamber he dreaded to enter. Finally, gathering his wits, he opened the door.

Hezekiah lay in a large canopy bed, being tended to by Milcah. Queen Adirah sat in a chair reading from a Bible. Tamino winced as he saw the large, ornately carved cane propped at the foot of the bed and the old King's precariously gaunt frame.

"Father, the White Cathedral has been completed, and they want me to go dedicate it. I know it was one of your pet projects, but I really don't think we should leave you right now. I think you need me."

"No, Wil'iah needs its King," Hezekiah responded. I know this may be difficult for you to accept"— the old man wheezed – "But I really can take care of myself. It is the duty of the king to dedicate new cathedrals built with royal funds. You need to go to Balthcutta. Don't worry about me." Tamino could tell that the words were more reassuring than what Hezekiah really believed. "I didn't pass my sword to you so you could neglect your duties, did I?"

"But father, what if—"

"We do not trade in unpleasant hypotheticals, my son, not when there is work to be done. Go, and take your family with you. Judith will love the little excursion. I don't think she's ever been to our newest city."

"Mother, are you alright with this?" Tamino asked Adirah.

"Your duties take you to Balthcutta," she responded. "We'll be alright here."

Hezekiah's eyes flashed to Milcah, who was busy mixing an elixir for the king in a valiant, though apparently vain, effort to combat his mysterious condition. "And Milcah, if Judith goes, you go too. Your place is with her."

Milcah protested. "But sir---"

"No 'buts.' I may not wear the crown anymore, but I'd like to think my wishes still warrant obedience."

"Very well. I will collect the child." Milcah saluted and left the room.

"Father, Mother, I love you," Tamino said simply.

"I love you too. Now, go dedicate that church!" Hezekiah took a sip of the elixir and coughed. "Goodness, I hate this stuff! If I didn't trust Milcah so much, I'd think she was trying to poison me!"

Tamino exited the chamber to go prepare to leave. He had one other major errand to complete. Another office lay two doors down from Tamino's main office. The door stood open, guarded by two stern nights. Tamino boldly stepped through.

Jeremiah sat hunched over his own desk, reading through a military report from the Army of Tjoritja, the local military unit responsible for the defense of the capital.

"What is it?" he asked as he looked up at his brother.

"Avora and I need to go to Balthcutta to dedicate the White Cathedral. I hate to leave right now, but Dad insists that we go. You know what that means. As sovereign protector, the defense of the city becomes your responsibility in the event of any …*adverse circumstances.*"

Jeremiah stood up abruptly, his intense eyes boring into

Tamino's soul. "You're right, I don't think it's a good idea for you to go right now, but it's your decision. As always, I vow that I will do my duty and defend this city to my dying breath, if that becomes necessary."

Tamino smiled grimly and nodded. "I always know I can count on you."

A few short hours later, the royal caravan began its long trek on the dusty road to Balthcutta.

CHAPTER SIXTY-NINE

DELILAH'S INVASION COUNCIL

Island of Ithaca, Frouzean Empire

*T*emur Khan stepped off the deck of his disguised "merchant" junk, casting a self-satisfied glance at the cargo hold, which ostensibly contained bales of silk, but really concealed three hundred soldiers. Gingerly walking down the gangway, he ruefully surveyed the grimy docks of the port town of Ithaca, a distant outpost of the Frouzean Empire on this nearly-forgotten island—at least it used to be. The dilapidated harbor teemed with activity as dozens of Mongol junks brought their secret human cargo to this muster point. Still others unloaded siege equipment, while poorly-maintained Frouzean galleys darted in and out of the harbor to begin to convey the cargo to the mainland.

Temur and his retinue proceeded up a cracked set of stairs to a large temple-like building that, even in its present condition, was impressive. A pair of Homeric guards with blank expressions swept the doors open for him.

Standing around a table in the center of the impressive colonnaded hall were a group of people, some of whom he recognized- his cousin Toghon, and the legendary generals Balin the Balaan and Nasir-al-din. The other Frouzeans he didn't know- but all had gathered here for a single purpose. Spread across the table was a map of the continent, with Wil'iah highlighted in a belligerent shade of red.

Despite the experience and seniority of the generals at the table, all attention was effortlessly commanded by Delilah, who wore an exceptionally loud garment that she referred to as "formal invasion wear." Her giant peaked shoulder pads and lurid cape were trimmed in bright orange silk intended to call to mind consuming flames. The shadow of her omnipresent snake headdress fell over the map as she described her plan.

"Wil'iah has three major population centers- their east and west coasts, and the region surrounding their detestable capital of Trukanamoa. If we can cut off these centers from each other and destroy them individually, Wil'iah is finished. Fortunately, we have at our disposal overwhelming superiority in numbers- Wil'iah's standing army is about one twelfth of what we have mustered." She pointed her scepter at the east coast.

"First, we will discuss the eastern theater of operations. Wil'iah's principal city in the region is Balthcutta, their second-most important port and most populous city. Balthcutta is well-defended and is expected to be a tough nut to crack. However, if we can cut it off from the surrounding territories, and destroy the naval forces defending it from the sea, we should be able to starve them into submission. To this end, our eastern forces will split into two main groups. One group, the coastal force, will be overseen by myself, General Toghon, and the Princes Minos of Ashkelon and Diomedes of Ekron," she said, nodding to two severe-looking men who stood to her right.

"The other group will proceed inland and attack Wil'iah's backcountry west of the mountains. This is their agricultural breadbasket. We will seize these food reserves for ourselves and deny them to the Wil'iahns, then drive north to cut off the populous east coast from the rest of the country, making any effort at reinforcement impossible. This effort will be led by Nasir al-Din and Ajax of Gath," she said, turning to Ajax.

"In addition, the Wil'iahns have built a string of fortifications in the mountains themselves. We expect these to present a threat to our rear as we proceed north into the country. To that end, Arigh Khaiya and Nestor of Ashdod will attack these fortifications."

"As for Balthcutta's naval defenses, our combined fleet, led by Admiral Omar Khan and Admiral Odysseus of Gath, will engage the Wil'iahn fleet, which is expected to sortie from Balthcutta to its defense. Once their fleet is destroyed, we will attack the city from the sea."

"Meanwhile," Delilah continued, "An equally-large force will attack Trukanamoa from the center. Trukanamoa presents a unique obstacle to us, as it is protected by a range of mountains that extends two hundred miles in either direction. While the main thrust of our attack will be from the south, this force will also split into ancillary side forces that will circumvent the mountains, destroy the fortifications guarding their approaches, and attack Trukanamoa from its less-heavily defended north."

Temur interjected. "There's a reason for the weaker northern defenses. Wil'iah can expect help from Manasseh to defend Trukanamoa's northern approaches."

Delilah laughed. "That's what they think. There won't be a Manasseh to turn to when Prince Jason's finished with them! His armies will simultaneously attack Issachar and Manasseh to ensure Wil'iah will get no help from its pitiful little friends. Command of the center operation will be given to you, Temur, in conjunction with Prince Menelaus of Gaza."

She now pointed her scepter to the west. "That leaves only one more operation for us! The accursed city of Trujustakanoa, Wil'iah's most important port. Fortunately, it is cut off from the rest of Wil'iah by a nearly impassable desert and is directly in the sights of the great army of Tanitania. Prince Hamilcar Barca of Tanitania will lead his armies first through the Pilbara Confederacy, which we expect to surrender in a matter of weeks, and then lay siege on Trujustakanoa itself. This concludes my wonderful plan!" She delightedly clapped her hands together, the long, red nails making a dissonant clacking sound.

Temur cleared his throat again. "This seems well-thought out, but surely the Wil'iahns will have made similar analyses of their weaknesses. Won't they be prepared for us?"

Delilah's mouth twisted into a wicked smile. "Ordinarily, yes, but we have a special surprise planned for them. We will attack them right when they are at their weakest, their most despondent – and their most unprepared."

She slammed her scepter down on the map. "Gentlemen, it's been a pleasure giving you orders. I look forward to watching your performance. Don't disappoint me."

The Mongol leaders curtly nodded and left the room to attend to their preparations. Delilah picked up a brush pen and dipped it in a florid, red inkwell. Then, with a flourish, she inscribed a great red X over the map of Wil'iah.

"Soon," she cooed.

The other Frouzean generals around her jeered with glee, then, one by one, left the room. Ajax the Lesser, now prince of Gath in the aftermath of his brother's demise, was the last to leave. Just before he exited the door, Delilah's hand caught his upper arm, stopping him. He turned to look back at her, a hungry look filling his eyes.

"Ajax, I have given you one of the most important assignments- the conquest of the backcountry. If you don't fail me, if you succeed…"

Ajax's fist clenched with emotion as his eyes burned with desire.

"What about your marriage to Kublai Khan?"

"I have a plan for him. Don't think about him. Every time you burn a Wil'iahn village and put its citizens to the sword, think of the rewards that await you. Think of *me.*"

With that, Delilah flounced out of the room, leaving Ajax staring wolfishly at the map of Wil'iah. Singling out the judge of Vrenga'nui, he brought his titanic fist hammering down on the table.

CHAPTER SEVENTY

FIRE ON THE MOUNTAIN

Balthcutta, Wil'iah

"**W**ell, that went well," Tamino said as he and Avora'tru'ivi stepped through the burnished double doors into the throne room of the Castle of Balthcutta. The room, located near the top of the resolute pile of whitewashed stone that rose in three tiers above the waves that crashed into the rocky outcropping that guarded the harbor, had a commanding view of the ships riding at anchor as well as the distant, blue-hazed mountains to the west. Overall, the glistening city of Balthcutta, recently built to a master-plan initiated by Hezekiah twenty years prior, represented the very best that Wil'iah had to offer, with harmonious, broad avenues, modern port facilities, impressive walls, lush gardens, and even a large tidal pool inhabited by flocks of native black swans. Also visible to the west was the magnificent White Cathedral, which Tamino and Avora'tru'ivi had just dedicated.

"It's a magnificent church. A credit to the country," the queen replied as she gathered her ceremonial skirts and bent to sit down in the plush silk throne that faced the open window, flanked by the Tahili standards of the king and queen and backed by a vertically-hanging Wil'iahn battle flag.

Before she could sit, the pounding of running feet echoed through the double doors from the hallway. Avora'tru'ivi stood with a start, and both she and Tamino whirled around to see a red-faced courier, drenched in sweat, stagger through the door, his chest heaving with effort. He was followed immediately by a peeved-looking member of the Judith Corps, who scowled at the courier.

"I'm sorry, your Faithfulnesses, I couldn't stop him on time." She panted at the monarchs.

"No..time…I had to tell…" wheezed the courier as he collapsed on the floor from exhaustion.

His eyes rapidly filling with alarm, Tamino stooped down to help the man to his feet.

"Tell us what?"

"His Faithfulness….Hezekiah..."

"What?" Avora'tru'ivi's eyebrows furrowed.

"He has…gone Home."

Tamino's stomach dropped to the floor as he involuntarily lost his grip on the man, who tumbled back down to the cool tiles. Tamino staggered back, reaching a hand behind him to search for the seat of the throne. Avora'tru'ivi ran forward and placed a steadying hand on his arm.

"I—I wasn't there." Tamino whispered, his eyes clouding with a mixture of anguish and guilt.

"Galbi—" the queen tried to interject.

"I knew I shouldn't have come here! He needed me!"

"Our place was here for the dedication. He would have wanted you to fulfill your national duties."

Slightly recovering from the initial shock, Tamino blinked as a single tear escaped the corner of his eye.

"We must make arrangements to return to Trukanamoa at once." He turned to the Judith Corps guard. "Notify the travel staff that we need to assemble a carava—."

The woman looked like she hadn't even heard him. Instead, her eyes, wide with disbelief, were locked on the window, her mouth quivering.

"Hoglah, I know we are all stunned by this, but—" Avora'tru'ivi's admonishment was cut short as her eyes followed the guard's westward gaze.

Atop the misty form of the tallest mountain in the distance was a single spark of light, its angry red blaze cutting through the haze of the Blue Mountains and searing itself into the queen's retinas.

"That's...that's..." Hoglah stammered.

"An invasion beacon." Avora'tru'ivi said matter-of-factly, the eerie calm of her voice belied by the wide-eyed terror that fell across her face.

She took a deep breath, gathered herself, and pursed her lips.

"Galbi, I don't think we should go back to Trukanamoa." Her final words were punctuated by a clanging sound as the brand-new bells of the distant White Cathedral sounded the alarm, joining a chorus of frightened and astonished shouts from below.

Tamino stood transfixed by the terrible image from the

window, his mouth slightly open in shock as his hands hung limply by his sides.

"Galbi."

Tamino shook himself free of the mesmerism of the beacon, stood about three inches taller, closed his mouth, and balled his fists. Turning to the queen, he locked eyes directly with her.

"No. You're right. We are needed here. We always knew something like this might happen. We have the plans that we need. Go get your armor, and meet me in the War Room." With that, he snapped away from his position in front of the window and strode out the double doors, pausing for a moment to look at the battle flag that hung resolutely behind the thrones. His eyes focused on the sixteen-pointed star fixed in the upper left-hand corner of the banner, from which the red, white, and blue rays emanated.

"God help us," he whispered, before briefly casting his eyes skyward.

OUR CHARACTERS WILL RETURN

IN

A LION ROARETH

Book Two of the Annals of Zebulon

Left to right: Top row: Briseis, Delilah, Avora'tru'ivi, Tamino, Middle Row: Salome, Ajax the Lesser, Kublai Khan, Adirah, Jeremiah. Bottom row: Jason, Achilles, Heracles, Lady Deborah, Jessica

GUIDE TO PEOPLE, PLACES, AND PRONUNCIATIONS

Achilles of Gath: Prince of Gath and champion of Frouzee Delilah

Adirah of Mangala: queen and co-founder of Wil'iah and mother of Tamino, Jessica, and Jeremiah; born 1226

Ajax the Great of Gath: Prince of Gath and father of Achilles and Ajax the Lesser

Ajax the Lesser of Gath: Prince of Gath and commander of the Imperial Army Group East

Allira: Prime Minister of the Council of Uluru, Wil'iah's representative legislature.

Arigh Khaiya: Mongol general. Real historical figure.

Avora'tru'ivi: A-VORE-uh troo EEvee: Princess of Ephraim and Manasseh and queen of Wil'iah; Born 1259

Balthcutta: Large city on the east coast of Wil'iah and Wil'iah's primary pacific port. Located at real-life Jervis Bay, in the Australian Capital Territories.

Bayan of the Baarin: Mongol general and mentor to Temur Khan. Real historical figure who led the conquest of China.

Briseis: Handmaiden to Frouzee Delilah

Chabi: Kublai Khan's late wife. Real historical figure.

Champa: Sovereign state in present-day southern Vietnam

Dai Viet: Sovereign state in present-day northern Vietnam ruled by the Tran Dynasty; also sometimes known as Annam.

Deborah of Dhirari: Captain of Zebulon, commander of Wil'iah's armed forces.

Delilah: Frouzee of the Frouzean Empire

Diomedes: Prince of Ashdod

Gamaliel IV: King of Manasseh and father of Avora'tru'ivi and Gideon

Gath: Capital city of Frouzea, located where real-life Melbourne is. Named for the hometown of the Biblical villain Goliath.

Gideon: Prince, later King, of Ephraim and Manasseh

Harijit: Crown Prince of Champa. Real historical figure

Hasdrubal: King of Tanitania and husband of Frouzee Delilah; a descendant of the famous real-life general Hannibal Barca, who attacked Rome with war elephants.

Heracles: Manservant and Champion of Frouzee Delilah

Hezekiah: founder and king of Wil'iah from 1256-1291. Born 1223.

Hoglah: Member of the Judith Corps, the queen of Wil'iah's elite guard

Hung Dao: General in command of the armies of Dai Viet; real historical figure

Italereme: King of the Arrernte Nation, an Aboriginal

people that live in central Australia.

Jason: Prince of Pelesetania

Jaya Indravarman V: King of Champa. Real historical figure

Jeremiah: Prince and Sovereign Protector of Wil'iah; Born 1262

Jessica: Princess of Wil'iah and commander of the Royal Wil'iahn Navy's Eastern Fleet; Born 1260

Karakorum: Former official capital of the Mongol Empire, located in present-day Mongolia

Kertanegara: King of Singhasari (modern-day Indonesia); real historical figure

Khanbaliq: Part-time capital of the Yuan Dynasty in China, present-day Beijing

Khmer Empire: Sovereign State in present-day Cambodia that submits to a tributary relationship with Kublai Khan

Kublai Khan: Emperor of the Yuan Dynasty and Great Khan of the Mongol Empire; real historical figure

Kurultai: The traditional Mongolian tribal process for choosing a new leader. Kublai Khan's kurultai was held in China, leading some of his rivals to question its legitimacy.

Liu: Chief advisor to Kublai Khan and one of his "three villainous ministers." Real historical figure, although in real life he was executed before the events of this story for corruption.

Lowanna: Woman who takes command of the defense of Trukanamoa

Lu Xiufu: Prime Minister of the Southern Song Dynasty and one of the "Three Loyal Princes of the Song." Real historical figure. In real life, he committed suicide with Emperor Zhao Bing at the conclusion of the Battle of Yamen, where this story begins.

Medea: escaped Frouzean slave

Milcah: MILL-kuh Maid and governess in the Court of Wil'iah

Minh: Associate of the Order of the Flame of Zebulon in Champa

Minos of Ashkelon: Prince of Ashkelon and commander of

the Imperial Army's Balthcutta attack force

Nasir-al-din: Mongol general of Persian descent. Real historical figure.

Pagan Empire: Sovereign state located in present-day Burma that submits to a tributary status with Kublai Khan. *Note that the term "Pagan" is unrelated to the religious term.*

Patroclus of Gaza: Prince of Gaza

Raden Wijaya: general of the Kingdom of Singhasari, and later founder of the Majahapit Empire. Real historical figure.

Salome: Handmaid to Frouzee Delilah and former harem girl of Achilles of Gath

Shechem: Capital city of the United Kingdom of Ephraim and Manasseh, located on the real-life Gulf of Carpentaria in northern Australia.

Sheerah: War queen of Ephraim and mother of Avora'tru'ivi and Gideon

Singhasari: Kingdom located on present-day Java, a forerunner to Indonesia.

Sogetu: Mongol general killed during the invasion of Champa in 1285. Real historical figure.

Tamino: Tuh-MEE-no; Born 1258, Prince, later King, of Wil'iah from 1291-1327.

Temur Khan: Grandson of Kublai Khan and second ruler of the Yuan (Mongol) Dynasty of China. Real historical figure

Thang Long: Capital of Dai Viet

Theseus of Ekron: Prince of Ekron

Tran Anh Tong: Crown prince, later emperor, of Dai Viet; ruled from 1293-1314. Real Historical Figure.

Tran Nanh Tong: Emperor of Dai Viet; ruled from 1278-1293. Real historical figure.

Tran Tranh Tong: Retired emperor of Dai Viet; ruled from 1258-1278. Real historical figure.

Tribhuwaneswari: Princess of Singhasari. Real historical figure

Trujustakanoa: TRUE-just-uh-kuh-nowa: large city on Wil'iah's west coast and former capital of the ancient Kingdom of Zebulon, located at real-life Derby, Western Australia, on

King Sound. Wil'iah's primary port for trade with Asia and the Indian Ocean.

Trukanamoa: TRUE-kahna-mowa: capital of Wil'iah, located where real-life Alice Springs stands at the center of Australia.

Toghon: Son of Kublai Khan, who led the disastrous invasion of Dai Viet in 1285 and later leads Mongol forces against Wil'iah. Real historical figure, who was exiled to Yangzhou and disowned by his father after failing to conquer Dai Viet.

Uluru: Also known as Ayers' Rock, a sacred site for Aboriginal Australians and, in this story, the site of the founding of Wil'iah.

Wen Tianxiang: One of the "Three Loyal Princes of the Song," a real historical figure.

Wil'iah: Will-Lee-Uh: country in Australia, formed from an alliance of Zebulite tribesmen descended from one of the Tribes of Israel and indigenous Aboriginal nations.

Xanadu (Shangdu): the legendary summer palace of Kublai Khan; real historical location described by Marco Polo.

Yamen: Location in the Pearl River Delta in Southern China, site of a disastrous battle between the Song Navy and the Mongol Navy that led to the fall of China.

Dowager Yang: Dowager Empress of the Song Dynasty and mother of Zhao Bing, who escapes to Wil'iah with her son. Real historical figure.

Zhang Shijie: Admiral of the Southern Song, and later Royal Wil'iahn, navies. One of the "Three Loyal Princes of the Song." Real historical figure. In real life, he disappeared at the Battle of Yamen (where this story begins) and was never heard from again.

Zhao Bing: Last emperor of the Song Dynasty, also known as the Xianxing Emperor. Real historical figure. In real life, he perished, at the age of seven, at the Battle of Yamen when Prime Minister Lu Xiufu and he jumped off of a warship to their deaths.

CONSTITUENT UNITS OF THE FROUZEAN EMPIRE

THE FIVE PRINCIPALITIES:

GATH,
GAZA
ASHDOD
ASHKELON
EKRON

IMPERIAL PROVINCES:

UPPER TANITANIA
 LOWER TANITANIA
ARBORIA
AURANIA

OUTER PRINCIPALITIES:

 PELESETANIA

TERRITORIES:

ITHACA
NULLARBOR
 OUTER FROUZEA

CONSTITUENT UNITS OF THE KINGDOM OF WIL'IAH

13ʰ-century Wil'iah is divided into judgates, administrative divisions that themselves contain individual sovereign Aboriginal nations. Two of these are semi-autonomous "Sovereign Judgates" with additional constitutional powers.

SOVEREIGN JUDGATES:

ANANGU
SOUTH MURRINUI

COUNCIL JUDGATES:

IYTWELYEPENTY
KATI-THANDA
KINIPAPA
MARANOA
MARDUWARRA
TANAMI
TJORITJA
VRENGA'NUI
WILUNA
YARINGA

ACKNOWLEDGEMENTS

The Author would like to thank Syd Abdella, Jimmy Applewhite, Jeri Fonte, Wade Waterstreet, and especially Ginger Clark and Beth Whittenbury for reading this book and providing enormously helpful feedback. Beth has been a constant source of support, ideas, and knowledge through the entire process of creating this book. He would like to thank the late, great Steve Irwin, whose 2002 film *The Crocodile Hunter: Collision Course* inspired a group of five-year-olds to create an imaginary country set in Australia, and those then-kids who shared in that imagination with the author. Lastly, he would like to thank all those who, throughout history, have stood up for what they believed in, even against incredible odds. The Kingdom of Wil'iah may not actually exist, but the spirit that it stands for most certainly does.

'Ivrae'ia Va'a'kau'lua!

ABOUT THE AUTHOR

William Whittenbury drew inspiration for this story from an imaginative game he played with his friends as a child. He previously co-authored the novel *The Shapeshifter's War* (2014) with the Bohemia Chapter of the National English Honor Society. In addition to writing, William is an aerospace engineer and holds a degree in Manufacturing and Design Engineering from Northwestern University. William is a heritage speaker for the US Naval Historical Foundation and the co-host of the maritime history podcast *In the Drydock*. He is also involved in efforts to save the critically-endangered vaquita porpoise.